Summer 99'
Phil 316

John Dewey

The Later Works, 1925–1953

Volume 9: 1933–1934

EDITED BY JO ANN BOYDSTON
TEXTUAL EDITOR, ANNE SHARPE
ASSOCIATE TEXTUAL EDITOR,
PATRICIA BAYSINGER
With an Introduction by Milton R. Konvitz

Southern Illinois University Press
Carbondale and Edwardsville

Copyright © 1989 by the Board of Trustees,
Southern Illinois University
All rights reserved
First published, October 1986
First paperbound printing, 1989
This edition printed in the United States of America

COMMITTEE ON
SCHOLARLY EDITIONS

AN APPROVED TEXT

MODERN LANGUAGE
ASSOCIATION OF AMERICA

The text of this reprinting is a photo-offset reproduction of the original cloth edition that contains the full apparatus for the volume awarded the seal of the Committee on Scholarly Editions of the Modern Language Association. Editorial expenses were met in part by a grant from the Editions Program of the National Endowment for the Humanities, an independent Federal agency.

The paperbound edition has been made possible by a special subvention from the John Dewey Foundation.

The Library of Congress catalogued the first printing of this work (in cloth) as follows:

Dewey, John, 1859–1952.
 The later works, 1925–1953.

   Vol. 9 has introd. by Milton R. Konvitz.
   Continues The middle works, 1899–1924.
   Includes bibliographies and indexes.
   CONTENTS: v. 1. 1925–[etc.]–v. 9. 1933–1934.
   1. Philosophy—Collected works. I. Boydston, Jo Ann, 1924–. II. Title.
B945.D41   1981   191   80-27285
ISBN 0-8093-1265-4 (v. 9)

ISBN 0-8093-1577-7 (paperback)

Contents

Introduction by Milton R. Konvitz	xi
A Common Faith	1
1. Religion versus the Religious	3
2. Faith and Its Object	21
3. The Human Abode of the Religious Function	40
ESSAYS	59
Steps to Economic Recovery	61
The Future of Radical Political Action	66
Unity and Progress	71
Imperative Need: A New Radical Party	76
What Keeps Funds Away from Purchasers	81
American Ideals (I): The Theory of Liberty vs. the Fact of Regimentation	87
Why I Am Not a Communist	91
The Supreme Intellectual Obligation	96
A Great American Prophet	102
Intelligence and Power	107
The Crisis in Education	112
Education and Our Present Social Problems	127
Dewey Outlines Utopian Schools	136

Shall We Abolish School "Frills"? No	141
Why Have Progressive Schools?	147
Education for a Changing Social Order	158
The Activity Movement	169
Education and the Social Order	175
Character Training for Youth	186
The Need for a Philosophy of Education	194
Can Education Share in Social Reconstruction?	205

REVIEWS 211

A God or The God? Review of *Is There a God?* by Henry Nelson Wieman, Douglas Clyde Macintosh, and Max Carl Otto	213
Dr. Dewey Replies	223
Social Stresses and Strains. Review of *Recent Social Trends in the United States*	229
Review of *Mr. Justice Brandeis*, edited by Felix Frankfurter	237
Santayana's Orthodoxy. Review of George Santayana's *Some Turns of Thought in Modern Philosophy*	240
Acquiescence and Activity in Communism. Review of Theodore B. H. Brameld's *A Philosophic Approach to Communism*	244

PEOPLE'S LOBBY BULLETIN 247

Unemployed and Underpaid Consumers Should Not Pay Billion Dollar Subsidy to Speculators	249
Relief Is Vital	252
The Banking Crisis	254

Congress Faces Its Test on Taxation	256
The Real Test of the "New Deal"	259
Superficial Treatment Must Fail	261
Inflationary Measures Injure the Masses	265
Wild Inflation Would Paralyze Nation	267
Lobby Asks Special Session on Debts	269
Unemployment Committee Asks Adequate Relief	271
Farm Processing and Other Consumption Taxes Must Be Repealed	273
The Next Session and the People's Lobby	275
President's Policies Help Property Owners Chiefly	277
New Deal Program Must Be Appraised	280
A Real Test of the Administration	282
America's Public Ownership Program	285
Facing the Era of Realities	287
No Half-Way House for America	289
MISCELLANY	291
Religions and the "Religious"	293
Reply to Edwin Ewart Aubrey and Henry Nelson Wieman in "Is John Dewey a Theist?"	294
Introduction to *Challenge to the New Deal*, edited by Alfred Mitchell Bingham and Selden Rodman	296
Foreword to George Raymond Geiger's *The Philosophy of Henry George*	299
Meaning, Assertion and Proposal	303

To Save the Rand School	305
The Drive against Hunger	307
Radio's Influence on the Mind	309
Preface to the English Edition of *Terror in Cuba*	310
Statement on Technocracy	312

REPORTS AND INTERVIEW 313

On the Grievance Committee's Report	315
The Report of the Special Grievance Committee of the Teachers Union	320
New York and the Seabury Investigation	346
Tomorrow May Be Too Late: Save the Schools Now	386

APPENDIXES 397

1. After Capitalism—What? by Reinhold Niebuhr	399
2. Shall We Abolish School "Frills"? Yes by H. L. Mencken	406
3. Mr. Wieman and Mr. Macintosh "Converse" with Mr. Dewey by Henry Nelson Wieman and Douglas Clyde Macintosh	412
4. John Dewey's Credo by Norbert Guterman	423
5. John Dewey's Common Faith by Henry Nelson Wieman	426
6. Is John Dewey a Theist? by Edwin Ewart Aubrey	435
7. Is John Dewey a Theist? by Henry Nelson Wieman	438

Checklist of Dewey's References	441
Index	445
Pagination Key to the First Edition of *A Common Faith*	467

Introduction

By Milton R. Konvitz

I.

When *A Common Faith* was published in 1934, John Dewey was seventy-five years of age. He knew as well as any other philosopher or scholar that it had become impossible to define the term "religion" in any meaningful way. In *A Common Faith* he put this conclusion forcefully:

> For we are forced to acknowledge that concretely there is no such thing as religion in the singular. There is only a multitude of religions. "Religion" is a strictly collective term and the collection it stands for is not even of the kind illustrated in textbooks of logic. It has not the unity of a regiment or assembly but that of any miscellaneous aggregate.[1]

Since religion cannot be defined, Dewey proposed the following terminology: make a distinction between "religion" as a noun substantive and "religious" as adjectival; and he followed this proposal with the following explanation:

> To be somewhat more explicit, a religion (and as I have just said there is no such thing as religion in general) always signifies a special body of beliefs and practices having some kind of institutional organization, loose or tight. In contrast, the adjective "religious" denotes nothing in the way of a specifiable entity, either institutional or as a system of beliefs. It does not denote anything to which one can specifically point as one can point to this and that historic religion or existing church. For it does not denote anything that can exist by it-

---

1. Dewey, *A Common Faith* (New Haven: Yale University Press, 1934), pp. 7–8 (this volume, p. 7). Subsequent page numbers in parentheses refer to this volume.

self or that can be organized into a particular and distinctive form of existence. It denotes attitudes that may be taken toward every object and every proposed end or ideal. (P. 8)

This proposal by Dewey, to avoid use of the term "religion" as a substantive and to use "religious" as an adjective has been the one feature of his book that has been most widely noted. There are other propositions in *A Common Faith* that have also attracted notice and criticism—notably its negative position with respect to the supernatural, and at the same time a degree of receptivity to the use of the term "God." These and other features of the book call for some discussion.

The main and basic lines of his thoughts on religion were sketched by Dewey in an autobiographical essay he published four years before *A Common Faith*.[2] In that essay he related that during his undergraduate days at the University of Vermont, he took a course in the philosophy of religion, which was concentrated on Bishop Butler's *The Analogy of Religion*. Dewey had been brought up in a conventionally evangelical atmosphere "of the more 'liberal' sort; and the struggles that later arose between acceptance of that faith and the discarding of traditional and institutional creeds came," he wrote, "from personal experiences and not from the effects of philosophical teaching." It was from personal experiences, whatever they may have been, that Dewey developed a "respect for concrete materials of experience," an emphasis on "the concrete, empirical, and 'practical'" that one finds in his later writings.[3]

Dewey referred ambiguously to "a trying personal crisis" because of the conflict between the traditional religious beliefs and the opinions which he could honestly entertain; but this conflict, he noted, "did not at any time constitute a leading philosophical problem." Instead of being strongly moved to cope with and possibly resolve this religious conflict, Dewey, from an early period, found that social interests and problems had for him "the intellectual appeal and provided the intellectual sustenance that

---

2. Dewey, "From Absolutism to Experimentalism," in George Plimpton Adams and William Pepperell Montague, eds., *Contemporary American Philosophy: Personal Statements* (New York: Macmillan Co., 1930), 2:13–27 [*The Later Works of John Dewey, 1925–1953*, ed. Jo Ann Boydston (Carbondale and Edwardsville: Southern Illinois University Press, 1984), 5:147–60].
3. Ibid., pp. 15–16, 17 [*Later Works* 5:149–50, 151].

many seem to have found primarily in religious questions." It was not, Dewey said, that he kept traditional religious beliefs and his own opinions apart; but he had the feeling that his genuinely sound religious experience "could and should adapt itself to whatever beliefs one found oneself intellectually entitled to hold." This became for him "a fundamental conviction." As a consequence, said Dewey, he had not been able to attach much importance to religion as a philosophical problem. An attachment of importance to religion as a philosophical problem "seems to be in the end," he said, "a subornation of candid philosophic thinking to the alleged but factitious needs of some special set of convictions."[4] Since he had been frequently criticized for "undue reticence about the problems of religion," he offered the following explanation:

> It seems to me that the great solicitude of many persons, professing belief in the universality of the need for religion, about the present and future of religion proves that in fact they are moved more by partisan interest in a particular religion than by interest in religious experience.[5]

His early model, apparently, was Plato, whose writings were Dewey's favorite reading in his undergraduate days and whose influence was sustained and lasting, for Dewey noted that Plato's highest flights of metaphysics always terminated with a social and practical turn; for Dewey, too, had learned to look toward "an integrated synthesis in a philosophy congruous with modern science and related to actual needs in education, morals, and religion."[6]

Four years later Dewey broke his "undue reticence" about religion with the publication of *A Common Faith*. At the outset, he said that his intention was to separate the religious phase of religion from the supernatural; to emancipate what is genuinely religious—to allow the religious aspect of experience to develop freely on its own account. This view, he said, will be unsatisfactory to two camps: to those who hold to traditional religions, and to those who hold that all religions are discredited and that everything of a religious nature should be dismissed.

4. Ibid., pp. 19, 20 [*Later Works* 5:153, 154].
5. Ibid., p. 20 [*Later Works* 5:154].
6. Ibid., p. 26 [*Later Works* 5:159].

In his autobiographical essay Dewey spoke of "religious experience," but in *A Common Faith* he takes the position that the religious experience cannot exist by itself. It is a quality that belongs to other experiences—aesthetic, scientific, moral, political. It is a quality that belongs to companionship, friendship. The religious is not an experience that one can have in isolation from some other experience. While Dewey does not himself use the term, it certainly must occur to a reader of the book that for its author the religious in experience is an epiphenomenon—not a primary, but a secondary happening. The religious quality in an experience "is the *effect* produced, the better adjustment in life and its conditions, not the manner and cause of its production. The way in which the experience operated, its function, determines its religious value" (p. 11). The religious quality in experience is sometimes brought about "by devotion to a cause; sometimes by a passage of poetry that opens a new perspective; sometimes . . . through philosophical reflection." The religious quality in experience can be found in "experiences having the force of bringing about a better, deeper and enduring adjustment in life." It occurs "frequently in connection with many significant moments of living." It is the quality which gives meaning to the "conditions of nature and human association that support and deepen the sense of values which carry one through periods of darkness and despair" (p. 11).

Thus far, then, we have two significant propositions: namely, (1) that there is no such thing as religion in general; there are specific religions, but the differences among them are so great that no common element among them can be extracted; and (2) there is a religious quality to or in certain experiences, but it is not an independently existing quality; it is an attitude that may be taken toward an object, an end, or an ideal; it is a quality that belongs to or is attached to other experiences.

The latter point receives much more elaboration from Dewey than does the former. Morality, he says, can become a religious experience. This happens when the ends of moral conviction arouse emotions that are intense and that are actuated by ends that unify the self. To make the experience a religious one, the "inclusiveness of the end in relation to both self and the 'universe' . . . is indispensable" (p. 16). This certainly sounds like an echo of Matthew Arnold's statement that "The true meaning of religion is thus not simply morality, but morality touched by emotion."[7]

The ends or ideals that actuate the emotions are unseen, but this does not make them supernatural. The ideal plays the role of an unseen power; all of our endeavors for the better are moved by faith in the unseen. The unseen motivates all of us—the parent, the artist, the scientist; all activity for a projected but as yet unseen end is religious in quality. Thus, all our normal, "natural" activities may involve the religious quality—indeed, the "realization of distinctively religious values [is] inherent in natural experience" (p. 20).

To achieve this wide forum for the religious quality to have its free life and play, it must be emancipated from what are conventionally conceived of as the religions. These religions are all relative to the conditions of social culture in which people have lived. They are full of historic encumbrances, dated cultural baggage. Since this is the fact, the logic of this admission is to press forward on the discarding of the outgrown traits of these (past) religions. Since we live in the present, the present state of culture should compel us to discard the outgrown ideas associated with past religions. We should start with a clean slate. If we do that, then whatever is basically religious in our experience will have an opportunity to express itself free from all historic encumbrances.

Among the encumbrances inherent in religions are intellectual beliefs, doctrines which are taken as true in an intellectual sense. These are all connected with the supernatural, and this connection is sapping the religious life itself; for religions have become subject to general skepticism and agnosticism. Great advances have been made in astronomy, geology, biology, anthropology, psychology, literary criticism, and other fields, with the result that some religions have had to abandon cosmic, historic, and theological beliefs, but have retained a minimum of intellectual content, and ascribe religious force to literary documents and certain personages, and insist on beliefs in theism and immortality. Overshadowing these facts, however, is the recognition that "There is but one sure road of access to truth," and that is: "observation, experiment, record and controlled reflection" (p. 23).

It is no longer a question of the truth of any one item of belief.

---

7. Arnold, *Literature and Dogma* (London: Smith, Elder and Co., 1883), p. 16.

The issue centers on the question of the method of inquiry, the method by which any and every intellectual belief is to be reached. Accordingly, if the religious quality or function in experience is to be emancipated, the emancipation can be effected "only through surrender of the whole notion of special truths that are religious by their own nature, together with the idea of peculiar avenues of access to such truths" (p. 23). The bifurcation of experiences into two categories, those subject to the scientific method and others not subject to this method—not subject to the scientific method or criterion or the scientific intellectual habit—has no justification. There are what are called mystical experiences, but their occurrence should lead to scientific inquiry into their causation.

The emancipation of the religious quality in experience will let it become attached to ideal ends or values. The reality of such ideal ends or values cannot be doubted—ideals such as justice, affection, truth. The union of their religious quality with such ideals or values should suffice without the need to encumber the religious attitude with dogma and doctrine. Thus the religious faith can aim towards "the unification of the self through allegiance to inclusive ideal ends, which imagination presents to us and to which the human will responds as worthy of controlling our desires and choices" (p. 23). In this context, God may be said to denote "the unity of all ideal ends arousing us to desire and actions" (p. 29).

These ideals are not illusions. Their reality is vouched for by their power in action. Ideals are things unrealized in fact, which come home to us and have power to stir us. The religious quality which comes with these ideal ends signifies a unity which is not a single Being, "but the unity of loyalty and effort evoked by the fact that many ends are one in the power of their ideal, or imaginative, quality to stir and hold us" (p. 30).

This power of ideals to stir us to action has no need of supernatural powers, which only divert attention from the ideals because men will then wait for external forces to do the work for them. If the forces that have been drafted into supernatural religions were used in natural ways, "the resulting reinforcement will be incalculable" (p. 34). The reduction or removal of evil can be accomplished without reliance on supernatural powers. For there are forces in society and nature that generate and support ideals. God can be said to be the *active* relation between the ideal and the actual.

The link between the ideal and the actual is not a mystical one; it is both natural and moral. It is not something given, but a uniting, an active joining. The goods of life are real but embryonic; their full actualization is dependent on our effort, and our effort is dependent upon our emotion. Now,

> whether one gives the name "God" to this union, operative in thought and action, is a matter for individual decision. But the *function* of such a working union of the ideal and actual seems to me to be identical with the force that has in fact been attached to the conception of God in all the religions that have a spiritual content. . . . (P. 35)

Rejecting both "traditional supernaturalism" and "aggressive atheism," Dewey wrote why he himself chose to use the name "God":

> One reason why personally I think it fitting to use the word "God" to denote that uniting of the ideal and actual . . . lies in the fact that aggressive atheism seems to me to have something in common with traditional supernaturalism. I do not mean merely that the former is mainly so negative that it fails to give positive direction to thought, though that fact is pertinent. What I have in mind especially is the exclusive preoccupation of both militant atheism and supernaturalism with man in isolation. . . . A religious attitude, however, needs the sense of a connection of man, in the way of both dependence and support, with the enveloping world that the imagination feels is a universe. Use of the words "God" or "divine" to convey the union of actual with ideal may protect man from a sense of isolation and from consequent despair or defiance. (P. 36)

Dewey tried to keep the term "divine" free of any supernatural meaning; it is, he said, "a term of human choice and aspiration" (p. 36). The "common faith" projected by the title of his book was envisioned by its author as a "humanistic religion" (p. 36). He asserted that Matthew Arnold's identification of God as "the enduring power, not ourselves, which makes for righteousness,"[8] was too narrow in two respects: namely, first, there is a suggestion of an external God in Arnold's statement, while "The powers that generate and support the good as experienced and as ideal, work *within* as well as without" (p. 36); and secondly, "the powers work to enforce values and ideals other than righteousness," such as beauty, truth, and friendship. Religion, if given naturalistic foundations, will be found to have "its natural place in every aspect of human experience that is concerned with estimate of possibilities, with emotional stir by possibilities as yet unrealized, and with all action in behalf of their realization. All that is significant in human experience falls within this frame" (p. 39).

In the temporal order, religions are generally identified with rites and ceremonies, legends and myths, cosmogonies and theologies. The community and the religion of the people were coterminous. Persons were born into a religious community; religion permeated its every aspect of life. But a great change has taken place in religion; namely, *membership in a religion is now voluntary.* Although persons may still be born into a religion, the organization of the religion is a special institution within a secular society. This is something new in history. While the intellectual conflict between scientific and religious beliefs has attracted much more attention, and is still receiving attention, "the change in the social centre of gravity of religion" (p. 41) has gone on steadily and has been generally accomplished, though the church/state conflict continues in some countries. The religious fundamentalists do not allow science to affect them intellectually, but of course their daily life is unavoidably affected by the results of science and technology. The social place and function of religion has radically changed—this has been the greatest revolution in religion in thousands of years. Secular associations now take up much of the interest of even believers.

Two facts particularly characterize this revolution: first, there is the personal choice in letting one's religious beliefs influence one's secular interests; and second, the very fact that the individual carries his religious attitude into secular affairs constitutes an enormous change. The religious attitude has thus become a floating, free-moving thing, independent of religion as an institution.

---

8. Ibid., p. 43.

While supernatural religion drew a line between the sacred and the profane, the idea that a religion can be independent of the supernatural has eliminated the need to make this distinction. Churches, however, have lagged behind in social movements, and when they have turned their attention to social problems, they have tended to pay attention to symptoms of social stress rather than to their causes.

The Renaissance was a new birth of secularism. In the eighteenth century the movement for a natural religion was a protest against ecclesiastical bodies. It did not deny supernatural ideas. It attempted, in fact, to justify theism and a belief in immortality, but through natural reason. Transcendentalism, too, did not escape from supernaturalism—it sought the diffusion of the supernatural throughout the secular life. But today even the idea of the supernatural has been loosened from ecclesiastical organization. Liberal religious circles today do not stress Original Sin, total depravity, or the corruption of nature. Today they stress that there are two systems of values, the natural and the supernatural, and that they are *complementary*. This is certainly an advance upon the traditional view. Well, then,

> if it be once admitted that human relations are charged with values that are religious in function, why not rest the case upon what is verifiable and concentrate thought and energy upon its full realization? (P. 48)

Liberal religion represents the second stage of growth in history, in which the ideals of human relations are seen as religious values, that is, values of a supernatural religion. If so, why not move to the third stage, in which the values prized in the religions shall be seen as "idealizations of things characteristic of natural association" (p. 48). This would avoid the dualism, which distracts energy—it would avoid the dualism of the secular and the spiritual, the religious and the profane.

The dualism can be overcome by putting the intelligence to work to solve man's social problems by looking at the causes rather than the mere symptoms. The evils are not normal expressions of social relations; they flow out of institutions that are molded by many forces. Many evils and many social relations are accidental and not inherent, and were not foreseen or intended. We must institutionalize, as it were, the "method of intelligence in action" and not refer evils or dispose of them by reference to "general moral causes," "abstract moral forces," the "sinfulness of man," "corruption of his heart," "his self-love and love of power." Social phenomena should not be referred to "general moral causes" (p. 51).

Dewey attacks "the emptiness of individuality in isolation" (p. 52). He belittles the idea of the individual salvation of individual souls, and a *laissez-faire* which denies the possibility of the radical intervention of the intelligence in the conduct of human life. The appeal for supernatural intervention may be an expression of a deep-seated *laissez-faireism*. Men must assume responsibility for making the will of God prevail, and this requires the intelligence "as distinct from the older conception of reason"— an intelligence that is "inherently involved in action" (p. 52). And there is no opposition between intelligence and emotion, for what is needed is passionate intelligence, "devotion, so intense as to be religious" (pp. 52–53). There must be a marriage of emotion with intelligence.

One must choose between alternatives: either the supernatural or the use of natural agencies. But this does not mean that we must destroy churches. There can be a celebration and reinforcement of human values with differing symbols by the churches. Questions of war and peace, economic injustice, political corruption, building the divine kingdom on earth—these are "signs of the times" (p. 55). The trouble is that Christianity stands committed to a spiritual aristocracy, the saved, and a rejection of the damned. This means a *laissez-faireism* with respect to human intervention, while giving lip service to the idea of the brotherhood of man. "I cannot understand," said Dewey,

> how any realization of the democratic ideal as a vital moral and spiritual ideal in human affairs is possible without surrender of the conception of the basic division to which supernatural Christianity is committed. (P. 56)

In his concluding remarks, Dewey rejects agnosticism and weak skepticism, for what is needed is a common faith, "explicit and militant." For we are all enmeshed in

> the widest and deepest symbol of the mysterious totality of being the imagination calls the universe. . . . It is the matrix within which our ideal aspirations are born and bred. . . .

. . . Ours is the responsibility of conserving, transmitting, rectifying and expanding the heritage of values we have received that those who come after us may receive it more solid and secure, more widely accessible and more generously shared than we have received it. Here are all the elements for a religious faith that shall not be confined to sect, class, or race. Such a faith has always been implicitly the common faith of mankind. (Pp. 56, 57–58)

II.

A year before *A Common Faith* was published, Dewey wrote a review of *Is There a God? A Conversation,* by Henry Nelson Wieman, Douglas Clyde Macintosh, and Max Carl Otto, which was published in the *Christian Century*.[9] Since this review, and his reply to the comments which it elicited,[10] were published almost contemporaneously with *A Common Faith,* it is reasonable to assume that Dewey considered his views as expressed in *Christian Century* to be wholly consistent with those expressed in his book.

Dewey in his review took to task the authors for affirming a belief in "*a* God" and for attaching special importance to "kinds of experience which are alone regarded by them as religious, because alone having to do with the unique objects which can evoke true religious attitudes" (p. 216). Dewey saw a contradiction between asserting the universality of God and yet demanding the limitation of human response and attitude that is appropriate "to the exclusive and jealous God of Israel" (p. 216). The authors, he said, "still insist upon a particular being or object, *a* God, and particular methods and channels of approach" (p. 216). Dewey also found a contradiction between an appeal to the supremacy of moral ideals as the ground for the content of religious ideas, "including that of God," and an insistence "upon a God to

9. Wieman's, Macintosh's, and Otto's discussion "Is There a God?" originally published in the *Christian Century* from February to August 1932, was published in the book *Is There a God? A Conversation* (Chicago and New York: Willett, Clark and Co., 1932).
10. Dewey, "Dr. Dewey Replies," *Christian Century* 50 (22 March 1933): 394–95 (this volume, pp. 223–28). For the article to which this is a reply, see "Mr. Wieman and Mr. Macintosh 'Converse' with Mr. Dewey," *Christian Century* 50 (1 March 1933): 299–302 (this volume, Appendix 3).

give moral ideals external and independent support . . ." (p. 218). He attacked "religious modernists" for, on the one hand, asserting the universality of God, and, on the other hand, clinging to "an earlier exclusive tradition and cult" (p. 218). "Mr. Macintosh wants a cosmic guarantee for our moral idealism and optimism. Mr. Wieman wants an objective counterpart for human love and devotion" (p. 219). Dewey identified his "main point" in the following passage:

> And to repeat once more my main point, the shift is from something too universal and inclusive in human experience to be identified with any historic religious tradition whatever, to say nothing of Christian theism, to something sufficiently "jealous" and exclusive to be an emotional carrier of one strain of traditional religious belief. (P. 220)

Admitting, said Dewey, that there are in existence conditions and forces which, apart from human desire and intent, bring about enjoyed and enjoyable goods, and that these goods can be secured and extended by attending to these conditions,

> does this admitted fact throw any light whatever upon the unity and singleness of the forces and factors which make for good? If not, Mr. Wieman's argument would seem to me to amount simply to a plea that in a time of transition and disturbance many persons will find it helpful and consoling to continue to use the *word* "God" to designate what actually are a collection of forces, unified only in their functional effect: the furtherance of goods in human life. . . . (Pp. 220–21)

In an issue of the same journal in the following month, Dewey tried to clear up some points. Citing the example of Buddhists and Comtean Positivists, Dewey asserted that it is possible to separate the religious experience from the question of the existence of God. His own experience, he said, as well as that of others, shows that what is ordinarily identified as a religious experience connected with God "can be had equally well in the ordinary course of human experience in our relations to the natural world and to one another as human beings related in the family, friendship, industry, art, science, and citizenship. *Either then the concept of God can be dropped out as far as genuinely religious experience is concerned, or it must be framed wholly in terms of natural and human relationship involved in our straight-away human experience."* [11]

In his argument with Wieman, Dewey states that unlike the latter, he would not say "God is the power which," etc. Dewey would turn the sentence around and say: "The power that makes for greatest good is God." And Dewey adds that "this mode of statement does not seem to be merely verbal . . ." (p. 225).

Dewey takes Wieman to task for his shift "between God as the power which *makes* for the greatest good and God as the Greatest Good" (p. 225). That which makes for good demands care, attention, watchfulness, but not love or adoration. "I can love a healthy person in a way that is enhanced by that person's health, and I can feel a grateful affection for the *person* who brings me greater health. I do not know just what love (or adoration) of the chemico-physical processes that basically determine health would be . . ." (pp. 225–26).

Again Dewey took occasion to state that "if any one wishes to give this humanly mediated ideal and fact . . . the *name* God, I do not see how anyone can say him nay . . ." (p. 226).

In these writings in the *Christian Century* Dewey anticipated the formulations of *A Common Faith*. The statements published in 1933 and 1934 are, I think, consistent one with the other, and the earlier statements, perhaps because they are made in a polemical setting, sometimes are even sharper and help a little to bring out his meaning.

III.

As we have noted, in his 1930 autobiographical essay Dewey said that he was aware of the fact that he had frequently been taken to task for his reticence on the problem of religion. It is regrettable that when he at last undertook to formulate his thoughts on this subject, he wrote one of his shortest books. Religion is a subject which has troubled and comforted mankind for thousands of years; it has disturbed and composed societies and empires, as well as countless men and women; it has troubled the thoughts of leading philosophers throughout the centuries.

---

11. "Dr. Dewey Replies," this volume, p. 223. Italics in original.

Yet Dewey did not undertake to deal with the subject until he was about seventy-five years of age, and then he dealt with it only in an extended essay. One cannot say that by that time Dewey was an old man and was mentally and physically too tired or weak to cope with so complex a question, for his magisterial *Logic: The Theory of Inquiry* followed *A Common Faith* four years later, in 1938, when Dewey was almost eighty years of age. In any case, *A Common Faith* leaves one disturbed and provoked. One wishes that Dewey had written on religion at greater length, allowed himself freer play of his intelligence and sensibilities. His style of writing in this little book is too confined, almost crabbed. He gives the feeling of having been in a hurry to get on and to get finished. What he says about God—a subject that fills a large library of books—he compresses in only a few ambiguous sentences. The book certainly has in it many valuable insights, but on the whole it creates the impression of a "hit-and-run" operation. As a consequence, while the book has been widely read and is referred to in bibliographies, its impact on religious thinking has not been commensurate with Dewey's standing in the community of American philosophers.

Dewey was not the first thinker to fail or refuse to recognize an independent status for the religious experience. Matthew Arnold, by identifying religious experience as "morality touched by emotion," in effect assigned to religion the status of an epiphenomenon. Religious experience, to Arnold, was the "righteousness" of the Hebrew Scriptures, but "touched, strengthened, and almost transformed, by the addition of feeling." Dewey, however, extended the reach or seat of the religious experience by making it a quality that belongs to other experiences, such as the aesthetic, scientific, or political, in addition to the moral. Arnold's proposition, according to Dewey, was too confining, too limited. What makes an experience religious is not the manner or cause of its production, but the way the experience operates, the function it performs. Devotion to a cause will make the experience religious in quality. The religious experience therefore occurs "frequently in connection with many significant moments of living." Whatever supports and deepens the sense of values "which carry one through periods of darkness and despair" is a religious experience; but this experience is not limited to such periods; it is a quality that may be said to belong also to companionship, to friendship, to the aesthetic enjoyment of poetry or other works of art. Dewey thus both agrees and disagrees with Arnold. Yes, he says, the religious experience does not have an independent status; but no, it is not attached only to morality.

Bernard Bosanquet, in his Gifford Lectures, *The Value and Destiny of the Individual*, published in 1913, expressed a view which now can be identified as Deweyite. Whatever, said Bosanquet, attaches us in the spirit to a reality of transcendent value, cannot be distinguished from religion. Wherever, he wrote,

> man fairly and loyally throws the seat of his value outside his immediate self into something else which he worships, with which he identifies his will, and which he takes as an object solid and secure at least relatively to his private existence—as an artist in his attitude to beauty or as a man of science to truth—there we have in its degree the experience of religion, and, also in its degree, the stability and security of the finite self.[12]

Thus, Bosanquet, like Arnold before him and like Dewey after him, removes the religious experience from an independent existence and attaches it to values such as the pursuit of truth or beauty, and both Bosanquet and Dewey, unlike Arnold, refuse to limit the religious experience to the realm of moral conduct or the pursuit of righteousness.

In *Literature and Dogma*, Arnold recognized the fact that other ancient peoples, besides Israel, recognized the need for moral order, but the genius and great contribution of Israel was to replace morality with religion; the devotion to and the pursuit of righteousness became the heart of Israel's religious experience, commitment, and mission. What Arnold undertook to do, it may be said, was to translate back religion into morality, to do the reverse of what he said Israel had done. Israel took morality and made it into its religion; Arnold took his religion and made it into morality—"morality touched by emotion"—"touched, strengthened, and almost transformed, by the addition of feeling." Dewey, it may be said, extended the process (as had been done by Bosanquet) to convert all essential values—the pursuit of truth in science, the pursuit of beauty in art, the enjoyment of

12. Bosanquet, *The Value and Destiny of the Individual* (London: Macmillan and Co., 1913), pp. 235, 240.

friendship and companionship, whatever gives value and meaning to human life—to the religious experience.

Common usage of the terms "religion" and "religious" makes it by this time impossible to confine these terms to any specific entity. They denote an attitude, as Dewey says, that may be taken toward any object or ideal. In taking this position, Dewey, I think, reflected what had become common usage and common understanding. For example, Thoreau in *Walden,* at one point wrote: "I got up early and bathed in the pond; that was a religious exercise...."[13] In his *Autobiography,* John Stuart Mill, writing about his wife, wrote: "Her memory is to me a religion."[14] In a lecture he delivered in 1844, Emerson said that he saw that the "religious party" had fallen away from the institutional church and were appearing in all sorts of social action associations, such as "temperance and non-resistance societies; in movements of abolitionists and of socialists; in Sabbath and Bible Conventions, ... even the insect world was to be defended."[15] Emerson was noting the fact that people were looking for the religious experience, not so much in churches as in other forms of activities—that religion had become something penumbral, an epiphenomenon.

While recognizing the fact that this has happened, it may still be asked if it is necessary to deny the existence of the religious experience as something independent and not simply as a sort of afterglow of other experiences, aesthetic, moral, scientific, or whatever they may be. Dewey, I think, should have recognized the fact that it was possible to have the religious experience as a primary experience, with the aesthetic or other values attached to it as secondary qualities. To cite only one example: For many persons, over the centuries, Psalm 23 has expressed what can be described as a purely religious experience. The person says: "In my relations with God, I feel Him to be as if He were my shepherd. In that relationship, I have no unsatisfied wants. In the material and social world in which I live, I have many wants that go

---

13. Henry David Thoreau, *Walden* (New York: Thomas Y. Crowell and Co., 1910), p. 115.
14. Mill, *Autobiography,* World's Classics (London: Oxford University Press, 1924), p. 213.
15. Ralph Waldo Emerson, "New England Reformers," *Essays,* 2d ser. (Boston: Houghton Mifflin Co., 1903).

unsatisfied, and I face many threats to my life and health and all other things I value, but on the level of my relationship with God, I lie down in green pastures and am led beside still waters, and my soul is restored. In my daily existence I know that I walk in the valley of the shadow of death, but on the level of existence where I see myself in relation to God, I fear no evil, for on that level God is with me, His rod and staff comfort me; on that level, I know that He has prepared a table for me—even in the presence of my enemies. On that level of life, my head is anointed with oil, and my cup runneth over."

I think it was a religious experience, pure in its essence and unattached to any other experience or value, that Josiah Royce had in mind when he wrote that one of the interests of the "higher religious consciousness" is that of "the baffled and disappointed soul in coming into the presence of some external truth, some reality that is perfect, that lacks our weakness, that is victorious even though we fail, that is good even though we are worthless."[16] In reflecting upon Spinoza's submissive form of piety, Royce said that a contemplative onlooker at the Everlasting, at the eternal God, accepting one's miseries, one's failures and defeats, may yet say: "His holiness I cannot create. Let me, if haply I may, see it, worship it, enjoy it as wondering, contemplative, adoring, helpless onlooker, consoled, if at all, by the knowledge that though I fail and am lost, he is from everlasting to everlasting."[17]

The term "religious," then, I would say, may in fact denote something in the way of a specific experience, existing by itself. While the term often denotes an attitude that may be taken toward any object or any ideal, it may also denote an experience that exists by itself, an experience that is primary and that is not an effusion from some other experience, that is not an epiphenomenon.

Moreover, I would submit that for some persons righteousness is not morality but religion. Matthew Arnold was right in his insistence that Israel achieved a revolution by replacing morality with religion and by making the pursuit of righteousness the core of its religion. But to the great prophets, religion was not "morality touched by emotion," religion was obedience of God's com-

16. Royce, *The Spirit of Modern Philosophy* (Boston and New York: Houghton Mifflin Co., 1892), p. 46.
17. Ibid., p. 50.

mandment to be righteous. Morality meant life in the presence of God. It did not mean the pursuit of happiness, or the pursuit of virtue, or the attempt to live by the dictates of reason. The object of what we would call morality was to the Hebrew prophets righteousness, which was the object of what we would call the religion of Israel (though Israel had no word for morality and no word for religion; it had words which meant the teachings or commandments of God). Thus Jeremiah cried out: "He judged the cause of the poor and the needy. . . . Is not this to know Me? saith the Lord."[18] This was the teaching of Micah: "He has showed you, O man, what is good; and what does the Lord require of you but to do justice, to love kindness, and to walk humbly with your God?"[19] And Amos made the same appeal: "Take away from Me the noise of thy songs; for I will not hear the melody of thy viols. But let justice well up as the waters and righteousness as a mighty stream."[20] In brief, obeying God's commandments did not mean living a moral life, it meant living a godly life, a religious life. "Cease to do evil, learn to do good," said Isaiah; "seek justice, correct oppression, defend the fatherless, plead for the widow."[21] Wrongdoing was a sin, an offense before the all-seeing God, a violation of His law. There were no laws of morality, no dictates of reason, no commands of the conscience, but simply and only the laws of God. I do not see why this does not point in the direction of a religious experience that is not superimposed upon or attached to morality. If anything, morality may be, in that setting, a derivative value or quality.

IV.

The religious experience should, Dewey says, become unencumbered by beliefs in the supernatural, for such beliefs sap the religious life itself. There is only one sure road to truth, and that is "observation, experiment, record and controlled reflection," and this one road to truth can have no commerce with the

18. Jer. 22:16.
19. Mic. 6:8.
20. Amos 5:23–24.
21. Isa. 1:16–17.

supernatural. Concern with the supernatural diverts attention from ideals because such concern leads persons to wait for God to actualize the ideals. If the forces that are directed toward the supernatural were used in natural ways, evils would be removed by the actions of human beings. Supernatural religions, therefore, are and have been obstacles standing in the way of human progress.

This states a truth which, I believe, can be supported by history. But it is only a partial truth. There have been and there are religions which are rooted in a belief in a transcendent God, or in supernaturalism, and yet are not otherworldly but are thisworldly. In the Hebrew Scriptures, e.g., there is no articulated belief in immortality or resurrection.[22] The great prophets did not point to a heaven but only to the earth and to the opportunity life offered to seek justice and righteousness as the law of God and the law of life. There are religions which teach that we are not to look for miracles, not to look for God to accomplish the tasks He has set for the offspring of Adam and Eve. God is represented as saying to man: "If you will lift the load, I will lift it too; but if you will not lift it, I will not."[23] Such religions teach that God will not give shelter to the homeless, nor feed the hungry, nor care for the widow, the orphan, and the stranger, but that He looks to man to perform these tasks; He says to man: "seek justice, correct oppression, defend the fatherless, plead for the widow"—God created an uncompleted world, and He looks to man to make the corrections, to work with God in completing and fulfilling the creation.

Just as man's historical record will show that men have been diverted from their God-given tasks by reliance on miracles and supernatural interventions, so, too, I think, the record would show that many persons, believing in a transcendent God, worked on the earth to do what God had left undone; that a belief in the supernatural inspired them with the courage and strength they needed to fulfill their ideals, which they saw as goals set for them by God.

22. Some biblical scholars find intimations of a belief in immortality in Psalms 16, 49, and 73, and in some passages in the Book of Job.
23. Talmud, Berakhoth. Quoted in Bernard Mandelbaum, *Choose Life* (New York: Random House, 1968), p. 32.

Dewey, as we have seen, finds in *A Common Faith* a place for God. Kant, it has been said, destroyed deism with the *Critique of Pure Reason*; then with the *Critique of Practical Reason* brought the corpse back to life.[24] Unsympathetic critics would say that Dewey has, with verbal magic, performed the same miracle. There is no room for the supernatural; there is nothing otherworldly; yet there is God. God, said Dewey, may denote "the unity of all ideal ends arousing us to desire and actions" (p. 29). God may be said to be the active relation between the ideal and the actual. Dewey's words in this context are very sparse and thin. It is, I think, impossible to interpret them in a way that will give them substance, force and life, without the fear that one is moving beyond Dewey and attributing ideas to him that he would deny. He wrote, with respect to God, a text on which it is impossible to construct a commentary.

This feeling is reinforced when one thinks of the fact that nowhere in his book does he condemn atheism. He attacks "aggressive atheism" and "militant atheism"; but what of an atheism that is not aggressive, not militant? Well, Dewey does not say, and one does not venture to say for him. But the fact remains that while he condemns supernaturalism, he finds a place for God—not much of a place, but still there it is; he condemns militant or aggressive atheism, but does not say he condemns atheism when it is not militant or aggressive.

There are, says Dewey, what are called mystical experiences, but he says nothing further about them except that their occurrences should lead to scientific inquiry into their causation. That is like saying that there is what is called love, but its occurrence should lead to scientific inquiry into its causation—as if such inquiry would dissipate the passion, excitement and delight of love. Is the mystical experience an illusion, the nature of which would be exposed by scientific research? Would research strip the experience of all mystery and deprive it of all earthly and transcendental value? Can the mystical experience, any more than the aesthetic or moral experience, or love, be "reduced" to physiological and psychological, physical and chemical components?

---

24. Paul Elmer More, *Shelburne Essays*, 6th ser. (Boston and New York: Houghton Mifflin Co., 1909), p. 3.

Since religions are culturally and historically conditioned, says Dewey, we should throw out all their dated cultural baggage and start with a clean slate. This, I think, overlooks the fact that one's connections with the past can be a sustaining tie rather than a constraining chain. To be disengaged from the past, to have no sense of history, to lack a sense of piety for one's origins, inheritance, and traditions, may leave a person rootless and alienated. A mind that is a *tabula rasa* may be as mortifying and harrowing as life in an empty house.

Perhaps John Dewey found himself substantially in the position in which John Stuart Mill found himself when he wrote his three essays on religion, which were published posthumously.[25] In the essay on "Utility of Religion" Mill argued that mental energy was being misspent to prop up religious beliefs, when the same mental powers should be directed toward other sources of virtue and happiness. Mill proposed that the whole domain of the supernatural should be removed from the area of belief to the area of hope; for the only rational attitude was skepticism as to belief in revelation, and skepticism as to atheism. There was, said Mill, legitimacy in the hope that there is providence and the hope that there is immortality; and there is room for the belief that God needs our help.

I cannot help but think that in some way Dewey had in mind the precedent of Mill as he grappled with the question of religion. One wishes that he had written more—or, as a less desirable alternative, that he had written less. Yet *A Common Faith* remains a provocative book, an intellectual and spiritual "teaser," an "essay" at a religious philosophy which no philosopher can wholly bypass.

When one thinks of this small book in the context of John Dewey's total contribution to American thought, there comes to mind Matthew Arnold's characterization of Marcus Aurelius, for in general the line of thought and action Dewey prescribes are such which

---

25. *The Philosophy of John Stuart Mill,* ed. Marshall Cohen (New York: Modern Library, 1961); John Stuart Mill, *Essays on Politics and Culture,* ed. Gertrude Himmelfarb (Garden City, N.Y.: Doubleday and Co., 1962).

every sound nature must recognize as right, and the motives he assigns are motives which every clear reason must recognize as valid. And so he remains the especial friend and comforter of all clear-headed and scrupulous, yet pure-hearted and upward-striving men, in those ages most especially that walk by sight and not by faith, and yet have no open vision; he cannot give such souls, perhaps, all they yearn for, but he gives them much; and what he gives them, they can receive.[26]

26. Arnold, *Essays in Criticism,* 1st ser. (London and New York: Macmillan and Co., 1891), p. 278.

A Common Faith

1. Religion versus the Religious

Never before in history has mankind been so much of two minds, so divided into two camps, as it is today. Religions have traditionally been allied with ideas of the supernatural, and often have been based upon explicit beliefs about it. Today there are many who hold that nothing worthy of being called religious is possible apart from the supernatural. Those who hold this belief differ in many respects. They range from those who accept the dogmas and sacraments of the Greek and Roman Catholic church as the only sure means of access to the supernatural to the theist or mild deist. Between them are the many Protestant denominations who think the Scriptures, aided by a pure conscience, are adequate avenues to supernatural truth and power. But they agree in one point: the necessity for a Supernatural Being and for an immortality that is beyond the power of nature.

The opposed group consists of those who think the advance of culture and science has completely discredited the supernatural and with it all religions that were allied with belief in it. But they go beyond this point. The extremists in this group believe that with elimination of the supernatural not only must historic religions be dismissed but with them everything of a religious nature. When historical knowledge has discredited the claims made for the supernatural character of the persons said to have founded historic religions; when the supernatural inspiration attributed to literatures held sacred has been riddled, and when anthropological and psychological knowledge has disclosed the all-too-human source from which religious beliefs and practices have sprung, everything religious must, they say, also go.

There is one idea held in common by these two opposite groups: identification of the religious with the supernatural. The question I shall raise in these chapters concerns the ground for and the consequences of this identification: its reasons and its value. In the discussion I shall develop another conception of the nature of the religious phase of experience, one that separates it from the supernatural and the things that have grown up about it. I shall try to show that these derivations are encumbrances and that what is genuinely religious will undergo an emancipation when it is relieved from them; that then, for the first time, the religious aspect of experience will be free to develop freely on its own account.

This view is exposed to attack from both the other camps. It goes contrary to traditional religions, including those that have the greatest hold upon the religiously minded today. The view announced will seem to them to cut the vital nerve of the religious element itself in taking away the basis upon which traditional religions and institutions have been founded. From the other side, the position I am taking seems like a timid halfway position, a concession and compromise unworthy of thought that is thoroughgoing. It is regarded as a view entertained from mere tendermindedness, as an emotional hangover from childhood indoctrination, or even as a manifestation of a desire to avoid disapproval and curry favor.

The heart of my point, as far as I shall develop it in this first section, is that there is a difference between religion, *a* religion, and the religious; between anything that may be denoted by a noun substantive and the quality of experience that is designated by an adjective. It is not easy to find a definition of religion in the substantive sense that wins general acceptance. However, in the *Oxford Dictionary* I find the following: "Recognition on the part of man of some unseen higher power as having control of his destiny and as being entitled to obedience, reverence and worship."

This particular definition is less explicit in assertion of the supernatural character of the higher unseen power than are others that might be cited. It is, however, surcharged with implications having their source in ideas connected with the belief in the supernatural, characteristic of historic religions. Let us suppose that one familiar with the history of religions, including those called primitive, compares the definition with the variety of known facts and by means of the comparison sets out to determine just what the definition means. I think he will be struck by three facts that reduce the terms of the definition to such a low common denominator that little meaning is left.

He will note that the "unseen powers" referred to have been conceived in a multitude of incompatible ways. Eliminating the differences, nothing is left beyond the bare reference to something unseen and powerful. This has been conceived as the vague and undefined Mana of the Melanesians; the Kami of primitive Shintoism; the fetish of the Africans; spirits, having some human properties, that pervade natural places and animate natural forces; the ultimate and impersonal principle of Buddhism; the unmoved mover of Greek thought; the gods and semi-divine heroes of the Greek and Roman Pantheons; the personal and loving Providence of Christianity, omnipotent, and limited by a corresponding evil power; the arbitrary Will of Moslemism; the supreme legislator and judge of deism. And these are but a few of the outstanding varieties of ways in which the invisible power has been conceived.

There is no greater similarity in the ways in which obedience and reverence have been expressed. There has been worship of animals, of ghosts, of ancestors, phallic worship, as well as of a Being of dread power and of love and wisdom. Reverence has been expressed in the human sacrifices of the Peruvians and Aztecs; the sexual orgies of some Oriental religions; exorcisms and ablutions; the offering of the humble and contrite mind of the Hebrew prophet, the elaborate rituals of the Greek and Roman Churches. Not even sacrifice has been uniform; it is highly sublimated in Protestant denominations and in Moslemism. Where it has existed it has taken all kinds of forms and been directed to a great variety of powers and spirits. It has been used for expiation, for propitiation and for buying special favors. There is no conceivable purpose for which rites have not been employed.

Finally, there is no discernible unity in the moral motivations appealed to and utilized. They have been as far apart as fear of lasting torture, hope of enduring bliss in which sexual enjoyment has sometimes been a conspicuous element; mortification of the flesh and extreme asceticism; prostitution and chastity; wars to extirpate the unbeliever; persecution to convert or punish the unbeliever, and philanthropic zeal; servile acceptance of imposed dogma, along with brotherly love and aspiration for a reign of justice among men.

I have, of course, mentioned only a sparse number of the facts which fill volumes in any well-stocked library. It may be asked by those who do not like to look upon the darker side of the history of religions why the darker facts should be brought up. We all know that civilized man has a background of bestiality and superstition and that these elements are still with us. Indeed, have not some religions, including the most influential forms of Christianity, taught that the heart of man is totally corrupt? How could the course of religion in its entire sweep not be marked by practices that are shameful in their cruelty and lustfulness, and by beliefs that are degraded and intellectually incredible? What else than what we find could be expected, in the case of people having little knowledge and no secure method of knowing; with primitive institutions, and with so little control of natural forces that they lived in a constant state of fear?

I gladly admit that historic religions have been relative to the conditions of social culture in which peoples lived. Indeed, what I am concerned with is to press home the logic of this method of disposal of outgrown traits of past religions. Beliefs and practices in a religion that now prevails are by this logic relative to the present state of culture. If so much flexibility has obtained in the past regarding an unseen power, the way it affects human destiny, and the attitudes we are to take toward it, why should it be assumed that change in conception and action has now come to an end? The logic involved in getting rid of inconvenient aspects of past religions compels us to inquire how much in religions now accepted are survivals from outgrown cultures. It compels us to ask what conception of unseen powers and our relations to them would be consonant with the best achievements and aspirations of the present. It demands that in imagination we wipe the slate clean and start afresh by asking what would be the idea of the unseen, of the manner of its control over us and the ways in which reverence and obedience would be manifested, if whatever is basically religious in experience had the opportunity to express itself free from all historic encumbrances.

So we return to the elements of the definition that has been given. What boots it to accept, in defense of the universality of religion, a definition that applies equally to the most savage and degraded beliefs and practices that have related to unseen powers and to noble ideals of a religion having the greatest share of moral content? There are two points involved. One of them is that there is nothing left worth preserving in the notions of unseen powers, controlling human destiny to which obedience, reverence and worship are due, if we glide silently over the nature that has been attributed to the powers, the radically diverse ways in which they have been supposed to control human destiny, and in which submission and awe have been manifested. The other point is that when we begin to select, to choose, and say that some present ways of thinking about the unseen powers are better than others; that the reverence shown by a free and self-respecting human being is better than the servile obedience rendered to an arbitrary power by frightened men; that we should believe that control of human destiny is exercised by a wise and loving spirit rather than by madcap ghosts or sheer force—when I say, we begin to choose, we have entered upon a road that has not yet come to an end. We have reached a point that invites us to proceed farther.

For we are forced to acknowledge that concretely there is no such thing as religion in the singular. There is only a multitude of religions. "Religion" is a strictly collective term and the collection it stands for is not even of the kind illustrated in textbooks of logic. It has not the unity of a regiment or assembly but that of any miscellaneous aggregate. Attempts to prove the universality prove too much or too little. It is probable that religions have been universal in the sense that all the peoples we know anything about have had *a* religion. But the differences among them are so great and so shocking that any common element that can be extracted is meaningless. The idea that religion is universal proves too little in that the older apologists for Christianity seem to have been better advised than some modern ones in condemning every religion but one as an impostor, as at bottom some kind of demon worship or at any rate a superstitious figment. Choice among religions is imperative, and the necessity for choice leaves nothing of any force in the argument from universality. Moreover, when once we enter upon the road of choice, there is at once presented a possibility not yet generally realized.

For the historic increase of the ethical and ideal content of religions suggests that the process of purification may be carried further. It indicates that further choice is imminent in which certain values and functions in experience may be selected. This possibility is what I had in mind in speaking of the difference between the religious and a religion. I am not proposing a religion, but rather the emancipation of elements and outlooks that may be called religious. For the moment we have a religion, whether that of the Sioux Indian or of Judaism or of Christianity, that moment the ideal factors in experience that may be called religious take on a load that is not inherent in them, a load of current beliefs and of institutional practices that are irrelevant to them.

I can illustrate what I mean by a common phenomenon in contemporary life. It is widely supposed that a person who does not accept any religion is thereby shown to be a non-religious person. Yet it is conceivable that the present depression in religion is closely connected with the fact that religions now prevent, because of their weight of historic encumbrances, the religious quality of experience from coming to consciousness and finding the expression that is appropriate to present conditions, intellectual and moral. I believe that such is the case. I believe that many persons are so repelled from what exists as a religion by its intellectual and moral implications, that they are not even aware of attitudes in themselves that if they came to fruition would be genuinely religious. I hope that this remark may help make clear what I mean by the distinction between "religion" as a noun substantive and "religious" as adjectival.

To be somewhat more explicit, a religion (and as I have just said there is no such thing as religion in general) always signifies a special body of beliefs and practices having some kind of institutional organization, loose or tight. In contrast, the adjective "religious" denotes nothing in the way of a specifiable entity, either institutional or as a system of beliefs. It does not denote anything to which one can specifically point as one can point to this and that historic religion or existing church. For it does not denote anything that can exist by itself or that can be organized into a particular and distinctive form of existence. It denotes attitudes that may be taken toward every object and every proposed end or ideal.

Before, however, I develop my suggestion that realization of the distinction just made would operate to emancipate the religious quality from encumbrances that now smother or limit it, I must refer to a position that in some respects is similar in words to the position I have taken, but that in fact is a whole world removed from it. I have several times used the phrase "religious elements of experience." Now at present there is much talk, especially in liberal circles, of religious experience as vouching for the authenticity of certain beliefs and the desirability of certain practices, such as particular forms of prayer and worship. It is even asserted that religious experience is the ultimate basis of religion itself. The gulf between this position and that which I have taken is what I am now concerned to point out.

Those who hold to the notion that there is a definite kind of experience which is itself religious, by that very fact make out of it something specific, as a kind of experience that is marked off from experience as aesthetic, scientific, moral, political; from experience as companionship and friendship. But "religious" as a quality of experience signifies something that may belong to all these experiences. It is the polar opposite of some type of experience that can exist by itself. The distinction comes out clearly when it is noted that the concept of this distinct kind of experience is used to validate a belief in some special kind of object and also to justify some special kind of practice.

For there are many religionists who are now dissatisfied with the older "proofs" of the existence of God, those that go by the name of ontological, cosmological and teleological. The cause of the dissatisfaction is perhaps not so much the arguments that Kant used to show the insufficiency of these alleged proofs, as it is the growing feeling that they are too formal to offer any support to religion in action. Anyway, the dissatisfaction exists. Moreover, these religionists are moved by the rise of the experimental method in other fields. What is more natural and proper, accordingly, than that they should affirm they are just as good empiricists as anybody else—indeed, as good as the scientists themselves? As the latter rely upon certain kinds of experience to prove the existence of certain kinds of objects, so the religionists rely upon a certain kind of experience to prove the existence of the object of religion, especially the supreme object, God.

The discussion may be made more definite by introducing, at this point, a particular illustration of this type of reasoning. A writer says: "I broke down from overwork and soon came to the verge of nervous prostration. One morning after a long and sleepless night ... I resolved to stop drawing upon myself so continuously and begin drawing upon God. I determined to set apart a quiet time every day in which I could relate my life to its Ultimate Source, regain the consciousness that in God I live, move and have my being. That was thirty years ago. Since then I have had literally not one hour of darkness or despair."

This is an impressive record. I do not doubt its authenticity nor that of the experience related. It illustrates a religious aspect of experience. But it illustrates also the use of that quality to carry a superimposed load of a particular religion. For having been brought up in the Christian religion, its subject interprets it in the terms of the personal God characteristic of that religion. Taoists, Buddhists, Moslems, persons of no religion including those who reject all supernatural influence and power, have had experiences similar in their effect. Yet another author commenting upon the passage says: "The religious expert can be more sure that this God exists than he can of either the cosmological God of speculative surmise or the Christlike God involved in the validity of moral optimism," and goes on to add that such experiences "mean that God the Savior, the Power that gives victory over sin on certain conditions that man can fulfill, is an existent, accessible and scientifically knowable reality." It should be clear that this inference is sound only if the conditions, of whatever sort, that produce the effect are called "God." But most readers will take the inference to mean that the existence of a particular Being, of the type called "God" in the Christian religion, is proved by a method akin to that of experimental science.

In reality, the only thing that can be said to be "proved" is the existence of some complex of conditions that have operated to effect an adjustment in life, an orientation, that brings with it a sense of security and peace. The particular interpretation given to this complex of conditions is not inherent in the experience itself. It is derived from the culture with which a particular person has been imbued. A fatalist will give one name to it; a Christian Scientist another, and the one who rejects all supernatural being still another. The determining factor in the interpretation of the experience is the particular doctrinal apparatus into which a person has been inducted. The emotional deposit connected with prior teaching floods the whole situation. It may readily confer upon the experience such a peculiarly sacred preciousness that all inquiry into its causation is barred. The stable outcome is so invaluable that the cause to which it is referred is usually nothing but a reduplication of the thing that has occurred, plus some name that has acquired a deeply emotional quality.

The intent of this discussion is not to deny the genuineness of the result nor its importance in life. It is not, save incidentally, to point out the possibility of a purely naturalistic explanation of the event. My purpose is to indicate what happens when religious experience is already set aside as something *sui generis*. The actual religious quality in the experience described is the *effect* produced, the better adjustment in life and its conditions, not the manner and cause of its production. The way in which the experience operated, its function, determines its religious value. If the reorientation actually occurs, it, and the sense of security and stability accompanying it, are forces on their own account. It takes place in different persons in a multitude of ways. It is sometimes brought about by devotion to a cause; sometimes by a passage of poetry that opens a new perspective; sometimes as was the case with Spinoza—deemed an atheist in his day—through philosophical reflection.

The difference between an experience having a religious force because of what it does in and to the processes of living and religious experience as a separate kind of thing gives me occasion to refer to a previous remark. If this function were rescued through emancipation from dependence upon specific types of beliefs and practices, from those elements that constitute a religion, many individuals would find that experiences having the force of bringing about a better, deeper and enduring adjustment in life are not so rare and infrequent as they are commonly supposed to be. They occur frequently in connection with many significant moments of living. The idea of invisible powers would take on the meaning of all the conditions of nature and human association that support and deepen the sense of values which carry one through periods of darkness and despair to such an extent that they lose their usual depressive character.

I do not suppose for many minds the dislocation of the religious from a religion is easy to effect. Tradition and custom, especially when emotionally charged, are a part of the habits that have become one with our very being. But the possibility of the transfer is demonstrated by its actuality. Let us then for the moment drop the term "religious," and ask what are the attitudes that lend deep and enduring support to the processes of living. I have, for example, used the words "adjustment" and "orientation." What do they signify?

While the words "accommodation," "adaptation," and "adjustment" are frequently employed as synonyms, attitudes exist that are so different that for the sake of clear thought they should be discriminated. There are conditions we meet that cannot be changed. If they are particular and limited, we modify our own particular attitudes in accordance with them. Thus we accommodate ourselves to changes in weather, to alterations in income when we have no other recourse. When the external conditions are lasting we become inured, habituated, or, as the process is now often called, conditioned. The two main traits of this attitude, which I should like to call accommodation, are that it affects *particular* modes of conduct, not the entire self, and that the process is mainly *passive*. It may, however, become general and then it becomes fatalistic resignation or submission. There are other attitudes toward the environment that are also particular but that are more active. We re-act against conditions and endeavor to change them to meet our wants and demands. Plays in a foreign language are "adapted" to meet the needs of an American audience. A house is rebuilt to suit changed conditions of the household; the telephone is invented to serve the demand for speedy communication at a distance; dry soils are irrigated so that they may bear abundant crops. Instead of accommodating ourselves to conditions, we modify conditions so that they will be accommodated to our wants and purposes. This process may be called adaptation.

Now both of these processes are often called by the more general name of adjustment. But there are also changes in ourselves in relation to the world in which we live that are much more inclusive and deep seated. They relate not to this and that want in relation to this and that condition of our surroundings, but pertain to our being in its entirety. Because of their scope, this modification of ourselves is enduring. It lasts through any amount of vicissitude of circumstances, internal and external. There is a composing and harmonizing of the various elements of our being such that, in spite of changes in the special conditions that surround us, these conditions are also arranged, settled, in relation to us. This attitude includes a note of submission. But it is voluntary, not externally imposed; and as voluntary it is something more than a mere Stoical resolution to endure unperturbed throughout the buffetings of fortune. It is more outgoing, more ready and glad, than the latter attitude, and it is more active than the former. And in calling it voluntary, it is not meant that it depends upon a particular resolve or volition. It is a change *of* will conceived as the organic plenitude of our being, rather than any special change *in* will.

It is the claim of religions that they effect this generic and enduring change in attitude. I should like to turn the statement around and say that whenever this change takes place there is a definitely religious attitude. It is not *a* religion that brings it about, but when it occurs, from whatever cause and by whatever means, there is a religious outlook and function. As I have said before, the doctrinal or intellectual apparatus and the institutional accretions that grow up are, in a strict sense, adventitious to the intrinsic quality of such experiences. For they are affairs of the traditions of the culture with which individuals are inoculated. Mr. Santayana has connected the religious quality of experience with the imaginative, as that is expressed in poetry. "Religion and poetry," he says, "are identical in essence, and differ merely in the way in which they are attached to practical affairs. Poetry is called religion when it intervenes in life, and religion, when it merely supervenes upon life, is seen to be nothing but poetry." The difference between intervening *in* and supervening *upon* is as important as is the identity set forth. Imagination may play upon life or it may enter profoundly into it. As Mr. Santayana puts it, "poetry has a universal and a moral function," for "its highest power lies in its relevance to the ideals and purposes of life." Except as it intervenes, "all observation is observation of brute fact, all discipline is mere repression, until these facts digested and this discipline embodied in humane impulses become the starting-point for a creative movement of the imagination, the firm basis for ideal constructions in society, religion, and art."

If I may make a comment upon this penetrating insight of Mr. Santayana, I would say that the difference between imagination that only supervenes and imagination that intervenes is the difference between one that completely interpenetrates all the elements of our being and one that is interwoven with only special and partial factors. There actually occurs extremely little observation of brute facts merely for the sake of the facts, just as there is little discipline that is repression and nothing but repression. Facts are usually observed with reference to some practical end and purpose, and that end is presented only imaginatively. The most repressive discipline has some end in view to which there is at least imputed an ideal quality; otherwise it is purely sadistic. But in such cases of observation and discipline imagination is limited and partial. It does not extend far; it does not permeate deeply and widely.

The connection between imagination and the harmonizing of the self is closer than is usually thought. The idea of a whole, whether of the whole personal being or of the world, is an imaginative, not a literal, idea. The limited world of our observation and reflection becomes the Universe only through imaginative extension. It cannot be apprehended in knowledge nor realized in reflection. Neither observation, thought, nor practical activity can attain that complete unification of the self which is called a whole. The *whole* self is an ideal, an imaginative projection. Hence the idea of a thoroughgoing and deep-seated harmonizing of the self with the Universe (as a name for the totality of conditions with which the self is connected) operates only through imagination—which is one reason why this composing of the self is not voluntary in the sense of an act of special volition or resolution. An "adjustment" possesses the will rather than is its express product. Religionists have been right in thinking of it as an influx from sources beyond conscious deliberation and purpose—a fact that helps explain, psychologically, why it has so generally been attributed to a supernatural source and that, perhaps, throws some light upon the reference of it by William James to unconscious factors. And it is pertinent to note that the unification of the self throughout the ceaseless flux of what it does, suffers, and achieves, cannot be attained in terms of itself. The self is always directed toward something beyond itself and so its own unification depends upon the idea of the integration of the shifting scenes of the world into that imaginative totality we call the Universe.

The intimate connection of imagination with ideal elements in experience is generally recognized. Such is not the case with respect to its connection with faith. The latter has been regarded as a substitute for knowledge, for sight. It is defined, in the Christian religion, as *evidence* of things not seen. The implication is that faith is a kind of anticipatory vision of things that are now invisible because of the limitations of our finite and erring nature. Because it is a substitute for knowledge, its material and object are intellectual in quality. As John Locke summed up the matter, faith is "assent to a proposition . . . on the credit of its proposer." Religious faith is then given to a body of propositions as true on the credit of their supernatural author, reason coming in to demonstrate the reasonableness of giving such credit. Of necessity there results the development of theologies, or bodies of systematic propositions, to make explicit in organized form the content of the propositions to which belief is attached and assent given. Given the point of view, those who hold that religion necessarily implies a theology are correct.

But belief or faith has also a moral and practical import. Even devils, according to the older theologians, believe—and tremble. A distinction was made, therefore, between "speculative" or intellectual belief and an act called "justifying" faith. Apart from any theological context, there is a difference between belief that is a conviction that some end should be supreme over conduct, and belief that some object or being exists as a truth for the intellect. Conviction in the moral sense signifies being conquered, vanquished, in our active nature by an ideal end; it signifies acknowledgment of its rightful claim over our desires and purposes. Such acknowledgment is practical, not primarily intellectual. It goes beyond evidence that can be presented to *any* possible observer. Reflection, often long and arduous, may be involved in arriving at the conviction, but the import of thought is not exhausted in discovery of evidence that can justify intellectual assent. The authority of an ideal over choice and conduct is the authority of an ideal, not of a fact, of a truth guaranteed to intellect, not of the status of the one who propounds the truth.

Such moral faith is not easy. It was questioned of old whether the Son of Man should find faith on the earth in his coming. Moral faith has been bolstered by all sorts of arguments intended to prove that its object is not ideal and that its claim upon us is not primarily moral or practical, since the ideal in question is already embedded in the existent frame of things. It is argued that the ideal is already the final reality at the heart of things that exist, and that only our senses or the corruption of our natures prevent us from apprehending its prior existential being. Starting, say, from such an idea as that justice is more than a moral ideal because it is embedded in the very make-up of the actually existent world, men have gone on to build up vast intellectual schemes, philosophies, and theologies, to prove that ideals are real not as ideals but as antecedently existing actualities. They have failed to see that in converting moral realities into matters of intellectual assent they have evinced lack of *moral* faith. Faith that something should be in existence as far as lies in our power is changed into the intellectual belief that it is already in existence. When physical existence does not bear out the assertion, the physical is subtly changed into the metaphysical. In this way, moral faith has been inextricably tied up with intellectual beliefs about the supernatural.

The tendency to convert ends of moral faith and action into articles of an intellectual creed has been furthered by a tendency of which psychologists are well aware. What we ardently desire to have thus and so, we tend to believe is already so. Desire has a powerful influence upon intellectual beliefs. Moreover, when conditions are adverse to realization of the objects of our desire—and in the case of significant ideals they are extremely adverse—it is an easy way out to assume that after all they are already embodied in the ultimate structure of what is, and that appearances to the contrary are *merely* appearances. Imagination then merely supervenes and is freed from the responsibility for intervening. Weak natures take to reverie as a refuge as strong ones do to fanaticism. Those who dissent are mourned over by the first class and converted through the use of force by the second.

What has been said does not imply that all moral faith in ideal ends is by virtue of that fact religious in quality. The religious is "morality touched by emotion" only when the ends of moral conviction arouse emotions that are not only intense but are actuated and supported by ends so inclusive that they unify the self. The inclusiveness of the end in relation to both self and the "universe" to which an inclusive self is related is indispensable. According to the best authorities, "religion" comes from a root that means being bound or tied. Originally, it meant being bound by vows to a particular way of life—as *les religieux* were monks and nuns who had assumed certain vows. The religious attitude signifies something that is bound through imagination to a *general* attitude. This comprehensive attitude, moreover, is much broader than anything indicated by "moral" in its usual sense. The quality of attitude is displayed in art, science and good citizenship.

If we apply the conception set forth to the terms of the definition earlier quoted, these terms take on a new significance. An unseen power controlling our destiny becomes the power of an ideal. All possibilities, as possibilities, are ideal in character. The artist, scientist, citizen, parent, as far as they are actuated by the spirit of their callings, are controlled by the unseen. For all endeavor for the better is moved by faith in what is possible, not by adherence to the actual. Nor does this faith depend for its moving power upon intellectual assurance or belief that the things worked for must surely prevail and come into embodied existence. For the authority of the object to determine our attitude and conduct, the right that is given it to claim our allegiance and devotion is based on the intrinsic nature of the ideal. The outcome, given our best endeavor, is not with us. The inherent vice of all intellectual schemes of idealism is that they convert the idealism of action into a system of beliefs about antecedent reality. The character assigned this reality is so different from that which observation and reflection lead to and support that these schemes inevitably glide into alliance with the supernatural.

All religions, marked by elevated ideal quality, have dwelt upon the power of religion to introduce perspective into the piecemeal and shifting episodes of existence. Here too we need to reverse the ordinary statement and say that whatever introduces genuine perspective is religious, not that religion is something that introduces it. There can be no doubt (referring to the second element of the definition) of our dependence upon forces beyond our control. Primitive man was so impotent in the face of these forces that, especially in an unfavorable natural environment, fear became a dominant attitude, and, as the old saying goes, fear created the gods.

With increase of mechanisms of control, the element of fear has, relatively speaking, subsided. Some optimistic souls have even concluded that the forces about us are on the whole essentially benign. But every crisis, whether of the individual or of the community, reminds man of the precarious and partial nature of the control he exercises. When man, individually and collectively, has done his uttermost, conditions that at different times and places have given rise to the ideas of Fate and Fortune, of Chance and Providence, remain. It is the part of manliness to insist upon the capacity of mankind to strive to direct natural and social forces to humane ends. But unqualified absolutistic statements about the omnipotence of such endeavors reflect egoism rather than intelligent courage.

The fact that human destiny is so interwoven with forces beyond human control renders it unnecessary to suppose that dependence and the humility that accompanies it have to find the particular channel that is prescribed by traditional doctrines. What is especially significant is rather the form which the sense of dependence takes. Fear never gave stable perspective in the life of anyone. It is dispersive and withdrawing. Most religions have in fact added rites of communion to those of expiation and propitiation. For our dependence is manifested in those relations to the environment that support our undertakings and aspirations as much as it is in the defeats inflicted upon us. The essentially unreligious attitude is that which attributes human achievement and purpose to man in isolation from the world of physical nature and his fellows. Our successes are dependent upon the cooperation of nature. The sense of the dignity of human nature is as religious as is the sense of awe and reverence when it rests upon a sense of human nature as a cooperating part of a larger whole. Natural piety is not of necessity either a fatalistic acquiescence in natural happenings or a romantic idealization of the world. It may rest upon a just sense of nature as the whole of which we are parts, while it also recognizes that we are parts that are marked by intelligence and purpose, having the capacity to strive by their aid to bring conditions into greater consonance with what is humanly desirable. Such piety is an inherent constituent of a just perspective in life.

Understanding and knowledge also enter into a perspective that is religious in quality. Faith in the continued disclosing of truth through directed cooperative human endeavor is more religious in quality than is any faith in a completed revelation. It is of course now usual to hold that revelation is not completed in the sense of being ended. But religions hold that the essential framework is settled in its significant moral features at least, and that new elements that are offered must be judged by conformity to this framework. Some fixed doctrinal apparatus is necessary for *a* religion. But faith in the possibilities of continued and rigorous inquiry does not limit access to truth to any channel or scheme of things. It does not first say that truth is universal and then add there is but one road to it. It does not depend for assurance upon subjection to any dogma or item of doctrine. It trusts that the natural interactions between man and his environment will breed more intelligence and generate more knowledge provided the scientific methods that define intelligence in operation are pushed further into the mysteries of the world, being themselves promoted and improved in the operation. There is such a thing as faith in intelligence becoming religious in quality—a fact that perhaps explains the efforts of some religionists to disparage the possibilities of intelligence as a force. They properly feel such faith to be a dangerous rival.

Lives that are consciously inspired by loyalty to such ideals as have been mentioned are still comparatively infrequent to the extent of that comprehensiveness and intensity which arouse an ardor religious in function. But before we infer the incompetency of such ideals and of the actions they inspire, we should at least ask ourselves how much of the existing situation is due to the fact that the religious factors of experience have been drafted into supernatural channels and thereby loaded with irrelevant encumbrances. A body of beliefs and practices that are apart from the common and natural relations of mankind must, in the degree in which it is influential, weaken and sap the force of the possibilities inherent in such relations. Here lies one aspect of the emancipation of the religious from religion.

Any activity pursued in behalf of an ideal end against obstacles and in spite of threats of personal loss because of conviction of its general and enduring value is religious in quality. Many a person, inquirer, artist, philanthropist, citizen, men and women in the humblest walks of life, have achieved, without presumption and without display, such unification of themselves and of their relations to the conditions of existence. It remains to extend their spirit and inspiration to ever wider numbers. If I have said anything about religions and religion that seems harsh, I have said those things because of a firm belief that the claim on the part of religions to possess a monopoly of ideals and of the supernatural means by which alone, it is alleged, they can be furthered, stands in the way of the realization of distinctively religious values inherent in natural experience. For that reason, if for no other, I should be sorry if any were misled by the frequency with which I have employed the adjective "religious" to conceive of what I have said as a disguised apology for what have passed as religions. The opposition between religious values as I conceive them and religions is not to be bridged. Just because the release of these values is so important, their identification with the creeds and cults of religions must be dissolved.

2. Faith and Its Object

All religions, as I pointed out in the preceding chapter, involve specific intellectual beliefs, and they attach—some greater, some less—importance to assent to these doctrines as true, true in the intellectual sense. They have literatures held especially sacred, containing historical material with which the validity of the religions is connected. They have developed a doctrinal apparatus it is incumbent upon "believers" (with varying degrees of strictness in different religions) to accept. They also insist that there is some special and isolated channel of access to the truths they hold.

No one will deny, I suppose, that the present crisis in religion is intimately bound up with these claims. The skepticism and agnosticism that are rife and that from the standpoint of the religionist are fatal to the religious spirit are directly bound up with the intellectual contents, historical, cosmological, ethical, and theological, asserted to be indispensable in everything religious. There is no need for me here to go with any minuteness into the causes that have generated doubt and disbelief, uncertainty and rejection, as to these contents. It is enough to point out that all the beliefs and ideas in question, whether having to do with historical and literary matters, or with astronomy, geology and biology, or with the creation and structure of the world and man, are connected with the supernatural, and that this connection is the factor that has brought doubt upon them; the factor that from the standpoint of historic and institutional religions is sapping the religious life itself.

The obvious and simple facts of the case are that some views about the origin and constitution of the world and man, some views about the course of human history and personages and incidents in that history, have become so interwoven with religion as to be identified with it. On the other hand, the growth of knowledge and of its methods and tests has been such as to make acceptance of these beliefs increasingly onerous and even impossible for large numbers of cultivated men and women. With such persons, the result is that the more these ideas are used as the basis and justification of a religion, the more dubious that religion becomes.

Protestant denominations have largely abandoned the idea that particular ecclesiastic sources can authoritatively determine cosmic, historic and theological beliefs. The more liberal among them have at least mitigated the older belief that individual hardness and corruption of heart are the causes of intellectual rejection of the intellectual apparatus of the Christian religion. But these denominations have also, with exceptions numerically insignificant, retained a certain indispensable minimum of intellectual content. They ascribe peculiar religious force to certain literary documents and certain historic personages. Even when they have greatly reduced the bulk of intellectual content to be accepted, they have insisted at least upon theism and the immortality of the individual.

It is no part of my intention to rehearse in any detail the weighty facts that collectively go by the name of the conflict of science and religion—a conflict that is not done away with by calling it a conflict of science with theology, as long as even a minimum of intellectual assent is prescribed as essential. The impact of astronomy not merely upon the older cosmogony of religion but upon elements of creeds dealing with historic events—witness the idea of ascent into heaven—is familiar. Geological discoveries have displaced creation myths which once bulked large. Biology has revolutionized conceptions of soul and mind which once occupied a central place in religious beliefs and ideas, and this science has made a profound impression upon ideas of sin, redemption, and immortality. Anthropology, history and literary criticism have furnished a radically different version of the historic events and personages upon which Christian religions have built. Psychology is already opening to us natural explanations of phenomena so extraordinary that once their supernatural origin was, so to say, the natural explanation.

The significant bearing for my purpose of all this is that new methods of inquiry and reflection have become for the educated man today the final arbiter of all questions of fact, existence, and intellectual assent. Nothing less than a revolution in the "seat of intellectual authority" has taken place. This revolution, rather than any particular aspect of its impact upon this and that religious belief, is the central thing. In this revolution, every defeat is a stimulus to renewed inquiry; every victory won is the open door to more discoveries, and every discovery is a new seed planted in the soil of intelligence, from which grow fresh plants with new fruits. The mind of man is being habituated to a new method and ideal: There is but one sure road of access to truth—the road of patient, cooperative inquiry operating by means of observation, experiment, record and controlled reflection.

The scope of the change is well illustrated by the fact that whenever a particular outpost is surrendered it is usually met by the remark from a liberal theologian that the particular doctrine or supposed historic or literary tenet surrendered was never, after all, an intrinsic part of religious belief, and that without it the true nature of religion stands out more clearly than before. Equally significant is the growing gulf between fundamentalists and liberals in the churches. What is not realized—although perhaps it is more definitely seen by fundamentalists than by liberals—is that the issue does not concern this and that piecemeal *item* of belief, but centres in the question of the method by which any and every item of intellectual belief is to be arrived at and justified.

The positive lesson is that religious qualities and values if they are real at all are not bound up with any single item of intellectual assent, not even that of the existence of the God of theism; and that, under existing conditions, the religious function in experience can be emancipated only through surrender of the whole notion of special truths that are religious by their own nature, together with the idea of peculiar avenues of access to such truths. For were we to admit that there is but one method for ascertaining fact and truth—that conveyed by the word "scientific" in its most general and generous sense—no discovery in any branch of knowledge and inquiry could then disturb the faith that is religious. I should describe this faith as the unification of the self through allegiance to inclusive ideal ends, which imagination presents to us and to which the human will responds as worthy of controlling our desires and choices.

It is probably impossible to imagine the amount of intellectual energy that has been diverted from normal processes of arriving at intellectual conclusions because it has gone into rationalization of the doctrines entertained by historic religions. The set that has thus been given the general mind is much more harmful, to my mind, than are the consequences of any one particular item of belief, serious as have been those flowing from acceptance of some of them. The modern liberal version of the intellectual content of Christianity seems to the modern mind to be more rational than some of the earlier doctrines that have been reacted against. Such is not the case in fact. The theological philosophers of the Middle Ages had no greater difficulty in giving rational form to all the doctrines of the Roman church than has the liberal theologian of today in formulating and justifying intellectually the doctrines he entertains. This statement is as applicable to the doctrine of continuing miracles, penance, indulgences, saints and angels, etc., as to the trinity, incarnation, atonement, and the sacraments. The fundamental question, I repeat, is not of this and that article of intellectual belief but of intellectual habit, method and criterion.

One method of swerving aside the impact of changed knowledge and method upon the intellectual content of religion is the method of division of territory and jurisdiction into two parts. Formerly these were called the realm of nature and the realm of grace. They are now often known as those of revelation and natural knowledge. Modern religious liberalism has no definite names for them, save, perhaps, the division, referred to in the last chapter, between scientific and religious experience. The implication is that in one territory the supremacy of scientific knowledge must be acknowledged, while there is another region, not very precisely defined, of intimate personal experience wherein other methods and criteria hold sway.

This method of justifying the peculiar and legitimate claim of certain elements of belief is always open to the objection that a positive conclusion is drawn from a negative fact. Existing ignorance or backwardness is employed to assert the existence of a division in the nature of the subject-matter dealt with. Yet the gap may only reflect, at most, a limitation now existing but in the future to be done away with. The argument that because some province or aspect of experience has not yet been "invaded" by scientific methods, it is not subject to them, is as old as it is dangerous. Time and time again, in some particular reserved field, it has been invalidated. Psychology is still in its infancy. He is bold to the point of rashness who asserts that intimate personal experience will never come within the ken of natural knowledge.

It is more to the present point, however, to consider the region that is claimed by religionists as a special reserve. It is mystical experience. The difference, however, between mystic experience and the theory about it that is offered to us must be noted. The experience is a fact to be inquired into. The theory, like any theory, is an interpretation of the fact. The idea that by its very nature the experience is a veridical realization of the direct presence of God does not rest so much upon examination of the facts as it does upon importing into their interpretation a conception that is formed outside them. In its dependence upon a prior conception of the supernatural, which is the thing to be proved, it begs the question.

History exhibits many types of mystic experience, and each of these types is contemporaneously explained by the concepts that prevail in the culture and the circle in which the phenomena occur. There are mystic crises that arise, as among some North American Indian tribes, induced by fasting. They are accompanied by trances and semi-hysteria. Their purpose is to gain some special power, such perhaps as locating a person who is lost or finding objects that have been secreted. There is the mysticism of Hindoo practice now enjoying some vogue in Western countries. There is the mystic ecstasy of Neoplatonism with its complete abrogation of the self and absorption into an impersonal whole of Being. There is the mysticism of intense aesthetic experience independent of any theological or metaphysical interpretation. There is the heretical mysticism of William Blake. There is the mysticism of sudden unreasoning fear in which the very foundations seem shaken beneath one—to mention but a few of the types that may be found.

What common element is there between, say, the Neoplatonic conception of a super-divine Being wholly apart from human needs and conditions and the medieval theory of an immediate union that is fostered through attention to the sacraments or through concentration upon the heart of Jesus? The contemporary emphasis of some Protestant theologians upon the sense of inner personal communion with God, found in religious experience, is almost as far away from medieval Christianity as it is from Neoplatonism or Yoga. Interpretations of the experience have not grown from the experience itself with the aid of such scientific resources as may be available. They have been imported by borrowing without criticism from ideas that are current in the surrounding culture.

The mystic states of the shaman and of some North American Indians are frankly techniques for gaining a special power—*the* power as it is conceived by some revivalist sects. There is no especial intellectual objectification accompanying the experience. The knowledge that is said to be gained is not that of Being but of particular secrets and occult modes of operation. The aim is not to gain knowledge of superior divine power, but to get advice, cures for the sick, prestige, etc. The conception that mystic experience is a normal mode of religious experience by which we may acquire knowledge of God and divine things is a nineteenth-century interpretation that has gained vogue in direct ratio to the decline of older methods of religious apologetics.

There is no reason for denying the existence of experiences that are called mystical. On the contrary, there is every reason to suppose that, in some degree of intensity, they occur so frequently that they may be regarded as normal manifestations that take place at certain rhythmic points in the movement of experience. The assumption that denial of a particular interpretation of their objective content proves that those who make the denial do not have the experience in question, so that if they had it they would be equally persuaded of its objective source in the presence of God, has no foundation in fact. As with every empirical phenomenon, the occurrence of the state called mystical is simply an occasion for inquiry into its mode of causation. There is no more reason for converting the experience itself into an immediate knowledge of its cause than in the case of an experience of lightning or any other natural occurrence.

My purpose, then, in this brief reference to mysticism is not to throw doubt upon the existence of particular experiences called mystical. Nor is it to propound any theory to account for them. I have referred to the matter merely as an illustration of the general tendency to mark off two distinct realms in one of which science has jurisdiction, while in the other, special modes of immediate knowledge of religious objects have authority. This dualism as it operates in contemporary interpretation of mystic experience in order to validate certain beliefs is but a reinstatement of the old dualism between the natural and the supernatural, in terms better adapted to the cultural conditions of the present time. Since it is the conception of the supernatural that science calls in question, the circular nature of this type of reasoning is obvious.

Apologists for a religion often point to the shift that goes on in scientific ideas and materials as evidence of the unreliability of science as a mode of knowledge. They often seem peculiarly elated by the great, almost revolutionary, change in fundamental physical conceptions that has taken place in science during the present generation. Even if the alleged unreliability were as great as they assume (or even greater), the question would remain: Have we any other recourse for knowledge? But in fact they miss the point. Science is not constituted by any particular body of subject-matter. It is constituted by a method, a method of changing beliefs by means of tested inquiry as well as of arriving at them. It is its glory, not its condemnation, that its subject-matter develops as the method is improved. There is no special subject-matter of belief that is sacrosanct. The identification of science with a particular set of beliefs and ideas is itself a hold-over of ancient and still current dogmatic habits of thought which are opposed to science in its actuality and which science is undermining.

For scientific method is adverse not only to dogma but to doctrine as well, provided we take "doctrine" in its usual meaning—a body of definite beliefs that need only to be taught and learned as true. This negative attitude of science to doctrine does not indicate indifference to truth. It signifies supreme loyalty to the method by which truth is attained. The scientific-religious conflict ultimately is a conflict between allegiance to this method and allegiance to even an irreducible minimum of belief so fixed in advance that it can never be modified.

The method of intelligence is open and public. The doctrinal method is limited and private. This limitation persists even when knowledge of the truth that is religious is said to be arrived at by a special mode of experience, that termed "religious." For the latter is assumed to be a very special kind of experience. To be sure it is asserted to be open to all who obey certain conditions.

Yet the mystic experience yields, as we have seen, various results in the way of belief to different persons, depending upon the surrounding culture of those who undergo it. As a method, it lacks the public character belonging to the method of intelligence. Moreover, when the experience in question does not yield consciousness of the presence of God, in the sense that is alleged to exist, the retort is always at hand that it is not a genuine religious experience. For by definition, only that experience *is* religious which arrives at this particular result. The argument is circular. The traditional position is that some hardness or corruption of heart prevents one from having the experience. Liberal religionists are now more humane. But their logic does not differ.

It is sometimes held that beliefs about religious matters are symbolic, like rites and ceremonies. This view may be an advance upon that which holds to their literal objective validity. But as usually put forward it suffers from an ambiguity. Of what are the beliefs symbols? Are they symbols of things experienced in other modes than those set apart as religious, so that the things symbolized have an independent standing? Or are they symbols in the sense of standing for some transcendental reality—transcendental because not being the subject-matter of experience generally? Even the fundamentalist admits a certain quality and degree of symbolism in the latter sense in objects of religious belief. For he holds that the objects of these beliefs are so far beyond finite human capacity that our beliefs must be couched in more or less metaphorical terms. The conception that faith is the best available substitute for knowledge in our present estate still attaches to the notion of the symbolic character of the materials of faith; unless by ascribing to them a symbolic nature we mean that these materials stand for something that is verifiable in general and public experience.

Were we to adopt the latter point of view, it would be evident not only that the intellectual articles of a creed must be understood to be symbolic of moral and other ideal values, but that the facts taken to be historic and used as concrete evidence of the intellectual articles are themselves symbolic. These articles of a creed present events and persons that have been made over by the idealizing imagination in the interest, at their best, of moral ideals. Historic personages in their divine attributes are materializations of the ends that enlist devotion and inspire endeavor.

They are symbolic of the reality of ends moving us in many forms of experience. The ideal values that are thus symbolized also mark human experience in science and art and the various modes of human association: they mark almost everything in life that rises from the level of manipulation of conditions as they exist. It is admitted that the objects of religion are ideal in contrast with our present state. What would be lost if it were also admitted that they have authoritative claim upon conduct just because they are ideal? The assumption that these objects of religion exist already in some realm of Being seems to add nothing to their force, while it weakens their claim over us as ideals, in so far as it bases that claim upon matters that are intellectually dubious. The question narrows itself to this: Are the ideals that move us genuinely ideal or are they ideal only in contrast with our present estate?

The import of the question extends far. It determines the meaning given to the word "God." On one score, the word can mean only a particular Being. On the other score, it denotes the unity of all ideal ends arousing us to desire and actions. Does the unification have a claim upon our attitude and conduct because it is already, apart from us, in realized existence, or because of its own inherent meaning and value? Suppose for the moment that the word "God" means the ideal ends that at a given time and place one acknowledges as having authority over his volition and emotion, the values to which one is supremely devoted, as far as these ends, through imagination, take on unity. If we make this supposition, the issue will stand out clearly in contrast with the doctrine of religions that "God" designates some kind of Being having prior and therefore non-ideal existence.

The word "non-ideal" is to be taken literally in regard to some religions that have historically existed, to all of them as far as they are neglectful of moral qualities in their divine beings. It does not apply in the same *literal* way to Judaism and Christianity. For they have asserted that the Supreme Being has moral and spiritual attributes. But it applies to them none the less in that these moral and spiritual characters are thought of as properties of a particular existence and are thought to be of religious value for us because of this embodiment in such an existence. Here, as far as I can see, is the ultimate issue as to the difference between *a* religion and the religious as a function of experience.

The idea that "God" represents a unification of ideal values that is essentially imaginative in origin when the imagination supervenes in conduct is attended with verbal difficulties owing to our frequent use of the word "imagination" to denote fantasy and doubtful reality. But the reality of ideal ends as ideals is vouched for by their undeniable power in action. An ideal is not an illusion because imagination is the organ through which it is apprehended. For *all* possibilities reach us through the imagination. In a definite sense the only meaning that can be assigned the term "imagination" is that things unrealized in fact come home to us and have power to stir us. The unification effected through imagination is not fanciful, for it is the reflex of the unification of practical and emotional attitudes. The unity signifies not a single Being, but the unity of loyalty and effort evoked by the fact that many ends are one in the power of their ideal, or imaginative, quality to stir and hold us.

We may well ask whether the power and significance in life of the traditional conceptions of God are not due to the ideal qualities referred to by them, the hypostatization of them into an existence being due to a conflux of tendencies in human nature that converts the object of desire into an antecedent reality (as was mentioned in the previous chapter) with beliefs that have prevailed in the cultures of the past. For in the older cultures the idea of the supernatural was "natural," in the sense in which "natural" signifies something customary and familiar. It seems more credible that religious persons have been supported and consoled by the reality with which ideal values appeal to them than that they have been upborne by sheer matter of fact existence. That, when once men are inured to the idea of the union of the ideal and the physical, the two should be so bound together in emotion that it is difficult to institute a separation, agrees with all we know of human psychology.

The benefits that will accrue, however, from making the separation are evident. The dislocation frees the religious values of experience once for all from matters that are continually becoming more dubious. With that release there comes emancipation from the necessity of resort to apologetics. The reality of ideal ends and values in their authority over us is an undoubted fact. The validity of justice, affection, and that intellectual correspondence of our ideas with realities that we call truth, is so assured in its hold upon humanity that it is unnecessary for the religious attitude to encumber itself with the apparatus of dogma and doctrine. Any other conception of the religious attitude, when it is adequately analyzed, means that those who hold it care more for force than for ideal values—since all that an Existence can add is force to establish, to punish, and to reward. There are, indeed, some persons who frankly say that their own faith does not require any guarantee that moral values are backed up by physical force, but who hold that the masses are so backward that ideal values will not affect their conduct unless in the popular belief these values have the sanction of a power that can enforce them and can execute justice upon those who fail to comply.

There are some persons, deserving of more respect, who say: "We agree that the beginning must be made with the primacy of the ideal. But why stop at this point? Why not search with the utmost eagerness and vigor for all the evidence we can find, such as is supplied by history, by presence of design in nature, which may lead on to the belief that the ideal is already extant in a Personality having objective existence?"

One answer to the question is that we are involved by this search in all the problems of the existence of evil that have haunted theology in the past and that the most ingenious apologetics have not faced, much less met. If these apologists had not identified the existence of ideal goods with that of a Person supposed to originate and support them—a Being, moreover, to whom omnipotent power is attributed—the problem of the occurrence of evil would be gratuitous. The significance of ideal ends and meanings is, indeed, closely connected with the fact that there are in life all sorts of things that are evil to us because we would have them otherwise. Were existing conditions wholly good, the notion of possibilities to be realized would never emerge.

But the more basic answer is that while if the search is conducted upon a strictly empirical basis there is no reason why it should not take place, as a matter of fact it is always undertaken in the interest of the supernatural. Thus it diverts attention and energy from ideal values and from the exploration of actual conditions by means of which they may be promoted. History is testimony to this fact. Men have never fully used the powers they possess to advance the good in life, because they have waited upon some power external to themselves and to nature to do the work they are responsible for doing. Dependence upon an external power is the counterpart of surrender of human endeavor. Nor is emphasis on exercising our own powers for good an egoistical or a sentimentally optimistic recourse. It is not the first, for it does not isolate man, either individually or collectively, from nature. It is not the second, because it makes no assumption beyond that of the need and responsibility for human endeavor, and beyond the conviction that, if human desire and endeavor were enlisted in behalf of natural ends, conditions would be bettered. It involves no expectation of a millennium of good.

Belief in the supernatural as a necessary power for apprehension of the ideal and for practical attachment to it has for its counterpart a pessimistic belief in the corruption and impotency of natural means. That is axiomatic in Christian dogma. But this apparent pessimism has a way of suddenly changing into an exaggerated optimism. For according to the terms of the doctrine, if the faith in the supernatural is of the required order, regeneration at once takes place. Goodness, in all essentials, is thereby established; if not, there is proof that the established relation to the supernatural has been vitiated. This romantic optimism is one cause for the excessive attention to individual salvation characteristic of traditional Christianity. Belief in a sudden and complete transmutation through conversion and in the objective efficacy of prayer, is too easy a way out of difficulties. It leaves matters in general just about as they were before; that is, sufficiently bad so that there is additional support for the idea that only supernatural aid can better them. The position of natural intelligence is that there exists a *mixture* of good and evil, and that reconstruction in the direction of the good which is indicated by ideal ends, must take place, if at all, through continued cooperative effort. There is at least enough impulse toward justice, kindliness, and order so that if it were mobilized for action, not expecting abrupt and complete transformation to occur, the disorder, cruelty, and oppression that exist would be reduced.

The discussion has arrived at a point where a more fundamental objection to the position I am taking needs consideration. The misunderstanding upon which this objection rests should be pointed out. The view I have advanced is sometimes treated as if the identification of the divine with ideal ends left the ideal wholly without roots in existence and without support from existence. The objection implies that my view commits one to such a separation of the ideal and the existent that the ideal has no chance to find lodgment even as a seed that might grow and bear fruit. On the contrary, what I have been criticizing is the *identification* of the ideal with a particular Being, especially when that identification makes necessary the conclusion that this Being is outside of nature, and what I have tried to show is that the ideal itself has its roots in natural conditions; it emerges when the imagination idealizes existence by laying hold of the possibilities offered to thought and action. There are values, goods, actually realized upon a natural basis—the goods of human association, of art and knowledge. The idealizing imagination seizes upon the most precious things found in the climacteric moments of experience and projects them. We need no external criterion and guarantee for their goodness. They are had, they exist as good, and out of them we frame our ideal ends.

Moreover, the ends that result from our projection of experienced goods into objects of thought, desire and effort exist, only they exist *as* ends. Ends, purposes, exercise determining power in human conduct. The aims of philanthropists, of Florence Nightingale, of Howard, of Wilberforce, of Peabody, have not been idle dreams. They have modified institutions. Aims, ideals, do not exist simply in "mind"; they exist in character, in personality and action. One might call the roll of artists, intellectual inquirers, parents, friends, citizens who are neighbors, to show that purposes exist in an *operative* way. What I have been objecting to, I repeat, is not the idea that ideals are linked with existence and that they themselves exist, through human embodiment, as forces, but the idea that their authority and value depend upon some prior complete embodiment—as if the efforts of human beings in behalf of justice, or knowledge or beauty, depended for their effectiveness and validity upon assurance that there already existed in some supernal region a place where criminals are humanely treated, where there is no serfdom or slavery, where all facts and truths are already discovered and possessed, and all beauty is eternally displayed in actualized form.

The aims and ideals that move us are generated through imagination. But they are not made out of imaginary stuff. They are made out of the hard stuff of the world of physical and social experience. The locomotive did not exist before Stevenson, nor the telegraph before the time of Morse. But the conditions for their existence were there in physical material and energies and in human capacity. Imagination seized hold upon the idea of a rearrangement of existing things that would evolve new objects. The same thing is true of a painter, a musician, a poet, a philanthropist, a moral prophet. The new vision does not arise out of nothing, but emerges through seeing, in terms of possibilities, that is, of imagination, old things in new relations serving a new end which the new end aids in creating.

Moreover the process of creation is experimental and continuous. The artist, scientific man, or good citizen, depends upon what others have done before him and are doing around him. The sense of new values that become ends to be realized arises first in dim and uncertain form. As the values are dwelt upon and carried forward in action they grow in definiteness and coherence. Interaction between aim and existent conditions improves and tests the ideal; and conditions are at the same time modified. Ideals change as they are applied in existent conditions. The process endures and advances with the life of humanity. What one person and one group accomplish becomes the standing ground and starting point of those who succeed them. When the vital factors in this natural process are generally acknowledged in emotion, thought and action, the process will be both accelerated and purified through elimination of that irrelevant element that culminates in the idea of the supernatural. When the vital factors attain the religious force that has been drafted into supernatural religions, the resulting reinforcement will be incalculable.

These considerations may be applied to the idea of God, or, to avoid misleading conceptions, to the idea of the divine. This idea is, as I have said, one of ideal possibilities unified through imaginative realization and projection. But this idea of God, or of the divine, is also connected with all the natural forces and conditions—including man and human association—that promote the growth of the ideal and that further its realization. We are in the presence neither of ideals completely embodied in existence nor yet of ideals that are mere rootless ideals, fantasies, utopias. For there are forces in nature and society that generate and support the ideals. They are further unified by the action that gives them coherence and solidity. It is this *active* relation between ideal and actual to which I would give the name "God." I would not insist that the name *must* be given. There are those who hold that the associations of the term with the supernatural are so numerous and close that any use of the word "God" is sure to give rise to misconception and be taken as a concession to traditional ideas.

They may be correct in this view. But the facts to which I have referred are there, and they need to be brought out with all possible clearness and force. There exist concretely and experimentally goods—the values of art in all its forms, of knowledge, of effort and of rest after striving, of education and fellowship, of friendship and love, of growth in mind and body. These goods are there and yet they are relatively embryonic. Many persons are shut out from generous participation in them; there are forces at work that threaten and sap existent goods as well as prevent their expansion. A clear and intense conception of a union of ideal ends with actual conditions is capable of arousing steady emotion. It may be fed by every experience, no matter what its material.

In a distracted age, the need for such an idea is urgent. It can unify interests and energies now dispersed; it can direct action and generate the heat of emotion and the light of intelligence. Whether one gives the name "God" to this union, operative in thought and action, is a matter for individual decision. But the *function* of such a working union of the ideal and actual seems to me to be identical with the force that has in fact been attached to the conception of God in all the religions that have a spiritual content; and a clear idea of that function seems to me urgently needed at the present time.

The sense of this union may, with some persons, be furthered by mystical experiences, using the term "mystical" in its broadest sense. That result depends largely upon temperament. But there is a marked difference between the union associated with mysticism and the union which I had in mind. There is nothing mystical about the latter; it is natural and moral. Nor is there anything mystical about the perception or consciousness of such union. Imagination of ideal ends pertinent to actual conditions represents the fruition of a disciplined mind. There is, indeed, even danger that resort to mystical experiences will be an escape, and that its result will be the passive feeling that the union of actual and ideal is already accomplished. But in fact this union is active and practical; it is a *uniting*, not something given.

One reason why personally I think it fitting to use the word "God" to denote that uniting of the ideal and actual which has been spoken of, lies in the fact that aggressive atheism seems to me to have something in common with traditional supernaturalism. I do not mean merely that the former is mainly so negative that it fails to give positive direction to thought, though that fact is pertinent. What I have in mind especially is the exclusive preoccupation of both militant atheism and supernaturalism with man in isolation. For in spite of supernaturalism's reference to something beyond nature, it conceives of this earth as the moral centre of the universe and of man as the apex of the whole scheme of things. It regards the drama of sin and redemption enacted within the isolated and lonely soul of man as the one thing of ultimate importance. Apart from man, nature is held either accursed or negligible. Militant atheism is also affected by lack of natural piety. The ties binding man to nature that poets have always celebrated are passed over lightly. The attitude taken is often that of man living in an indifferent and hostile world and issuing blasts of defiance. A religious attitude, however, needs the sense of a connection of man, in the way of both dependence and support, with the enveloping world that the imagination feels is a universe. Use of the words "God" or "divine" to convey the union of actual with ideal may protect man from a sense of isolation and from consequent despair or defiance.

In any case, whatever the name, the meaning is selective. For it involves no miscellaneous worship of everything in general. It selects those factors in existence that generate and support our idea of good as an end to be striven for. It excludes a multitude of forces that at any given time are irrelevant to this function. Nature produces whatever gives reinforcement and direction but also what occasions discord and confusion. The "divine" is thus a term of human choice and aspiration. A humanistic religion, if it excludes our relation to nature, is pale and thin, as it is presumptuous, when it takes humanity as an object of worship. Matthew Arnold's conception of a "power not ourselves" is too narrow in its reference to operative and sustaining conditions. While it is selective, it is too narrow in its basis of selection—righteousness. The conception thus needs to be widened in two ways. The powers that generate and support the good as experienced and as ideal, work *within* as well as without. There seems to be a reminiscence of an external Jehovah in Arnold's statement. And the powers work to enforce other values and ideals than righteousness. Arnold's sense of an opposition between Hellenism and Hebraism resulted in exclusion of beauty, truth, and friendship from the list of the consequences toward which powers work within and without.

In the relation between nature and human ends and endeavors, recent science has broken down the older dualism. It has been engaged in this task for three centuries. But as long as the conceptions of science were strictly mechanical (mechanical in the sense of assuming separate things acting upon one another purely externally by push and pull), religious apologists had a standing ground in pointing out the differences between man and physical nature. The differences could be used for arguing that something supernatural had intervened in the case of man. The recent acclaim, however, by apologists for religion of the surrender by science of the classic type of mechanicalism[1] seems ill-advised from their own point of view. For the change in the modern scientific view of nature simply brings man and nature nearer together. We are no longer compelled to choose between explaining away what is distinctive in man through reducing him to another form of a mechanical model and the doctrine that something literally supernatural marks him off from nature. The less mechanical—in its older sense—physical nature is found to be, the closer is man to nature.

In his fascinating book, *The Dawn of Conscience*, James Henry Breasted refers to Haeckel as saying that the question he would most wish to have answered is this: Is the universe friendly to man? The question is an ambiguous one. Friendly to man in what respect? With respect to ease and comfort, to material success, to egoistic ambitions? Or to his aspiration to inquire and discover, to invent and create, to build a more secure order for human existence? In whatever form the question be put, the answer cannot in all honesty be an unqualified and absolute one. Mr. Breasted's answer, as a historian, is that nature has been friendly to the emergence and development of conscience and character. Those who will have all or nothing cannot be satisfied with this

---

1. I use this term because science has not abandoned its beliefs in working mechanisms in giving up the idea that they are of the nature of a strictly mechanical contact of discrete things.

answer. Emergence and growth are not enough for them. They want something more than growth accompanied by toil and pain. They want final achievement. Others who are less absolutist may be content to think that, morally speaking, growth is a higher value and ideal than is sheer attainment. They will remember also that growth has not been confined to conscience and character; that it extends also to discovery, learning and knowledge, to creation in the arts, to furtherance of ties that hold men together in mutual aid and affection. These persons at least will be satisfied with an intellectual view of the religious function that is based on continuing choice directed toward ideal ends.

For, I would remind readers in conclusion, it is the intellectual side of the religious attitude that I have been considering. I have suggested that the religious element in life has been hampered by conceptions of the supernatural that were imbedded in those cultures wherein man had little control over outer nature and little in the way of sure method of inquiry and test. The crisis today as to the intellectual content of religious belief has been caused by the change in the intellectual climate due to the increase of our knowledge and our means of understanding. I have tried to show that this change is not fatal to the religious values in our common experience, however adverse its impact may be upon historic religions. Rather, provided that the methods and results of intelligence at work are frankly adopted, the change is liberating.

It clarifies our ideals, rendering them less subject to illusion and fantasy. It relieves us of the incubus of thinking of them as fixed, as without power of growth. It discloses that they develop in coherence and pertinency with increase of natural intelligence. The change gives aspiration for natural knowledge a definitely religious character, since growth in understanding of nature is seen to be organically related to the formation of ideal ends. The same change enables man to select those elements in natural conditions that may be organized to support and extend the sway of ideals. All purpose is selective, and all intelligent action includes deliberate choice. In the degree in which we cease to depend upon belief in the supernatural, selection is enlightened and choice can be made in behalf of ideals whose inherent relations to conditions and consequences are understood. Were the naturalistic foundations and bearings of religion grasped, the religious element in life would emerge from the throes of the crisis in religion. Religion would then be found to have its natural place in every aspect of human experience that is concerned with estimate of possibilities, with emotional stir by possibilities as yet unrealized, and with all action in behalf of their realization. All that is significant in human experience falls within this frame.

3. The Human Abode of the Religious Function

In discussing the intellectual content of religion before considering religion in its social connections, I did not follow the usual temporal order. Upon the whole, collective modes of practice either come first or are of greater importance. The core of religions has generally been found in rites and ceremonies. Legends and myths grow up in part as decorative dressings, in response to the irrepressible human tendency toward story-telling, and in part as attempts to explain ritual practices. Then as culture advances, stories are consolidated, and theogonies and cosmogonies are formed—as with the Babylonians, Egyptians, Hebrews and Greeks. In the case of the Greeks, the stories of creation and accounts of the constitution of the world were mainly poetic and literary, and philosophies ultimately developed from them. In most cases, legends along with rites and ceremonies came under the guardianship of a special body, the priesthood, and were subject to the special arts which it possessed. A special group was set aside as the responsible owners, protectors, and promulgators of the corpus of beliefs.

But the formation of a special social group having a peculiar relation to both the practices and the beliefs of religion is but part of the story. In the widest perspective, it is the less important part. The more significant point as regards the social import of religion is that the priesthoods were official representatives of some community, tribe, city-state or empire. Whether there was a priesthood or not, individuals who were members of a community were born into a religious community as they were into social and political organization. Each social group had its own divine beings who were its founders and protectors. Its rites of sacrifice, purification, and communion were manifestations of organized civic life. The temple was a public institution, the focus of the worship of the community; the influence of its practices extended to all the customs of the community, domestic, economic, and political. Even wars between groups were usually conflicts of their respective deities.

An individual did not join a church. He was born and reared in a community whose social unity, organization and traditions were symbolized and celebrated in the rites, cults and beliefs of a collective religion. Education was the induction of the young into community activities that were interwoven at every point with customs, legends and ceremonies intimately connected with and sanctioned by a religion. There are a few persons, especially those brought up in Jewish communities in Russia, who can understand without the use of imagination what a religion means socially when it permeates all the customs and activities of group life. To most of us in the United States such a situation is only a remote historic episode.

The change that has taken place in conditions once universal and now infrequent is in my opinion the greatest change that has occurred in religion in all history. The intellectual conflict of scientific and theological beliefs has attracted much more attention. It is still near the focus of attention. But the change in the social centre of gravity of religion has gone on so steadily and is now so generally accomplished that it has faded from the thought of most persons, save perhaps the historians, and even they are especially aware of it only in its political aspect. For the conflict between state and church still continues in some countries.

There are even now persons who are born into a particular church, that of their parents, and who take membership in it almost as a matter of course; indeed, the fact of such membership may be an important, even a determining, factor in an individual's whole career. But the thing new in history, the thing once unheard of, is that the organization in question is a *special* institution within a secular community. Even where there are established churches, they are constituted by the state and may be unmade by the state. Not only the national state but other forms of organization among groups have grown in power and influence at the expense of organizations built upon and about a religion. The correlate of this fact is that membership in associations of the latter type is more and more a matter of the voluntary choice of individuals, who may tend to accept responsibilities imposed by the church but who accept them of their own volition.

If they do accept them, the organization they join is, in many nations, chartered under a general corporation law of the political and secular entity.

The shift in what I have called the social centre of gravity accompanies the enormous expansion of associations formed for educational, political, economic, philanthropic and scientific purposes, which has occurred independently of any religion. These social modes have grown so much that they exercise the greater hold upon the thought and interest of most persons, even of those holding membership in churches. This positive extension of interests which, from the standpoint of a religion, are non-religious, is so great that in comparison with it the direct effect of science upon the creeds of religion seems to me of secondary importance.

I say, the *direct* effect; for the indirect effect of science in stimulating the growth of competing organizations is enormous. Changes that are purely intellectual affect at most but a small number of specialists. They are secondary to consequences brought about through impact upon the *conditions* under which human beings associate with one another. Invention and technology, in alliance with industry and commerce, have, needless to say, profoundly affected these underlying conditions of association. Every political and social problem of the present day reflects this indirect influence, from unemployment to banking, from municipal administration to the great migration of peoples made possible by new modes of transportation, from birth control to foreign commerce and war. The social changes that have come about through application of the new knowledge affect everyone, whether he is aware or not of the source of the forces that play upon him. The effect is the deeper, indeed, because so largely unconscious. For, to repeat what I have said, the *conditions* under which people meet and act together have been modified.

The fundamentalist in religion is one whose beliefs in intellectual content have hardly been touched by scientific developments. His notions about heaven and earth and man, as far as their bearing on religion is concerned, are hardly more affected by the work of Copernicus, Newton, and Darwin than they are by that of Einstein. But his actual life, in what he does day by day and in the contacts that are set up, has been radically changed by political and economic changes that have followed from applications of science. As far as strictly intellectual changes are concerned, creeds display great power of accommodation; their articles undergo insensible change of perspective; emphases are altered, and new meanings creep in. The Catholic Church, particularly, has shown leniency in dealing with intellectual deviations as long as they do not touch discipline, rites, and sacraments.

Among the laity only a small number, the more highly educated section, is directly affected by changes in scientific beliefs. Certain ideas recede more or less into the background but are not seriously challenged; nominally they are accepted. Probably most educated people thought the conception of biological evolution had been accepted as a commonplace until legislation in Tennessee and the Scopes trial brought about an acute crisis that revealed how far that was from being the case. Within an ecclesiastic organization, on the other hand, the class of professionals does not sense the change in perspective and emphasis of values in the general mind until some acute situation reveals it. Then they vigorously deny the validity of the new interests that have arisen. But since they are working against interests rather than merely against ideas, their desperate efforts are not convincing except for those already convinced.

Changes in practice that affect collective life go deep and extend far. They have been operating ever since the time we call the Middle Ages. The Renaissance was essentially a new birth of secularism. The development of the idea of "natural religion," characteristic of the eighteenth century, was a protest against control by ecclesiastic bodies—a movement foreshadowed in this respect by the growth of "independent" religious societies in the preceding century. But natural religion no more denied the intellectual validity of supernatural ideas than did the growth of independent congregations. It attempted rather to justify theism and immortality on the basis of the natural reason of the individual. The transcendentalism of the nineteenth century was a further move in the same general direction, a movement in which "reason" took on a more romantic, more colorful, and more collective form. It asserted the diffusion of the supernatural through secular life.

These movements and others not mentioned are the intellectual reflex of the greatest revolution that has taken place in religions during the thousands of years that man has been upon earth. For, as I have said, this change has to do with the *social* place and function of religion. Even the hold of the supernatural upon the general mind has become more and more disassociated from the power of ecclesiastic organization—that is, of any particular form of communal organization. Thus the very idea that was central in religions has more and more oozed away, so to speak, from the guardianship and care of any particular social institution. Even more important is the fact that a steady encroachment upon ecclesiastic institutions of forms of association once regarded as secular has altered the way in which men spend their time in work, recreation, citizenship, and political action. The essential point is not just that secular organizations and actions are legally or externally severed from the control of the church, but that interests and values unrelated to the offices of any church now so largely sway the desires and aims of even believers.

The individual believer may indeed carry the disposition and motivation he has acquired through affiliation with a religious organization into his political action, into his connection with schools, even into his business and amusements. But there remain two facts that constitute a revolution. In the first place, conditions are such that this action is a matter of personal choice and resolution on the part of individuals, not of the very nature of social organization. In the second place, the very fact that an individual imports or carries his personal attitude into affairs that are inherently secular, that are outside the scope of religion, constitutes an enormous change, in spite of the belief that secular matters *should* be permeated by the spirit of religion. Even if it be asserted, as it is by some religionists, that all the new movements and interests of any value grew up under the auspices of a church and received their impetus from the same source, it must be admitted that once the vessels have been launched, they are sailing on strange seas to far lands.

Here, it seems to me, is the issue to be faced. Here is the place where the distinction that I have drawn between a religion and the religious function is peculiarly applicable. It is of the nature of a religion based on the supernatural to draw a line between the religious and the secular and profane, even when it asserts the rightful authority of the Church and its religion to dominate these other interests. The conception that "religious" signifies a certain attitude and outlook, independent of the supernatural, necessitates no such division. It does not shut religious values up within a particular compartment, nor assume that a particular form of association bears a unique relation to it. Upon the social side the future of the religious function seems preeminently bound up with its emancipation from religions and a particular religion. Many persons feel perplexed because of the multiplicity of churches and the conflict of their claims. But the fundamental difficulty goes deeper.

In what has been said I have not ignored the interpretation put, by representatives of religious organizations, upon the historic change that has occurred. The oldest organization, the Roman Catholic church, judges the secularization of life, the growing independence of social interests and values from control by the church, as but one evidence the more of the apostasy of the natural man from God: the corruption inherent in the will of mankind has resulted in defiance of the authority that God has delegated to his designated representatives on earth. This church points to the fact that secularization has proceeded *pari passu* with the extension of Protestantism as evidence of the wilful heresy of the latter in its appeal to private conscience and choice. The remedy is simple. Submission to the will of God, as continuously expressed through the organization that is his established vicegerent on earth, is the sole means by which social relations and values can again become coextensive with religion.

Protestant churches, on the contrary, have emphasized the fact that the relation of man to God is primarily an individual matter, a matter of personal choice and responsibility. From this point of view, one aspect of the change outlined marks an advance that is religious as well as moral. For according to it, the beliefs and rites that tend to make relation of man to God a collective and institutional affair erect barriers between the human soul and the divine spirit. Communion with God must be initiated by the individual's heart and will through direct divine assistance. Hence the change that has occurred in the social status of organized religion is nothing to deplore. What has been lost was at best specious and external. What has been gained is that religion has been placed upon its only real and solid foundation: direct relationship of conscience and will to God. Although there is much that is non-Christian and anti-Christian in existing economic and political institutions, it is better that change be accomplished by the sum total of efforts of men and women who are imbued with personal faith, than that they be effected by any wholesale institutional effort that subordinates the individual to an external and ultimately a worldly authority.

Were the question involved in these two opposed views taken up in detail, there are some specific considerations that might be urged. It might be urged that the progressive secularization of the interests of life has not been attended by the increasing degeneration that the argument of the first group implies. There are many who, as historical students, independent of affiliation with any religion, would regard reversal of the process of secularization and return to conditions in which the Church was the final authority as a menace to things held most precious. With reference to the position of Protestantism, it may be urged that in fact such social advances as have taken place are not the product of voluntary religious associations; that, on the contrary, the forces that have worked to humanize human relations, that have resulted in intellectual and aesthetic development, have come from influences that are independent of the churches. A case could be made out for the position that the churches have lagged behind in most important social movements and that they have turned their chief attention in social affairs to moral *symptoms*, to vices and abuses, like drunkenness, sale of intoxicants, divorce, rather than to the causes of war and of the long list of economic and political injustices and oppressions. Protest against the latter has been mainly left to secular movements.

In earlier times, what we now call the supernatural hardly meant anything more definite than the extraordinary, that which was striking and emotionally impressive because of its out-of-the-way character. Probably even today the commonest conception of the natural is that which is usual, customary and familiar. When there is no insight into the cause of unusual events, belief in the supernatural is itself "natural"—in this sense of natural. Supernaturalism was, therefore, a genuinely social religion as long as men's minds were attuned to the supernatural. It gave an "explanation" of extraordinary occurrences while it provided techniques for utilizing supernatural forces to secure advantages and to protect the members of the community against them when they were adverse.

The growth of natural science brought extraordinary things into line with events for which there is a "natural" explanation. At the same time, the development of positive social interests crowded heaven—and its opposite, hell—into the background. The function and offices of churches became more and more specialized; concerns and values that had been regarded, in an earlier contrast, as profane and secular grew in bulk and in importance. At the same time, the notion that basic and ultimate spiritual and ideal values are associated with the supernatural has persisted as a kind of vague background and aura. A kind of polite deference to the notion remains along with a concrete transfer of interest. The general mind is thus left in a confused and divided state. The movement that has been going on for the last few centuries will continue to breed doubleness of mind until religious meanings and values are definitely integrated into normal social relations.

The issue may be more definitely stated. The extreme position on one side is that apart from relation to the supernatural, man is morally on a level with the brutes. The other position is that all significant ends and all securities for stability and peace have grown up in the matrix of human relations, and that the values given a supernatural locus are in fact products of an idealizing imagination that has laid hold of natural goods. There ensues a second contrast. On the one hand, it is held that relation to the supernatural is the only finally dependable source of motive power; that directly and indirectly it has animated every serious effort for the guidance and rectification of man's life on earth. The other position is that goods actually experienced in the concrete relations of family, neighborhood, citizenship, pursuit of art and science, are what men actually depend upon for guidance and support, and that their reference to a supernatural and other-worldly locus has obscured their real nature and has weakened their force.

The contrasts outlined define the religious problem of the present and the future. What would be the consequences upon the values of human association if intrinsic and immanent satisfactions and opportunities were clearly held to and cultivated with the ardor and the devotion that have at times marked historic religions? The contention of an increasing number of persons is that depreciation of natural social values has resulted, both in principle and in actual fact, from reference of their origin and significance to supernatural sources. Natural relations, of husband and wife, of parent and child, friend and friend, neighbor and neighbor, of fellow workers in industry, science, and art, are neglected, passed over, not developed for all that is in them. They are, moreover, not merely depreciated. They have been regarded as dangerous rivals of higher values; as offering temptations to be resisted; as usurpations by flesh of the authority of the spirit; as revolts of the human against the divine.

The doctrine of original sin and total depravity, of the corruption of nature, external and internal, is not especially current in liberal religious circles at present. Rather, there prevails the idea that there are two separate systems of values—an idea similar to that referred to in the previous chapter about a revelation of two kinds of truth. The values found in natural and supernatural relationships are now, in liberal circles, said to be complementary, just as the truths of revelation and of science are the two sides, mutually sustaining, of the same ultimate truth.

I cannot but think that this position represents a great advance upon the traditional one. While it is open logically to the objections that hold against the idea of the dual revelation of truth, practically it indicates a development of a humane point of view. But if it be once admitted that human relations are charged with values that are religious in function, why not rest the case upon what is verifiable and concentrate thought and energy upon its full realization?

History seems to exhibit three stages of growth. In the first stage, human relationships were thought to be so infected with the evils of corrupt human nature as to require redemption from external and supernatural sources. In the next stage, what is significant in these relations is found to be akin to values esteemed distinctively religious. This is the point now reached by liberal theologians. The third stage would realize that in fact the values prized in those religions that have ideal elements are idealizations of things characteristic of natural association, which have then been projected into a supernatural realm for safe-keeping and sanction. Note the role of such terms as Father, Son, Bride,

Fellowship and Communion in the vocabulary of Christianity, and note also the tendency, even if a somewhat inchoate one, of terms that express the more intimate phases of association to displace those of legal, political origin: King, Judge, and Lord of Hosts.

Unless there is a movement into what I have called the third stage, fundamental dualism and a division in life continue. The idea of a double and parallel manifestation of the divine, in which the latter has superior status and authority, brings about a condition of unstable equilibrium. It operates to distract energy, through dividing the objects to which it is directed. It also imperatively raises the question as to why having gone far in recognition of religious values in normal community life, we should not go further. The values of natural human intercourse and mutual dependence are open and public, capable of verification by the methods through which all natural facts are established. By means of the same experimental method, they are capable of expansion. Why not concentrate upon nurturing and extending them? Unless we take this step, the idea of two realms of spiritual values is only a softened version of the old dualism between the secular and the spiritual, the profane and the religious.

The condition of unstable equilibrium is indeed so evident to the thoughtful mind that there are attempts just now to revert to the earlier stage of belief. It is not difficult to make a severe indictment of existing social relations. It is enough to point to the war, jealousy, and fear that dominate the relations of national states to one another; to the growing demoralization of the older ties of domestic life; to the staggering evidence of corruption and futility in politics, and to the egoism, brutality, and oppression that characterize economic activities. By piling up material of this sort, one may, if one chooses, arrive at the triumphant conclusion that social relations are so debased that the only recourse is to supernatural aid. The general disorder of the Great War and succeeding decades has led to a revival of the theology of corruption, sin, and need for supernatural redemption.

The conclusion does not follow, however, from the data. It ignores, in the first place, that all the positive values which are prized, and in aid of which supernatural power is appealed to, have, after all, emerged from the very scene of human associations of which it is possible to paint so black a picture. Something in the facts has been left out of the picture. I shall not bring forward again at this place what was earlier said as to the effect upon actual conditions of diversion of the thought and action of those who are peculiarly sensitive to ideal considerations into supernatural channels. I shall raise a more directly practical issue. Society is convicted of being "immoral" by evoking all the evils of institutions as they now exist, and the unexpressed premise is that the institutions as they exist are normal expressions of social relations in their own nature.

Were this premise stated, the enormous gap between it and the conclusion set forth would be apparent. The problem of the relation between social relations and institutions that are dominant at a particular time is the most intricate problem presented to social inquiry. The idea that the latter are a direct reflex of the former ignores the multiplicity of factors that historically have entered into the shaping of institutions. Historically speaking, many of these factors are accidental with respect to the institutional form that has been given to social relations. One of my favorite quotations is a statement of Clarence Ayres that "our industrial revolution began, as some historians say, with half a dozen technical improvements in the textile industry; and it took us a century to realize that anything of moment had happened to us, beyond the obvious improvement of spinning and weaving." This statement must serve in lieu of long argument to suggest what I mean by the "accidental" relation of institutional developments to the primary facts of human association. The relation is accidental because institutional consequences that have resulted were not foreseen or intended. To say this, is to say that social intelligence in the sense in which there is intelligence about physical relations is in so far nonexistent.

Here is the negative fact that renders argument for the necessity of supernatural intervention to effect significant betterment only just another instance of the old, old inference to the supernatural from the basis of ignorance. We lack, for example, knowledge of the relation of life to inanimate matter. Therefore supernatural intervention is assumed to have effected the transition from brute to man. We do not know the relation of the organism—the brain and nervous system—to the occurrence of thought. Therefore, it is argued, there is a supernatural link. We do not know the relation of causes to results in social matters, and consequently we lack means of control. Therefore, it is inferred, we must resort to supernatural control. Of course, I make no claim to knowing how far intelligence may and will develop in respect to social relations. But one thing I think I do know. The needed understanding will not develop unless we strive for it. The assumption that only supernatural agencies can give control is a sure method of retarding this effort. It is as sure to be a hindering force now with respect to social intelligence, as the similar appeal was earlier an obstruction in the development of physical knowledge.

Even immediately, without awaiting the development of greater intelligence in relation to social affairs, a great difference would be made by use of natural means and methods. It is even now possible to examine complex social phenomena sufficiently to put the finger on things that are wrong. It is possible to trace to some extent these evils to their causes, and to causes that are something very different from abstract moral forces. It is possible to work out and work upon remedies for some of the sore spots. The outcome will not be a gospel of salvation but it will be in line with that pursued, for example, in matters of disease and health. The method if used would not only accomplish something toward social health but it would accomplish a greater thing; it would forward the development of social intelligence so that it could act with greater hardihood and on a larger scale.

Vested interests, interests vested with power, are powerfully on the side of the *status quo*, and therefore they are especially powerful in hindering the growth and application of the method of natural intelligence. Just because these interests are so powerful, it is the more necessary to fight for recognition of the method of intelligence in action. But one of the greatest obstacles in conducting this combat is the tendency to dispose of social evils in terms of general moral causes. The sinfulness of man, the corruption of his heart, his self-love and love of power, when referred to as causes are precisely of the same nature as was the appeal to abstract powers (which in fact only reduplicated under a general name a multitude of particular effects) that once prevailed in physical "science," and that operated as a chief obstacle to the generation and growth of the latter. Demons were once appealed to in order to explain bodily disease and no such thing as a strictly natural death was supposed to happen. The importation of general moral causes to explain present *social* phenomena is on the same intellectual level. Reinforced by the prestige of traditional religions, and backed by the emotional force of beliefs in the supernatural, it stifles the growth of that social intelligence by means of which direction of social change could be taken out of the region of accident, as accident has been defined. Accident in this broad sense and the idea of the supernatural are twins. Interest in the supernatural therefore reinforces other vested interests to prolong the social reign of accident.

There is a strong reaction in some religious circles today against the idea of mere individual salvation of individual souls. There is also a reaction in politics and economics against the idea of *laissez faire*. Both of these movements reflect a common tendency. Both of them are signs of the growing awareness of the emptiness of individuality in isolation. But the fundamental root of the *laissez faire* idea is denial (more often implicit than express) of the possibility of radical intervention of intelligence in the conduct of human life. Now appeal for supernatural intervention in improvement of social matters is also the expression of a deep-seated *laissez-faireism*; it is the acknowledgment of the desperate situation into which we are driven by the idea of the irrelevance and futility of human intervention in social events and interests. Those contemporary theologians who are interested in social change and who at the same time depreciate human intelligence and effort in behalf of the supernatural, are riding two horses that are going in opposite directions. The old-fashioned ideas of doing something to make the will of God prevail in the world, and of assuming the responsibility of doing the job ourselves, have more to be said for them, logically and practically.

The emphasis that has been put upon intelligence as a method should not mislead anyone. Intelligence, as distinct from the older conception of reason, is inherently involved in action. Moreover, there is no opposition between it and emotion. There is such a thing as passionate intelligence, as ardor in behalf of light shining into the murky places of social existence, and as zeal for its refreshing and purifying effect. The whole story of man shows that there are no objects that may not deeply stir engrossing emotion. One of the few experiments in the attachment of emotion to ends that mankind has not tried is that of devotion, so intense as to be religious, to intelligence as a force in social action.

But this is only part of the scene. No matter how much evidence may be piled up against social institutions as they exist, affection and passionate desire for justice and security are realities in human nature. So are the emotions that arise from living in conditions of inequity, oppression, and insecurity. Combination of the two kinds of emotion has more than once produced those changes that go by the name of revolution. To say that emotions which are not fused with intelligence are blind is tautology. Intense emotion may utter itself in action that destroys institutions. But the only assurance of birth of better ones is the marriage of emotion with intelligence.

Criticism of the commitment of religion to the supernatural is thus positive in import. All modes of human association are "affected with a public interest," and full realization of this interest is equivalent to a sense of a significance that is religious in its function. The objection to supernaturalism is that it stands in the way of an effective realization of the sweep and depth of the implications of natural human relations. It stands in the way of using the means that are in our power to make radical changes in these relations. It is certainly true that great material changes might be made with no corresponding improvement of a spiritual or ideal nature. But development in the latter direction cannot be introduced from without; it cannot be brought about by dressing up material and economic changes with decorations derived from the supernatural. It can come only from more intense realization of values that inhere in the actual connections of human beings with one another. The attempt to segregate the implicit public interest and social value of all institutions and social arrangements in a particular organization is a fatal diversion.

Were men and women actuated throughout the length and breadth of human relations with the faith and ardor that have at times marked historic religions the consequences would be incalculable. To achieve this faith and *élan* is no easy task. But religions have attempted something similar, directed moreover toward a less promising object—the supernatural. It does not become those who hold that faith may move mountains to deny in advance the possibility of its manifestation on the basis of verifiable realities. There already exists, though in a rudimentary form, the capacity to relate social conditions and events to their causes, and the ability will grow with exercise. There is the technical skill with which to initiate a campaign for social health and sanity analogous to that made in behalf of physical public health. Human beings have impulses toward affection, compassion and justice, equality and freedom. It remains to weld all these things together. It is of no use merely to assert that the intrenched foes of class interest and power in high places are hostile to the realization of such a union. As I have already said, if this enemy did not exist, there would be little sense in urging *any* policy of change. The point to be grasped is that, unless one gives up the whole struggle as hopeless, one has to choose between alternatives. One alternative is dependence upon the supernatural; the other, the use of natural agencies.

There is then no sense, logical or practical, in pointing out the difficulties that stand in the way of the latter course, until the question of the alternative is faced. If it is faced, it will also be realized that one factor in the choice is dependence upon enlisting only those committed to the supernatural and alliance with all men and women who feel the stir of social emotion, including the large number of those who, consciously or unconsciously, have turned their backs upon the supernatural. Those who face the alternatives will also have to choose between a continued and even more systematic *laissez faire* depreciation of intelligence and the resources of natural knowledge and understanding, and conscious and organized effort to turn the use of these means from narrow ends, personal and class, to larger human purposes. They will have to ask, as far as they nominally believe in the need for radical social change, whether what they accomplish when they point with one hand to the seriousness of present evils is not undone when the other hand points away from man and nature for their remedy.

The transfer of idealizing imagination, thought and emotion to natural human relations would not signify the destruction of churches that now exist. It would rather offer the means for a recovery of vitality. The fund of human values that are prized and that need to be cherished, values that are satisfied and rectified by *all* human concerns and arrangements, could be celebrated and reinforced, in different ways and with differing symbols, by the churches. In that way the churches would indeed become catholic. The demand that churches show a more active interest in social affairs, that they take a definite stand upon such questions as war, economic injustice, political corruption, that they stimulate action for a divine kingdom on earth, is one of the signs of the times. But as long as social values are related to a supernatural for which the churches stand in some peculiar way, there is an inherent inconsistency between the demand and efforts to execute it. On the one hand, it is urged that the churches are going outside their special province when they involve themselves in economic and political issues. On the other hand, the very fact that they claim if not a monopoly of supreme values and motivating forces, yet a unique relation to them, makes it impossible for the churches to participate in promotion of social ends on a natural and equal human basis. The surrender of claims to an exclusive and authoritative position is a *sine qua non* for doing away with the dilemma in which churches now find themselves in respect to their sphere of social action.

At the outset, I referred to an outstanding historic fact. The coincidence of the realm of social interests and activities with a tribal or civic community has vanished. Secular interests and activities have grown up outside of organized religions and are independent of their authority. The hold of these interests upon the thoughts and desires of men has crowded the social importance of organized religions into a corner and the area of this corner is decreasing. This change either marks a terrible decline in everything that can justly be termed religious in value, in traditional religions, or it provides the opportunity for expansion of these qualities on a new basis and with a new outlook. It is impossible to ignore the fact that historic Christianity has been committed to a separation of sheep and goats; the saved and the lost; the elect and the mass. Spiritual aristocracy as well as *laissez faire* with respect to natural and human intervention, is deeply embedded in its traditions. Lip service—often more than lip service—has been given to the idea of the common brotherhood of all men. But those outside the fold of the church and those who do not rely upon belief in the supernatural have been regarded as only potential brothers, still requiring adoption into the family. I cannot understand how any realization of the democratic ideal as a vital moral and spiritual ideal in human affairs is possible without surrender of the conception of the basic division to which supernatural Christianity is committed. Whether or no we are, save in some metaphorical sense, all brothers, we are at least all in the same boat traversing the same turbulent ocean. The potential religious significance of this fact is infinite.

In the opening chapter I made a distinction between religion and the religious. I pointed out that religion—or religions—is charged with beliefs, practices and modes of organization that have accrued to and been loaded upon the religious element in experience by the state of culture in which religions have developed. I urged that conditions are now ripe for emancipation of the religious quality from accretions that have grown up about it and that limit the credibility and the influence of religion. In the second chapter, I developed this idea with respect to the faith in ideals that is immanent in the religious value of experience, and asserted that the power of this faith would be enhanced were belief freed from the conception that the significance and validity of the ideal are bound up with intellectual assent to the proposition that the ideal is already embodied in some supernatural or metaphysical sense in the very framework of existence.

The matter touched upon in the present chapter includes within itself all that has been previously set forth. It does so upon both its negative and positive sides. The community of causes and consequences in which we, together with those not born, are enmeshed is the widest and deepest symbol of the mysterious totality of being the imagination calls the universe. It is the embodiment for sense and thought of that encompassing scope of existence the intellect cannot grasp. It is the matrix within which our ideal aspirations are born and bred. It is the source of the values that the moral imagination projects as directive criteria and as shaping purposes.

The continuing life of this comprehensive community of beings includes all the significant achievement of men in science and art and all the kindly offices of intercourse and communication. It holds within its content all the material that gives verifiable intellectual support to our ideal faiths. A "creed" founded on this material will change and grow, but it cannot be shaken.

What it surrenders it gives up gladly because of new light and not as a reluctant concession. What it adds, it adds because new knowledge gives further insight into the conditions that bear upon the formation and execution of our life purposes. A one-sided psychology, a reflex of eighteenth-century "individualism," treated knowledge as an accomplishment of a lonely mind. We should now be aware that it is a product of the cooperative and communicative operations of human beings living together. Its communal origin is an indication of its rightful communal use. The unification of what is known at any given time, not upon an impossible eternal and abstract basis but upon that of its bearing upon the unification of human desire and purpose, furnishes a sufficient creed for human acceptance, one that would provide a religious release and reinforcement of knowledge.

"Agnosticism" is a shadow cast by the eclipse of the supernatural. Of course, acknowledgment that we do not know what we do not know is a necessity of all intellectual integrity. But generalized agnosticism is only a halfway elimination of the supernatural. Its meaning departs when the intellectual outlook is directed wholly to the natural world. When it is so directed, there are plenty of particular matters regarding which we must say we do not know; we only inquire and form hypotheses which future inquiry will confirm or reject. But such doubts are an incident of faith in the method of intelligence. They are signs of faith, not of a pale and impotent skepticism. We doubt in order that we may find out, not because some inaccessible supernatural lurks behind whatever *we* can know. The substantial background of practical faith in ideal ends is positive and outreaching.

The considerations put forward in the present chapter may be summed up in what they imply. The ideal ends to which we attach our faith are not shadowy and wavering. They assume concrete form in our understanding of our relations to one another and the values contained in these relations. We who now live are parts of a humanity that extends into the remote past, a humanity that has interacted with nature. The things in civilization we most prize are not of ourselves. They exist by grace of the doings and sufferings of the continuous human community in which we are a link. Ours is the responsibility of conserving, transmitting, rectifying and expanding the heritage of values we have received that those who come after us may receive it more solid and secure, more widely accessible and more generously shared than we have received it. Here are all the elements for a religious faith that shall not be confined to sect, class, or race. Such a faith has always been implicitly the common faith of mankind. It remains to make it explicit and militant.

Essays

Steps to Economic Recovery

You have heard much about various steps that should be taken to promote economic recovery. I propose this evening to concentrate attention upon one step, a step absolutely fundamental to permanent recovery of the sick patient as distinct from remedies that dope the patient into a temporary hectic burst of activity; a step so simple and so basic as to be generally neglected.

The one thing uppermost in the minds of everybody to-day is the appalling existence of want in the midst of plenty, of millions of unemployed in the midst of idle billions of hoarded money and unused credit as well as factories and mills deteriorating for lack of use, of hunger while farmers are burning grain for fuel. No wonder people are asking what sort of a crazy economic system we have when at a time when millions are short of adequate food, when babies are going without the milk necessary for their growth, the best remedy that experts can think of and that the Federal Government can recommend, is to pay a premium to farmers to grow less grain with which to make flour to feed the hungry and pay a premium to dairymen to send less milk to market.

Henry George called attention to this situation over fifty years ago. The contradiction between increasing plenty, increase of potential security, and actual want and insecurity is stated in the title of his chief work, *Progress and Poverty*. That is what his book is about. It is a record of the fact that as the means and appliances of civilization increase, poverty and insecurity also increase. It is an explanation of why millionaires and tramps multiply together. It is a prediction of why this state of affairs will con-

[First published as a pamphlet by the Robert Schalkenbach Foundation (New York, 1933), 16 pp., from a 28 April 1933 radio address on the WEVD University of the Air.]

tinue; it is a prediction of the plight in which the nation finds itself to-day. At the same time it is the explanation of why this condition is artificial, man-made, unnecessary, and how it can be remedied. So I suggest that as a beginning of the first steps to permanent recovery there be a nation-wide revival of interest in the writings and teachings of Henry George, and that there be such an enlightenment of public opinion that our representatives in legislatures and public places be compelled to adopt the changes he urged.

Do not the following words sound as if they were written to-day? "So true it is that poverty does not come from the inability to produce more wealth, that from every side we hear that power to produce is in excess of the ability to find a market; that the constant fear seems to be not that too little, but that too much, will be produced! Do we not maintain a high tariff, and keep at every port a horde of Custom-House officers, for fear the people of other countries will overwhelm us with their goods? Is not a large part of our machinery constantly idle? Are there not, even in what we call good times, an immense number of unemployed men who would gladly be at work producing wealth if they could only get the opportunity? Do we not, even now, hear from every side of embarrassment from the very excess of productive power and of combinations to reduce production? ... This seeming glut of production, this seeming excess of productive powers runs through all branches of industry and is evident all over the civilized world."

Yet these words were penned in 1883, just fifty years ago, by George in his work called *Social Problems*, every word of which applies to our present condition, only in a more intense degree. Nor did our people have to wait for the advent of technocrats to hear that the machine and the control of power make it *possible* to abolish poverty while *actually* improvements in the machinery of production and distribution are working in the opposite direction. Fifty years ago, George pointed out the same contrast. On the one hand, as he said: "Productive power in such a state of civilization as ours is sufficient, did we give it play, to so enormously increase the production of wealth as to give abundance to all." On the other hand, now as when George wrote: "The tendency of all the inventions and improvements so wonderfully augmenting productive power is to concentrate enormous wealth in the hands of a few, to make the condition of the many more hopeless . . . Without a single exception I can think of, the effect of all modern industrial improvements is to production upon a large scale, to the minute division of labor, to the giving of large capital an overpowering advantage . . . The tendency of the machine is in everything not merely to place it out of the power of the workman to become his own employer, but to reduce him to the position of a mere feeder or attendant; to dispense with judgment, skill and brains . . . He has no more control of the conditions that give him employment than has the passenger in the railway train over the motion of the train." And yet machine and scientific technology contains in itself the possibility of the complete abolition of want and poverty. What is the trouble?

Go to the work of Henry George himself and learn how many of the troubles from which society still suffers, and suffers increasingly, are due to the fact that a few have monopolized the land, and that in consequence they have the power to dictate to others access to the land and to its products—which include waterpower, electricity, coal, iron and all minerals, as well as the foods that sustain life—and that they have the power to appropriate to their private use the values that the industry, the civilized order, the very benefactions, of others produce. This wrong is at the very basis of our present social and economic chaos, and until it is righted, all steps toward economic recovery may be temporarily helpful while in the long run useless.

I suppose my hearers have heard the following line of consolation put forth by professional optimists like Mr. Charles Schwab and his imitators. "To be sure," they say, "we have a bad depression, but we have had in our history at least nine such depressions, before, and yet have come out of them all to enjoy even better times than went before." What a wonderful consolation, and what a wonderful system! We can get out of our present hole and climb up in order to fall into a tenth, and eleventh and twelfth hole, and so on, each deeper than the one before! Is it not about time that instead of patching up here and there we try to go to the roots of our troubles?

Consequently instead of attempting a technical explanation of the moral and economic philosophy of Henry George, I want to urge my hearers to acquaint themselves with his own works, to study them, and then to organize to see that his principle is carried into effect. What are the most evident sore spots of the present? The answer is clear. Unemployment; extreme inequality in the distribution of the national income; enormous fixed charges in the way of interest on debts; a crazy, cumbrous, inequitable tax system that puts the burden on the producer, and the ultimate consumer, and lets off the parasites, exploiters and the privileged,—who ought to be relieved entirely of their gorged excess,—very lightly, and indeed in many cases, as in that of the tariff, pays them a premium for imposing a burden on honest industry and on the means of production; a vicious and incompetent banking system, with billions of money, the hope for the future of millions of hard-working peoples, still locked up, while the depositors lose their homes and walk the streets in vain; the greater part of our population, in the nation of the earth most favored by nature, still living either in slums or in homes without the improvements indispensable to a healthy and civilized life.

You cannot study Henry George without learning how intimately each of these wrongs and evils is bound up with our land system. One of our great national weaknesses is speculation. Everybody recognizes that fact in the stock market orgy of our late boom days. Only a few realize the extent to which speculation in land is the source of many troubles of the farmer, the part it has played in loading banks and insurance companies with frozen assets and compelling the closing of thousands of banks, nor how the high rents, the unpayable mortgages and the slums of the cities are connected with speculation in land values. All authorities on public works hold that the most fruitful field for them is slum clearance and better housing. Yet only a few seem to realize that with our present situation this improvement will put a bonus in the pockets of landlords, and the land speculator will be the one to profit financially—for after all buildings are built on land.

So with taxation. There are all sorts of tinkering going on, but the tinkers and patchers shut their eyes to the fact that the socially produced annual value of land—not of improvements, but of ground-rent value—is about five billion dollars and that its appropriation by those who create it, the community, would at once relieve the tax burden and ultimately would solve the tax problem. Of late the federal government has concerned itself with the problems of home ownership, but again by methods of tinkering that may easily in the long run do more harm than good. The community's acquisition of its own creation, ground-rent value, would both reduce the price of land and entirely eliminate taxes on improvement, thus making ownership easier. And how anyone expects to solve the unemployment question by putting the sanction of both legality and high pecuniary reward upon the ability of the few to keep the many from equal access to land and to the raw material, without which labor is impossible, I do not see—and no one else does. For the tinkerers assume that unemployment must continue, only with government assistance to those who are necessarily out of work. By all means let us help those that now need it, but for the future let us prevent the cause instead of merely mitigating the effects.

So if there were time, one could go through every one of our problems and show its intimate connection with a just solution of the land problem.

I do not claim that George's remedy is a panacea that will cure by itself all our ailments. But I do claim that we cannot get rid of our basic troubles without it. I would make exactly the same concession and the same claim that Henry George himself made: "I do not say that in the recognition of the equal and unalienable right of each human being to the natural elements from which life must be supported and wants satisfied, lies the solution of all social problems. I fully recognize that even after we do this, much will remain to do. We might recognize the equal right to land, and yet tyranny and spoliation be continued. But whatever else we do, as long as we fail to recognize the equal right to the elements of nature, nothing will avail to remedy that unnatural inequality in the distribution of wealth which is fraught with so much evil and danger. Reform as we may, until we make this fundamental reform our material progress can but tend to differentiate our people into the monstrously rich and the frightfully poor. Whatever be the increase of wealth, the masses will still be ground toward the point of bare subsistence—we must still have our great criminal classes, our paupers and our tramps, men and women driven to degradation and desperation from inability to make an honest living."

The Future of Radical Political Action

The last election did not settle the future of political parties in the United States. It rather demonstrated the discontent of at least seven million voters with existing alignments. The general trend was definitely in behalf of policies which would use the agencies of government for the social control of industry and finance. It was far from an expression of confidence that the Democratic Party is capable of bringing about such control. For all who, like the present writer, believe that it is thoroughly incapable of doing the needed work, the article of Norman Thomas in the *Nation* of December 14 on "The Future of the Socialist Party" raises the question of what instrumentality will be the efficient agent for radical political change. Mr. Thomas holds that the Socialist Party alone has the philosophy which meets the political needs. Such a position certainly simplifies the situation. But it also narrows it. In view of the size of the Socialist vote, and of the extent to which it was in part an expression of confidence in Mr. Thomas personally, and in another part a protest vote from non-Socialist liberals, it narrows the problem perhaps unduly.

It is natural that Mr. Thomas should feel that the Socialist Party is the only way out. He has been twice the candidate of his party for the Presidency. There are divergences within the party, such as were manifest in the Milwaukee convention. It is not surprising that he should take the opportunity to set forth his solidarity with the section which officially controls the party; and that he should wish, even at the risk of ungraciousness to the non-Socialists who supported him and of indulging in recriminations, to clear his skirts of any leaning toward those who do not accept the *ipsissima verba* of official Socialist doctrine. But for the millions of the politically discontented who are outside the

[First published in *Nation* 136 (4 January 1933): 8–9.]

Socialist Party, the exigencies of the internal strategy of that party cannot go far to settle the larger question of the future of unified political action aiming at social control.

In discussing the matter I feel free to approach it from the angle of the League for Independent Political Action. I do not do so because of Mr. Thomas's unfortunate references to that organization. The league is not a party and has no ambition to become a party. Its function is to promote education and organization looking toward the organization of the desired new alignment. Since it aims to act as a connecting link, and as far as may be as a clearing-house, for groups and individuals who are seeking similar ends, it may stand at least as a symbol for one type of approach to the problem. We agree that a philosophy is needed as a basis for an effective political movement. We have never prejudged the question as to just how far that philosophy agrees or disagrees with that which Mr. Thomas says is the only possible philosophy. I shall not now try to pass on that question. I shall rather set forth our philosophy positively, leaving it to the reader, Socialist or non-Socialist, to judge our degree of divergence and agreement.

The first point in our political philosophy may be stated in connection with the charge brought by Mr. Thomas that the league holds "an intellectualized version of a watered-down socialism." For the statement shows a radical misconception of what our stand is. It is quite true that many of our planks are socialistic and agree with the more immediate demands of the Socialist platform. It is true that we recognize the educational work done by the party and by Mr. Thomas and are grateful to them. But the league's agreements are not imitative. It has not first borrowed and then diluted. We believe that actual social conditions and needs suffice to determine the direction political action should take, and we believe that this is the philosophy which underlies the democratic faith of the American people. The belief is the mark of a positive philosophy, not of the absence of one. If charges against the League for Independent Political Action signify that our program is, in an ultimate sense, partial and tentative, experimental and not rigid, we do more than accept them as a compliment. We claim them as indications of our philosophy. We are confronted with a situation in which certain long-span economic forces are operative and which are sufficiently definite to provide a basis for a constructive political program. But we know that this situation bristles with unknowns and we cannot assume that all issues are settled in advance.

In saying this I am not charging the Socialists with being dogmatic or doctrinaire. I notice that Mr. Thomas in his statement calls for government ownership of the "principal" means of production and distribution. As far as the Socialist Party accepts the distinction between "principal" and other means, it inclines in the direction of what in the case of the League for Independent Political Action is dismissed as a "watered-down socialism." For how can "principal" ones be settled upon, save on the basis of actual conditions and tendencies? And while collective ownership of *all* natural resources is called for, there is evidence that the Socialist Party recognizes a gradation in importance and in urgency, and would concentrate first of all upon coal and the water power from which electric power is derived. So far, then, as the Socialist Party is not doctrinaire, there are no differences which are not subject to discussion and conferences—and not so much *with* the L.I.P.A. itself as, through it, with the other groups which are concerned with bringing about a new type of politics in this country.

We are thus led to the second main point in the philosophy of the L.I.P.A. This is the belief that politics is a struggle for possession and use of power to settle specific issues that grow out of the country's needs and problems. There is very little difference of opinion among radical groups as to what these issues at present are; there is more difference, though not to an amount insuperable for unity, as to how they should be dealt with. Since it believes that politics is a struggle for power to achieve results, the philosophy of the league stands for that strength which can be had only by unity. It believes in working for agreement, not for emphasizing and magnifying the differences that stand in the way of union. I do not charge the Socialist Party with standing for sectarianism and division. I do say that *we* desire a union of forces to which Socialists can and should contribute.

Because we desire a union of forces instead of that isolation and division which have so weakened liberal and radical forces in the past, we are strongly opposed to all slurs and sneers at the farmers, engineers, teachers, social workers, small merchants, clergy, newspaper people, and white-collar workers who constitute the despised middle class. Since they also constitute a great part of the American nation, and since they are influential and are sensitive to the injustices and inequalities of the present economic order, we do not indulge in the fantasy that effective power can be gained by taking pains to alienate them, by assuming, for example, that they are animated by anti-social class motives. This attitude does not signify that we think their present political views are, upon the whole, sufficiently enlightened to afford the basis of a political program, but that we do believe that they are readily capable of education under competent leadership.

It is nothing less than misrepresentation based on ignorance to assert that this effort to reach the elements just spoken of is connected with disregard of the interests of the manual workers, to say nothing about those who go into the field of motives to search out unworthy ones, similar, for example, to those which members of the Communist Party constantly attribute to the Socialist Party. It has been a constant aim of the L.I.P.A. to find labor groups which believe in independent political action, to bring them together, and to carry on education among those labor groups which have not yet seen the light. We *are* opposed to the defeatist policy which assumes that there can be no effective radical political action in this country until the majority of the population have sunk into the "proletariat." We are not yet convinced that the Socialist Party has taken this latter position even though individual Socialists have done so.

Because we are an organization working to secure unity of action where division now exists, we are necessarily exploring the field. We cannot prejudge the amount of unity that can be achieved. For this reason, we are proposing to have a conference of all progressive and radical groups in 1933 to consider this very question. Naturally we shall be disappointed if Socialist leaders slam the door in advance on all hope of cooperation.

Since Mr. Thomas in his *As I See It* states that the essential is to achieve the substance rather than the name, we hope he may be willing, "without prejudice" as to any ulterior commitment, to recommend to the party of which he is the honored head that it enter upon the exploration discussions which are the necessary preliminary to the united action which alone will achieve desired results. But in any and every case the L.I.P.A. invites the cooperation to this end of all individuals and all groups who are of like mind about the need for political action to bring about radical changes in our present economic and financial system.

Unity and Progress

It will be in the interest of continuity, I take it, if I try to make some connection between my own article and that of Dr. Niebuhr which opened this series. My intent, however, is not to write negatively, as would be the case if my article's main purpose and effect were criticism of Dr. Niebuhr's view, with considerable portions of which I am in agreement. I hope to use one aspect of his article as a background for introducing my own analysis, such as it is, of the American political need.

The thing that most strikes me in Dr. Niebuhr's exposition is its implication (provided of course that I read it aright) that a general philosophy of history is a prerequisite of a political analysis which will direct political action. It happens, of course, that European philosophies of history, from the time of St. Augustine's *City of God*, were of the nature of Christian theodicies. They were intended to justify the ways of God to man as manifested in human history, and specifically to interpret the general course of history as part of the great drama of human sin and final judgment in redemption or condemnation.

As secular interests grew and supernatural interests ebbed, as historical research into particulars developed, interest in a comprehensive philosophical interpretation of history declined. The present-day successors of even the great German idealists of the early nineteenth century, that is, of the men who attempted to translate a theological philosophy of history into metaphysical terms, avoid with virtual universality any attempt to apply their spiritualistic interpretation of the universe to the scene of history. In an extremely interesting way it happened, however, that the real heirs of the idea of a comprehensive philosophy of history

[First published in *World Tomorrow* 16 (8 March 1933): 232–33. For Reinhold Niebuhr's article to which this is a response, see Appendix 1.]

were a group of non-Christian and anti-religious thinkers who attempted a comprehensive philosophy of history from the standpoint of economic life. As I read Dr. Niebuhr's article, he is also one who believes that no analysis of political and economic tendencies can be made except upon the basis of an inclusive philosophy of history of economic type. Agreement or disagreement upon this fundamental point will accordingly deeply affect one's whole conception of the method and criterion of political judgment and action.

Dr. Niebuhr makes no reference to a philosophy of history. Lest I be thought guilty of introducing the phrase in a gratuitous and prejudicial manner, let me briefly explain what I mean. He engages in long range views and predictions. He seems to me to predicate political policies for the present upon a conception of what the future is practically sure to be. Amid the confused welter of social phenomena he has no doubt as to what the dominant forces are and what is to be their certain outcome. This is what I mean by basing oneself upon a philosophy of history. It seems to me to reverse the effective procedure in politics. I should begin, if I could, with finding out what are the urgent needs of the present and then try to shape policies to meet those needs. On this basis politics would then be used to help determine the future. Instead of trying to form a present line of policy on the basis of highly dubious forecasts of a long-range future, I would form a conception of what future society might become on the basis of actualities in the present, and then strive to bring this future about. As far as the kind of future to be worked for is concerned, I do not suppose I differ much from Dr. Niebuhr. I should want to see politics used to forward the formation of a genuinely cooperative society, where workers are in control of industry and finance as directly as possible through the economic organization of society itself rather than through any form of superimposed state socialism, and where work ensures not only security, leisure and opportunity for cultural development, but also such a share in control as will contribute directly to intellectual and moral realization of personality. Moreover, I believe that measures which effectively deal with present needs will operate to bring about this social end, and that only such measures will.

If I am right in my understanding of the tenor of Dr. Niebuhr's article, his reversal of what seems to me the right procedure accounts for what strikes me as a deplorable vagueness about what needs to be done and how to do it. I think any point of view that is more concerned with the question of deciding what will come "after capitalism" than in discovering what needs to be done during the present crisis in capitalism, and how it is to be done, is bound to be vague in spite of whatever is said about the need of "realism." The vagueness is evident, to my mind, not only in what is omitted as to a present working program, but in the oscillation regarding the method by which changes are to come about. On one hand, there is the emphasis on class conflict and struggle, and on the fact that no dominant group gives up power until compelled (connected with a somewhat theological view of collective egoism and the natural depravity of human nature), and on the other hand, there is deprecation of struggle carried to the point of violence and a vague picture of some future peaceful triumph of social righteousness. I can understand thoroughgoing pacifism, and I can understand the Communistic version of a violent struggle ending in the victory of the proletariat. But Dr. Niebuhr's position escapes me. I mention this point not to charge him with personal inconsistency, but because some such outcome seems to follow naturally from his inverted mode of approach.

It seems to me, then, that the basic question for those who agree upon the necessity of radical transformation of the economic foundations of present society is that of political procedure, of method of action. It is for this reason, as I hope the previous discussion has made clear, that I have conditioned my statement of my own conception of the right mode of attack upon a critical consideration of Dr. Niebuhr's article. The method of considering, on the one hand, urgent needs and ills and measures which will cope with them, and, on the other hand, of forming an idea of the kind of society we desire to bring into existence, which will give continuity of direction to political effort, is very different from that which Dr. Niebuhr criticizes under the name of "liberalism." It has nothing in common with the sentimentalism to which he gives that name. There has been and still is an immense amount of political immaturity and economic illiteracy in the American citizenship, and I am not questioning either the existence or the futility of what Dr. Niebuhr calls liberalism. I am concerned only to point out the irrelevancy of his description and condemnation to the kind of procedure which I am proposing.

I do not believe there is any great difference among those on the radical and near-radical front (meaning those who believe in the necessity of basic changes in the existing order of society) as to what the urgent needs of the present are. There is, however, still need of a great deal of definite and constructive thinking as to the best measures of dealing with these ills, best from the standpoint of meeting the causes of the trouble and of forwarding a better social order. We must doubtless, in any case, find our way experimentally. But in spite of the immense amount of discussion called out by the acute crisis and tragic breakdown, there is not as yet an adequate consensus, even among those who desire radical measures, as to the definite and precise line of policies to be undertaken. There are experts in many fields who can be enlisted in a consideration of such policies who will balk at subscribing to some ultimate comprehensive social doctrine. There is pressing need of union for consideration and adoption of definite policies and for a united attack in their behalf.

We are confronted with perhaps the most curious political situation the civilized world has ever seen. In the midst of the breakdown, with almost universal criticism of the present order, with a very general acceptance, I should say, by 90 per cent of the intelligent portion of the community, of the need of drastic changes, there is no significant organized political action of a radical sort. Either the American people are so politically inept and incompetent that we are bound to drift into greater chaos, or there has been something wrong in the basic method of approach of those groups that are interested in directing the processes of change. I believe that unity, union of thought and action, is the prerequisite of curing this anomalous condition. I believe that this unity is hindered by the type of view represented in Dr. Niebuhr's article, and that it is attainable on the basis of the two conditions I have mentioned. In the past, especially in the period of "prosperity," it is easy to understand that radical groups should have felt themselves forced away from a policy of action into one of somewhat remote speculation and rationalization. (The economic philosophy of history, with its doctrine of inevitable final change of a specified sort which many Marxians derived from Marx, is a typical rationalization of a condition of immediate powerlessness.)

Because I believe the greatest immediate need is exploration of the possibilities and conditions of unified thought and action on the radical front, I have written as I have. I am not writing in behalf of any particular group or in behalf of any pet conceptions of my own. I fear the consequences if radicals do not combine to work out and work for a definite political program.

Imperative Need: A New Radical Party

Those who have power, rule. This is a necessity, not something to complain of. Democracy was born of the idea that political institution of the ballot and officials elected for a term would give the people power, the people and not a class. For a time the scheme worked, even though haltingly. Why have power and rule passed from the people to a few? Everybody knows who the few are, and the class-status of the few answers the question. They are not engineers, scientists, any more than they are an aristocracy of birth. They are an oligarchy of wealth. They rule over us because they control banks, credit, the land, and big organized means of production (like the U.S. Steel Corporation and General Motors as examples that are outstanding and yet only examples), the railways and other means of transportation, and, with exceptions, the public press.

Power today resides in control of the means of production, exchange, publicity, transportation and communication. Whoever owns them rules the life of the country, not necessarily by intention, not necessarily by deliberate corruption of the nominal government, but by necessity. Power is power and must act, and it must act according to the nature of the machinery through which it operates. In this case, the machinery is business for private profit through private control of banking, land, industry, reinforced by command of the press, press agents and other means of publicity and propaganda.

In order to restore democracy, one thing and one thing only is essential. The people will rule when they have power, and they will have power in the degree they own and control the land, banks, the producing and distributing agencies of the nation. Ravings about Bolshevism, communism, socialism are irrelevant

[First published in *Common Sense* 2 (September 1933): 6–7.]

to the axiomatic truth of this statement. They come either from complaisant ignorance or from the deliberate desire of those in possession of power and rule to perpetuate their privilege.

For a brief period, that of the "new economic era," the real rulers of the country came near admitting the fact of their domination. For they justified it on the ground that they were responsible for the prosperity of the country, and that through them it seeped down to labor that was enjoying, because of the beneficent rule of those at the top, constantly increasing wages and increased power to share in the higher standard of living and the security vouchsafed them by the almoners of divine providence.

Events have proved that while those in private control of industry and wealth rule they do not and cannot govern. For government implies order and security at the very least. And what we have is tragic insecurity and essential anarchy. I need not call the roll of the millions of unemployed, of the millions living scantily and precariously upon the dole of waning private charity, of the combination, that would be incredible if it were not actual, of piled up real wealth of food and goods with privation and poverty. I allow myself one minor instance. At the time when public officials are calling upon police and militia to keep dairy farmers from emptying milk, the federal government is paying a premium to other farmers for plowing under millions of acres of corn and cotton. If that is not anarchy, no one knows what anarchy is.

This situation continues only because the mass of the people refuse to look facts in the face and prefer to feed on illusions, produced and circulated by those in power with a profusion that contrasts with their withholding of the necessities of life. The day that the mass of the American people awake to the realities of the situation, that day the restoration of democracy will commence, for power and rule will revert to the people.

We are in the midst of the third great crisis that has occurred in this nation. The first was in the revolutionary and post-revolutionary days. The second was the Civil War which "freed" black slaves and began the entrenchment of wealth. Because of the greater size and bigger population of the country and the complexity of social affairs, and the possibility of a secure and abundant life for all, the present economic crisis overshadows in importance both of the others. We make the choice between a continuation of anarchy, disguised and externally suppressed—

for a time—by what is called Fascism, leading to inevitable catastrophe, and a political revolution by which the people will resume power—that is to say, not tinkering with the details of legislation and administration but taking over the means of power.

I am willing to admit that Franklin Roosevelt and some of his advisors mean well, and that some of the things they are doing are the sort of things that are needed preparatory to the nationalization, or better the popularization, of power of production, distribution and exchange. But consider the two main alternatives—leaving out of account a complete breakdown of their efforts and the return, possibly next winter, of the conditions of last winter on an aggravated scale. Let us suppose that a reasonable modicum of prosperity returns, that employment picks up considerably and so on. What will happen? An enormous organized move, supported by all the strength of the agencies of publicity and ballyhoo, for another "return to normalcy." The argument will be simple and plausible. Roosevelt's measures were fine in an emergency; we gladly and patriotically supported them. But the emergency has passed. Government must now take its hands off business and allow the innate energy and wisdom of the leaders of business to conduct their affairs in their own wise and successful way—the truly "American" way. The plea will of course be tremendously reinforced by the officially temporary character of the methods—licensing of corporations for example for only one year.

It will not require any obvious surrender or loss of face on the part of President Roosevelt to accede to the clamor and pressure. He can, if he chooses, claim credit for the temporary nature of the emergency measures and take the lead in declaring that now they have been so successful that they have accomplished their purpose. It is impossible to exaggerate the pressure that will be brought to bear upon him. It will come from the representatives of big interests who will have no difficulty in presenting "evidence" that the good work is now accomplished and that business will be strangled and the permanent return of prosperity prevented by a continuation of the emergency measures. Those most active in bringing the pressure to bear upon the Administration will be some of the big business men now among his advisors.

The pressure will not be confined to President Roosevelt and his

Cabinet. It will be brought upon the Democratic party and the politicians who are the henchmen of the present system. And it will also come from within, from the most influential leaders of the present Democratic party, already sullen and discontented, proclaiming that the present leadership is betraying the party and the people "for a mess of communistic pottage."

The only way to preserve as well as to extend whatever is good in the Rooseveltian measures is the formation of a strong united radical new party.

The above is on the assumption that Roosevelt and his immediate advisors and supporters have both an intelligent and sincere understanding of existing needs and the remedies for them. There is another alternative. It is possible, on the whole more probable in my opinion, that they are both somewhat blind and half-hearted, and their chief desire is to bolster and repair the present system—which means as sure as night follows day an ultimate return of complete power and rule to the very elements that have brought the nation to its present pass.

There are some conspicuous indications that point this way. There is the complete failure so far to deal in any fundamental way with the banking and credit situation. Popular opinion was ripe for something thorough-going, for the genuine social control of money and credit—the greatest single source of power in the existing system of class privilege and power. The opportunity has not been seized. The same may be said of popular control of the railway system. Whether the dangerous and almost surely destructive policy of deliberate inflation is to be entered upon is still uncertain as I write. But one thing is certain. The alternative of a drastic writing down of debts and all fixed charges has not even received consideration.

Then there is the likelihood that the ultimate effect of present measures, without an extension of them that the Administration has not suggested, will ultimately strengthen the big business interests at the expense of the smaller units. And there is the surrender of the interests of labor in the matter of genuine collective bargaining as to wages. That "company unions" will be effective in raising wages to the point to secure the essential increase of buying and consuming power is a notion too absurd to entertain. To mention only one other point, there is the eager willingness of the Administration to use the methods of coercion, intimidation, suppression and organized ballyhoo that were used in war-time. Just as happened after the war, the methods will continue and will be ready to suppress free discussion and to mislead opinion when the time for the absolutely certain movement for "government hands off business" arrives. The power of the forces now being set in motion cannot be over-estimated.

Upon this alternative also there is but one conclusion to be reached: *The need is imperative for the immediate formation of a strong united radical third party.*

What Keeps Funds Away from Purchasers

Want and scarcity in an age of plenty for all is the contradiction that now stares us in the face. Lack of purchasing power stalls the entire agricultural and industrial machine. The cause for this destructive absence of purchasing power is simple and evident. The income that goes to property—that is, to investors through dividends, rent, and interest—is out of all proportion to that which goes to farmers, to workers in factories, stores, and offices. Hence the mass purchasing power of the Nation as a whole is paralyzed.

Only about 1 percent of the total population, some 340,000 persons, has, according to official income-tax figures, a taxable income of $5,000 or over. Moreover, two thirds of the total income of this group of 1 percent of all families came from dividends and interest, omitting even at that all income from tax-exempt bonds.

The National Bureau of Economic Research reports that for 1932 the total national income from every source was a little less than fifty billions, and that one third of this whole sum was income on property, namely, dividends, interest, rent, and withdrawals of accumulated surplus. The 1 percent already referred to got three fifths of the total amount paid out in dividends.

These facts prove that the great mass of the people—farmers, laborers, and the white-collar class—do not get much more than a subsistence income on the average. How can they be expected to furnish the mass purchasing power absolutely necessary to provide permanent recovery?

It is absurd to suppose that 1 percent or even 10 percent, hav-

[First published in *Congressional Record*, 73d Cong., 2d sess., 1934, 78, pt. 7: 7384–85, from a speech to the Joint Committee on Unemployment on 21 April 1934 in Washington, D.C., broadcast over WRC.]

ing excess income, can keep the industrial and agricultural machinery going. Moreover, the most conservative estimate made by engineers and business executives is that present plant is not producing more than three fifths of what it could turn out if all of it were brought up to the level of the most efficient enterprises. How is work going to be supplied to the eight or ten million now supported by charity (if at all), because of their lack of work, unless mass purchasing power is created by much higher levels of income for the mass of the population, so as to provide the sale of goods that will enable farmers and manufacturers to sell what they are capable of producing?

The demand exercised by invested capital for dividends on stocks and interest on bonds and loans is thus the chief single cause for lack of adequate mass buying power.

Apart from radical change in the whole system, there is but one way of increasing mass purchasing power. The Government must become an employer of labor on a much larger scale than at present. A much more extensive program of housing than is now contemplated would give direct employment to many and indirectly provide labor and income for more persons through stimulation of capital goods industries. Government ownership of natural monopolies and quasi-monopolies would increase mass purchasing power by relieving the consumer of the present diversion of what he pays into dividends and interest. The change in our taxation system required, if the Government is to become a large scale employer, would assist in directing a larger part of the national income into channels where it would provide mass buying power.

The conservative propertied interests of the country are the ones most directly interested in having a redistribution of national income that will increase mass purchasing power and so prevent the present creeping paralysis from rendering the productive plant of the Nation increasingly idle and nonproductive.

The farmers know they are exploited because they are forced to sell the products they produce at prices fixed by someone else and invariably below the cost of production. The consumers know they are exploited because they must buy at prices fixed by someone else and often exorbitant. They know that the cost of living is so high that many of the average families cannot buy the food products that are needed to prevent hunger and preserve health. The producer is exploited in the sale of his products at prices over which he has no control, and the consumer is exploited in the purchase of food products and other necessities at prices over which he has no control.

A concerted effort is constantly being made to lead the consuming public to believe that the farmers are responsible for the high cost of living and that the bulk of the high prices they pay goes to the farmers.

The three A's of the Agricultural Department issues a biweekly bulletin called the *Consumers' Guide*. In the issue of April 9 they explain where your food dollar goes. In 1929, on 14 principal food products, 52 cents went to the processors and distributors, and 48 cents to the farmer. In 1933, 69 cents went for processing and distributing, and 31 cents to the farmer. In March 1934, according to this bulletin, 62 cents of your food dollar went to the processors and distributors, and 38 cents to the farmer.

They state in another issue that in 1932 the farmer got 33 cents of the total consumer's dollar, and in 1933 the farmer got 35 cents. At that rate, during the last 2 years, for a product for which the farmer received $1, the consumer paid $3.

The spread is too wide. It is impossible for the average consumer to absorb the 65- to 67-cent spread in each dollar's worth of food products that he buys. This is the result of the exploitation through the profit system which is largely responsible for the present so-called "depression" and has all but wrecked our whole economic structure.

The dairy farmer receives from 2 to 4 cents per quart for milk, and the consumer pays from 10 to 16 cents. The cost of distribution plus the profit of the distributors is the big item in the price the consumer pays for milk. The bulk of the milk is handled by holding companies or what amounts to a Milk Trust. This Milk Trust makes an enormous profit and pays their officials enormous salaries. The farmer is robbed in the price he receives and the consumer is robbed in the price he pays.

Out of the meat dollar the producer gets 31 cents, the packer 38 cents, and the retailer 31 cents.

Recently I received a newspaper clipping from North Dakota which listed the local price of wheat at 66 cents per bushel. There was also an "ad" of a local flour mill, quoting the price of flour at $6 per barrel, and feed at $16 per ton.

The price of wheat was based on the Minneapolis price, 400 miles away, less the freight; and the price of flour manufactured in the local mill was based on the Minneapolis price plus the freight. The value of wheat that went into a barrel of flour, at quoted prices, is $2.97; deducting this from the price of a barrel of flour is $3.03, plus 56 cents, the value of the feed, makes $3.59, and represents the amount received by the miller for grinding the barrel of flour, which is 62 cents more than the farmer received for producing the wheat and hauling it to the mill.

Bread at that time was selling for 8 cents per loaf. Approximately 292 one-pound loaves are made from a barrel of flour, and the consumer pays $23.36 for the bread made from $2.97 worth of wheat. The farmer gets a little less than 1 cent for the wheat in a pound loaf of bread; the miller gets a little over 1 cent for grinding the flour that goes into the loaf; the baker gets about 4 cents for baking, and the retailer gets 2 cents for handing the loaf of bread over the counter. They all get a profit but the farmer who produces the wheat. The processor and the distributor must get their profit even though the farmer sells at a loss.

There is an old saying among the farmers—take the gambler out of the bread basket. It is impossible to give the farmer an honest market as long as the speculators and gamblers manipulate and fix his prices. Last year the Chicago Board of Trade bought and sold over 10,000,000,000 bushels of wheat, which was 20 times as much as all the wheat produced in the whole United States last year.

Under the N.R.A. program, codes have been put into effect having for their purpose the regulation of prices to provide for cost of production for the processor and manufacturer, the wholesaler, jobber, and distributor, and in many instances the prices have gone up. All industries are being taken care of under the N.R.A., with the exception of agriculture, on a cost-of-production and a fair-profit basis.

The three A's, through the processing tax and the allotment payments, are attempting to increase farm prices to what is known as the "pre-war parity price." It is admitted that a portion of the processing tax has been passed back to the producer, and a part of it has been passed on to the consumer. It is also conceded that if farm prices are brought up to the parity price, they will still be under cost of production, and therefore agriculture will not be a prosperous business even with the parity price—which they are not getting.

The latest A.A.A. figures on parity prices—April 4—are to the effect that wheat is only 65 percent of parity price; cotton, 77 percent of parity; corn, 57.1 percent; butterfat, only 65.8 percent; beef cattle, only 63.2 percent; and hogs, only 41 percent of parity price.

The Agricultural Department seems to be carrying out the Biblical instruction of not letting the right hand know what thy left hand doeth.

The A.A.A.'s division of the Agricultural Department is advocating a drastic reduction of acreage of production of certain crops, like corn and wheat, in order to reduce the so-called "surplus." Another division of the Agricultural Department is putting out a bulletin advocating that an adequate diet of wheat flour per capita at moderate cost is 122 pounds, which would be a reduction of per capita consumption of wheat flour of 48 pounds per year. This, if carried out, would reduce consumption materially while the A.A.A. are at the same time reducing the acreage to cut down production to the present needs.

There is also another division putting out a bulletin which instructs the farmer how to produce a larger yield per acre of corn, and the A.A.A. are insisting on the reduction of acreage at the same time to cut down the production.

A marketing bill (S. 3333) has been introduced in both the House and Senate to provide for the purchase and sale of farm products. It sets up a Farmers and Consumers Financing Corporation, with authority to control the processing and distribution of products from the producer to the consumer. The purpose of the act is to provide a market for the sale of agricultural products and to eliminate, as far as possible, the commissions and charges that are exacted upon agricultural products from the time such products leave the producer until the same reaches the consumer, and to thereby increase the price which the producer receives and decrease the price the consumer pays.

There should be more cooperation between the producers and the consumers. The cost of processing and handling farm products must be cut down. Unnecessary middlemen must be eliminated.

The farmer is entitled to cost of production just as much as anyone else in any other line of business, and the consumer is equally entitled to buy these farm products at a reasonable price.

If codes are to be continued, give the farmer a code based on cost of production just as the codes for the other industries; eliminate the gambler in food products and other necessities of life; let us have a market control that will eliminate the exploiters; cut out graft; provide for efficient distribution at reasonable cost and give the consumers service instead of exploitation. Cooperation between the producers and consumers will easily bring about these results.

American Ideals (I)
The Theory of Liberty vs. the Fact of Regimentation

It is a significant and sinister fact that at the present time those who cry "liberty" with the greatest vehemence are representatives of the class that is more responsible than any other for the loss of actual liberty by the mass of our citizens. They would make the grand idea of liberty the monopoly of the business man and the employer in the conduct of their affairs. They loudly profess adherence to the glory of the Constitution as the protector of human liberties. But when the guaranteed freedom of speech and public assembly are violently interfered with by organized gangs, these men are strangely—or not so strangely—silent. They rather devote themselves to asserting that the Civil Liberties Union and others interested in maintaining the civil rights guaranteed by the Constitution are subversive of Americanism and are even financed from Moscow.

If we want to find authentic cases of regimentation in both action and opinion we should look for them in the state of the average worker in any well "organized" industry under the capitalistic regime. The regimentation does not apply merely to manual laborers and operators of machines. It affects the white collar class and even the specially trained engineers who are so necessary for the management of great industrial enterprises. In their cases, however, regimentation goes by the euphemistic name of loyalty. In the state of New York and other states, teachers in private and public schools are now regimented. Although every citizen in order to vote has to state that he will support the Constitution, teachers are now singled out for a special additional oath. He is naïve indeed who supposes that the object of the oath is anything but to produce regimentation of opinion and its expression through producing an atmosphere of intimidation.

[First published in *Common Sense* 3 (December 1934): 10–11.]

In the last few days I have seen a document signed by a number of young people who work in the Wall Street area. It is full of fine sentiments about liberty and the dangers of regimentation. In mentioning a questionaire sent out to workers in the field the document records that "in our questionaire we asked 'Have you faith in the American form of government?' and the answers are 100% yes." This is indeed encouraging. But what would have happened to the job of a young man who replied in the negative? The document also says and in italics, "*We are unalterably opposed to any form of regimentation of individual liberties that our forefathers wrested for us.*" This too is a noble sentiment. But one recalls that the financial authorities of this area all proclaimed with a single voice that the Securities Act and the Act regulating trading in stock exchanges were cases of regimentation. The regimentation which is vigorously opposed is any kind of social control of private business.

I quote one passage at length. "*What the American youth holds dearest is the American dream of freedom of opportunity and choice of occupation.* It is an American tradition to hold before the youth of this country, the equality of opportunity. Our country has become great through following such an ideal. Were once this golden dream of opportunity to vanish before the eyes of youth, our country would not be known as the land of opportunity any longer, but as a regimented government." It requires a calloused cheek to write the first sentences in the face of the millions who cannot find any opportunity to work at anything, much less to have freedom of choice in the line of work. But what I would call especial attention to is the closing words. It is not a regimented *society* we have to fear; to say that might call attention to the fact that the dream, of freedom of opportunity, golden, silver or paper, has already vanished for millions upon millions. No, the only regimentation we have to fear is that of *government*. No words could convey more clearly the belief that social control of big business and finance is the only kind of regimentation that is thought of.

The document closes with the hope, in which I heartily share, that "*democratic government will again re-assert itself as a living embodiment and expression of free men.*" But the meaning of the hope as it is entertained under the influence of financial centres is expressed in the following phrase: "The capitalistic order *upon which democratic government is based.*" (In this case, the italics are mine.) In short, a state that is the living embodiment of free men is identical with the unhampered flourishing of capitalism. That is not our idea of democracy.

A leading representative, in fact the publicity agent of the Liberty League, Mr. Shouse, has recently attacked the disposition to oppose property rights and personal rights. Property, he says, has no rights. The right in property is a right of a person; there are only personal rights. So there you are. Nobody can believe that this sophism can be effective unless he has already identified rights, or liberty, with property interests. It is not the right to *obtain* property which is defended; to secure that right to the great mass of our citizens would involve basic changes in our economic system. No, it is *the right of those who are already the propertied class to be free from social control* that is zealously contended for.

It is highly important that those who wish to see great changes in our economic order brought about, should not fall into the trap that is set for them. What *we* want is liberty, a liberty that does not exist in the present system. The economic and financial system that is now administered is the great foe of this liberty; it is what makes the "golden dream" of our forefathers a hideous nightmare for uncounted millions.

The liberty of concentrated wealth to do as it pleases is that which practically reduces so many to a condition of serfdom. Control of credit and control of the instruments of production may give liberty to a small class but it shuts millions out from any significant share in liberty. The word regimentation comes from a military fact, from war. If Mr. Du Pont and other members of the Liberty League are really opposed to regimentation let them turn their energies against war, including the liberty to make private profits by the manufacture of munitions and armaments. For war is synonymous with regimentation of action and opinion.

The liberty that we want is more than the liberty to work and to get a living wage that is now denied, although it more than includes that factor. The nation today is possessed of abundant resources, of agricultural and factory means of production, along with the technical knowledge and skill that will bring an abundant material life to all. But the culture of the world in science and art, in all their varied forms, is also our heritage. Liberty to share freely in this rich heritage is the goal towards which economic liberty for all, and not just for a small class, is the means. How many of those who are now shouting for liberty of private business enterprise on the part of the entrepreneur are active, I wonder, in protecting the public schools, the most rudimentary form of liberty of access to the cultural heritage of the race, against the forces that are weakening the schools? And how many are busy concocting schemes for reducing their taxes by crippling public education?

Let radicals make it clear that an infinitely greater amount of real liberty is possible than our present system provides for. Let them make clear that *they* are the ones who would extend the liberties for which our forefathers fought till they include all members of society and until every normal human being has the opportunity to develop to the full, in peace and security, the capacities with which he is naturally endowed. Regiment *things* and free human beings. Regiment machines and money and other inanimate things, and give liberty to human beings.

Why I Am Not a Communist

Having had the opportunity to see the contribution of Mr. Bertrand Russell, I have doubts as to whether I can say much that he has not already said. But I begin by emphasizing the fact that I write with reference to being a Communist in the Western world, especially here and now in the United States, and a Communist after the pattern set in the U.S.S.R.

1. *Such* Communism rests upon an almost entire neglect of the specific historical backgrounds and traditions which have operated to shape the patterns of thought and action in America. The autocratic background of the Russian Church and State, the fact that every progressive movement in Russia had its origin in some foreign source and has been imposed from above upon the Russian people, explain much about the form Communism has taken in that country. It is therefore nothing short of fantastic to transfer the ideology of Russian Communism to a country which is so profoundly different in its economic, political, and cultural history. Were this fact acknowledged by Communists and reflected in their daily activities and general program, were it admitted that many of the practical and theoretical features of Russian Communism (like belief in the plenary and verbal inspiration of Marx, the implicit or explicit domination of the Communist party in every field of culture, the ruthless extermination of minority opinion in its own ranks, the verbal glorification of the mass and the actual cult of the infallibility of leadership) are due to local causes, the character of Communism in other countries might undergo a radical change. But it is extremely unlikely that this will take place. For official Communism has made the practical traits of the dictatorship *of* the proletariat and *over* the proletariat, the suppression of the civil

liberties of all non-proletarian elements as well as of dissenting proletarian minorities, integral parts of the standard Communist faith and dogma. It has imposed and not argued the theory of dialectic materialism (which in the U.S.S.R. itself has to undergo frequent restatement in accordance with the exigencies of party factional controversy) upon all its followers. Its cultural philosophy, which has many commendable features, is vitiated by the absurd attempt to make a single and uniform entity out of the "proletariat."

2. Particularly unacceptable to me in the ideology of official Communism is its monistic and one-way philosophy of history. This is akin to the point made above. The thesis that all societies must exhibit a uniform, even if uneven, social development from primitive communism to slavery, from slavery to feudalism, from feudalism to capitalism, and from capitalism to socialism, and that the transition from capitalism to socialism must be achieved by the same way in all countries, can be accepted only by those who are either ignorant of history or who are so steeped in dogma that they cannot look at a fact without changing it to suit their special purposes. From this monistic philosophy of history, there follows a uniform political practice and a uniform theory of revolutionary strategy and tactics. But where differences in historic background, national psychology, religious profession and practice are taken into account—and they must be considered in every scientific theory—there will be corresponding differences in political methods, differences that may extend to general policies as well as to the strategy of their execution. For example, so far as the historic experience of America is concerned, two things among many others are overlooked by official Communists whose philosophy has been projected on the basis of special European conditions. We in the United States have no background of a dominant and overshadowing feudalism. Our troubles flow from the oppressive exercise of power by financial over-lords and from the failure to introduce new forms of *democratic* control in industry and government consonant with the shift from individual to corporate economy. It is a possibility overlooked by official Communists that important social changes in the direction of democratization of industry may be accomplished by groups working *with* the working-class although, strictly speaking, not *of* them. The other point ignored by the

Communists is our deeply-rooted belief in the importance of individuality, a belief that is almost absent in the Oriental world from which Russia has drawn so much. Not to see that this attitude, so engrained in our habitual ways of thought and action, demands a very different set of policies and methods from those embodied in official Communism, verges to my mind on political insanity.

3. While I recognize the existence of class-conflicts as one of the fundamental facts of social life to-day, I am profoundly skeptical of class war as *the* means by which such conflicts can be eliminated and genuine social advance made. And yet this is a basic point in Communist theory and is more and more identified with the meaning of dialectic materialism as applied to the social process. Historically speaking, it may have been necessary for Russia in order to achieve peace for her war-weary soldiers, and land for her hungry peasants, to convert incipient class-war into open civil war culminating in the so-called dictatorship of the proletariat. But nonetheless Fascism in Germany and Italy cannot be understood except with reference to the lesson those countries learned from the U.S.S.R. How Communism can continue to advocate the kind of economic change it desires by means of civil war, armed insurrection and iron dictatorship in face of what has happened in Italy and Germany I cannot at all understand. Reliable observers have contended that the communist ideology of dictatorship and violence together with the belief that the communist party was the foreign arm of a foreign power constituted one of the factors which aided the growth of Fascism in Germany. I am firmly convinced that imminent civil war, or even the overt threat of such a war, in any western nation, will bring Fascism with its terrible engines of repression to power. Communism, then, with its doctrine of the necessity of the forcible overthrow of the state by armed insurrection, with its doctrine of the dictatorship of the proletariat, with its threats to exclude all other classes from civil rights, to smash their political parties, and to deprive them of the rights of freedom of speech, press and assembly—which Communists *now* claim for themselves under capitalism—Communism is itself, an unwitting, but nonetheless, powerful factor in bringing about Fascism. As an unalterable opponent of Fascism in every form, I cannot be a Communist.

4. It is not irrelevant to add that one of the reasons I am not a Communist is that the emotional tone and methods of discussion and dispute which seem to accompany Communism at present are extremely repugnant to me. Fair-play, elementary honesty in the representation of facts and especially of the opinions of others, are something more than "bourgeois virtues." They are traits that have been won only after long struggle. They are not deep-seated in human nature even now—witness the methods that brought Hitlerism to power. The systematic, persistent and seemingly intentional disregard of these things by Communist spokesmen in speech and press, the hysteria of their denunciations, their attempts at character assassination of their opponents, their misrepresentation of the views of the "liberals" to whom they also appeal for aid in their defense campaigns, their policy of "rule or ruin" in their so-called united front activities, their apparent conviction that what they take to be the end justifies the use of *any* means if only those means promise to be successful—all these, in my judgment, are fatal to the very end which official Communists profess to have at heart. And if I read the temper of the American people aright, especially so in this country.

5. A revolution effected solely or chiefly by violence can in a modernized society like our own result only in chaos. Not only would civilization be destroyed but the things necessary for bare life. There are some, I am sure, now holding and preaching Communism who would be the first to react against it, if in this country Communism were much more than a weak protest or an avocation of literary men. Few communists are really aware of the far-reaching implications of the doctrine that civil war is the *only* method by which revolutionary economic and political changes can be brought about. A comparatively simple social structure, such as that which Russia had, may be able to recover from the effects of violent, internal disturbance. And Russia, it must be remembered, had the weakest middle class of any major nation. Were a large scale revolution to break out in highly industrialized America, where the middle class is stronger, more militant and better prepared than anywhere else in the world, it would either be abortive, drowned in a blood bath, or if it were victorious, would win only a Pyrrhic victory. The two sides would

destroy the country and each other. For this reason, too, I am not a Communist.

I have been considering the position, as I understand it, of the orthodox and official Communism. I cannot blind myself, however, to the perceptible difference between communism with a small *c*, and Communism, official Communism, spelt with a capital letter.

The Supreme Intellectual Obligation[1]

The scientific worker faces a dilemma. The nature of his calling necessitates a very considerable remoteness from immediate social activities and interests. His vocation is absorbing in its demands upon time, energy and thought. As men were told to enter their closets to pray, so the scientific man has to enter the seclusion of the laboratory, museum and study. He has, as it is, more than enough distractions to contend with, especially if, as so often happens, he is also a teacher and has administrative and committee duties. Moreover, the field of knowledge cannot be attacked en masse. It must be broken up into problems, and as a rule, detailed aspects and phases of these problems must be discriminated into still lesser elements. A certain degree of specialization is a necessity of scientific advance. With every increase of specialization, remoteness from common and public affairs also increases. Division of labor is as much a necessity of investigation into the secrets of nature and of man as it is of industry.

Nor does aloofness reach an end in this point. The language in use for common communication does not fit the needs of statement of scientific inquiries and results. It was developed for other purposes than that of accurate and precise exposition of science, and is totally unfitted to set forth comprehensive generalizations in exact form. The result is that the scientist speaks what for the mass of men is an unknown tongue, one that requires much more training to acquire than any living speech or than any dead language. He can speak directly about his own affairs and problems only to a comparatively small circle of the initiated.

These considerations define one horn of the dilemma. The

1. Address delivered at the dinner held in honor of James McKeen Cattell at the University Club, Boston, Wednesday, December 27, 1933.

[First published in *Science Education* 18 (February 1934): 1–4.]

other horn is constituted by the fact that the scientist lives in the same world with others, and a world that is being made over by the fruits of his labors. There is hardly a single detail of our common and collective life, whether in transportation of persons and goods, in modes of communication, in household appliances and conveniences, in medicine, in agriculture and all the varied forms of productive industry, that is not what it is today because of what science has discovered. The scientist may be aloof in his work and language, but the results of his work pervade and permeate, they determine, every aspect of social life. The inventor, the engineer and the business man are unremittingly occupied with translating what is discovered in the laboratory into applications of utensil, device, tool and machine, which have largely revolutionized the conduct of life in the home, the farm and amusement as well as industry. I could easily spend many times my allotted time in a partial cataloging of things unknown fifty years ago that are now everyday necessities.

These consequences of science extend their influence far beyond what anthropologists call material culture. They affect institutions and great modes of interest and activity. We have broken with the intellectual traditions of the past and the mass of men have not had the nature of the change interpreted to them, although science set the terms on which men associate together. They transform life in ways that have created social problems of such vastness and complexity that the human mind stands bewildered. The intellect is at present subdued by the results of its own intellectual victories. It has become a commonplace to refer to consequences of chemistry in its application to warfare. High explosives, with their allies of steel and airplane derived from physics, are capable of destroying every city on the face of the earth, and we are even threatened with bacterial warfare. If the problems of peace and war have assumed a new and unprecedented form—which, alas, the nations are meeting for the most part only by increased expenditure for armament—it is because of applications of scientific knowledge.

I have selected but one aspect of the question. The economic problem which weighs so heavily upon us today affords another illustration of the new social impact of science. Here too it is a commonplace that mankind in advanced industrial countries and especially in the United States confronts the paradox of want in the midst of plenty. It is science, which through technological applications has produced the potentiality of plenty, of ease and security for all, while lagging legal and political institutions, unaffected as yet by the advance of science into their domain, explain the want, insecurity and suffering that are the other term of the paradox.

My title is the supreme intellectual obligation. But every obligation is moral, and in its ultimate consequences social. The demands of the situation cannot be met, as some reactionaries urge, by going backward in science, by putting restrictions upon its productive activities. They cannot be met by putting a gloss of humanistic culture over the brute realities of the situation. They can be met only by human activity exercised in human directions. The wounds made by applications of science can be healed only by a further extension of applications of knowledge and intelligence; like the purpose of all modern healing the application must be preventive as well as curative. This is the supreme obligation of intellectual activity at the present time. The moral consequences of science in life impose a corresponding responsibility.

As with almost everything in contemporary life, it is easier to diagnose the ill than to indicate the remedy. But there are some suggestions that occur to all who reflect upon the problem. The field of education is immense and it has hardly been touched by the application of science. There are, indeed, courses in science installed in high schools and colleges. That much of the educational battle has been won, and we owe a great debt to those who waged the battle against the obstacles of tradition and the inertia of institutional habit. But the scientific attitude, the will to use scientific method and the equipment necessary to put the will into effect, is still, speaking for the mass of people, inchoate and unformed. The obligations incumbent upon science cannot be met until its representatives cease to be contented with having a multiplicity of courses in various sciences represented in the schools, and devote even more energy than was spent in getting a place for science in the curriculum to seeing to it that the sciences which are taught are themselves more concerned about creating a certain mental attitude than they are about purveying a fixed body of information, or about preparing a small number of persons for the further specialized pursuit of some particular science.

I do not mean of course that every opportunity should not be afforded the comparatively small number of selected minds that have both taste and capacity for advanced work in a chosen field of science. But I do mean that the responsibility of science cannot be fulfilled by educational methods that are chiefly concerned with the self-perpetuation of specialized science to the neglect of influencing the much larger number to adopt into the very make-up of their minds those attitudes of open-mindedness, intellectual integrity, observation and interest in testing their opinions and beliefs that are characteristic of the scientific attitude.

The problem is of course much broader than the remaking of courses in science which is nevertheless requisite. Every course in every subject should have as its chief end the cultivation of these attitudes of mind. As long as acquisition of items of information, whether they be particular facts or broad generalizations, is the chief concern of instruction, the appropriation of method into the working constitution of personality will continue to come off a bad second. Information is necessary, yes, more than is now usually obtained. But it should not stand as an end in itself. It should be an integral part of the operations of learning that construct the scientific attitude; that are, indeed, a part of that attitude since the scientific inquirer is above all else a continuing and persistent learner. As long as intellectual docility is the chief aim, as long as it is esteemed more important for the young to acquire correct beliefs than to be alert about the methods by which beliefs are formed the influence of science will be confined to those departments in which it has won its victories in the past. I cannot refrain from saying that one great obstacle is that many scientific men still hold, implicitly if not expressly, that there is a region of beliefs, social, religious, and political, which is reserved for sheer acceptance and where unbiased inquiry should not intrude.

There is, moreover, a virgin field practically untouched by the influence of science. Elementary education is still a place for acquiring skills and passively absorbing facts. It is generally now admitted that the most fundamental attitudes are formed in childhood, many of them in the early years. The greatest indictment that can be brought against present civilization, in its intellectual phase, is that so little attention is given to instilling, as a part of organic habit, trust in intelligence and eager interest in its active manifestation. I take little interest in demonstrations of the average low level of native intelligence as long as I am aware how little is done to secure full operation of what native intellectual capacity there is, however limited it may be. Speaking generally, it is now everywhere subordinated to acquisition of special skills and the retention of more or less irrelevant masses of facts and principles—irrelevant, that is, to the formation of the inquiring mind that explores and tests. Yet childhood is the time of the most active curiosity and highest interest in continual experimentation. The chief responsibility for the attainment of a system of education in which the groundwork of a habit and attitude inspired and directed by something akin to the method of science lies with those who already enjoy the benefits of special scientific training.

I have spoken chiefly with respect to the education of the schools. But the problem and the responsibility of education go deeper. There are some signs of a rebirth of the educational interest that marked the Greeks who thought of it, as far as we can gather from the records, chiefly in terms of adults. The theme of adult education is in the air. There was never a time in the history of the world in which power to think with respect to conduct of social life and the remaking of traditional institutions is as important as it is today in our own country. There is an immense amount of knowledge available, knowledge economic, historical, psychological, as well as physical. The chief obstacle lies not in lack of the information that might be brought to bear, experimentally, upon our problems. It lies on the one hand in the fact that this knowledge is laid away in cold storage for safe-keeping, and on the other hand in the fact that the public is not yet habituated to desire the knowledge nor even to belief in the necessity for it. Hunger is lacking and the material with which to feed it is not accessible. Yet appetite grows with eating. The trouble with much of what is called popularization of knowledge is that it is content with diffusion of information, in diluted form, merely as information. It needs to be organized and presented in its bearing upon action. Here is a most significant phase of the obligation incumbent upon the scientifically trained men and women of our age. When there is the same energy displayed in applying knowledge to large human problems as there is today in applying it to physical inventions and to industry and commerce many of our present problems will be well on their way to solution.

I cannot close without reference to the pertinence of the theme discussed, however inadequate its mode of presentation, to the honored guest of the evening. James McKeen Cattell is himself an active scientific worker, one who has initiated in his own field of psychology many movements that have borne rich fruit. But he has found time, thought and energy to devote to the larger questions of the bearing of science upon life. He has given himself without stint to the better organization of scientific workers in all fields; he has striven valiantly for moral and financial improvement of the condition of academic workers; he has been the leader to the task of editing and diffusing the achievements of scientific inquiry. I do not need to press home the moral in connection with the intellectual obligation of which I have spoken. Laboring of the point is unnecessary as long as we have Cattell with us. He is a living example of the ways in which a scientific man can perform the supreme intellectual duty and as such we gladly greet and honor him this evening.

A Great American Prophet

In his *Equality*, Bellamy states, through the mouth of Dr. Leete as exponent, the device that marks off his picture of a social Utopia from all other literary Utopias. Explaining why men of our day do not see the meaning of facts that stare them constantly in the face, he says: "It was precisely because they stared you and your contemporaries so constantly in the face that you lost the faculty for judging their meaning. They were too near the eyes to be seen aright." This statement gives the key to the literary device which Bellamy employs in both *Looking Backward* and *Equality*. He uses his picture of the new order as a means of making us realize by force of contrast the realities of the social world in which we now actually live.

I do not mean that Bellamy did not take his picture, in its main outlines, seriously. But I do mean that it was evolved by his own brooding on the injustices, oppressions and wreckage attendant on the present economic system, and that when he had seen these things for himself, he employed his imagination of a social order based on economic equality to enable others to see what he had himself seen and felt. Many persons have indicted the present system. But what enabled Bellamy's books to circulate by the hundreds of thousands was that his indictment operated through imagination setting forth what was possible. The result is a sense of the terrible gulf between what is possible and what is actual.

Upon the page next to that from which the above quotation is taken, he gives a statement of the principle that, from a technical intellectual point of view, underlies his indictment of the present economic system. The system starts from the sound principle that *things*, physical nature, have no rights as against human beings. From this principle was derived in practice the conclusion

[First published in *Common Sense* 3 (April 1934): 6–7.]

that individuals might acquire an unlimited ownership of things as far as their abilities permit. "But this view absolutely ignores the social consequences which result from the unequal distribution of material things in a world where everybody absolutely depends for life and all its uses on their share of those things." In this simple sentence, Bellamy has given the unanswerable reply to those moralists who unwittingly defend the existing order by making a sharp separation between the material on one side and the ethical and ideal on the other. Bellamy's communism rests on an ethical base rather than upon a view that is sometimes called "scientific" because of its abstraction from considerations of human well-being. But his ethical principle always takes cognizance of the dependence of human life and its supreme values upon equal access to and control over material things. In doing that, it makes ample place for all the factors that "scientific" communists have emphasized, regarding the political and social power that is exercised by economic relations of production and distribution.

Bellamy was an American and a New Englander in more than a geographical sense. He was imbued with a religious faith in the democratic ideal. But for that very reason he saw through the sham and pretence that exists or can exist in the present economic system. I could fill pages with quotations in which he exposes his profound conviction that our democratic government is a veiled plutocracy. He was far from being the originator of this idea. But what distinguishes Bellamy is the clear ardor with which he grasped the *human* meaning of democracy as an idea of equality and liberty, and portrayed the complete contradiction between our present economic system and the realization of human equality and liberty. No one has carried through the idea that equality is obtainable only by complete equality of income more fully than Bellamy. Again, what distinguishes him is that he derives his zeal and his insight from devotion to the American ideal of democracy.

This approach inevitably suggests comparison and contrast with that of Marx. Bellamy's most obvious indebtedness to Marx is in connection with his adoption of the idea that the present system is resulting in greater and greater concentration of capital (Bellamy wrote in the period of the overt emergence of trusts) and the fact that this concentration would result in the organization and socialization of labor, while the final outcome would be a society economically communist in nature. The most obvious point of contrast is found in Bellamy's conviction that the revolution would be essentially peaceful in nature. He imagined that by the end of the nineteenth century the trust movement would have resulted in the practical consolidation of the entire capital of the nation, so that the "logical" next step in evolution would be its nationalization and administration for the benefit of the people.

The issue raised is too large to be discussed here. But it is fairly evident that Bellamy was too much under the influence of the idea of evolution in its Victorian sense. Consequently he thought on the one hand that the mass of the people would realize the great transitional service rendered by the system of consolidated capitalism, while on the other hand it is implied that those who control this system would be impotent in the face of the public demand that the final logical step be taken. It is a moderate comment that Bellamy was not conscious of how long the capitalist psychology would remain active, even among the laborers and farmers, after the capitalist system had broken down, and that he did not realize the extent of sabotage, so brilliantly exposed by Veblen, that prevails among the capitalist class—witness the manipulations by insiders carried on at the expense of stockholders.

There is another point in Bellamy's theory in relation to Marx's that remains ambiguous. The administrative government plays a large part in Bellamy's theory. On the face of it there is no "withering away of the state." At the same time, in view of Marx's definition of the state as the agent of class domination, it may be that the difference is more verbal than real. For Bellamy's administrative government is certainly the expression of a classless society.

I wish that those who conceive that the abolition of private capital and of energy expended for profit signify complete regimentation of life and the abolition also of all personal choice and all emulation, would read with an open mind Bellamy's picture of a socialized economy. It is not merely that he exposes with extraordinary vigor and clarity the restriction upon liberty that the present system imposes but that he pictures how socialized industry and finance would release and further all those personal and private types of choice of occupation and use of leisure that men and women actually most prize today. His picture of a reign of brotherly love may be overdrawn. But the same cannot be said of his account of freedom in personal life outside of the imperative demand for the amount of work necessary to provide for the upkeep of social capital. In an incidental chapter on the present servility to fashion he brings out the underlying principle. "Equality creates an atmosphere which kills imitation, and is pregnant with originality, for every one acts out himself, having nothing to gain by imitating any one else." It is the present system that promotes uniformity, standardization and regimentation.

From the standpoint of their immediate task in Europe, Marx and Lenin may have been right in being chary of prognosis of the future classless society. It seemed to them part of a hated "idealism" to indulge in imaginative picturization. But the value of judging the present in terms of imagination of what is possible in the future, nowhere appears more clearly than in Bellamy's account of private life and the direction that emulation takes under a system of socialized production and distribution.

However, even with respect to the latter, he exhibits a good deal of prescience. There is little in Technocracy's picture of a possible future that is not foreshadowed by Bellamy—even to the amount of personal income that would be available. While he was wise in not going into detail, he foresaw an enormous increase in productivity by means of power, and a consequent release from the onerous forms of labor. Yet his interest is in the psychological emancipation that will result more than in the material mechanism, clearly though he sketches many features of the working structure of the latter. Nothing is further from the truth than the criticism often advanced that he pictures simply a millennium of material ease and comfort.

It is not surprising that during the present bankruptcy of economic class control, there is a great revival of interest in Bellamy. It is an American communism that he depicts, and his appeal comes largely from the fact that he sees in it the necessary means of realizing the democratic ideal. Limitations of space compel me to pass by in silence a multitude of interesting points, but I hope that what I have said will lead some to consult his *Equality* which is more thorough than the more popular *Looking Backward*, as he himself intended. The chapters on the "Economic Suicide of the Profit System" and "'The Parable of the Water Tank'" are priceless—and not in its slang sense. The chapter on "What Started the Revolution" and its sequel are extraordinary summaries of contemporary history. It is encouraging to know that Bellamy Societies are starting almost spontaneously, but with the aid of a central organization, all over the country. It is a good omen and I do not believe that a mirage of prosperity will again bring about the eclipse of Bellamy's teachings that occurred in the post-war period. In this country the problem of industrial socialization is much more of a psychological problem than, it seems to me, it is in any European country. The worth of Bellamy's books in effecting a translation of the ideas of democracy into economic terms is incalculable. What *Uncle Tom's Cabin* was to the anti-slavery movement Bellamy's book may well be to the shaping of popular opinion for a new social order. Moreover there is one difference. Bellamy's work is definitely constructive. While it is filled with fundamental criticisms of the present anarchy (which the demands of language have compelled me to refer to at times as an order or system!) there is no tinge of bitterness in it. It accords with American psychology in breathing the atmosphere of hope.

Intelligence and Power

Those who contend that intelligence is capable of exercising a significant role in social affairs and that it would be well if it had a much larger influence in directing social affairs can readily be made to appear ridiculous. From the standpoint of past human history it not only appears but is ridiculous. It takes little acquaintance with the past to realize what the forces have been that have determined social institutions, arrangements and changes. There has been oligarchical despotic power, political, ecclesiastic and economic, sometimes exercised openly, more often by all sorts of indirect and subtle means. Habit, custom and tradition have had a weight in comparison with which that of intelligence is feeble. Custom and tradition have originated in all sorts of ways, many of them accidental. But, once established, they have had weight independent of the conditions of their origin and have reinforced the power of vested interests. At critical times, widespread illusions, generated by intense emotions, have played a role in comparison with which the influence of intelligence is negligible.

What critics overlook is that there would be no point in urging the potential claims of intelligence unless the latter had been submerged in such ways as have been indicated. The net outcome of the domination of the methods of institutional force, custom and illusion does not encourage one to look with great hope upon dependence on new combinations among them for future progress. The situation is such that it is calculated to make one look around, even if from sheer desperation, for some other method, however desperate. And under such circumstances, it also seems as if the effort to stimulate resort to the method of intelligence

[First published in *New Republic* 78 (25 April 1934): 306–7.]

might present itself as at least one desperate recourse, if not the only one that remains untried. In view of the influence of collective illusion in the past, some case might be made out for the contention that even if it be an illusion, exaltation of intelligence and experimental method is worth a trial. Illusion for illusion, this particular one may be better than those upon which humanity has usually depended.[1]

The success of this method in obtaining control over physical forces and conditions has been offered as evidence that the case for trying it in social matters is not altogether desperate nor yet illusory. This reference has also been misunderstood by critics. For it is not held that the particular techniques of the physical sciences are to be literally copied—though of course they are to be utilized wherever applicable—nor that experimentation in the laboratory sense can be carried out on any large scale in social affairs. It is held that the attitude of mind exemplified in the conquest of nature by the experimental sciences, and the method involved in it, may and should be carried into social affairs. And the force of the contention depends on the consideration already mentioned: What are the alternatives? Dogmatism, reinforced by the weight of unquestioned custom and tradition, the disguised or open play of class interests, dependence upon brute force and violence.

It is stated, however, that a fundamental difference in the two cases of physical and social intelligence is ignored. "The physical sciences, it is said, gained their freedom when they overcame the traditionalism based on ignorance, but the traditionalism which the social sciences face is based upon the economic interest of the dominant social classes who are trying to maintain their special privileges in society" (Niebuhr). Of course it is. But it is a naïve view of history that supposes that dominant class interests were not the chief force that maintained the tradition against which the new method and conclusions in physical science had to make their way. Nor is it supposed for a moment that the new scientific

---

1. "The truest visions of religion are illusions which may be partially realised by being resolutely believed. For what religion believes to be true is not wholly true but ought to be true; and may become true if its truth is not doubted." Reinhold Niebuhr, *Moral Man and Immoral Society*, page 81.

method would have won its way in a comparatively few centuries—not that it has completely conquered even yet in the physical field—unless it had found a lodgment in other social interests than the dominant ones and been backed by the constantly growing influence of other interests.

Here we come to the nub of the matter. Intelligence has no power *per se*. In so far as the older rationalists assumed that it had, they were wrong. Hume was nearer the truth, although guilty of exaggeration on the other side, when he said "reason is and always must be the slave of passion"—or interest. But dominant interest is never the exclusive interest that exists—not when there is a struggle taking place. The real problem is whether there are strong interests now active which can best succeed by adopting the method of experimental intelligence into their struggles, or whether they too should rely upon the use of methods that have brought the world to its present estate, only using them the other way around.

Intelligence becomes a *power* only when it is brought into the operation of other forces than itself. But power is a blanket term and covers a multitude of different things. Everything that is done is done by some form of power—that is a truism. But violence and war are powers, finance is a power, newspapers, publicity agents and propaganda are powers, churches and the beliefs they have inculcated are powers, as well as a multitude of other things. Persuasion and conference are also powers, although it is easy to overestimate the degree of their power in the existing economic and international system. In short, we have not said anything so long as we have merely said power. What first is needed is discrimination, knowledge of the distribution of power.

Intelligence becomes a power only as it is integrated into some system of wants, of effective demands. The doctrine that has prevailed in the past regarding the nature of intelligence is itself a reflex of its separation from action. It has been conceived as something complete in itself, action following after and upon it as a merely external expression of it. If I held that notion of intelligence I should more than agree with the critics who doubt that intelligence has any particular role in bringing about needed social change. For the notion is simply one aspect of the divorce of theory and practice that has obtained throughout most of the history of mankind. The peculiar significance of the method of the physical sciences is that they broke through this idea that had for so long hypnotized mankind, demonstrating that action is a necessary part of intelligence—namely, action that changes conditions that previously existed.

Hence the first effect of acceptance of the idea that the operation of control of social forces has something to learn from the experimental method of the physical sciences is a radical alteration in the prevailing conception of social knowledge. The current assumption is that knowledge comes first and then action may—or may not—proceed from it. Critics who have attacked the idea that intelligence has an important role to play have based their attack upon acceptance of this idea; they have criticized me on the basis of attributing to me the very idea that I have been concerned to overthrow. Thus on the basis of a passage in which I denied that any amount of fact-finding apart from action aiming at control of social processes—in other words, a planned economy—could ever build up social knowledge and understanding, Mr. Niebuhr imputes to me middle-class prejudices in ignoring the role of class interest and conflict in social affairs! He imputes to me a great exaggeration of the potentialities of education in spite of the fact that I have spent a good deal of energy in urging that no genuine education is possible without active participation in actual conditions, and have pointed out that economic interests are the chief cause why this change in education is retarded and deflected.

The question at issue is not a personal one, however, and it is not worth notice on personal grounds. Just because dominant economic interests are the chief cause for non-use of the method of intelligence to control social change, opponents of the method play into the hands of these interests when they discourage the potentialities of this method. In my judgment they perpetuate the present confusion, and they strengthen the forces that will introduce evil consequences into the result of any change, however revolutionary it may be, brought about by means into which the method of intelligence has not entered. "Education" even in its widest sense cannot do everything. But what is accomplished without education, again in its broadest sense, will be badly done and much of it will have to be done over. The crucial problem is how intelligence may gain increasing power through incorporation with wants and interests that are actually operating. The very fact that intelligence in the past has operated for narrow ends and in behalf of class interests is a reason for putting a high estimate upon its possible role in social control, not a reason for disparaging it.

The Crisis in Education [1]

Mr. Chairman, Friends, Fellow Teachers: It is always an inestimable pleasure to me to meet with a group of fellow teachers. Whatever I have done or tried to do in life, the thing that I prize the most of all is the fact that I have been for many years—more years than perhaps I would want to admit—a teacher, and it is a particular pleasure to me that I am speaking to a body of teachers under the auspices of the local union of the American Federation of Teachers, for in my career as a teacher there is nothing which I prize more than the fact that ever since there has been a teachers union in New York City I have been a member of that union and entitled to carry my union card.

The two largest cities in this country, New York and Chicago, have recently witnessed the spectacle of extra-legal bodies arrogating to themselves some such responsibility as is implied in the title "Citizens' Committee," that are dictating civic policies, including matters that directly affect public schools. These committees are composed mostly of bankers, of industrialists, and of real estate dealers, the groups in fact which more than any other special groups in this country have helped bring on the present economic and financial crisis.

According to their own statements, these groups in these cities (typical of what is going on all over the country) intervene in the interest of economy. But how do they conceive of economy? What does economy mean to them? What do they think it is? Is it basic reform of municipal administration in order to cut out waste, graft, unnecessary duplication of units, official favoritism, the sacrifice of public to private interests? Are they attacking this

1. Address before Yale Local No. 204 of the American Federation of Teachers and the New Haven Teachers Association, at Hotel Taft, New Haven, January 28, 1933.

[First published in *American Teacher* 17 (April 1933): 5–9.]

problem of economy in any fundamental way? No, and for one reason, many of these organizations are themselves too closely linked up with the sources of waste, too dependent upon favors dealt to them by politicians to undertake anything so needed and so fundamental. By economy they mean a reduction of wages and of salaries of all persons on the municipal pay roll. Experience all over the country shows that the teaching body of the country is the group of public employees upon whom and against whom this kind of economy is most regularly applied.

It happened, as I came up this morning, I bought a paper, the *Herald-Tribune*, to read and I found something from an address of Professor McGoldrick of the Department of Public Administration of Columbia University, an address to the bankers themselves in their state convention. The heading is "Bankers Told They Shirk City Responsibility." Here you have an authority in the field of public administration, talking to an audience of bankers, and using more definite and harsh words than I have used. He shows how all the economy measures have been pointed in the direction of reduction of salaries of public employees, and that this fact means still greater deflation of the purchasing power of the community, actually damaging the economic condition of the city itself, certain to be reflected in the general volume of business, and likely to be reflected even in rents. And furthermore this group did not accompany the demand with one for a balanced budget. They did not show any way a balanced budget could be brought about. They asked merely and wholly for a reduction of expenses. The speaker ends by saying, "The banks are the most important agency for control under our present arrangement. This is not an opportunity but a responsibility. It is a responsibility to be exercised with consideration of the best interests of the investing and general public. There is little room for pride in the way these responsibilities were exercised in the last decade. I think we can confidently predict that if the bankers do not show that they are now prepared to act with a greater regard to general well-being in the next decade, they will be superseded by some other form of social control." Those are the words of an expert in the field from the standpoint of his expert knowledge, not of a radical or a sensational speaker.

I shall not here go into the question of whether or not further deflation of salaries and wages with its corresponding reduction of an already depleted purchasing power is any way to get out of the present crisis. I content myself with recording the practically unanimous conclusion of the economists of the country to the contrary. I do point out that this organized drive against the public school system of the country, typified in the action of representatives of concentrated wealth in the two largest cities of the country, and being taken up all over the country is against the public welfare and that it comes from those who have the least amount of personal concern with public education. Their children for the most part do not attend the public schools. The cultural life of their own families would hardly suffer at all if public schools should be completely closed instead of as at present having their activities curtailed. They are the ones who have steadily fought from the start all enrichment of the curriculum, calling art, music, physical education, handicrafts, etc.—the things which they demand as a matter of course for their own children, in their own homes—fads and frills when they are to be made a part of the educational facilities for the poor and for the masses. Their plea for economy is part of their effort to protect the tax bills of the concentrated wealth of the country, the element which is most able to pay taxes, and moreover the element which has profited the most, both directly and indirectly, from the results of the spread of knowledge and skill through our public school system of education.

It is slight wonder that an ex-president of the American Federation of Teachers at a public meeting in Chicago asked whether this movement was not one, "under cover of the depression, ruthlessly to slash selected public services and costs in the interest of the big taxpayers with little regard for the needs of the masses of the people and their children." It is no wonder that he protested against "surrendering the control of the school to organized large tax payers who are not dependent upon the public schools for an education of their children as the mass of the people are." It is no cause for surprise that the legislative representative of the New York Teachers Union, a part of the American Federation of Teachers, pointed out in a public address recently that twenty-one of the fifty-one directors of the so-called Citizens' Budget Commission of the City of New York are affiliated with the twenty-five leading banks of the city, and that a large part of the others are representatives of the speculative real estate agencies of the city, and showed that their policy regarding cuts in salaries of public servants, which came before the special session of the legislature in Albany recently, was dictated and controlled by the heads of the two biggest banks of New York City and of the nation. And he went on to show that the average rate of dividends declared by these banks last year has been 20%, some of them running to 60%. These bankers are holding up New York City for the money they loan for five times the rate of interest which they are charging the Federal Government. He then went on to raise the question whether we are already in process of having a dictatorship of banking and financial interests superimposed upon the nominal government of this country.

Again returning to what the first speaker to whom I referred said. He said that in view of the concentrated attack upon public education in many places, "a nationwide conspiracy against the public schools is not too strong a description of the facts."

We are a tolerant and a good-humored people in this country. Certainly the mass of the teaching body is, and I suppose there are many who will regard this statement as too strong and will hesitate to endorse it. Incidentally, I should like to call attention to the leading article in the issue of the *Saturday Evening Post*, which bears the date of the meeting here today, January 28. I hate to advertise this because I am afraid somebody will go out and buy the *Post*, and I would much rather urge something in quite the opposite direction.

The social and economic position of this writer and the general humaneness of his point of view are sufficiently indicated by the fact that he states that the income tax is communistic and is the beginning of communism in this country, and then goes on to say that taxes ought to be levied per capita irrespective of difference of income and not per dollar on the dollars of the taxpayers. But he then goes on—and this is the thing in which I am particularly interested—and picks out the public schools of the country and the wages of the public school teachers as the chief topic in his plea for reduced taxation. The entire tone of the article is to create the feeling that the public school teacher is a pampered, petted creature living at the expense of the hard working and hard pressed tax payers. This is one of the many points where a group representing large financial interests—you have already heard about the United States Chamber of Commerce—is already organizing a campaign, using the depression not in order to secure legitimate and desirable changes in the internal workings and administration of a government devoted in undue measure to serving privilege, not to secure a new method of tax revision in the whole system and method of taxation, but to make public servants and especially school teachers the goat. The very same persons who on every other occasion deprecate every reference to "classes" as an effort to create discord among our citizens are now deliberately appealing to envy and jealousy in order to carry through a so-called economy which in fact is only reduction of wages in the interest of big taxpayers—that element of society best able to stand the burden of taxation.

As the campaign is already actively waging and week by week is going to become more acute, teachers should not permit themselves to be put on the defensive. They should be in possession of the facts and be active in making these facts known. I am not going to apologize for presenting some of these facts even in statistical form, although figures are not very interesting nor easy to listen to and carry in the mind. These facts all come from the most efficient and authoritative sources that are available.

In the first place, the total amount raised by taxes for school purposes in this country has never been more than four per cent of the total annual income of the country. 1930 is the last date for which figures are available. It was then three and one-third per cent of the total national income. Because of the depreciation of income since then the ratio has now probably become somewhat larger. As for salaries, there are large sections of the country, located for the most part in the southeastern section, in which the average rural and elementary school teacher's salary is less than $621 per year. The average salary in what is in the total probably the largest single group of sections scattered over the country is less than $787 a year, that is of the elementary and rural groups. There is a portion, about as large roughly speaking as the lowest section, situated mainly in the states just across the Mississippi, in which the salaries of this group are between $788 and $952. There is another group, mainly in New York and New England in the east and in the Rocky Mountain states in the west, where the average salary is between $953 and $1167, and there is a portion, including Connecticut, New Jersey, and parts of New York in the east and California, Nevada, Arizona, parts of Wyoming and Washington State in the west in which the salary of this group averages over $1167.

These figures are taken from the report of the committee authorized first by Congress with an appropriation from Congress; then, during the economy drive, the appropriation was not continued and the General Education Board financed the continuation of the study. A group of experts, college men, and men not merely in education but in public finance and business men, conducted a survey that was extended into every county of every state in the United States. This map, which may be obtained by addressing the American Council of Education in Washington or by addressing the Bureau of Educational Service, Teachers College, New York City, shows by the different markings these five groups and their distribution. Teachers ought to be in possession of these facts and this graphic presentation of them.

It is doubtless significant that the author of the *Saturday Evening Post* article picked out one of the states where teachers are paid the highest rates, namely New Jersey, as an example of how petted and pampered the school teacher is and how he is fattened at the expense of the tax payer. Anybody who thinks that from $3 to $4 a day, which is the average in the rural and elementary school, is an adequate wage in the richest country of the world, is a wage that will call educated men and women to the teaching profession and hold them there, that it is a wage which will enable the teachers to care for the education of their own children and maintain a decent status in the community, is past all argument.

Of the total amount of money raised by taxation in the entire country, federal, state and local, for all purposes, a little less than one-fifth goes to the public schools. I think we would all agree that the part that goes to the public schools is the part which the ordinary tax payer pays most willingly, and yet of the whole tax bill of the country only one-fifth goes to the support of the public school system. This is slightly less than the total amount spent for redemption of and interest on debts of the branches of government in this country. It is only one-fifth of the amount which the American people spend annually for the purchase and upkeep of automobiles; more than one-third more than the whole tax paid for the school bill of the country goes to the purchase of premiums on life insurance. It is less than half of the annual bill that is spent for physical construction, the construction of buildings; and again I think that the American people will agree that the building of the youth and citizenship of the country approaches in importance the building of skyscrapers, or of highways, etc.

For one I do not believe that the average American citizen, parent and tax payer, wants to see the gains which have been made eliminated. The task is to make the people of the country realize the facts amid the cloud of misrepresentation, of the screen of poison gas which is emitted from selfish quarters. One of the stock items in the concerted attack upon the public school and the school teacher is the rise in the total cost of education. There is no doubt about this rise. There has been an increase of a little over 300% since 1914—just before the war. Statistical study by economic experts, whose figures have not been challenged, shows, however, that over 48% of this increase, almost one-half that is, is due to the depreciation of the purchasing power of the dollar. During the war and for years afterwards teachers' wages remained practically stationary, while the cost of living increased, as we know, enormously. During the twenties hard work secured, at least in the more prosperous and enlightened parts of the country, a definite gross increase in salaries, but by 1930 the salary measured in purchasing power was hardly equal to that of 1914.

In the second place there has been a very great increase in school attendance since 1914, a total increase of a little over one-third in the number of those to whom schools are required to give instruction. In addition attendance has become much more regular and the school year up to 1930 was lengthened so that from these two causes there was an actual increase of school days of 60%. In this increase of student attendance, much the greater part took place in the more expensive part of the school system, the high school. In these 16 years the number of high school students increased from 1,200,000 to 4,300,000, a marvelous increase unprecedented in the whole history of education, of 261%; while the days of schooling in high schools increased 340%. These various increases take care of 27% more of the increase in school expenses, the two items together, 75%. This leaves about one-quarter of the total amount of the increase chargeable to extension in the quantity and quality of service rendered by the public school in the years between 1914 and 1930. Let the reactionaries, especially those who do not utilize in any way the service of the public school system or believe in the service of the public school teacher for the children, do their clamoring for the elimination of these improvements. Again I cannot believe that the American public, if the facts can be got before them, will support this campaign.

This is one side of the picture—that which most intelligent people will regard as the bright side of the picture—this increase of the number going to school and of school facilities. This is the bright side, I say, in spite of the efforts of the hired Hessians of big financial interests to make American people ashamed of what they have done for public education in the United States. There was a dark side, even before the depression came on. I will quote again from the findings of this official committee, headed by Professor Paul Mort. According to this report, nine and one-half million American children, about 40% of those in schools, are deprived of essential schooling because of a breakdown in the traditional methods of financing the schools. It is not surprising perhaps that this committee, which has studied the matter impartially, does not follow the chorus of bankers and industrialists and financiers in urging that the support of the schools be cut down still further. It deals with causes, not with effects. It states "that drastic tax revision in virtually all of the 48 states is indicated by the survey as immediately necessary if the poorer local communities are to be relieved of present crushing burdens and if a minimum program of care and education is to be set up for the children of those communities." We are not questioning the need of revision of methods of taxation and distribution of taxation. We are pleading for going back to the causes to get real economy in these ways instead of beginning merely by slashing. What is needed is the revision of the methods of the tax system itself, not merely reduction of wages—a revision which is imperative if bad conditions are not to grow worse.

It is difficult to secure up to date figures as to the exact effect of the depression upon the schools, but between the report of this committee and that of the Citizens Conference on the Crisis in Education called by President Hoover, presided over by Secretary Wilbur, we have the beginnings of the facts. The Mort Committee reports that "thousands of communities throughout the country find themselves unable, under present methods of taxation, to make even elemental provision for the care and education of their children and youth. Scores of thousands of youth of high school age are wandering through the country; an even larger number, including hosts of younger children are suffering from malnutrition and inadequate care in both rural and urban sections. So serious are the dangers to American children that immediate steps should be taken by State Legislatures to prevent the deepening of the disaster." These are not statements from radicals or sensationalists but from an official body of investigating experts. And the answer of the self-constituted extra-legal bodies who have taken it upon themselves to regulate civic finance is to reduce school facilities and school expenses still more!

The title of the conference called by President Hoover is also significant. It is a Conference on the Crisis in Education. The title is sufficiently striking in itself to save one from being called upon to be sensational in what he says about the menace to public education. Secretary Wilbur who presided at the conference and who has not been accused either of radicalism or sensationalism, closed the conference by saying, "If you are going to pay school teachers, you have got to get the money, and that money now is going to be sought for from a dozen sources. So we must take an aggressive attitude for the schools if we are going to see our children through. It is not a matter of passing resolutions; it is a matter of fighting, and there is no better thing to fight for than the American school child, and I want to leave with you as you go that challenge. Fight through for these American school children. Fight the highways, fight the politicians, fight all the groups—it's worth while." That from Secretary Wilbur regarding the present crisis.

To the honor of President Hoover, not only for calling the meeting but for what he said when he opened the Conference, let it be recorded that he stated, "Our nation faces the acute responsibility of providing a right of way for the American child. In spite of economic, social, and governmental difficulties, our future citizenry must be built up now." The contrast between building it up and cutting down the school facilities of the country need not be dwelt upon here.

The Conference itself brought out clearly the reason for calling the present situation a crisis. The agenda prepared in advance called attention to the fact the situation might be put in four words: "Increasing responsibilities, decreasing resources." The depression has actually led to an increase in school enrollment and the schools have many problems to meet due to the effect of unemployment on home life. Teachers are themselves voluntarily supplying clothes and at least one free meal a day to children. The public school teachers of New York City have given, according to official records, over two million and a quarter dollars out of their salaries to relief funds in the city of New York, and we may safely challenge every group in the community to show a record of voluntary service in the present crisis equal of that of the teaching group in the public schools.

But the schools are having to deal with this situation with reduced funds. School revenues last year were cut down at least six per cent throughout the country, and there is no doubt the reduction will be much greater when the returns for the current year are in. In some large cities even last year reductions ran to 25% and 30%. Teachers' salaries were reduced to a slightly less extent. In city school systems it amounted however to 10% and over. In one state of the Union the wage of the rural school teacher has declined 40% in three years, and in three other states it amounts to 25% for the same time. Capital outlay, that for grounds, buildings, equipment, went down in the cities which reported 28% year before last and 40% last year, evidently at the expense of increase in school population. In other words buildings are not being kept up, equipment is not being provided to meet even the normal increase in the schools. To meet the decrease in funds, the size of classes, already too large per teacher, which teachers organizations have been working to cut down, have been increased; many teachers have been dismissed; graduates of training and normal schools, trained to go into teaching, are put upon the waiting list (New York City alone is said to have 5,000 such persons); the length of the school year is cut, in some cases by a month or more; some schools have been closed entirely and a larger number threatened with having to shut their doors; in many places payment of salaries is long in arrears; and, as already indicated, building activities have been arrested and needed repairs postponed, while many schools are reported operating with an abnormal lack of equipment.

In many respects the curtailment and impoverishment of the

curriculum, the elimination of important modes of service, are even more serious than the points mentioned. Art and manual training, home economics and physical training, are crippled; special classes for crippled and backward children are eliminated; night classes and evening schools are dropped; many cities have given up kindergarten and sub-primary classes. In New York City, the richest city in the world, there has been curtailment of continuation classes, playground facilities, and provision for adult education, in addition to other eliminations. It is not exaggerating to say that the enrichment of educational services, which is the outstanding gain of American public education during the last forty years, is today seriously and fundamentally threatened. There is no doubt about the reality of the crisis and it is foolish for both teachers and the public interested in the public schools to conceal from themselves the seriousness of the condition.

And yet once more, the sole method of meeting the crisis which is put forward from powerful sources, probably as things stand today the most powerful in the Nation, backed by an influential press, catered to by politicians who owe their power and often their income to dealings with the invisible government of the country, is to cripple the schools still more. Every single day deliberate efforts are put forth to represent the teacher as a petted and semi-parasitic element in the community, unwilling to share with the rest of the community a fair portion of the burden of the depression. I have read, I think, all of the important utterances made by representatives of the American Federation of Teachers. They all point out the fact to which I called attention earlier, the deliberate false conception of economy which is put forth and is being implanted in the public mind. They have been concrete and definite in suggesting methods by which waste and extravagance could have been eliminated and a system of taxation made more effective and more just. And they have all ended with expressing the willingness of teachers to stand their share of whatever is then shown to be needed after these reforms have been undertaken in good faith. I agree completely with them in saying that if the teaching body yields without a fight to show the difference between true and false economy, without an effort to show up the motives of organized finance, the teachers will not only harm themselves and the cause of education, but will also become the accomplices of politicians in continuing to do business in the old way at the old stand.

Above all, it behooves the teachers in behalf of the community, of the educational function which they serve, and not merely because of their personal interest in a fit wage for what they do—self respecting and honorable as is that motive—to make clear beyond a peradventure that public education is not a business carried on for pecuniary profit, that it is not therefore an occupation to be measured by the standards which the bankers and real estate men and the big industrialists seek for themselves in working for personal gain and measuring success and failure by the ledger balance, but that money spent on education is a social investment—an investment in future well being, moral, economic, physical, and intellectual, of the country. Teachers are simply means, agents in this social work. They are performing the most important public duty now performed by any one group in society. Any claims which they can rightfully make are not made in behalf of themselves as private persons, but in behalf of society and the nation. These will be what they are and are not in the future largely because of what is done and not done in this day and generation in the schools of the country.

Why have I brought coals to Newcastle in calling these familiar facts to the attention of those engaged in teaching, many of whom are already suffering and likely to suffer more? Fundamentally I have done so for one reason only. As I see it the great question before the teachers is the question of *How*. By what method shall teachers make clear to a confused public, a public deliberately misled by powerful agencies, the rightful claims of public schools in this time of crisis? I know of but one basic answer. It is found in the old saying of Benjamin Franklin, "We must hang together or we shall all hang separately." Organization, union, combined and concerted thought and action, is the answer, and the only answer I can see to the adequate solution of the problem of the crisis. There is a militant organization serving as the organ and instrument of this effort already in existence. It is the American Federation of Teachers, affiliated with the American Federation of Labor. Some years ago, I wrote a little document which was printed by the Union as to why I was a member of the Union. I am going to take the liberty of quoting briefly from one part of it that bears upon a difficulty (which to my mind is wholly gratuitous) in the minds of many teachers, namely, the affiliation with the American Federation of Labor. That statement was made years before the present depression and it is milder than I should make now. "*Our whole educational system suffers from the divorce between head and hand, between work and books, between action and ideas, a divorce which symbolizes the segregation of teachers from the rest of the workers who form the great mass of the community. If all teachers were within the Teachers Union and if they were in active contact with the working men and women of the country and their problems, I am sure more would be done to reform and improve our education and to put into execution the ideas and ideals written about and talked about by progressive educators than by any other one cause whatsoever, if not more than by all other causes together.*"

Then we have the present crisis. I have referred to that conference held in Washington. It is altogether likely, though I cannot prove this statement, that it was first intended to make this conference a further agent of the forces that wish to put through the program of reduction of teachers' salaries and curtailment of the services rendered by the public school. It did not do that. On the whole it came out on the opposite side, and the reason, more than any other, for the position finally taken at Washington was the efforts of the American Federation of Labor, which called into consultation Dr. Linville, the president of the American Federation of Teachers, Mrs. Hanson and others, and got their view of the situation and presented it actively to the meeting. They prepared an emergency program on the crisis in education.

Again I cannot read it all, but I will read part of Labor's statement to emphasize this conflict between the forces of organized labor and of organized finance to show who are our friends and upon whom we shall rely and with whom we shall unite in this present crisis.

"We believe that public welfare demands and should be insistent on standards of education, no curtailment of activities, or employment of teachers of lower standards. That is going on all over the country—curtailment in length of school year, unduly increasing the size of classes," lowering the standard of teachers, etc.

These people are at least sufficiently educated to know there is a difference between cuts in wages and economy. I should like to read: "Cities have had to face the problem of rapidly mounting demands for relief of the unemployed. There isn't a city in the country that isn't suffering and isn't urging some kind of reduction of expense because of appropriations for relief. Instead of recognizing that responsibility for relief is a government responsibility to be shared by all, nation, state, homes, the major responsibility has been shifted to the local unit."

Now if the teachers organizations, through the American Federation of Teachers, can join the movement to make the federal government do its share, there will be a relief of local funds which will take away a large part of this pressure for the reduction of the salary of the public servants of the community. Get this program of organized labor and contrast it with the program of the representative of the National Manufacturers Association at the Washington conference. Contrast it with the twenty suggestions of the United States Chamber of Commerce, and then ask: Who are the friends of the teachers and of the public school in the present crisis? Are not public school teachers paying too high a price for maintaining a kind of intellectual and social exclusiveness, an academic snobbery, in keeping aloof from any contact with organized labor in this country?

It was through the agency of the American Federation of Teachers that a bill has already been introduced in Congress authorizing the Reconstruction Finance Corporation to make loans to the various units of the country in charge of the schools for school purposes.

Some teachers have the idea that the sole object of a teachers union and the American Federation of Teachers is to protect teachers' wages. I have no apologies to make for that phase. I don't see why any workers should not have an organization to secure a decent living standard. The laborer is worthy of his hire. But the foundations of the teachers unions of the American Federation of Teachers are very much wider and I should like to have you study together the history of unions representing even a minority of teachers, often a small minority, in such cities as Chicago, New York, Minneapolis, Atlanta, and others, to see that they have stood in the van of all movements calculated to improve public education, to introduce the principles and ideals of progressive education into the schools attended by the mass of the children; that they have been the most active instrument there is, not merely in protecting teachers from individual abuse, but in standing against the efforts of politicians to use the public school system for their own purposes. I should like to assure any doubting Thomases on this point that if they investigate the actual records of the unions already in existence they will find good reason to be proud to be associated with the teachers who have already organized and combined in these unions.

In closing I want to say that all of these other teacher organizations are very valuable. They raise the standard of teaching in the field of scholarship and improved methods of teaching. But there is none of them that I know of except the American Federation of Teachers that stands constantly, openly, and aggressively for the realization of the social function of the profession and for raising the moral, the intellectual, and the social level of the profession as a profession on the basis of the social rights and the social responsibilities of the group of teachers as a professional group in the community.

Education and Our Present Social Problems[1]

The present interest in social reconstruction and the present desire of many educators to have the schools assume greater responsibility for achieving it remind me of a somewhat similar stir in the last years of the World War. At that time, too, it was in the air that a great social transformation was imminent and educators were urged to play their part in bringing it about. We all know what happened. There was a hurried and thoughtless "return to normalcy" and in the years following affairs generally were more completely in the grip of reactionaries than ever before in our history.

I do not wish to suggest that the two situations are wholly similar and the present outcome likely to be that of the early twenties. Much less do I wish to join the chorus of those who point to such episodes as proof of the futility of all liberal aspiration for social reform. There are doubtless reasons why the thinking and discussion that attend the present stir will not be as transitory as they were fourteen years ago. But I think the earlier experience conveys a warning and raises a question. At least I shall employ reference to it to state a question which in any case is important. Instead of considering our social problems as such, I shall ask: What is the method by which educators should approach them? Where shall he take his stand in viewing them? Is there any road of approach that will help us ward off the failure which has accompanied so many idealistic and humane movements in the past?

The question is not raised in a complete vacuum nor even in the upper air. There are, it seems to me, already signs of an approach on the part of educators which is not likely to be produc-

1. An address delivered before the Department of Supervisors and Directors of Instruction at Minneapolis, Minnesota, March 1, 1933.

[First published in *School and Society* 37 (15 April 1933): 473–78.]

tive of enduring results. Of late years we have got in the habit of starting out by listing objectives to be attained. Now this procedure in itself is intelligent and admirable. We want to know what we are after, what we are striving to accomplish. But there is an underlying question. Whence shall we derive our objectives? Do we pluck them out of the air, dig them out of the ground about us, extract them from our inner desires or what? Much of what we like to think of as American idealism, and which we congratulate ourselves upon, frames ends out of what appears to be desirable in general, apart from means at hand. I have for instance quite lately heard good people ask whether it was quite moral to use the debts which foreign nations owe us as a means of securing drastic reduction of armaments, by making this reduction a condition of abating the debts. And educators may set up social objectives which are inherently fine and noble by starting too remote from present conditions and needs, and hence isolated from the only means by which what they wish can be attained.

A union of idealism of purpose with realistic survey and utilization of existing conditions seems to me the only way in which our objectives can be saved from becoming empty, sentimental, and doomed to defeat. We must frame our social objectives on the basis of knowing the forces and causes which produce the evils from which we suffer, and must frame them on the basis of those forces and conditions in the actual situation which supply means for their realization. I do not know whether charity always begins at home. But I am sure that understanding and the framing of practicable ends and ideals begin as nearly at home as possible. If this principle is applied to education in relation to social problems, it will prevent us as educators from going too far afield at the beginning, and will fix our minds on asking what we can do in terms of the means at hand for doing what we want to do. It is better to do something positive and enduring than to ascend into the high heavens in a balloon that hits the ground with a bump as soon as the gas gives out.

If we adopt this course, we shall begin with the situation in which education now finds itself, with the predicament of the schools affecting students and teachers alike. Ascertaining as best we can the full facts regarding this situation, we shall then try to find out the causes for this state of things, the forces which are responsible for the evils from which the schools are suffering and the even greater evils which are threatened. We shall then move out to the whole social field in which these forces are operating and inquire what counteracting and remedial forces there are with which we may cooperate, and shall frame our ends and objectives on the basis of these surveys.

I can not pretend to go into the full consideration of the immediate troubles in education in relation to the social and economic forces which have produced them. There are at least two recent authoritative statements. One is that of the official committee headed by Professor Mort; the other is that of the Citizens Conference in Washington held in January at the call of President Hoover. The title of that Conference, as nearly official as anything of the sort can be, tells the essential story: The Crisis in Education. Those gathered here know, if the general public does not, the various elements which define the crisis. They know about reduced appropriations at the time when the schools have increased responsibilities put upon them by increased number of pupils and other factors due to the economic collapse; they know about closed schools, reduced school years, enlarged classes; failure to build and equip to keep up with increase in population and obsolescence of old equipment; the closing of kindergartens; elimination of manual training, art work, music, physical training, domestic arts; abolition of special classes for the backward and handicapped; scores of thousands of graduates of normal schools and training colleges added to the unemployed; salaries cut and unpaid; night and continuation schools abandoned. These are samples of forces which are threatening (I speak without exaggeration) to wipe out the gains in security of teachers and in enrichment of instruction which are the great gains of the last forty years. And, of course, we are in the early stage of the movement, not at its close.

In effect and to some degree, how great it is hard to judge, in deliberate intent, the public schools are under attack. The fountain heads of the attack everywhere are large taxpayers and the institutions which represent the wealthier and privileged elements in the community. Those who make the least use of the public schools, who are the least dependent upon them because of superior economic status, who give their children at home by means of private teachers the same things which they denounce as extravagances when supplied in less measure to the children of the masses in schools, these are the ones most active in the attack upon the schools. Under cover of the depression and the cry of economy (interpreted to mean reduction of expense and not removal of sources of waste and disorder) the efficiency and attractiveness of the schools are being threatened. The standards won by hard work over many years are being undermined.

That the causes of the situation do not lie within the schools is too obvious to need exposition. That the causes are in the general state of society itself is equally evident. And any child who can listen and read knows that they lie in the economic institutions and arrangements of present society. On one side is the crisis in education. On the other side are the social problems. There is no doubt about the close connection of the two. The causes of the economic catastrophe are the causes of the educational crisis. Whatever will remove or mitigate the forces which brought about the collapse of industry, the terrible insecurity of millions of our people, the breakdown in government due to decrease of revenues, will have the same beneficial effect on education. There is no other way out. We must do what we can at once to protect the schools from the forces which are imperilling them. In so doing we shall not be defending merely our personal interests. Of various suggestions regarding "economy" in school expense passed on "by way of illustration" from the National Chamber of Commerce to local Chambers, only two *directly* affect the income of teachers in service. Others include reduction of the length of school day and year, increase in size of classes, discontinuance of kindergartens and continuation schools, postponement of capital outlay (thus incidentally keeping up unemployment), simplification of curricula—an obvious euphemism—taking away one year from both elementary and high school students, imposition of fees on high school students, etc.[2]

I have indicated but not described in any detail the situation

---

2. The Chamber of Commerce has issued an apologetic statement to the effect that the suggestions did not originate in their office but in the agenda of the Citizens Conference, and were enclosed in a questionnaire by way of illustration. The Chamber of Commerce forgot to mention who prepared the agenda, and the fact that these items were deliberately rejected by the Conference, and it omitted to enclose even by way of illustration the contrary suggestions adopted by the Conference. It is not surprising accordingly that their document made no reference to the spirited opposition of the American Federation of Labor.

which educators find themselves in if they take the advice to begin the study of their relation to social problems at home, in what lies closest to them. This method of approach will not merely disclose, as I have already said, the economic nature of the social problems now pressing upon the nation and world, but it will, if it is pursued any distance at all, remove from teachers the illusion which many of them have entertained—that their vocation and vocational interest are so distinctive, so separated from that of other wage earners and salaried persons, as to justify them in an attitude of aloofness. The demonstration that the vocation of education is not and can not be shut off and shut up within itself is complete. The educator as a human being, as a member of the community and as an educator, whether teacher or administrator, must concern himself with economic interests, conditions, needs, possibilities, plans for reconstruction, if he is to be secure and effective in performing his educational function.

Here, then, we are to look for an avenue of approach to social problems which is most likely to produce results that will be enduring and so direct activities that they will not evaporate with a change in the curve of the economic cycle. As the educator travels this road he will see that social problems are not something outside him and his work, but are directly his own concern, and, once more, that they are not so just because they affect his own tenure and wage, but because of education itself. For this very reason he will see that "social problems" signify problems which affect large numbers in common. They are not things like thunderstorms or cyclones, to be looked at from outside; they arise from general social causes and have general social effects and hence are to be dealt with socially, that is, by the educator in common with others. There is a curious quirk in human nature which makes us think of social problems as something external although their effects are something personal and private. We as educators need first of all to recognize that the social problems are something of our own; that they, and not simply their consequences, are ours; that we are part of the causes which bring them about in what we have done and have refrained from doing, and that we have a necessary share in finding their solution. Moreover, we have it not just in any outside way called "social" but in the educational interest which is an integral part of society.

In short, a social problem is one which the educator has in

common with the farmer, with the factory worker, the small merchant, the white collar worker. The problem is social because it is common. Put in another way, the causes which produce the suffering of men and women in these groups are the causes which have generated the crisis in education. Hence, if we begin to study the social problem from where the educator is at home so to speak, we shall learn that our interests as teachers are one with those of these other persons. Unless we realize the identity of interest which binds us together I fear our interest in the social problems will remain on the academic level. Or, at best, it will be more sentimental than practical.

This community of interest is not confined to the fact that teachers, like members of the other groups, require personal security and due reward for their work. Security of useful function, of service necessary to society, is at stake. The educator is aware that he performs an indispensable social function. Present conditions make him alive to the fact that the performance of that function requires protection. But the same is true of every other group. Society could not exist without the farmers, the workers in factories and shops. All the groups alike are victims of anti-social forces. For nothing can be imagined more fundamentally anti-social than the conditions and factors which cripple and paralyze those engaged in performing necessary social work, which prevent them from doing their work and thus deprive society as a whole of what it needs, while it also demoralizes the workers themselves. Unless the world is a crazy bedlam, unless order and justice are foreign to its constitution, such a state can not indefinitely continue.

The relation of education to social problems is not, then, external and academic. It resides first of all in the community of interest of educators with all workers who are genuine producers of social necessities. This community of interest has both its negative and positive poles. Educators and others alike need protection against personal unsettlement, insecurity, overhanging disaster. Both must have guaranteed to them the effective ability to perform the services which the whole community requires. I would insist then that the first step for educators to take is the full recognition of this community of interest. Unless the start is made at this point I fear lest the newly aroused interest of teachers in basic social problems will operate at arm's length and, lacking leverage, will with a return of moderate prosperity grow faint.

The second step which follows naturally upon realization of community of interest is of course an alliance in sympathy and in action. The province and function of education are not of course limited to children, though teachers as a whole have had their share in execution of this function limited to children and youth, leaving to the press and other agencies formation of the judgments and sentiments of adults. As long as educators think of their work as something apart from that of other workers and of their interests as separate, this state of affairs is practically sure to persist. The alliance of educators with others who are at a disadvantage because of the chaotic and inequitable economic order of society is, as far as I can see, the only way of changing this state of things so as to enable educators to take part in the normal education of adults.

One reason they can not do so at present is that they are not prepared to do so, even intellectually. They share in the economic illiteracy which is so common. And much of this ignorance is due in turn to remoteness of teachers from the mass of people upon whom the disordered economic scheme weighs most heavily. Educators themselves can get the education which will enable them to help others only through the effective realization of the community of interest of which I have been speaking. The same identification of sympathy and thought will also break down the moral barriers which now divide teachers from members of other groups and make the latter more or less suspicious of them.

A great deal is now said about the importance of social planning in order to secure the integration and coordination which our sick society so badly needs. As I read the report of the Committee on Social Trends, the trend most emphasized is that toward a condition of unbalance due to the independent and unrelated growth of the different parts of the social mechanism. And according to those who report, with scientific moderation, on the trends, the unrelated development of the economic phase, both as a whole in relation to other interests, and internally in the relation of its parts to one another, is the thing chiefly responsible for the existing unbalance. Today the need for planning and coordination is, in theory at least, almost a commonplace. But it can not be realized on paper nor by means of plans on paper however perfect in theoretical principle. The problem is more than one of adjusting certain impersonal functions, like production and consumption. The human element comes in. The work has got to be done by people. It will not be done as long as people, as human beings, do not understand one another and sympathize with one another. Teachers will not have even a modest share in building a new social order unless they have broken down personal remoteness and indifference as to the things they have in common with farmers, factory workers, the white collar class generally, and have ceased to think of their interests as being separate or exclusively linked with those of purely professional groups.

The work that has to be done in the further social education of the teachers themselves in economic matters and in the work they have to do with the young can not, in short, be properly performed except as teachers, beginning at home with their own activities and function, widen their outlook and sympathy until they come into that practical association with other workers which will create common bonds and exchange of experiences and ideas in a common practical effort. The duty to educate the young for citizenship is universally recognized in words. At present much of the work done in this line is barren because the importance of the economic factor in good citizenship does not receive attention. I do not see how it can get proper attention without that realization of community of interest and consequent alliance in sympathy and understanding for which I have been pleading.

In conclusion, let me say that one of the first steps to be taken practically in effecting a closer connection of education with actual social responsibilities is for teachers to assert themselves more directly about educational affairs and about the organization and conduct of the schools: assert themselves I mean both in the internal conduct of the schools by introducing a greater amount of teacher responsibility in administration, and outside in relation to the public and the community. The present dictation of policies for the schools by bankers and other outside pecuniary groups is more than harmful to the cause of education. It is also a pathetic and tragic commentary on the lack of possession of social power by the teaching profession. Teachers will not do much for the general settlement of social problems, outside of the indirect influence of academic discussion, much less help build a new social order until they have asserted themselves by taking an active share in the settlement of the educational problems which most directly concern teachers in their own local communities. Beginning at home is again the lesson to be learned.

Dewey Outlines Utopian Schools

The most Utopian thing in Utopia is that there are no schools at all. Education is carried on without anything of the nature of schools, or, if this idea is so extreme that we cannot conceive of it as educational at all, then we may say nothing of the sort at present we know as schools. Children, however, are gathered together in association with older and more mature people who direct their activity.

The assembly places all have large grounds, gardens, orchards, greenhouses, and none of the buildings in which children and older people gather will hold much more than 200 people, this having been found to be about the limits of close, intimate personal acquaintance on the part of people who associate together.

And inside these buildings, which are all of them of the nature of our present open-air schools in their physical structure, there are none of the things we usually associate with our present schools. Of course, there are no mechanical rows of screwed-down desks. There is rather something like a well-furnished home of today, only with a much greater variety of equipment and no messy accumulations of all sorts of miscellaneous furniture; more open spaces than our homes have today.

Then there are the workshops, with their apparatus for carrying on activities with all kinds of material—wood, iron, textiles. There are historic museums and scientific laboratories, and books everywhere as well as a central library.

The adults who are most actively concerned with the young have, of course, to meet a certain requirement, and the first thing that struck me as a visitor to Utopia was that they must all be

[First published in *New York Times*, 23 April 1933, Education section, p. 7, from an address on 21 April 1933 to the Conference on the Educational Status of the Four- and Five-Year-Old Child at Teachers College, Columbia University.]

married persons and, except in exceptional cases, must have had children of their own. Unmarried, younger persons occupy places of assistance and serve a kind of initiatory apprenticeship. Moreover, older children, since there are no arbitrary divisions into classes, take part in directing the activities of those still younger.

The activity of these older children may be used to illustrate the method by which those whom we would call teachers are selected. It is almost a method of self-selection. For instance, the children aged say from about 13 to 18 who are especially fond of younger children are given the opportunity to consort with them. They work with the younger children under observation, and then it soon becomes evident who among them have the taste, interest and the kind of skill which is needed for effective dealing with the young.

As their interest in the young develops, their own further education centres more and more about the study of processes of growth and development, and so there is a very similar process of natural selection by which parents are taken out of the narrower contact with their own children in the homes and are brought forward in the educational nurture of larger numbers of children.

The work of these educational groups is carried on much as painters were trained in, say, Italy, when painting was at its height. The adult leaders, through their previous experience and by the manner of their selection, combine special knowledge of children with special gifts in certain directions.

They associate themselves with the young in carrying on some line of action. Just as in these older studios younger people were apprentices who observed the elders and took part along with them in doing at first some of the simpler things and then, as they got more experience, engaged directly in the more complex forms of activity, so in these directed activities in these centres the older people are first engaged in carrying on some work in which they themselves are competent, whether painting or music or scientific inquiry, observation of nature or industrial cooperation in some line. Then the younger children, watching them, listening to them, begin taking part in the simpler forms of the action—a minor part, until as they develop they accept more and more responsibility for cooperating.

Naturally I inquired what were the purposes, or, as we say now, the objectives, of the activities carried on in these centres. At first nothing puzzled me more than the fact that my inquiry after objectives was not at all understood, for the whole concept of the school, of teachers and pupils and lessons, had so completely disappeared that when I asked after the special objectives of the activity of these centres, my Utopian friends thought I was asking why children should live at all, and therefore they did not take my questions seriously.

After I made them understand what I meant, my question was dismissed with the remark that since children were alive and growing, "of course, we, as the Utopians, try to make their lives worth while to them; of course, we try to see that they really do grow, that they really develop." But as for having any objective beyond the process of a developing life, the idea still seemed to them quite silly. The notion that there was some special end which the young should try to attain was completely foreign to their thoughts.

By observation, however, I was led to the conclusion that what we would regard as the fundamental purposes were thoroughly ingrained in the working of the activities themselves. In our language it might be said to be the discovery of the aptitudes, the tastes, the abilities and the weaknesses of each boy and girl, and then to develop their positive capacities into attitudes and to arrange and reinforce the positive powers so as not to cover up the weak points but to offset them.

I inquired, having a background of our own schools in mind, how with their methods they ever made sure that the children and youth really learned anything, how they mastered the subject matter, geography and arithmetic and history, and how they ever were sure that they really learned to read and write and figure. Here, too, at first I came upon a blank wall. For they asked, in return to my question, whether in the period from which I came for a visit to Utopia it was possible for a boy or girl who was normal physiologically to grow up without learning the things which he or she needed to learn—because it was evident to them that it was not possible for any one except a congenital idiot to be born and to grow up without learning.

When they discovered, however, that I was serious, they asked whether it was true that in our day we had to have schools and teachers and examinations to make sure that babies learned to walk and to talk.

It was during these conversations that I learned to appreciate how completely the whole concept of acquiring and storing away things had been displaced by the concept of creating attitudes by shaping desires and developing the needs that are significant in the process of living.

The Utopians believed that the pattern which exists in economic society in our time affected the general habits of thought; that because personal acquisition and private possession were such dominant ideals in all fields, even if unconsciously so, they had taken possession of the minds of educators to the extent that the idea of personal acquisition and possession controlled the whole educational system.

They pointed not merely to the use in our schools of the competitive methods of appeal to rivalry and the use of rewards and punishments, of set examinations and the system of promotion, but they also said that all these things were merely incidental expressions of the acquisitive system of society and the kind of measure and test of achievement and success which had to prevail in an acquisitive type of society.

So it was that we had come to regard all study as simply a method of acquiring something, even if only useless or remote facts, and thought of learning and scholarship as the private possession of the resulting acquisition. And the social change which had taken place with the abolition of an acquisitive economic society had, in their judgment, made possible the transformation of the centre of emphasis from learning (in our sense) to the creation of attitudes.

They said that the great educational liberation came about when the concept of external attainments was thrown away and when they started to find out what each individual person had in him from the very beginning, and then devoted themselves to finding out the conditions of the environment and the kinds of activity in which the positive capacities of each young person could operate most effectually.

In setting creation, productivity, over against acquiring, they said that there was no genuine production without enjoyment. They imagined that the ethics of education in the older period had been that enjoyment in education always had to be something deferred; that the motto of the schools, at least, was that man never is, but always is to be, blest; while the only education that really could discover and elicit power was one which brought these powers for immediate use and enjoyment.

Naturally, I inquired what attitudes they regarded as most important to create, since the formation of attitudes had taken the place with the young of the acquisition of information. They had some difficulty in ranking attitudes in any order of importance, because they were so occupied with an all-around development of the capacities of the young. But, through observation, I should say that they ranked the attitude which would give a sense of positive power as at least as basic and primary as the others, if not more so.

This attitude which resulted in a sense of positive power involved, of course, elimination of fear, of embarrassment, of constraint, of self-consciousness; eliminated the conditions which created the feeling of failure and incapacity. Possibly it included the development of a confidence, of readiness to tackle difficulties, of actual eagerness to seek problems instead of dreading them and running away from them. It included a rather ardent faith in human capacity. It included a faith in the capacity of the environment to support worthwhile activities, provided the environment was approached and dealt with in the right way.

Shall We Abolish School "Frills"? No

There exists today an organized attack upon what has been accomplished in the last thirty or forty years in enriching the material of instruction and of life in the public schools. The attack is made in the interest of economy. It is proposed to eliminate from the schools such things as health service, work with wood, metal, tools, domestic arts, music, drawing, and dramatics, on the ground that they are "frills" and costly frills at that. I do not question the desirability of every legitimate economy in the conduct of the schools. I deny absolutely that saving money at the expense of the lives of young people, now and in the future, is economy.

Economy is something more than reducing expenditure of funds. If it were not, it would be economy to save the money now spent in buying food, shelter, and clothing for the millions of unemployed. It is as heartless and as foolish to starve the minds and characters of the young as it is to starve the bodies of their parents. The real question is not economy versus waste but whether things scornfully named frills are or are not important things in the education of mind and brain; whether they are luxuries or whether they are necessities in the present state of society.

Early in its history the United States committed itself to a system of education for all, conducted at public expense. This was not accidental but was a manifestation of our fundamental national faith. Our educational system has always had enemies but they have been those who had no faith in any part of our democratic social experiment. The economic crisis has encouraged these people to come back to the attack. They make a great fuss about "frills." Their real opposition is to the belief in human ca-

[First published in *Rotarian* 42 (May 1933): 18–19, 49. For H. L. Mencken's article to which this is a reply, see Appendix 2.]

pacity, the belief in the right of every human being to have a chance to develop, the desire of parents that their children shall have better opportunities than they enjoyed—the beliefs that created the tax-supported American public-school system. Show me a man who is active in attacking our schools because of their "frills" and I will show you either a large tax-payer who sends his own children to a private school or else one who disbelieves in the whole democratic endeavor.

At every period of American life the schools have responded to the social conditions of the time. In pioneer days, life was simple and so was schooling. The subjects taught were reading, writing, spelling, and arithmetic, and the method used was memorizing and drilling. This kind of education did not exist because pedagogues or wise men chose to have it this way. It existed because of the general social and economic conditions. Life outside of school, in the home, on the farm, in the neighborhood shops, gave adequate training in all that was indispensable except the Three R's. Life put definite responsibilities upon all young people and developed character and judgment. The struggle for existence was too pressing to permit more than a few to go on to higher education. Even as late as 1890 only two hundred thousand boys and girls went to high school.

Today over four million go. The larger part of the increase is due to the fact that young people were attracted to school and held there by the very things that are denounced as frills. Do the parents of this nation wish to return to the times when high schools were only for the children of the distinctly well-to-do? If so, all they have to do is to eject the things called frills from the schools.

Why do twenty times as many young people go to high school now as went forty years ago? The things that explain this are the things that also explain the expansion of the studies, activities, and equipment of the schools. Industries once carried on in the home have moved to factories. So manual training, machine-shop work, cooking, dress-making, millinery, and so on, were introduced into school, in order that children might not be wholly unprepared for the world in which they were to live and work. As the machine age made it possible for great masses of people to live at a level above that of mere subsistence, these masses demanded cultivated enjoyments for their leisure. The school answered this demand; music, drawing, dramatics, clay-modelling became part of the daily work.

The community learned more about the protection of health, the prevention of disease; it also spent more of its time living in cramped urban quarters. The schools did what they could to meet the improved health standards. Physical training, playgrounds, instruction in "safety," medical inspection, and, in favored places, dental clinics, were introduced. Boys and girls not wanted in industry, or shut out from entering it at an early age by the humane sentiment of the community, went to school, more of them, more days a year, and because of "frills" high-school attendance was multiplied twenty-fold.

Cut off from the training of body, hand, and eye, formerly given by neighborhood industry, deprived of the training of judgment and character once gained in the old fashioned self-supporting and self-contained home, American children today find in school some of the discipline and education that in pioneer days came from their life outside school.

Imagine every study, every activity, every piece of equipment and facility, that is today condemned as a frill, eliminated from schools. Imagine that the schools have gone back to what their critics still believe to be the essentials. How attractive would these schools be?

Do reading, writing, spelling, and arithmetic seem to be adequate preparation for life in times like these? Have parents in cultivated homes ever regarded music, drawing, opportunity for physical development, careful medical inspection, dancing, and so on, as frills for their own boys and girls? No, it is only when these things are brought at public expense to those whom they despise as the masses, as the common, average people, that they become trivial and luxuries.

Eliminating the newer studies as useless frills, is in effect, and often in intention, part and parcel of the movement to restrict all education to the most elementary basis, except that for the favored few. This would be bad enough even if there were any assurance that the children of the wealthy were sure to have more intelligence and character than the children of the poor. There is no such assurance. The only way that society can make sure of enlisting the talents of youth is to make all schools attractive enough to hold the mass and to make their instruction sufficiently varied so that abilities other than the strictly literary can have a chance to develop.

It is as absurd to suppose that schools could remain unchanged during the tremendous social expansions and reorganizations of the last forty years, as it is to suppose that the old local gristmills, saw-mills, and blacksmith shops could continue to serve new conditions, or that the old dirt roads could meet the needs of an automobile age. There is no measure, fixed and unchanging from age to age, by which to decide what is a frill and what an essential in education. The only true gauge is social conditions and needs.

The change from the home life of families living in their own houses, having their own yard and gardens, to crowded city apartments with no play space save dangerous, traffic-crowded streets is alone enough to have required a great readjustment in school life. Special classes for the blind, deaf, crippled, the handicapped, and kindergartens for little children, may not be included among the frills that are to be cut out in the name of economy. But they are the products of the same social and humane forces that produced the things called frills. If the latter are wiped out, so will be the former.

The best defense, in the end the only defense for "frills," is that they are not frills but legitimate and practical responses to social conditions and needs.

The belief they are frills is found in different quarters. There are persons of a literary turn of mind, those who make their living by writing, who are often given to thinking that everything, except some ability in mathematics, beyond their own trade tools, are frilly. This view is strengthened by the fact that for centuries schools concentrated on language and symbols, so that many who are romantically attached to the past and afraid of change reinforce the literary folk.

Then there are the successful men who pride themselves on being hard-headed and who point out that they have risen in the world on the basis of the old-style Three R's, and conclude that what was good enough for them is good enough for anybody. Not all of these put together would be powerful enough to pry the masses of parents loose from attachment to schools that give their children the things needed for development. But at present they are reinforced by the wealthy who do not like to pay large school taxes and who send their own children to private schools. An amusing feature of the situation is that while public schools cost, on the average, fifty cents a day a pupil, these complaining tax-payers pay four or five times as much as this for the privilege of being exclusive.

The question of frills or no frills reduces itself to this simple question: Do we want to build up and strengthen a class division by means of schools for the masses that confine education to a few simple and mechanical skills, while the well-to-do send their children to schools where they get exactly the things that are branded as frills when they are given at public expense to the children of the masses? The parent who contemplates this possibility and who thinks of his own children having to be content with that kind of school while his millionaire neighbors send their children where they can get everything denied his own children can be trusted to decide the question of "frills."

No great change in education or anything else could occur as rapidly as our educational expansion and be unaccompanied by mistakes and excrescences. In defending the studies and activities in health, music, dramatics, wood and metal craft, cooking, dress-making, and so on, that have changed schools from places of mechanical routine to centres of life, it is not necessary to defend every particular thing done in their name. It is easy, and it is as cheap as it is easy, to pick out extravagances here and there and use them to condemn the whole movement. It is better, however, to pick out specific things and confine criticism to them.

So I shall mention one point that in my judgment may be legitimately attacked as a frill. In many of the large cities of the United States, so-called vocational education has been converted into specific trade-training, with costly building and a multiplicity of elaborate and expensive specialized shops. Educators who do not really believe in this method have yielded in order to get money from the federal board appropriating funds under the Smith-Lever Bill and actuated by a mechanical "job analysis" philosophy.

To provide a shop for every specialized industry and to install machinery for each minute process of that industry, to analyze the job as it is carried on in expert factories and insist upon reproducing every step is not only expensive, but is wasteful education. Often both machines and processes have changed before the graduates get into industry. An understanding of basic principles is needed much more than specialized detail. It is one thing, however, to criticize an abuse and try to eliminate it and it is another to make an indiscriminate attack on the underlying principle and movement.

Teachers and schools must indeed do what they can to rescue communities from the dangers of bankruptcy through excessive taxation. But the expense of even the excrescences that could be lopped off is nothing compared with political frills in job-holding and in complication of taxing agencies. Let the gentlemen who are making a drive on the schools turn toward extravagances and corruption in politics, and not take it out on helpless children.

The contribution made to economy by schools should not be such that schools will revert to the old-fashioned dame schools where pupils can learn just enough to make a docile peasantry and fodder for factories, with their culture confined to the headlines of tabloids.

The schools represent the interest of the young. The young do not constitute a vested interest; they are not organized nor powerful. But they stand for what is most precious in American life and for the future country that is to be. For these reasons I do not think the ridicule of literary folk nor the direct assault of big tax-payers will be successful.

Why Have Progressive Schools?

One of the commonest charges brought against the progressive schools and schoolmasters who advocate modern methods is that they express the aims of their kind of education in vague and general terms. What they say sounds well, but what does it mean?

What is any education for? Let the reader try to answer this question. He will evolve a generalized formula much like those of the specialists. However definite his own picture of what he means may be, the words he uses will be capable of as many interpretations as he has listeners. This is as true of the statements of the aims of old-fashioned education as of those of the most advanced schools. Some of the shortest and simplest answers are: A preparation for life; to learn to live; to give the child what he needs, or will need, to know; to develop good citizens; to develop well-rounded, happy, efficient individuals. Can the reader point to any one of these and say with confidence, "This belongs to the new," or, "This rules out the new"? No, not of these, nor of any other definitions of the purpose of education. He cannot because the differences of opinion about what education should be lie, not in the purpose of education, but in personal views about people and society.

The purpose of education has always been to every one, in essence, the same—to give the young the things they need in order to develop in an orderly, sequential way into members of society. This was the purpose of the education given to a little aboriginal in the Australian bush before the coming of the white man. It was the purpose of the education of youth in the golden age of Athens. It is the purpose of education today, whether this education goes on in a one-room school in the mountains of Tennessee or in the

[First published in *Current History* 38 (July 1933): 441–48.]

most advanced progressive school in a radical community. But to develop into a member of society in the Australian bush had nothing in common with developing into a member of society in ancient Greece, and still less with what is needed today. Any education is, in its forms and methods, an outgrowth of the needs of the society in which it exists.

No one is surprised that the educational methods in Soviet Russia are different from those here. That other methods will develop in a Hitlerized Germany is easy to understand. Yet even within two such rigid and controlled societies as these two countries are at present striving for, there is and will be experimentation, discussion and difference of opinion among teachers as to the best methods of developing members of those societies. There will be satisfied parents and dissatisfied parents. There will be happy children who like the schools and adjust to them easily, and children who do not adjust and whose difficulties are blamed on the schools.

The Australian aboriginal, the Athenian, the Soviet citizen, the Hitlerite had, or have, societies that can be defined in definite terms; the aims of which, whatever we think of them, can be recognized by any one. Accept these aims and there will be comparatively little difference of opinion about the kind of education that should be given youth in any one of the societies. In our American democracy aims have, until recently, been stated in terms of the individual, not in those of the society he is to be educated for.

In the early days of education in this country all that seemed to be necessary for the attainment of the ideals of democracy was to give every child an equal start in life by furnishing him with certain fundamentals of learning, then turn him loose and let him do the rest.

The little red school houses of the country were started with a curriculum that did just this and no more. Higher schools of learning were not thought of as general educational institutions, but as strictly professional schools where ministers, lawyers, doctors and teachers learned the technical facts they needed for the pursuit of their vocations. This system of education worked, not because it was an inspired program for assuring the workings of the ideals of democracy, but because life was simple and the country offered almost unlimited opportunity for the individual.

Life centred in the home. There, or in a neighborhood shop where his father worked, the child saw the industries of the country being carried on—baking, canning, dressmaking, farming, carpentry, blacksmithing, printing, wheelwrighting and so on. There, by taking part in the daily life, he learned habits of industry and perseverance and imbibed his ethical and moral standards. The small homogeneous community life of the early days enabled him to learn civics at first hand, through seeing and hearing about the running of his own town. There were space, air, fields and trees everywhere accessible, so that his play needed no specialized facilities and supervision. The only opportunities that this sharing in the life of the home and the village did not offer were for "book learning"—the Three Rs. The child went to school to learn to read, write and figure. His life outside school gave him the rest of the training he needed.

Then life began to change. The things once made at home were now made in factories and the child knew nothing of them. The inventions and discoveries in science brought railroads, the telegraph and telephone, gas and electricity, farm machinery—a host of things about which one could not really know without far more training than was given by mere practice in using the finished product. Industrialization brought the big city, with its slums and palaces, its lack of play space, its sharp distinction between city and country. Finally it brought the automobile, the movies and the radio, with their enormous influence in taking the family out of the home and making even the little child much more part of the great world than had ever been dreamed of in the past.

These changes did not happen all at once. If they had, perhaps it would have been necessary to scrap the simple curriculum of the first schools and begin afresh with one that recognized all these new and tremendously different factors at once. Instead, what happened was that gradually, as one new need was felt, a new subject was added to the course of study. The simple device of teaching reading, writing and arithmetic through the medium of the new subject did not occur to any one. Even literature and reading, and penmanship and writing, became four separate subjects. The great increase in leisure and in the well-to-do classes made its contribution, too, to the number of subjects taught. Parents began to demand that schools teach some of the things that would enrich the use of leisure, some of the things that it would be nice to have children know, as well as the things that were necessary to enable the child to get along in the world. Thus art, music, dancing, French, and so on, were introduced into the schools. The growth of wealth and leisure also enormously increased the number of pupils in the schools of higher learning. Gradually the academy or preparatory school and the colleges ceased to be merely places for technical training and became places where one might go to go on being educated more or less regardless of what specific thing one was being educated for. And these schools, too, added more subjects to their curricula as the number of students and their demands increased.

Just as subjects were added one by one to the once-sufficient Three Rs, so the methods that had been adequate for the three continued and were used unchanged. When the child's educational life, in the larger sense, was lived at home, what he needed was practice and drill in the Three Rs, so that he could take them home and use them. So the new subjects were taught by drill, whether the home he would take them to offered any opportunities for their use or not. If these methods were not as successful with the new subjects, the fault lay not in the method but in the fact that because these subjects were new they were frills, lacking in the inherent disciplinary value of the old fundamentals.

The science of individual psychology began to develop after the enrichment of the curriculum was well on its way, so that the two developments went on in parallel lines touching almost not at all. The discoveries of the former about the way people learn, about individual differences and the interrelation of effort and interest, were unknown to schoolmasters, or were thought of as too newfangled for consideration. It was a little as if no one had been willing to put radios on the market because it was obviously an absurd idea that sound can be transmitted for vast distances through mountains and brick walls without special means like wires. And although these psychological discoveries are many of them as well established today as the facts of the radio, they are still temperamentally abhorrent to a great many schoolmasters and parents. A great many others are willing to admit them when stated in general terms, but feel the strongest emotional reluctance to giving children the benefit of them by applying them to teaching methods. In brief, these three discoveries may be stated as follows:

1. The human mind does not learn in a vacuum; the facts presented for learning, to be grasped, must have some relation to the previous experience of the individual or to his present needs; learning proceeds from the concrete to the general, not from the general to the particular.

2. Every individual is a little different from every other individual, not alone in his general capacity and character; the differences extend to rather minute abilities and characteristics, and no amount of discipline will eradicate them. The obvious conclusion of this is that uniform methods cannot possibly produce uniform results in education, that the more we wish to come to making every one alike the more varied and individualized must the methods be.

3. Individual effort is impossible without individual interest. There can be no such thing as a subject which in and by itself will furnish training for every mind. If work is not in itself interesting to the individual or does not have associations or by-products which make its doing interesting, the individual cannot put his best efforts into it. However hard he may work at it, the effort does not go into the accomplishment of the work, but is largely dissipated in a moral and emotional struggle to keep the attention where it is not held.

The progressive education movement is the outgrowth of the realization by educators of the fact that our highly complex, rapid, crowded civilization demands and has been met by changes in school subjects and practice; that to make these changes effective something more is needed than simply the addition of one subject after another. The new subjects should be introduced with some relation to each other and the ways in which they operate and integrate in the world outside of school. It is also the outgrowth of the desire to put into practice in the classroom what the new science of psychology has discovered about individual learning and individual differences.

The kinds of schools, together with the methods used in them, which have developed from the desire to adjust the curriculum to society and to use the new psychology to increase the pupil's learning are numerous, almost as numerous as the schools themselves. When an individual or a group tries to adjust the curriculum to society, it immediately becomes necessary to formulate a conception of what that society is. What are its strengths that should be stressed in the schools, what its weaknesses that children should understand?

Is it a good thing to bring up the young with desires and habits that try to preserve everything just as it is today, or should they be able to meet change, to weigh the values and find good in the new? How much of the background and development of our civilization do children need to be able to understand what is in the world today? How much do they need to become cultivated individuals, able to enjoy leisure and carry on worth-while traditions? The answers to these and many other questions and the skill used in translating them into practice will determine the kind of school. Both these factors will differ according to the temperament, beliefs, background and experience of the individuals who answer them. This to the writer does not seem to be an indictment of progressive schools.

In a world changing as rapidly as ours, in a democracy with so short a history to draw on for choice of the best ways to succeed, expression of differences of opinions by different kinds of schools is a wholesome sign. In developing anything new, it is a good plan to have different methods working side by side, to experiment, to compare. This kind of difference has nothing whatever to do with whether a particular school is a good school or a bad school, with whether children learn what they are taught and are happy and successful at school and at home. Nor does this mean that all progressive schools just by the fact of being labeled "progressive" are good schools. It simply means that progressive education has not one formula, is not a fixed and finished thing about which it is legitimate and safe to make generalizations. It is as ridiculous to say that all progressive schools are good, as it is to say that the principles of progressive education are bad and unworkable because one school is poor, or because one child does not succeed in one school.

We are used to the faults of traditional schools, so used to them that when any difficulty arises we tend to lay the blame on the child or the home he comes from. There are, however, good teachers and bad teachers in traditional schools, and no curriculum, no matter how old, how cut and dried, how uniform it is, can possibly give a higher quality of output than the quality of the teacher who is using it. Probably nine-tenths of the violent criticism of progressive schools as progressive, that is so popular, would melt away like Summer snows if we would look at traditional schools as we look at modern schools, or if we expected only the same amount from them. A progressive school to escape damnation has to be practically perfect, has to give each child just what his particular parents think he should have, has to succeed with every child, if he is a genius or just average, if he is nervously unstable, if he changes schools every year, however queer or unadjusted at home he may be. A traditional school is not expected to make good unless the child fits in, conforms and raises no problems. Two instances of the kind of criticism that is commonly leveled at a progressive school and practically never at an old-fashioned school are the matters of learning to read and of discipline.

Some children are backward about learning to read. They either have great difficulty learning or are so slow about it that their parents begin to think they never will. When this happens in an old-fashioned school the child either gets "left back," and has to repeat the work of the first or second grade, or the school tells the mother that she will have to teach the child to read at home if he is to go on with his class. And without any special fuss every one assumes that there is something the matter with the child. When this happens in a progressive school the chances are that parents and friends immediately assume that it is the school's fault, that the school does not even bother to teach reading, or at least does not think it important enough to "make" the child learn; the child would of course be reading fluently long ago were it not for the school's lax methods. We know today that certain children have reading difficulties, due sometimes to eye peculiarities, sometimes to left-handedness, sometimes to other more obscure causes. The only way to tell why one child does not learn to read is often a rather elaborate examination into all these possibilities. Experience has shown that if the child is mentally normal he will learn to read anyway by the time he is ten or so, and that in after life it is impossible to tell these late readers from the children who teach themselves when they are three.

In the matter of discipline the progressive school is even more subject to attack. If a child misbehaves in an old-fashioned school, he is naughty and his parents meekly undertake to see that he stops giving trouble. If he misbehaves in a modern school, the school is spoiling him, it has no standards of conduct, it sets no store by those sterling qualities obedience and orderliness. It is probably true that a progressive school seems disorderly to visitors who cannot imagine a school except as a place where rows of silent children sit quietly at desks until told to do something by a teacher. But modern education does not aim at this kind of order. Its aim is the kind of order that exists in a roomful of people, each one of whom is working at a common task. There will be talking, consulting, moving about in such a group whether the workers are adults or children. The standard for order and discipline of a group is not how silent is the room, or how few and uniform the kinds of tools and materials that are being used, but the quality and amount of work done by the individuals and the group. A different technique is required of the teacher in such a room from that required by a teacher in a room where each pupil sits at a screwed down desk and studies the same part of the same lesson from the same textbook at the same time. There are progressive teachers who have not mastered the technique. There are good teachers and poor teachers in progressive schools just as there are in traditional schools. But there is absolutely no scientific objective evidence to support the view that behavior problems are relatively more common in progressive schools than in traditional schools, or that the former are less successful in straightening out those that do arise than the latter.

Another common criticism of progressive education is that individual development and the training of special abilities or talents are stressed at the expense of learning social adjustment, good manners, how to get along with adults—that all progressive schools have a highly individualistic philosophy. If we confine ourselves to the philosophy, just the opposite seems to be the truth. It is the modern schools that have formulated their aims in definite social terms. It is they that are trying to work out some method of achieving harmony between the democratic belief in the liberty of the individual and his responsibility for the welfare of the group. A group of conservatives are already attacking them because they have expressed the belief that the schools have a responsibility to educate so that recurrence of present economic conditions will be impossible.

Individualism run riot is laid at the doors of modern schools, probably because it is these schools that first adopted teaching methods based on the new knowledge of individual psychology and on the recent findings about the growth of young bodies. To many the mere fact that children are free to move about, to seek help from others, to undertake pieces of work in small groups is taken as evidence that the aim of the methods must be to develop individualists, to let the children do as they please. These methods were, in fact, introduced because we know that physical freedom is necessary to growing bodies and because psychological investigations have proved that learning is better and faster when the learner understands his problem as a whole and does his work under his own motive power rather than under minute, piecemeal dictation from a boss.

Many others who grow up under the stern old adage, "Spare the rod and spoil the child," cannot bear, apparently, to believe that any more pleasant or congenial method of learning can possibly be good for the young. They cherish many vestiges of the old idea that children are little limbs of Satan and that the only way to bend them to the uses of civilization is force and long training in doing things just because they are told to do them, regardless of whether or not the work is of any immediate use or interest. Without this training, they claim, one will never be able to see a difficult or dull job through to completion in later life. The strong moralistic bias that colors these views seems to make it impossible for their holders to see that in giving meaning, in his own daily life, to the work a child does, there is actually a gain in the disciplinary value of the work, rather than a loss. There is gain because the work is immediately valuable and satisfactory to the child. Therefore his best effort goes into it and his critical powers and initiative are exercised and developed. Moral and intellectual powers increase in vigor when the force of the worker's spontaneous interest and desire to accomplish something are behind them. This is as true of children as of adults. It is these powers that the progressive schools seek to release. If they sometimes fail, if they sometimes make mistakes, it must be remembered that their techniques are still being developed, that they are new. We should remember, too, that the time-honored and hoary techniques of the traditional school do not always succeed in teaching every pupil to extract square roots fluently, or to be able to push every difficult and wearisome task through to a triumphant conclusion. How much shirking and bluffing goes on in old-fashioned schools?

It is also frequently said that progressive methods may work with young children, but that when the high school is reached these schools are forced to give up their methods and go back to the old so that their pupils can pass college entrance examinations. It is true that college entrance examinations require the accumulation of such a vast number of specific facts that a great deal of drill and cramming is necessary if a pupil is to know enough answers to pass. This does not mean, however, that as children grow older the only way they can learn is by drill and cramming, or that progressive methods applied at the high-school age fail to educate. It simply means that to get into college a young person has to spend a great deal of time memorizing details so that he can answer a great many detailed questions.

Some colleges have for a number of years made exceptions in entrance requirements for the graduates of a few progressive schools. Reports are that these pupils have been able to carry on college work with records as good as, if not better than, pupils from conventional high schools. At present nearly twenty progressive schools have completed arrangements with almost all the accredited colleges and universities to begin, in 1936, admitting their graduates on other bases than the passing of the regular entrance examinations. The school will furnish a recommendation to the effect that the graduate has the necessary intelligence to do college work, has serious interests and purposes, and has demonstrated ability to work in one or more fields in which the college gives instruction. It will also furnish a careful record of the student's school life, including his records in the school examinations and his scores in various kinds of diagnostic tests. This will allow these schools to develop the curricula and teaching methods they believe best suited to the education of their students while they are in school, instead of forcing them to train for one special event in the child's future. After a reasonable number of pupils, whose high-school studies were carried on under this system, have graduated from college we shall have an authoritative answer as to whether progressive methods can be used in high schools with pupils who are going to college. If the plan works it will probably do more to reconcile the public to the fact that change and experimentation are needed in education than any other one thing.

Meantime, change and experimentation will go on anyway because life outside the school is changing, because scientific knowledge of the nature of growth is developing, and because parents want things for their children that they did not obtain when they went to school. The real measure of the success of the progressive schools is the modifications that finally take place in conservative schools because of the experimental pioneering. Judged by that standard alone, the progressive movement is making good.

I have emphasized the movement rather than schools as schools. For by the nature of the case, the various progressive schools differ widely from one another, more widely than traditional schools that have only to adhere to well-recognized standards. But also by the nature of the case, the progressive schools have something in common. They all aim at greater attention to distinctively individual needs and characteristics. Hence they are pervaded by a great degree of freedom of action and discussion. Secondly, they all utilize the outgoing activities of students to a much larger degree than does the traditional school. In other countries, especially in Latin countries, their popular name is "schools of action." Thirdly, they aim at an unwonted amount of cooperation of pupils with one another and of pupils with teachers. The latter function as fellow-workers in the activities that are going on rather than as rulers set on high. This fact determines the distinctive character of discipline in progressive schools. It is meant to be self-discipline as far as is possible, gained through sharing in work and play in which all have a common interest.

Within the limits of these three principles, there remain great possibilities of variation. But in spite of differences, their like elements sum up in the conviction that every worth-while education is a direct enrichment of the life of the young and not merely a more or less repellent preparation for the duties of adult life. They all believe that life is growth, that growth, while it involves meeting and overcoming obstacles, and hence has hard and trying spots, is essentially something to be enjoyed now. That learning is not necessarily a disagreeable process is the discovery, or re-discovery, of modern progressive education.

Education for a Changing Social Order

Education for a changing social order means fundamentally an education that introduces students into the realities of the present order—or disorder, order being a courtesy name for the present chaos. As Andy replied when Amos asked him the meaning of *status quo*, "It's a name for the mess we are in." Nobody knows what the future is going to be. The only sure thing is that it will change as the present is changing; changing so rapidly that we could almost say it *is* change.

Probably there were a few people ten years ago or so who thought they knew what the future was going to be. Ten years is a short time and yet the wisest did not know what the intervening years were going to bring forth. Certainly no one knew what the year of grace 1934 was going to be politically, economically and internationally. If we cannot see ten years ahead, the prospects are surely poor for our predicting what social affairs are going to be a generation from now, or even by the time the younger pupils in the school will be going out into active life.

People dissatisfied with the present are only too apt to flee, according to their respective temperaments, either to the past or to the future. It is easier to look backward and pleasanter to imagine what may be ahead than it is to face the present. Yet it is out of the present with all its cross currents that the future will be born. We can and should project our hopes and aspirations. But it is the way we treat present social forces that will determine how far our hopes are realized in the future. And we cannot administer these forces unless we first of all know what they are and how they are working.

In other words, there are three choices that education can

[First published in *Peabody Reflector and Alumni News* 7 (April 1934): 123–24, 142–43, from an address on 23 February 1934 to the American Association of Teachers Colleges in Cleveland, Ohio.]

take. It can go on dwelling in the past; it can set ideal pictures for the future and strive to educate on the basis of that picture; or we can strive through our schools to make pupils vividly and deeply aware of the kind of social world in which they are living. For these reasons I am glad that the assigned subject is "education for a changing social order" rather than education for a *new* social order:—not that we do not need a new social order, but that the fundamental condition of attaining it is to begin where we are, with the present, and having found out something about that, learn where education is to throw its weight; learn what existing forces are to be weakened and replaced, and what are to be supported and reinforced.

In the first place, let me say that it would be almost an educational revolution if we even recognized that we lived in a changing social order and proceeded to act upon that recognition in our schools. For speaking in the broad way which time alone permits, our educational system has been an education for a static, a relatively fixed, social order. One evidence of that fact is the emphasis put upon getting what are called the right answers to problems that are laid down by text and teacher, instead of putting the emphasis upon finding out what the problems are, finding out by having the boys and girls themselves take an active part in studying the conditions that set the problem.

The idolizing of correct knowledge and correct views is not confined of course to social matters. It is bad there as I shall try to show in a few minutes. But a fixed mental set is given in almost all subjects. Whether or not there is transfer of the external effects of learning, there is no doubt that an attitude that is formed persists, and waits to be ready to be applied to all subjects. Unconsciously students form the habit of supposing that things in general, aside from a few details, are all settled; that some one has the right solution and that it only remains for the student to learn it.

The result is that many young people leave school with the attitude of wanting and expecting to be *told*, rather than with the attitude of realizing that they must look into things, must inquire and examine. There is complaint, and rightly, that the population is too amenable, on the whole, to the influence of propaganda. But why is it? Why are so many people so ready to swallow what is persistently told them, or told them with an air of authority?

Why is there so much gullibility? I do not believe that it is mainly from lack of native intelligence. It is because they have acquired the habit of listening and of accepting, instead of that of inquiry, and, if you please, of intelligent scepticism.

There are other causes for this mental passivity. Men and women working mechanically all day, tending machines, are not likely to be especially alert. But I think the schools have to accept some responsibility for the prevalence of this habit of mind.

While methods of teaching in arithmetic, history, geography, in fact, almost all school subjects, aid in establishing the mental habit of passive acceptance, while docility at the expense of an inquiring disposition, is too generally cultivated, the evil culminates in the attitudes that are formed in political, social and economic matters. I give one particular illustration not perhaps important in itself, but as typical. I saw the other day a little pamphlet designed for high school teachers and students. The idea behind it was an excellent one. It was devoted to the National Recovery Act and the activities carried on under its administration. Here surely is a topic related to the world in which we are living. Acquaintance on the part of students with this present line of governmental activity is valuable in itself as a preparation of students for the duties of citizenship. Even more important this study could easily be made a doorway through which students could be led to a study of almost any phase of present industrial and business life, including the position of the consumer and the wage earner.

So far, so good. But the central theme of the pamphlet was whether the NRA should be continued indefinitely, and not only that but the pamphlet took a definite position on the matter. It was calculated to lead students to a certain view as the correct one. Now, I do not suppose there was anything wrong about this desire in the intention of the writer. But I do think it was educationally wrong. I think the fact is an illustration of the prevailing tendency to have everything settled, to have students arrive at correct views on every topic that comes up for fear lest their minds be left hanging in uncertainty.

Since, however, events themselves are hanging in the air, since the world itself is in a state of uncertainty as to what is impending, the point that is most important educationally was omitted. The tendency to develop closed minds was strengthened. Can any one believe that the educational result would not have been much better if the facts had been presented, even the arguments pro and con, so that the nature of the problem stood out clearly, and then the matter left there for the students' own continuous inquiry? Was it better to have the matter settled as far as the minds of the boys and girls were concerned or better to arouse curiosity and an abiding interest in the question for the future?

I have taken this particular illustration not because it is especially bad. On the contrary, it is an example of something much better than what has often gone on in the schools. It is an attempt to bring instruction into relation with the changing social scene. Upon the whole I do not think it is too much to say that when the schools have touched upon political and economic affairs it has been at arm's length in comparison with which the instance referred to is almost a hand-to-hand grapple.

School contacts have been too large, remote and highly general. And they have often been so much in the way of laudation of what was done in the past as to give students a highly *unreal* idea of actual conditions. It is recognized that our forefathers a century and a half ago had real problems to deal with both in revolutionary days and the years that followed till the Constitution was adopted. It is recognized that Civil War days were times of real stress and strain. But comparatively little has been done to make students aware that we live in the midst of new problems that are as urgent and in many ways even more complex.

It has even been regarded as unpatriotic to say or teach anything that would give pupils the idea that our Constitution and the system under which we live are not so perfect that any serious problems remain. Those who call attention to the fact that a system adopted in the era of the stage-coach and candle light are not perfectly adapted to the era of the railway, electricity and airplane have been stigmatized as disturbers and wilful agitators, if not actual revolutionaries bent on overthrowing our system. Patriotism has been identified with complacency.

I might say, speaking broadly, that not only have we paid more attention to the past than to the present, but that we have educated on the basis of a fixed or static social order instead of one that is dynamic, changing more rapidly than at any time in the entire past. Well educated people have been wont to think with pity of the efforts of states like Tennessee and Arkansas to forbid the teaching of biological evolution in the public schools. But the fact is that when it comes to economic and political matters we have all of us lived in an atmosphere of fundamentalism, and that atmosphere has penetrated the schools. After all, the evolution of institutions is of much greater concern to the average person than is the evolution of plant and animal life. But those who feel enlightened, because they are willing to admit that the latter have been a constant scene of change, have felt that it was necessary to hold firmly to fixity of economic and political institutions, beliefs and loyalties. Or if they have accepted the idea of evolution in social affairs they have regarded it as a very slow gradual process that takes place automatically without the intervention of purpose and directed action on the part of human beings.

So I come back to my main theme. Education for a changing social order must be based on an understanding of the facts of the changes that are going on, and especially on insight into the causes that are producing these changes—the forces that are at work. Take, for example, the eclipse of democratic government in so many European countries. Many countries are living under dictatorships that have abolished all forms of representative government and that mention democracy only as a term of contempt. There are many influential persons in this country who uniformly speak with scorn of Congress and tell us how the business world breathes freely only when it is not in session. I do not suppose that all of them want a dictatorship, perhaps only a few do. But their attitude involves, whether they are aware of it or not, profound disrespect for representative government and democratic institutions.

There is no need here to go into the causes that have brought about the European situation. Let us stay close to home affairs. The country was founded upon faith in democracy with its ideals of liberty and democracy. Not many students in our high schools and only a comparatively few in the colleges are made aware of the fact that the Constitution was adopted in a time of distrust of the people and that many measures designed to curb the political power of the masses were embedded in it—a fact that was the cause of the adoption of all the earlier amendments at a time when popular sentiment was less under the influence of the reactionaries. But nevertheless Thomas Jefferson and Abraham Lincoln, the sturdiest defenders of democratic ideas, have always been the great national heroes. Why has the faith grown dimmer? And why is there so little interest in politics that hardly more than one-half of those entitled to vote go to the polls in a hotly contested election where parties have immense campaign funds at their disposal?

The question of course is a complicated one. But there is one fact so outstanding and so plain that it must be reckoned with. Economic conditions now are entangled at every point with politics, and economic forces decide political activity. Nevertheless, the determining economic conditions operate in ways that are not open and clear to the mass of the citizens. In theory and to a large degree practically in the minds of the average citizen politics and economics are kept apart. In spite of the fact that every important political issue arises out of industry, business and finance, we are constantly led to suppose that political and legal institutions work on independent and separate lines, lines that were laid down long ago and that are thoroughly democratic.

The simple fact is that power rules and that the real government is carried on not in Washington and our state capitals but wherever power resides. We live in a time when money not only talks but acts. There is an accumulation and concentration of wealth. Our industrial and commercial system is carried only by means of capital that is amassed and organized. I do not complain of this fact. I only say that it is an outstanding fact and affects politics.

When our country was in process of creation, the men who transported goods carried them with horses and wagons which they owned themselves. The men who made the goods made them in their own neighborhoods with tools which they worked by their own hands, and even when they did not own the raw materials upon which they used their tools, they at least mostly owned the tools and they worked with a few neighbors whom they knew personally and who had a common stake in their local community. This was the time when rugged individualism had a meaning and it was the time when democratic institutions were born.

You cannot imagine the railway system by which the great mass of raw materials and manufactured goods are transported today being owned and managed in that personal way. It takes a large amount of capital to build and run a railway system. Corporations with issuance of bonds and stocks that bring about the accumulation of large capital drawn from a great variety of individuals were necessities if we were to use steam and electricity instead of depending upon horses and wagons.

Compare the old forge and blacksmith shop in which ironwares were produced with the mills and factories of the United States Steel or Bethlehem Corporations of today, and you have at least a symbol of the corresponding change that has taken place in productive industry. Or compare the old-fashioned wagon-works with the big automobile factories in Detroit and you see why it is that capital has been gathered together and organized on a vast scale. We could not have our present type of civilization without the change from personally managed production and transportation dependent, comparatively speaking, upon personal means, without the aggregation of impersonal capital.

For this reason I said I was not complaining of the mere fact. The real point concerns the question of *how the aggregated capital is controlled and how it is used*—what is the social effect of the way it is used. And since I am not making a political speech I am not mentioning even this fact to complain of it at this time. The point is the bearing of it upon education for citizenship in our present order. The point is that our youth cannot possibly understand the problems and forces of political life unless they understand its background in industry, trade and finance.

If we contrast the actual situation with instruction in civics as that is given in most of our schools, we see how pathetically meagre the latter is. The latter is almost shoved into a corner. But the nature of the usual instruction given is still more serious. While there has been great improvement in recent years, and there is not so much merely formal study of the legal anatomy of government as there once was, it is still true that an understanding of the situation cannot be had by a single course set apart from others. What is required is something fundamental by way of a pretty complete overhauling of the curriculum from the fifth grade onwards through the high school. The whole course of study should be oriented toward the world of the present, not toward the past, and its great aim should be to make those who go out from the school conscious of the forces that are changing the conditions of life for everybody.

Of course such a reorganization is not easy and cannot be performed over night. There must be preparation. There are none in such a strategic position to make the preparation for the change as the training schools for teachers, and in this group the colleges and schools for teachers connected with the universities of the country hold a central place. For this reason in what I have said so far I have spoken of the education that is needed in the schools. For the kind of instruction they are to receive and the methods that are to be used should decide what is to be done in the training of teachers. The constant temptation of such training schools is either to prepare in a cut and dried way for the details of the school room or else to develop under the name of science and philosophy ideas that are too far away from school life and action.

I do not think that I am over bold in saying that at the present time the institutions that train teachers have a unique opportunity. It is a few of the larger features of this opportunity that I should like to outline. If teachers are to be trained to educate the young for a changing social order, the institutions that train them cannot, in the first place, accept the present curriculum as setting the standard for their work. Those who give instruction in them must inquire critically and cooperatively into the relationship of this curriculum to a changing order. They must start on the development of plans of study for the schools generally that are organized about the idea of social life as indeed a life, a moving changing thing.

I do not think that the method of approach can be too bold or too challenging. The execution of the plans in actual practice will be a much slower thing, and there will be plenty of obstacles to slow down its execution. But the method of approach is an intellectual matter, and while conservatism will affect practice, the approach cannot be too radical—radical in the sense of trying to get at the root of the matter. We have never had in this country centralized governmental departments of education such as exist in the cabinets of European countries. Progress has been by voluntary efforts and by a process of permeation and osmosis. In the long run I believe this method is better than dictation from above. But the method imposes a peculiar responsibility on teacher-training institutions.

In the absence of official leadership it is for them to be leaders. There is a strong tendency for them to be followers. I do not mean by this statement that they are consciously servile in their attitude. I mean rather that a great many forces converge to make the readiest and simplest course the acceptance of the existing system and to prepare their students for taking an efficient part in it, improving it of course, but improving it within the limits set by it as it is in its existing framework. Teachers must find positions and their fitness is likely to be judged by their preparation as it enables them to fit in. The eyes of those who direct these institutions are unconsciously kept upon existing practices and their ideal is to carry on the investigations and instill the ideals that will better those practices without attempting to change the general framework.

Under ordinary conditions such policies are all that could be expected, and there is no doubt of the good work that has been done in these directions. For we are living in a time to which the mildest word that can be applied is emergency; one that most of us do not hesitate to call a crisis, and which may be one of the turning points in history that occur every century or two. Everybody knows that ideas and proposals that would have been hooted at a few years ago are now promulgated and listened to. It is only in emergencies that far-reaching changes can be initiated. The opportunity for serious educational changes, that I referred to a few moments ago, is determined in a large measure by the state of the public mind at the present time. No one knows how long this particular situation will continue; if and when it disappears educational changes that could be accomplished with comparative ease during the crisis will be almost impossible to accomplish.

But now the idea of a New Deal is not only on everybody's lips but in everybody's minds. There are critics of course, but unless I misjudge the state of public opinion the mass of the people are hoping that it will go much further; they are waiting for an onward movement to take place. If educators hold back, the public will be indifferent to the schools, more indifferent than in the past. If the public sees that educators are awake to the situation and are trying to do their part to meet the new situation, there will be hearty support for changes that would have aroused an opposition impossible to overcome a few years ago.

The opportunity is such as comes not once in a generation but once in a century. Indeed, it was in the thirties of the nineteenth century that there was a great ferment in education and that the foundations of free public education were laid and that the movement for special education of teachers was set on foot. It was in the thirties a century ago that Horace Mann and Henry Barnard began the publication of their educational journals. It would be interesting to know whether it is a mere coincidence that the thirties of a century ago were also a period of extreme depression. At all events, there was an opportunity and it was taken advantage of by educators. How far can we rise to the present opportunity?

It would be absurd for me to attempt to lay down even in outline a program for an education for teachers that would put them in a position where they could in turn enable students to do their part in directing the changes that are going on so that we would move to a juster, more humane and more secure social order. But it is pertinent to point out certain facts. In the first place, the material for developing such a program is at hand in more abundant measure than at any previous time. There is much material conservatively presented in reports of the Commission on Social Trends. The N.E.A. has a Committee on Social and Economic Goals for America. An American Committee on Economic Policy has been formed as a clearing house and distributing centre of information. While aimed more directly at adult education, the material will be significant for any educational reorganization. A committee for the reorganization of secondary education has been formed and is at work. The Commission on Social Studies will soon make a report and it is understood that it will contain an analysis of present social conditions and forces. These are a few of the high spots with reference to available material.

In the second place, there is no cause for fear of fixed inculcation—which, according to the dictionary, originally signified a mere stamping in. We have a great deal of that in the interest of striving to maintain the order of the past that has so completely broken down. What we need to substitute for this fixed indoctrination, which has exercised an oppressive and coercive influence in the past, is an intelligent understanding of actual conditions that will stimulate individual inquiry and enable the minds of students and teachers alike to think in a straightforward and competent way and reach their own conclusions.

In the third place, the entire curriculum should be organized about a social centre and oriented toward social ends. At present, the curricula of the schools are so centrifugal, so dispersed and overloaded, so lacking in intellectual organization and unity of purpose, that unification is needed on every ground. For the sake of educational coherence as well as for educating a generation that can deal intelligently with our social troubles, a centre of unity is imperatively needed. We have gone for a long time on the policy of piece-meal additions of courses and studies. What we need is a thoroughgoing reorganization about a centre which will include within its circumference whatever is relevant to present needs. Will the institutions that prepare teachers take the lead?

The Activity Movement

It is obvious that the term "activity" is exceedingly broad. It does not lose this breadth in connection with educational programs. It runs a whole gamut. Of itself it says nothing about *kinds* of activity, and of itself it says nothing about the source of activity or about its locus and residence. It decides nothing, for example, about the ratio of physical, emotional, and intellectual factors. It says nothing about who or what starts the activity going, or whether its residence is collective or individual; evidently solo and chorus singing are both activities. Of course many of these ambiguities are mitigated, if not eliminated, in educational matters by the context, by the actual things that the word is used to denote. But a survey of literature, including the various definitions reported in this volume, shows that the term is elastic enough to cover dissimilar affairs in education. Hence different judgments as to the value of an "activity" program are more or less connected with the different views as to what is meant by the term.

It has consequently occurred to me that perhaps the most helpful thing I can do is to set forth some of the conceptions that, in their extreme forms, are opposed to one another, and to indicate the problems that these oppositions give rise to. The statement of the problems may both clarify the situations by showing how differences of view arise and indicate the general directions in which their settlement is to be looked for.

1. To some minds the term "activity" suggests doing something overt, something sufficiently gross or macroscopic to be readily perceptible by others. Such persons might not deny that a child engrossed in reading a book or listening quietly to music is

active, but they would not take the clue to an educational activity program from such "inner" acts. Since it is bodily activity that is gross and easily visible, while thinking is an implicit action, the educational equivalents of such a conception are evident without amplification.

The cause of the educational movement that emphasizes the importance of overt doing is not far to seek. It is primarily a reaction against the bad consequences of the externally enforced passivity characteristic of the traditional school with its imperative demand for quiet, silence, immobility, folded arms, set positions. When the reaction was positively supported by carrying into the school the results of child study, which showed that the young child is predominantly motor, the doors were thrown wide open to an activity program in the sense of emphasis of perceptible bodily activities, of doings and makings, of play and work. The educational problem that emerges is to discover, with different individuals and in the same individual at different stages of growth, the part played in the whole scheme of growth by the factor of doing.

With respect to chronological growth, a scale or spectrum exists. Speaking generally, the younger the child, the greater the role of overt, as distinct from implicit, activity. Upon the whole the infant when awake is *doing* something with sense organs and muscular equipment. With increasing maturity, the ratio of implicit activity increases. But there are also great individual differences. In adult life, we all recognize the distinction between the executive and the inquiring and artistic types. Persons of the first sort think for the sake of doing; those of the second type act (in the sense of doing and making) chiefly for the sake of directing and enriching emotional and intellectual experience. Differences show themselves early in life. Some children are distracted and confused by the amount of doing that is a stimulus to others, while the latter are benumbed by conditions that are suited to the former.

In short, there is nothing in the bare concept of activity that gives helpful direction to the educational program. There must be the kind and amount of doing that conduces to health and vigor, that produces observation and reflection, that clarifies and tests ideas, that tempers while it expresses emotions. No set program can be deduced from these generalities. They define a problem to be met by continued observation and experimentation, the solutions never being twice alike with different individuals or different groups. The settled point is that activity as doing is a means rather than an end.

2. Activity may be judged and evaluated according to its concrete and tangible results or according to the contribution it makes to a relatively intangible personal development. In theory, it may be measured by both without their conflicting with one another. In practice, one or the other so tends to predominate that different, almost opposed, types of educational procedure may result. Measurement in its quantitative, statistical, form fixes attention upon near-by, fairly direct results of action. Personal development is a thing of much longer time-span and lends itself to qualitative rather than quantitative judgment. It is open to the objection that it is "subjective." On the other hand, the more mature and experienced the teacher, the less will he or she be dependent upon tangible, directly applicable, external tests, and will use them, not as final, but as guides to judgment of the direction in which development is taking place. The more fully the processes of long-term growth are studied, the more objective will be the estimates of what is going on in particular individuals, while too much reliance upon special tangible tests tends to prevent attention to the conditions and laws of general growth.

What has been said applies directly to the mooted question of educational "ends" and "objectives." The valuation of activity on the basis of close-by, tangible results tends toward formation of one type of ends and objectives; namely, those that are specific and externally definable and measurable. Consequently, acceptance of this view will dictate a program that will, although it is an activity program, differ radically from the activity program in which concrete tangible results are subordinated to an enduring long-span growth. While my own philosophy leans decidedly in the latter direction, I am here concerned more with pointing the distinction that will explain differences in so-called activity programs and aid in clarifying thinking and decision on the subject than in settling the question. From the standpoint of activity as itself a continuing growth of the whole being (not divided into inner and outer, or into doing, thinking, and emotion as separate things), ends and objectives are not so much things to be definitely achieved by students as they are points to be borne in mind by the educator in surveying the progress of individuals to make sure that it is fairly balanced.

While space will not allow of the development of the points, it should be noted that the conflict between activity directed at acquiring skill and acquiring definite bodies of formal knowledge, and activity growing out of and expressing the existing state of experience belong in the category just discussed. Again there is no opposition in theory. There cannot be general growth unless skills and information are acquired and retained. But practically, educational systems differ as to where the emphasis is placed. Are skills and special modes of knowledge made the specific goals of activity, or are they treated as means for carrying on and enriching experience as a going concern? If the implications of this question are borne in mind when examining actual or recommended forms of activity programs, it will be found, I think, that ambiguities are cleared up, and special points will fall in place as members of an inclusive scheme. In that case, choice will at least be more conscious and intelligent.

3. Probably the point on which there is the greatest amount of controversial difference concerns the opposition often set up between the child's desires, preferences, and experiences on one side and social values and demands on the other. According to some, an activity program must grow directly out of the existing attitudes and contacts of those under instruction. To others, this course appears to be antagonistic not only to acquisition of subject matter in any organized way but also to preparation for meeting the inevitable requirements of later life. Others still evade the idea by setting up forms of activity that are practically uniform for all, so that the habit of conforming individual activity to that of others is established.

This problem, as far as theory is concerned, arises because a false antithesis is set up. There are multitudes of active tendencies in the young and a multitude of nascent preferences and dawning interests. There is a great deal of elasticity within an individual; individuality is rather a *direction of movement* than anything definitely formed. Selection and arrangement have to occur anyway unless everything is carried on at haphazard according to the caprice or pressure of the moment. The problem is therefore to discover *within* present experience those values that are akin to those which the community prizes, and to cultivate those tendencies that lead in the direction that social demands will take. If emphasis is put upon these points of community, not all clashes of personal desire and social claim will be avoided, but in the main there will be growth toward harmony.

The very dependence of the young establishes within their own make-up response to social demands. A good instance in the life of the preschool child is the learning of language. Ability to understand the language of others and to speak coherently is an imperative social claim. But no crisis of antagonism arises with the young child because within the active tendencies of the child there are already operative the desire and the tendency to communicate and be communicated with. By taking advantage of them the problem of reconciling present experience with social values and with preparation for future social requirements is met almost without consciousness that there is a problem.

Much of the practical difficulty and conflict that exist is due to a false idea of the definiteness and fixity of the desires and interest of childhood. When children are asked in an overt way what they want or what they would like to do, they are usually forced into a purely artificial state and the result is the deliberate creation of an undesirable habit. It is the business of the educator to study the tendencies of the young so as to be more consciously aware than are the children themselves what the latter need and want. Any other course transfers the responsibility of the teacher to those taught. Arbitrary "dictation" is not a matter of words or of form, but consists in imposing actions that do not correspond with tendencies that can be discovered within the experience of those who are growing up. The pupil also makes an arbitrary imposition on himself when, in response to an inquiry as to what he would like, he, because of ignorance of underlying and enduring tendencies and interest, snatches at some accidental affair. On the other side, those who strongly insist upon the priority of social claims and values to present experience usually overlook the leverage they might find in the latter for an uncoerced approach to their end, and they also exaggerate the fixity of social demands. There is nothing that society itself needs more than self-reliant personalities with habits of initiative, re-adaptability, and inherent decisiveness.

From the brief survey of these three points, the conclusion follows that the mere concept of activity *in general* no longer has any definite educational value. It did have when it stood in marked contrast with quiescence and passive absorption. But we have now reached a point where the problem is to study in a discriminating way from a variety of points of view various modes of activity, and to observe their respective consequences when they are employed. Otherwise an activity program will be in danger of being a catchword used to justify all sorts of things of greatly diverging values.

There must be some kind and amount of overt doing. But in the abstract this activity may be boisterous, rowdy, thoughtless, blindly emotional, passionate, mechanical, and perfunctory, swallowed up in doing what others are doing, or the opposite. Activity may consist of a succession of more or less spasmodic, because brief and interrupted, performances, or of a consecutively developing occupation evolving over a long period. It may be suggested by external, and more or less accidental, occasions, or it may be based upon competent study of the conditions of growth and the laws of cause and effect in formation of mind and character. Let it be recognized that all existing tendencies are multiple, often conflicting; that present experience is complex, containing a variety of possible values; that it is a continuous and moving thing that can be understood only by taking long sections into account where what is done now has consequences far beyond immediate tangible and visible ones; that what can be seen is valuable only as a sign of a slow development not itself perceptible; and then the principle of activity will take its place in its just perspective within the whole educational scheme.

Education and the Social Order

It is significant that the great movement for tax-supported public education had its strong impetus in the thirties of the nineteenth century, a time of general economic depression. For the fact is not wholly a coincidence. Labor leaders were among the chief backers of the movement. This is not the place for a review of the positive accomplishments of the movement. They are familiar and are often eulogized, and not without just reason. In many of the States of the Union Huxley's ladder from the kindergarten through the university is an established fact. But now, a century later, in the midst of a still greater economic crisis, there is again a period of a new educational demand and unrest. It is a time to take stock and to consider why and how the existing educational system has failed to meet the needs of the present and the imminent future.

Part of the reason is found in the educational tradition itself. Elementary schooling was everywhere in the past devoted to the promotion of literacy. It was identified with acquiring skill in reading, writing and figuring. Our ancestors would have been possessed of uncanny insight and imagination if they had thought of the purpose of the common school in any other than traditional terms. Higher education was almost equally controlled by concern for symbols, namely, advanced mathematics and foreign languages.

The Pioneer Era

Moreover, aside from the tradition of the schools, there were especial reasons for the emphasis put upon elementary lit-

[First published as a pamphlet by the League for Industrial Democracy (New York, 1934), 16 pp.]

eracy in this country. The "Three Rs" are at all times the tools for introduction into higher studies; they have to be mastered if further initiation is to occur. And there were definite industrial and political causes for emphasis upon them in pioneer America. Manhood suffrage was becoming general. A mass of illiterate voters was an obvious menace. Industrialization was commencing, and the shop worker had a greater need for letters than the agrarian peasant of the Old World. Above all the idea of opportunity was in the social atmosphere. Ambition that children should have a better chance than their parents was almost universal. The mastery of letters was the open sesame. Sparse pioneer communities had few cultural facilities. Reading matter was scanty and yet was the only means of access to the world's culture. The legend of Abraham Lincoln poring over his books by the light of the candle is an authentic symbol of the general reverence for letters.

The social and intellectual climate inevitably strengthened the old type of school education. For life outside the school, at least until after the Civil War, provided abundant opportunity for "practical" education. Many industries were still domestic, and the village had its quota of small shops combining hand work with elementary machine processes. Moreover, unlike the modern big factory, the processes were open to view as well as simple and readily understood. The young people as they grew up "learned by doing." They participated in what was going on practically, as well as by observation and in imagination. What is now called vocational education took care of itself to a large extent by the force of conditions in the home, farm and shop; this fact operated to reinforce the traditional devotion of the school to letters.

Educational Discipline

The method and the aim of education corresponded to the conditions. The method was essentially inculcation—stamping in, in its literal sense. The main material of study was foreign and in a sense artificial. Dogberry to the contrary notwithstanding, reading and writing do not come by nature. Symbols are remote and alien, even when the material they convey are as familiar as "the cat on the mat." Imposition, accompanied by penalties for non-compliance and rewards for submission, was upon the whole the acknowledged method. Pioneer life outside the school contained enough stimulus to free movement and personal initiative to confirm the traditional idea that youth was averse to learning. Thus habits bred outside school created conditions inside the school that made recourse to external imposition and enforced receptivity seem necessary. The traditional notion of "discipline" was developed under these circumstances. The little red school-house of our ancestors was a struggle of wits and often of main strength between pupils and teachers.

Individual Success

The motivation, however, among the abler students was distinctly the appeal to getting on in the world, material success. In this respect, school conditions were in harmony with conditions out of school, however much they were unlike in other respects. With a sparse population and seemingly unlimited natural resources, the appeal to personal ambition was almost boundless. There were always new lands awaiting the enterprising, and mechanical invention was constantly opening new opportunities. The social situation produced by the developing process of industrialization was radically different from that of the saturated industrialization we now have.

In his *The American Road to Culture*, Dr. Counts has summarized the conditions that produced the distinctively American system of schools. One chapter has the significant title: *Individual Success*. It opens with these words: "There is no principle that is more characteristic of the American theory and mode of life and that has played a larger part in shaping the development of the American educational system than the principle of individual success." Under the conditions just alluded to, while the possibility that any school boy might become President was actually appealed to, for the most part "success" was identified with economic advancement. Political ambition was satisfied for the most part through becoming the local party boss, or, more important, controlling by means of pecuniary power the party bosses.

Nor was the energy thus stimulated wholly selfish. Rugged individualism was not always a myth, nor were enterprise, initiative, sturdiness and personal thrift always such as to depress other members of the community. The country needed capital for its development of natural resources. Individualistic energy rendered real service to the community and the contrast between the lazy and idle, the thrifty and the ne'er-do-well had a genuine moral significance.

But educationally the important point is that the spirit of getting ahead and the idea that personal advancement was the best way to "serve the community" pervaded the school. It furnished the common ideal and operated as the dominant motive. And under the method of indoctrination which prevailed it became the chief article in the moral and economic faith that was inculcated. It would be a great mistake to read back the situation of the last twenty years or so, and suppose that this indoctrination was the deliberate act of a capitalist class bent on securing its own supremacy.

The common faith was the cult of individual success by means of individual effort. Indoctrination is always most successful when it is both unconsciously given and unconsciously received. When indoctrination was the prevailing method in all subjects, the only cause for surprise would be if it had not been resorted to in promoting the gospel of individual salvation, worldly as well as other-worldly. And in this moral field, it fell in line with the influences of everyday life outside the school, instead of going contrary as it did in most other subjects. Pupils were already inoculated by the atmosphere they breathed. The school enabled the germs to flourish and to make the ideal conscious.

Educational Change

Needless to say, I have been speaking of the pioneer phase of the schools—of the period before the industrial expansion that was stimulated by the Civil War and its aftermath, and which acquired a momentum during the nineties of the last century that swept all before it. The last forty years have been a time of constant educational change. Most teachers are honestly bewildered when they are charged with conservatism or reactionary tendencies in their field. They can point in rebuttal to changes in their own school buildings that, compared with the curriculum and methods of a generation ago, seem nothing short of revolutionary.

Relations of teacher and pupils have been humanized to a large extent. Older methods of "discipline" have been abolished or fallen into disuse. Much greater provision for activity within the school has been made in compensation for the curtailments enforced outside the school. Indoctrination in the school subjects has become more skilful and sugar-coated. Above all, new subjects and new courses of study have been introduced with almost startling rapidity. The world has never seen such a growth of school population in secondary and college education as in this country in the last forty years. School expansion in subjects, in courses, open to students and in numbers of students has kept pace with the industrial expansion.

Nevertheless there has been no fundamental change in spirit and motivation. Indeed, as industry and trade have expanded and wealth and the opportunities for enjoyment and power offered have grown the individualistic philosophy of success and material advancement has also grown. The current psychology of the people has been capitalistic far beyond the confines of the capitalists. It has permeated not only farmers but the working class. Indeed, while some of the more idealistic immigrants have come here because of anticipated blessings of liberty, the great mass came because they identified liberty with an opportunity for material advancement of themselves, their children and children's children.

The persistence of the earlier psychological and moral motivation has given the many sweeping educational changes to which I have referred a rather external character. Apart from change in basic attitudes, no thoroughgoing re-organization is possible. Indeed, the very addition of new subjects, going on as continually as it has done, has itself produced an educational problem.

It is a common complaint that there is multiplication of studies to the point of confusion and congestion, with the result of constant danger of superficiality and miscellaneous scattering, so that students get a smattering of many subjects and a thorough mastery of none. The situation is a reflex of social aimlessness and dispersiveness. A society that is largely held together by the aim of many individuals to get on as individuals is not really held together at all. Changes occur with breathless rapidity, but they have little organization and next to no centre and unified tendency. The curriculum of the schools reflects that situation.

The Need for a Social Purpose

The argument, which is that of history itself, indicates the present dilemma, the present choice that must be made, and the present opportunity. There is only one way out of the existing educational confusion and drift. That way is the definite substitution of a social purpose, controlling methods of teaching and discipline and materials of study, for the traditional individualistic aim. And, in the schools as in society generally, that change will signify more genuine development of individuality for the mass of individuals. For, in the first place, it signifies the substitution of methods of inquiry and mutual consultation and discussion for the methods of imposition and inculcation. I do not wish to imply that this method still exists in all its ancient force. In fact, teachers have worked out the technique already for the method that needs to be substituted.

But the new method is not widely used and is still, even when employed, definitely limited in its range of application, and for two reasons. One of them concerns the emphasis that is put upon getting things under discussion settled, or in the vocabulary of the teacher making sure that pupils get the "right answer." It is impossible, I think, to exaggerate the hold that this attitude has upon teaching in the schools. Problems are brought up but only that they may be solved and put to bed. There is current the opinion that the only alternative to this course is to leave students' minds in a state of confusion. To some extent such is the result, but it is mainly because they have already been imbued through texts and teachers with the notion there is already in existence the "right" answer to every question that is brought up.

The Need for Curiosity

The real alternative to settling questions is not mental confusion, but the development of a spirit of curiosity that will keep the student in an attitude of inquiry and of search for new light. If the result is simply to leave the student with the idea that there are two sides to the question and that there is a great deal to be said on both sides, the effect may be only a new version of the right answer affair; there are now two sides instead of just one. But the open mind is a nuisance if it is merely passively open to allow anything to find its way into a vacuous mind behind the opening. It is significant only as it is the mark of an actively searching mind, one on the alert for further knowledge and understanding. The basic trouble with much teaching, which on some grounds is excellent, is that it does not create wants in the mind, wants in the sense of demands that will go on operating on their own initiative.

This fact brings me to the other reason why the method of external imposition is only scotched, not killed. We live in a world that is changing, not settled and fixed. Even the best established of the natural sciences, physics, is full of unsolved questions and charged with rapid change. But the obvious matter is that the social world is in a state of flux, and that we go on teaching as if the Constitution and our forefathers had finally determined all important social and political questions—a method that leaves pupils later in life ready victims of propaganda and publicity agents. Method is relative to subject-matter and not much of the subject-matter of actual economic and social facts and forces finds its way into even the average high-school.

In short we teach the doings and impart the skills of the past, and severely leave alone the forces of the present that are creating the future in which the graduates of our schools will some day find themselves. We educate for a static social order which does not exist. We educate for the *status quo* and when the students go forth they do not find anything so settled that it can be called any thing of a static kind. What I have said about studying the past does not apply alone nor even chiefly to history. In general the students are concerned to learn the *achievements* of the past, whether it be history, geography, arithmetic, science or civics. They do not learn how these achievements were brought about nor do they learn the relation of the present to these achievements.

Shall We Indoctrinate?

There is a small but growing number of educators who think the remedy for the drift and aimlessness, which undoubtedly results, is to pursue a policy of deliberate indoctrination on the basis of a new social order. They are perhaps moved by what is going on in European countries where the schools are a definite instrumentality of promoting new social and economic orders. They are doing a valiant work in arousing teachers to think more about existing conditions, and in exposing the kind and amount of indoctrination for a reactionary social order that now goes on in the schools. I should not wish any words of mine to encourage teachers in a state of complacency and lethargy, and I fear that considerable opposition to the group in question proceeds from just such sources. But I think it ignores the fact that indoctrination for a new order works in European countries just because a great change has already taken place in their political structures; that, as I have already said, indoctrination works inevitably and smoothly when it is in line with what is already largely taken for granted in a community. There is an important difference between education *with respect to a new social order* and indoctrination into settled convictions about that order.

The New Social Order and Educators

The first activity in my judgment is necessary. Even with respect to conditions inside the schools themselves, it is the surest way out of present overloading and aimlessness. But from the standpoint of preparation for taking part in *directing* the changes that are going on anyway to a desirable end it is even more necessary. The first great step, as far as subject-matter and method are concerned, is to make sure of an educational system that informs students about the present state of society in a way that enables them to understand the conditions and forces at work. If only this result can be accomplished, students will be ready to take their own active part in aggressive participation in bringing about a new social order.

Organize the Teachers

The above statements are general in character. More specifically I would urge organization of teachers in connection with the Federation of Labor. Teachers in the public schools are public servants. Those who engage and dismiss them have great power. It is often exercised irresponsibly, and in many places there is a process of subtle or overt pressure and even intimidation. In order to get courage to revise instruction, teachers need the active support not only of organization among themselves but in connection with the elements of the community that have common ends with them and that are already organized. The depression has hit the teachers and the children of the country with great severity. Business interests concerned with reducing their own load of taxation have been active in measures of so-called economy that are crippling public education. Teachers have learned that they are in the wage-earning class. They are now more ready than in the past to act in behalf of a change of conditions that, in protecting the wage-earner, will also protect not merely their personal interests but the youth of the country and the future of society. The opportunity must be taken advantage of and teachers with social insight should take the lead.

Economic Illiteracy

Secondly, teachers and administrators should undertake among themselves organization for the study of economics and social problems. Economic illiteracy prevails throughout the country and it exists among educators. It would do no harm to declare a temporary moratorium on technical professional discussions. For the last twenty years, the attention of teachers has been directed almost exclusively to matters of psychological techniques. The effect has been to divert their thought and study from the social relations of public education. The emphasis should be decidedly changed. The most direct way of effecting this change is for socially progressive teachers to start upon a course of economic education of themselves and others. This can be done through formation of voluntary groups and through use of the stated teachers' meetings.

The School as a Cooperative Community

In the third place, educators should move steadily toward organization of the school itself as a cooperative community. The individualistic trend of education—in the narrow sense of individualism—has stimulated the use of competitive methods and appeals in the schools. The unconscious effect of these methods in conditioning students for a dying and bankrupt social regime is greater than the conscious result. Mere instruction that is not accompanied with direct participation in school affairs upon a genuine community basis will not go far. As far as possible, especially among high-school and college students, this participation should extend beyond the school and include an active part in some phases of the larger community life. Re-organization upon a cooperative basis should not be confined, moreover, to pupils. It should extend to administration so that oligarchical management from above may be abolished.

Adult Education

These considerations lead, in the fourth place, to the importance of continuing education. Social and industrial conditions are so complex that it is absurd to expect boys and girls who leave their schools in great numbers at the ages of fourteen and fifteen to be prepared for intelligent and active citizenship. The subject of adult education is now a live topic. Some hundreds of thousands of adults have already been reached by state and federal aid. The latter was designed primarily to give employment to thousands of teachers who were among the unemployed. But there is a start that should not be allowed to lose momentum. Adult education should be construed broadly enough to include the education of all youth after leaving their regular schools.

Moreover, it should not be too technical and narrowly vocational. I do not mean that every opportunity should not be afforded for reeducation away from occupational lines which have led into blind alleys. But I mean that the continuing education should also provide for adequate instruction for a new type of citizenship in which political questions will be seen in their economic background and bearings.

Fifth, all of these considerations reach their culmination in re-organization of subject-matter of study and methods upon a directly social basis and with a social aim. The new program remains to be worked out in detail. It can only be brought about by cooperative discussion and effort among a great multitude of teachers. But there are already some schools in the country that are genuine community centres and in which the influence of the school ramifies to take in the main interests of the community in such things as nutrition, health, recreation, etc. In a few cases, the influence has affected the industrial pursuits of the community. There are other schools, more of them in number, in which cooperative technique in instruction and learning and in administration and discipline have been highly developed. Too often, however, these schools have remained rather insulated from the larger community, and the influence of their changes in scholastic methods is thereby limited. In order to secure lasting improvements in education, parents and the leaders in community life must also be educated to move in unison with changes within the school.

Education vs. Dictatorship

I have referred to the dispersion and aimlessness of education in the schools. The needed unification can be obtained only as all subjects are organized with reference to their bearing upon the direction of social life. Social planning can be had only by means approaching dictatorship unless education is socially planned. That instruction in science, history, geography, etc., can be more vital as well as more coherent by relating it to actual social movements, forces and need is an idea that has still to be worked out. Unless the idea is carried into the concrete material and methods of the schools, the work of the latter will remain scattered and diffuse. For this reason, school education if not re-organized, will tend toward the perpetuation of present disorder and social chaos.

I do not think that the re-organization upon a social basis with a social aim can be accomplished over-night. For this reason I have dwelt upon the importance of re-education of teachers and administrators. But the opportunity was never so great nor the emergency so pressing as at present. If an organized movement can be initiated it will gain momentum and power with a rapidity truly surprising. The essential thing is that educators should actively recognize the need and opportunity.

Character Training for Youth

There is a good deal of alarm just now at what seems to be a deterioration of character among the young. There is a growing increase of juvenile criminality. Revelations of breach of trust and shady practices among men the community had looked up to as leaders have led to questioning of the value of the education they received when they were young. The prevalence of racketeering has added to the force of the question. In consequence, many persons are blaming the school for inattention to the importance of moral education. There are many who demand that systematic moral and religious instruction be introduced into the schools.

How far are the charges against the schools justified?

What is the place of the schools in the moral education of the young?

Anyone interested in these questions should be clear about at least two things. In the first place, the roots of character go deep and its branches extend far. Character means all the desires, purposes, and habits that influence conduct. The mind of an individual, his ideas and beliefs, are a part of character, for thought enters into the formation of desires and aims. Mind includes imagination, for there is nothing more important than the nature of the situations that fill imagination when a person is idle or at work. If we could look into a person's mind and see which mental pictures are habitually entertained we should have an unsurpassed key to his character. Habits are the fibre of character, but there are habits of desire and imagination as well as of outer action.

The second point follows from the first. Just because character is such an inclusive thing, the influences that shape it are equally extensive. If we bear this fact in mind when we ask what the schools are doing and can do in forming character, we shall not expect too much from them. We shall realize that at best the schools can be but one agency among the very many that are active in forming character. Compared with other influences that shape desire and purpose, the influence of the school is neither constant nor intense. Moral education of our children is in fact going on all the time, every waking hour of the day and three hundred and sixty-five days a year. Every influence that modifies the disposition and habits, the desires and thoughts of a child is a part of the development of his character.

In contrast with their power, the school has the children under its influence five hours a day, for not more than two hundred days a year (on the average much less), and its main business is teaching subject-matter and promoting the acquisition of certain skills, reading, writing, figuring, that from the children's standpoint have little to do with their main interests. The information given is largely from books, is remote from daily life, and is mainly committed to memory for reproduction in recitations rather than for direct manifestation in action outside the school. Industry, promptness, and neatness are indeed insisted upon, but even the good habits formed in these matters are so specialized that their transfer over into out-of-school matters is largely a matter of accident. Because the material is remote, the effect on character is also remote.

In short, formation of character is going on all the time; it cannot be confined to special occasions. Every experience a child has, especially if his emotions are enlisted, leaves an impress upon character. The friends and associates of the growing boy and girl, what goes on upon the playground and in the street, the newspapers, magazines, and books they read, the parties and movies they attend, the presence or absence of regular responsibilities in the home, the attitude of parents to each other, the general atmosphere of the household—all of these things are operating pretty constantly. And their effect is all the greater because they work unconsciously when the young are not thinking of morals at all. Even the best conscious instruction is effective in the degree in which it harmonizes with the cumulative result of all these unconscious forces.

Character, in short, is something that is *formed* rather than something that can be taught as geography and arithmetic are taught. Special things about character can be taught, and such teaching is important. It is usually given, both at home and in school, when something is done that is irregular and is disapproved. The child is disobedient, quarrelsome, has shirked doing some assigned task, has told a lie, etc. Then his attention is called to some specific moral matter. Even so, a great deal depends upon the way this moral instruction is managed. Reproof may be given in such a way that dislike of all authority is inculcated. Or a child develops skill in evasion and in covering up things that he knows are disapproved of.

Negativism, fear, undue self-consciousness often result. Consequently the net effect of even direct moral instruction cannot be foretold, and its efficacy depends upon its fitting into the mass of conditions which play unconsciously upon the young.

A few of the indirect forces may be noted by way of illustration. Recent investigations, conducted with scientific care, have shown that many boys and girls have been stimulated in unwholesome ways by the movies. Parents in good homes are likely to underestimate the influences of the movies upon children coming from other kinds of homes. The influence of movies upon children is fixed by the general tone and level of the child's surroundings.

A boy or girl from a cramped environment that provides few outlets reacts very differently from one in which the movie is not the main vent for romance, and for acquaintance with conditions very different from those that habitually surround him. The luxury of scenes depicted on the screen, the display of adventure and easy sex relations, inoculate a boy or girl living in narrow surroundings with all sorts of new ideas and desires. Their ambitions are directed into channels that contrast vividly with actual conditions of life. The things that a boy or girl from a well-to-do and cultivated home would discount or take simply as part of a show are for other children ideals to be realized—and without especial regard for the means of their attainment. The little moral at the close has no power compared with the force of desires that are excited.

A child who is one of a family of from four to six or seven children living in two rooms in a congested tenement district lives also on a congested street. The father is away most of the day and comes home tired from monotonous work. The mother, needless to say, has no servant. The children are under foot save when at school. They are "naughty" and scolded in the degree in which they get in her way or make added work. The street is their natural outlet and the mother gets relief in the degree they are out of the two rooms of the home. The effect of such conditions in creating a type of life in which the discipline and example of the gang count much more than that of family instruction cannot be exaggerated.

The homes of many of the well-to-do suffer from opposite conditions. There is excess of luxury and deficit of responsibility, since the routine of the household is cared for by servants.

To "pass the buck" and to find "alibis" is natural to all of us. When the public is faced by the sum total of the bad results of the conditions—of which only one or two have been selected as illustrations—a cry goes up that the schools are not doing their duty. I am not trying to set forth an alibi in turn for the schools, and I do not mean to assert that they have done and are doing all that can be done in shaping character. But take a look in imagination at the schoolroom. There are forty children there, perhaps fifty since the depression. The children are there five or five and a half hours a day. The teacher takes care of the "order" of the room, hears lessons in six or seven subjects, corrects papers, and has more or less semi-janitorial work to do. In the average schoolroom even today most of the time of the children is spent, when not reciting, in conning their textbooks, doing "sums" and other written work. They are active beings and yet have little outlet for their active impulses. How many parents would undertake to do much training of character, save of a negative and repressive sort, under such conditions?

The answer that is often given is to add one more study. Give direct instruction in morals, or in religion combined with morals. Now I cannot go into the merits and demerits of direct instruction of this sort. But it is a matter of common experience in other subjects that formal instruction often leaves no great impress. It is one thing to learn words and sentences by heart and another thing to take them to heart so that they influence action. At the best, this method has no great force in comparison with the indirect effect of conditions that are operating all the time in school and out. It is an old and true saying that example is more powerful than precept, and example is but one of the forces that act constantly on the young.

Those who are inclined to think that more of direct moral instruction would be almost a panacea for present evils usually look back to earlier times when such instruction was customary in home and school. They forget that it was effective because it was part of the general conditions and atmosphere. It was reinforced by many other things that are now lacking. It is a fallacy to suppose that the social trend and context can be radically changed and special methods be as effective as they were under other conditions.

It would be absurd to omit the effect upon the plastic and forming character of the young of the economic conditions that prevailed about them. Till recently, youth has grown up in a social atmosphere in which emphasis upon material success was enormous, both consciously and unconsciously. The fact that multitudes of persons were engaged in steady and honest industry was not sensational. Save where the young were faced with that fact in their own home and neighborhood, it did not have the effect that conspicuous cases of great financial careers exerted. And many children were faced by the fact that in their own homes, industry and honesty brought no great material reward. They came to feel that possession of money was the key to the things they most desired.

There is no great amount of tangible evidence that can be cited on this point. But the very fact that so many persons have come to think that the great thing is to "get by," and that if a person attains material success no great attention will be paid by society to the means by which he "got away" with it, should be evidence enough. If material success is glorified by current public opinion, the effect of that glorification upon the young cannot be offset by occasional moralizing from pulpit, press, teacher and parent.

In pointing out that the concrete state of social relations and activities is the most powerful factor in shaping character, I do not wish it inferred that I think schools have no responsibility and no opportunity. The conclusion to be drawn is that the schools are only one among many factors, and that their shaping influence will be most helpful when it falls in line with social forces operating outside the schools.

I think the depression has had one healthy effect. It has led to a more general questioning of the primacy of material values. Events have disclosed the demoralizing effect of making success in business the chief aim of life. But I think that still greater economic reconstruction must take place before material attainment and the acquisitive motive will be reduced to their place. It is difficult to produce a cooperative type of character in an economic system that lays chief stress upon competition, and wherein the most successful competitor is the one who is the most richly rewarded and who becomes almost the social hero and model. So I should put general economic change as the first and most important factor in producing a better kind of education for formation of character.

As long as society does not guarantee security of useful work, security for old age, and security of a decent home and of opportunity for education of all children by other means than acquisition of money, that long the very affection of parents for their children, their desire that children may have a better opportunity than their parents had, will compel parents to put great emphasis upon getting ahead in material ways, and their example will be a dominant factor in educating children.

As I have already intimated, better education of parents would be a large element in bringing about better moral education of children and youth. Psychology is still in its infancy. But the increase of knowledge of human nature, and of how it develops and is modified, has grown enormously in the last generation. It has grown especially with respect to how relations between persons—between parents with respect to each other and with respect to their offspring—affect character. The important movement for parental education has developed out of this increase of knowledge. But there are still multitudes of parents who have not had the most rudimentary contact with the new knowledge and who are totally unaware of the influences that are most powerfully affecting the moral fibre of their children.

I would put parental education second among the factors demanded in the improvement of character education.

In recent years there has been great advance in provision of recreation for the young, and yet hardly more than a beginning in comparison with what remains to be done. There are regions in New York City where "cellar clubs" flourish and are attended by school boys and girls. There are large regions in which, in spite of the efforts of social settlements, public playgrounds, and school fields, the great mass of growing youth resort to the streets for an outlet in the day time, and to dance halls, movies, and the like, in the evening.

The two dominant impulses of youth are toward activity and toward some kind of collective association. Our failure to provide for these two impulses, under the changed conditions of rural as well as city life, is at least a partial measure of why we are getting unsatisfactory results in character development.

If I put the school fourth and last it is not because I regard it as the least important of factors in moral training but because its success is so much bound up with the operation of the three others. I shall mention only two changes that would help. Few schools are organized on a social basis. Moral instruction through conference and discussion would be much more effective if it grew out of concrete situations present in the experience of the young instead of centering about general discussions of virtues and vices in the abstract. The more the school is organized as a community in which pupils share, the more opportunity there is for this kind of discussion and the more surely it will lead to the problems of larger social groupings outside the school. Moreover, such organization would give practice in the give and take of social life, practice in methods of cooperation, and would require assumption of definite responsibilities on the part of the young people—adapted of course to their age and maturity.

The other change is provision of greater opportunity for positive action, with corresponding reduction of the amount of passivity and mere absorption that are still current. The latter style of school organization and instruction involves a degree of suppression that stimulates unguided and unruly activity as compensation beyond the school walls. It does not arouse tastes and desires that would be followed up in constructive ways outside the school. It leaves boys and girls, especially those more active by nature, an easy prey to mere excitement.

In short, as far as schools are concerned, the present interest in more effective character education may have two different results. If it is satisfied by merely adding on a special course for direct instruction in good behavior, I do not think it can accomplish much. If it leads public attention to the changes that are needed in the schools in order that they may do more to develop intelligent and sturdy character in the young, it may well be the beginning of a most important movement.

It seems to me especially important that organizations of business and professional men should exercise an influence along the lines mentioned. They have already done a great deal in promoting the growth of the playground movement. They can determine to a great extent the treatment of delinquents, with respect to both prevention and cure. They are in a better position than any other one class to realize what slums and bad housing do to foster juvenile criminality. They can exercise a powerful influence upon the kind of movies that are shown in the community. Instead of throwing their powerful influence for so-called economy measures that eliminate provision for activity in lines of useful work in the schools, retaining only the driest and most formal subjects, they can effectively cooperate with school authorities to promote school subjects that give a healthy outlet to those impulses for activity that are so strong in the young. Through active parent associations they can bring more of the outside world into the school, breaking down that isolation of the school room from social life which is one of the chief reasons why schools do not do more effective work in the formation of character.

The Need for a Philosophy of Education

"Progressive education" is a phrase at least of contrast with an education predominantly static in subject-matter, authoritarian in methods, and mainly passive and receptive from the side of the young. But the philosophy of education must go beyond any method of education that is formed by way of contrast, reaction, and protest, as an attempt to discover what education *is* and how it takes place. Only as identified with schooling does a definition of actual education seem simple, though such definition gives the only criterion for judging and directing the work of schools.

Some suppose that the philosophy of education should tell what education *should* be and set up ideals and norms for it. In a sense this proposition is true, but not in the sense usually implied. For the only way of deciding what education should be, and which does not take us too far away from actual conditions and from tangible processes, is discovery of what actually takes place when education really occurs. Any ideal that is a genuine help in carrying on activity must rest upon a prior knowledge of concrete actual occurrences. A metallurgist's ideal of the best possible steel must rest upon knowledge of actual ores and of natural processes. Otherwise his ideal is not a directive idea but a fantasy.

So too with the ideal of education as affecting the philosophy of education we have to know how human nature is constituted in the concrete just as the steel-worker has to know about his raw material, to know about the working of actual social forces and about the operations through which basic raw materials are

[First published in *New Era in Home and School* 15 (November 1934): 211–14, from an address to the South African Education Conference in Capetown and Johannesburg, July 1934.]

modified into things of greater value. The need for a philosophy of education is thus fundamentally the need for finding out what education really *is*. We have to take those cases in which we find there is a real development of desirable powers, find out how this development took place, and then project what has taken place as a guide for directing our other efforts. The need for this discovery and this projection is the need for a philosophy of education.

What then is education when we find actual satisfactory specimens of it in existence? Firstly, it is a process of development—of growth, and the *process*, not merely the end result, is important. A truly healthy person is not something fixed and completed. He is one who through his processes and activities will continue to be healthy. He cannot say "I am healthy" and stop at that as if health were bound to continue automatically, otherwise he would soon find himself ill. Similarly, an educated person has the power to go on and get more education, to grow and to expand his development. Hence sometimes learned, erudite persons, as having parted with the capacity to grow, are not educated.

What is growth? What is development? Early philosophers, like Rousseau and his followers, made much use of the analogy of the development of a seed into the full-grown plant, deducing the conclusion that in human beings there are latent capacities which, left to themselves, will ultimately flower and bear fruit. So they framed the notion of a *natural* development, as far as possible left alone, as opposed to a directed growth, direction here being an interference resulting in distortion and corruption of natural powers.

This idea has two fallacies. In the first place seed-growth is limited as compared with human growth; its future is much more prescribed by its antecedent nature; its line of growth is comparatively fixed; it has not the capacities for growth in different directions toward different outcomes characteristic of the human young, which is also, if you please, a seed embodying germinal powers but may develop any of many forms.

This fact suggests the second fallacy. Even the seed of a plant does not grow simply of itself without atmospheric aids. Its development is controlled by external conditions and forces. Native inherent forces must interact with external if there is to be life and development. In brief, development, even with a plant, depends on the *kind of interaction* between itself and its environment. A stunted oak, or a stalk of maize with few ears of scattered grains, exhibits natural development as truly as the noblest tree or the prize-winning ear of maize. The difference in result is due not only to native stock but also to environment; the finest native stock would come to an untimely end, or give a miserable product, if its own energies could not interact with favourable atmospheric conditions.

There being two factors involved in any interaction (and hence in every kind of growth) the idea and ideal of education must take account of both. Native capacities of growth and inherent traits provide the raw material. What is lacking cannot interact with even the very best of conditions; there is then no leverage, nothing with which to cooperate. Traditional school methods and subject-matter fail in three ways to take this factor into account. In the first place, they ignore the *diversity* of capacities and needs of different human beings which constitute *individuality*. They virtually assume that, for purposes of education, all human beings are as much alike as peas in a pod, hence their provision of a uniform curriculum, the same lessons assigned for all, and the same conduct of the recitation.

In the second place, they fail to recognize that the *initiative* in growth comes from the needs and powers of the pupil. The *first* step in the interaction for growth comes from the reaching out of the tentacles of the individual, from an effort, at first blind, to procure the materials that his potentialities demand if they are to come into action and find satisfaction. With the body, hunger and power of taking and assimilating food are the first necessities. Without the inner demand and impetus the most nutritious food is offered in vain; repulsion and indigestion result. No proper system of education could tolerate the common assumption, that the mind of the individual is naturally averse to learning, and has to be either browbeaten or coaxed into action. Every mind, even of the youngest, is naturally seeking for those modes of active operation within the limits of its capacities. The problem is to discover what tendencies are especially seeking expression at a particular time and just what materials and methods will serve to evoke and direct a truly educative development.

The practical counterpart of this failure to see the source of initiative lies in the method of imposition by the teacher and of reception by the pupil. The idea of drill is only too suggestive of drilling a hole into a hard and resistant rock by means of repeated monotonous blows. Unwillingness to learn naturally follows failure to take into account tendencies urgent in the existing make-up of an individual. All sorts of external devices then are needed to achieve absorption and retention of imposed subject-matter and skills. This method of teaching may be compared to inscribing records upon a passive phonograph disc to secure their return when the proper button is pressed. Or again the pupil's mind is treated as an empty cistern passively waiting to be filled, while teacher and text-book form the reservoir from which pipelines lead.

The third failure is the result of the two already mentioned. Every teacher must observe that there *are* real differences among pupils. But, because these are not carried back to concrete differences of individuality in needs, in desires, in direction of native interest, they are too often generalized under two main heads. Some pupils are bright, others dull and stupid! Some are docile and obedient, others unruly and troublesome! Inability to fit into a cast-iron scheme of subject-matter or to meet the requirements of the set discipline is taken as a sign of either radical intrinsic incapacity or deliberate wilfulness. Conformity then becomes the criterion of judgment in spite of the value of initiative, originality and independence in life.

While the raw material and the starting-point of growth are found in native capacities, the environing conditions to be furnished by the educator are the indispensable means of their development. They are not, and do not of themselves decide, the end. A gardener, a worker of metals, must observe and pay attention to the properties of his material. If he permits these properties in their original form to dictate his treatment, he will not get *anywhere*. If they decide his end, he will fixate raw materials in their primitive state. Development will be arrested, not promoted. He must bring to his consideration of his material an idea, an ideal, of possibilities not realized, which must be in line with the constitution of his plant or ore; it must not do violence to them; it must be *their* possibilities. Yet it cannot be extracted from any study of their present form but from seeing them imaginatively, reflectively, and hence from another source.

Similarly with the educator, save that the demand on him for imaginative insight into possibilities is greater. The gardener and worker in metals may take as their measures results already achieved with plants and ores, although originality and invention will introduce some variation. But the true educator while using results already accomplished cannot make them his final and complete standard. Like the artist he has the problem of creating something that is not the exact duplicate of some previous creation.

In any case, development and growth involve change and modification in definite directions. A teacher, under the supposed sanction of the idea of cultivating individuality, may fixate a pupil more or less at his existing level, confusing respect for individual traits with a catering for their present estate. Respect for individuality is primarily the *intellectual* study of the individual to discover material. With this sympathetic understanding the *practical* work then begins of modification, of changing, of reconstruction continued without end. The change must at least be toward more effective techniques, greater self-reliance, a more thoughtful and inquiring disposition more capable of persistent effort in meeting obstacles.

Some would-be progressive schools and teachers in their reaction from the method of external imposition stop short with the recognition of the importance of giving free scope to native capacities and interests. They do not examine closely or long enough what these may actually be; they judge too much from superficial and transitory reactions to accidental circumstances. In the second place, they are inclined to take the evident individual traits as finalities instead of as possibilities for suitable direction into something of greater significance. Under the alleged sanction of not violating freedom and individuality the responsibility for providing development conditions is overlooked. The idea persists that evolution and development are simply matters of automatic unfolding from within.

This is a natural reaction from the manifest evils of external imposition. But there is a radically different alternative between thinking of the young as clay to be moulded into traditional patterns and thinking of existing capacities and present interests and desires as laying down the whole law of development. Existing likes and powers are to be treated as possibilities necessary for any healthy development. But development involves a point of direction as well as a starting-point with constant movement in that direction, and the direction-point, as the temporary goal, is reached only as the starting-point of further reconstruction. The great problem of the educator is to see intellectually, and to feel deeply, the forces moving in the young as possibilities, as signs and promises, and to interpret them in the light of what they may become. Nor does the exacting task end there: it is bound up with the judging and devising of the conditions, the materials, the tools—physical, moral, and social—which will, once more by *interaction* with existing powers and preferences, bring about the desired transformation.

The old education emphasised the necessity for provision of definite subject-matter and activities, which *are* necessities for right education. The weakness was that its imagination did not go beyond provision of a rigid environment of subject-matter drawn from sources remote from any concrete experiences of the taught. Its conception of techniques was derived from the conventions of the past. The New Education needs more attention, not less, to subject-matter and to progress in technique for getting satisfactory results. More does not, however, mean more in quantity of the same old kind but an imaginative vision, which sees that no prescribed and ready-made scheme can determine the exact subject-matter for the educative growth of each individual, since each sets a new problem and calls for at least a somewhat different emphasis in either subject-matter or angle of presentation. Only blindly obtuse convention supposes that the actual contents of text-books will further the educational development of all children, or of any one child, if they be regarded as the prescription of a doctor to be taken just as they are. As Louis Stevenson remarked, "the world is full of a number of things," and no teacher can know too much or have too ingenious an imagination in selecting and adapting this and that aspect of some of the many things in the world to meet the requirements that make for growth in this and that individual.

In short, departure from the rigidity of the old curriculum is only the negative side. If we do not go on and go far in the positive direction of providing, through persistent intelligent study and experiment, a body of subject-matter much richer, more varied and flexible, and also more definite in terms of the experience of those being educated, we shall tend to leave an educational vacuum in which anything may happen. The old saying that "nature abhors a vacuum" embodies a definite truth. Complete isolation is impossible in nature. The young live in some environment constantly interacting with what the young bring to it, and the result is the shaping of their interests, minds and characters—either educatively or mis-educatively. If the professed educator abdicates his responsibility for judging and selecting the kind of environment conducive, in his best understanding, to growth, then the young are left at the mercy of all the unorganized and casual forces that inevitably play upon them throughout life. In the educative environment the knowledge, judgment, or experience of the teacher becomes a greater, not a smaller factor. He now operates not as a magistrate set on high and possessed of arbitrary authority but as a friendly co-partner and guide in a common enterprise.

There is a further truism about education as development, difficult to carry out in practice and easily violated. Development is a *continuous* process and continually signifies consecutiveness of action—the strong point of the traditional education at its best. The subject-matter of the classics and mathematics involved a consecutive and orderly development along definite lines. In the newer education it is comparatively easy to improvise, to try a little of this to-day and something else to-morrow, on the basis of some immediate stimulus but without sufficient regard to its objective or whether or not something more difficult is led up to naturally, raising new questions and calling for acquisition of more adequate technique and for new modes of skill. There is genuine need for taking account of spontaneous interest and activity but, without care and thought, it readily results in a detached multiplicity of isolated brief-lived activities or projects, not in continuity of growth. Indeed, the new educational processes require much more planning ahead by the teachers, for whom the old planning was all effected in advance by the fixed curriculum, etc.

But a sound philosophy of education also requires that the general term environment be specified as dominantly human with its values social. Through its influence each person becomes saturated with the customs, the beliefs, the purposes, skills, hopes and fears, of his own cultural group. The features of even his physical surroundings come to him through the eyes and ears of his community. His geographical, climatical, and atmospherical experiences are clothed with the memories and traditions, the characteristic associations, of his particular society. In the early stages, then, it is particularly important that subject-matter be presented in its human context and setting. Here the school often fails when, in proceeding from the concrete to the abstract, it forgets that to the child only that which has human value and function is concrete. In his nature study and geography, physical things are presented to him from the standpoint of the adult specialist as if independent and complete in themselves. But to the child these things have a meaning only as they enter into human life. Even those distinctively human products, reading and writing, whose purpose is the furthering of human communication and association, are treated as if they were subjects of and in themselves, not used as is friendly everyday speech, and so for the child they become abstract, a mystery belonging to the school but not to daily life.

The same separation of school studies from social or human setting and function deadens the traditional recitation which, instead of being a scene of friendly intercourse as are the conversations of home and of ordinary life, clarified and organised by definite purpose, becomes an artificial exercise in repeating uniformly the identical material of some one text-book and a mere test of the faithfulness of the preparation. It thus becomes a first cause of the isolation of school from out-of-school life and experience.

As the material of genuine development is that of human contacts and associations, so the end, the value that is the criterion and directing guide of educational work, is social. The acquisition however perfectly of skills is not an end in itself. They are things to be put to use as a contribution to a common and shared life. They are intended, indeed, to make an individual more capable of self-support and of self-respecting independence. But unless this end is placed in the context of services rendered to others, services which they need to the fulfilment also of their lives, skills gained will be put to an egoistic and selfish use as means of a trained shrewdness for personal advantage at the cost of others' claims and opportunities for the good life. Too often, indeed, the schools, through reliance upon the spur of competition and the bestowal of special honours and prizes as for those who excel in a competitive race or even battle, only build up and strengthen the disposition that in after-school life employs special talents and superior skill to outwit others and "get on" personally without respect for their welfare.

And as with skills acquired in school so also with knowledge gained in school. The educational end and the ultimate test of the value of what is learned is its use and application in carrying on and improving the common life of all. The background of the traditional educational system is a class society, and opportunity for instruction in certain subjects, especially literary ones, and in mathematics beyond the rudiments of simple arithmetical subjects, was reserved for the well-born and the well-to-do, and thus knowledge of these subjects became a badge of cultural superiority and social status, which marked off those who had it from the vulgar herd and for many persons was a means of self-display. Useful knowledge, on the other hand, was necessary only for those compelled by their class status to work for a living. A class stigma attached to it, and the uselessness of knowledge, save for purely personal culture, was proof of its higher quality.

Even after education in many countries was made universal for all, these standards of value persisted. There is no greater egotism than that of learning when treated simply as a mark of personal distinction to be cherished for its own sake. Yet to eliminate this quality of exclusiveness all conditions of the school environment must tend in actual practice to develop in individuals the realization that knowledge is a trust for the furthering of the well-being of all.

Perhaps the greatest need of and for a philosophy of education to-day is the urgent need that exists for making clear in idea and effective in practice the social character of its end and that the criterion of value of school practices is social.

The aim of education is development of individuals to the utmost of their potentialities. But this statement as such leaves unanswered the question of the measure of the development to be desired and worked for. A society of free individuals in which all, in doing each his own work, contribute to the liberation and enrichment of the lives of others is the only environment for the normal growth to full stature. An environment in which some are limited will always in reaction create conditions that prevent the full development even of those who fancy they enjoy complete freedom for unhindered growth.

There are two outstanding reasons why in existing world conditions a philosophy of education must make the social aim of education the central article in its creed. The world is being rapidly industrialized. Individual groups, tribes and races, once living completely untouched by the economic regime of modern capitalistic industry, now find almost every phase of their lives affected by its expansion. The principle of a report of the Geneva Commission based on a study of conditions of life of mine-Natives in South Africa holds good of peoples all over the world, "The investment of Western capital in African industries has made the Native dependent upon the demand of the world markets for the products of his labour and the resources of his continent." In a world that has so largely engaged in a mad, often brutal, race for material gain by means of ruthless competition the school must make ceaseless and intelligently organized effort to develop above all else the will for cooperation and the spirit which sees in every other individual an equal right to share in the cultural and material fruits of collective human invention, industry, skill and knowledge. The supremacy of this aim in mind and character is necessary, not merely as an offset to the spirit of inhumanity bred by economic competition and exploitation but to prepare the coming generation for an inevitable new and more just and humane society which, unless hearts and minds are prepared by education, is likely to come attended with all the evils of social changes by violence.

The other especially urgent need is connected with the present unprecedented wave of nationalistic sentiment, of racial and national prejudice, of readiness to resort to force of arms. For this spirit to have arisen on such a scale the schools must have somehow failed grievously. Their best excuse is maybe that schools and educators were caught unawares. But that excuse is no longer available. We now know the enemy; it is out in the open. Unless the schools of the world can unite in effort to rebuild the spirit of common understanding, of mutual sympathy and goodwill among all peoples and races, to exorcise the demon of prejudice, isolation and hatred, they themselves are likely to be submerged by the general return to barbarism, the sure outcome of present tendencies if unchecked by the forces which education alone can evoke and fortify.

It is to this great work that any ideal worthy of the name of education summons the educational forces of all countries.

Can Education Share in Social Reconstruction?

That upon the whole the schools have been educating for something called the *status quo* can hardly be doubted by observing persons. The fallacy in this attempt should be equally evident. There is no *status quo*—except in the literal sense in which Andy explained the phrase to Amos: a name for the "mess we are in." It is not difficult, however, to define that which is called the "*status quo*"; the difficulty is that the movement of actual events has little connection with the name by which it is called.

For the alleged *status quo* is summed up in the phrase "rugged individualism." The assumption is—or was—that we are living in a free economic society in which every individual has an equal chance to exercise his initiative and his other abilities, and that the legal and political order is designed and calculated to further this equal liberty on the part of all individuals. No grosser myth ever received general currency. Economic freedom has been either non-existent or precarious for large masses of the population. Because of its absence and its tenuousness for the majority, political and cultural freedom has been sapped; the legally constituted order has supported the ideal of *beati possidentes*.

There is no need here to review the historic change from a simple agrarian order, in which the idea of equal opportunity contained a large measure of truth, to a complex industrial order with highly concentrated economic and political control. The point is that the earlier idea and theory persisted after it had lost all relevance to actual facts, and was then used to justify and strengthen the very situation that had undermined it in practice. What then is the real *status quo*? Is it the condition of free individuality postulated by the ruling theoretical philosophy, or is it the increasing encroachment of the power of a privileged minor-

[First published in *Social Frontier* 1 (October 1934): 11–12.]

ity, a power exercised over the liberties of the mass without corresponding responsibility?

It would not be difficult to make out a case for a positive and sweeping answer in favor of the latter alternative. Let me quote, as far as schools are concerned, from Roger Baldwin. "On the whole, it may be said without question that the public schools have been handed over to the keeping of the militant defenders of the *status quo*—the Daughters of the American Revolution, the American Legion, the Fundamentalists, the Ku Klux Klan, and the War Department. Look at the twelve year record! Compulsory patriotic rites and flag saluting by law in most states; compulsory reading of the Protestant Bible in eighteen states, contrary to the provision for the separation of church and state; compulsory teaching of the Constitution by prescribed routine; making a crime of the teaching of evolution in three states; special oaths of loyalty not required of other public servants in ten states; loyalty oaths required of students as a condition of graduation in many cities; history textbooks revised under pressure to conform to prejudice; restriction or ban on teachers' unions affiliated with the labor movement; laws protecting tenure beaten or emasculated; compulsory military training in both high schools and colleges, with inevitable pressure on students and teachers by the military mind." To these forms of outward and overt pressure may be added—as indeed Mr. Baldwin does add—more powerful, because more subtle and unformulated, pressures that act constantly upon teachers and students.

It might seem then that, judged by the present situation, *limitation* upon the efforts of teachers to promote a new social order—in which the ideal of freedom and equality of individuals will be a fact and not a fiction—tremendously outweighs the element of *possibility* of their doing so. Such is not the case, however, great as are the immediate odds against effort to realize the possibility. The reason is that the actual *status quo* is in a state of flux; there *is* no *status quo*, if by that term is meant something stable and constant. The last forty years have seen in every industrialized society all over the world a steady movement in the direction of social control of economic forces. Pressure for this control of capital—or if you please for its "regimentation"—is exercised both through political agencies and voluntary organizations. Laissez faire has been dying of strangulation. Mr. Hoover, who gave currency to the phrase "rugged individualism" while President, acted repeatedly and often on a fairly large scale for governmental intervention and regulation of economic forces. The list of interferences with genuine educational freedom that has been cited is itself a sign of an effort, and often a conscious one, to stem a tide that is running in the opposite direction— that is, toward a collectivism that is hostile to the idea of unrestricted action on the part of those individuals who are possessed of economic and political power because of control of capital.

I hope the bearing of these remarks upon the theme of the limitations and the possibilities of educational effort for establishing a new social order is fairly evident. Teachers and administrators often say they must "conform to conditions" rather than do what they would personally prefer to do. The proposition might be sound if conditions were fixed or even reasonably stable. But they are not. They are highly unstable; social conditions are running in different, often opposed directions. Because of this fact the educator in respect to the relation of educational work to present and future society is constantly compelled to make a choice. With what phase and direction of social forces will he throw in his energies? The chief evil is that the choice is so often made unconsciously by accommodation to the exigencies of immediate pressure and of estimate of probability of success in carrying out egoistic ambitions.

I do not think, accordingly, that the schools can in any literal sense be the builders of a new social order. But the schools will surely, as a matter of fact and not of ideal, *share* in the building of the social order of the future according as they ally themselves with this or that movement of existing social forces. This fact is inevitable. The schools of America have furthered the present social drift and chaos by their emphasis upon an economic form of success which is intrinsically pecuniary and egoistic. They will of necessity, and again not as a matter of theory, take an active part in determining the social order—or disorder—of the future, according as teachers and administrators align themselves with the older so-called "individualistic" ideals—which in fact are fatal to individuality for the many—or with the newer forces making for social control of economic forces. The plea that teachers must passively accommodate themselves to existing conditions is but one way—and a cowardly way—of making a choice in favor of the old and the chaotic.

If the teacher's choice is to throw himself in with the forces and conditions that are making for change in the direction of social control of capitalism—economic and political—there will hardly be a moment of the day when he will not have the opportunity to make his choice good in action. If the choice is conscious and intelligent, he will find that it affects the details of school administration and discipline, of methods of teaching, of selection and emphasis in subject-matter. The educator is, even now, I repeat, making this choice, but too often is making it blindly and unintelligently. If he or she is genuinely committed to alliance with present forces that tend to develop a social order which will, through collective control and ownership, make possible a genuine and needed "rugged individualism" (in the sense of individuality) for all members of the community, the teacher will, moreover, not be content with generalities about the desired future order. The task is to translate the desired ideal over into the conduct of the detail of the school in administration, instruction, and subject-matter. Here, it seems to me, is the great present need and responsibility of those who think the schools should consciously be partners in the construction of a changed society. The challenge to teachers must be issued and in clear tones. But the challenge is merely a beginning. What does it mean in the particulars of work in the school and on the playground? An answer to this question and not more general commitment to social theory and slogans is the pressing demand.

In spite of the lethargy and timidity of all too many teachers, I believe there are enough teachers who will respond to the great task of making schools active and militant participants in creation of a new social order, provided they are shown not merely the general end in view but also the means of its accomplishment. Dr. Kandel, at the close of a somewhat scornful article as to the part of the schools in this task of social reconstruction, says of society in general: "It would welcome help from any direction to correct the existing abuses and make it true to itself; beyond that it would not permit the schools to go. If the teaching body, whose duty it is to define and interpret society's culture and ideal to the oncoming generation, undertook this much it would still be faced with a formidable task; it may lay the basis for a new social order, but society and not the teaching body will determine its particulars."

There are, in this statement, many words and phrases that I am tempted to underscore: correction of *abuses*; the *duty* of the teacher; the *basis* for a new social order; leaving *particulars* to society. But I content myself with asking what more can any educator, however "radical," want? Abuses cannot be corrected by merely negative means; they can be eliminated only by substitution of just and humane conditions. Laying the *basis*, intellectual and moral, for a new social order is a sufficiently novel and inspiring ideal to arouse a new spirit in the teaching profession and to give direction to radically changed effort. Those who hold such an ideal are false to what they profess in words when they line up with reactionaries by ridicule of those who would make the profession a reality. That task may well be left to educational fascists.

Reviews

A God or The God?

Is There a God? A Conversation, by Henry Nelson Wieman, Douglas Clyde Macintosh, and Max Carl Otto. Chicago and New York: Willett, Clark and Co., 1932.

I have found much of the discussion in these Conversations elusive and hard to follow. I have found it difficult to put my finger, intellectually speaking, on the subject under discussion. This has seemed to change without notice, and the effect is baffling. In consequence the most considerable part of my reflections has been devoted to trying to find an explanation of the trouble I have experienced in establishing a continuous identification of the subject under consideration, and I do not see how I can do better, from my standpoint, than to try to put the reader in possession of the explanation which I finally arrived at.

The conclusion may perhaps be at least suggested if I say that the difficulty seems to centre about the use of the indefinite article in the title: Is there *a* God? I should not have experienced a similar difficulty if the question were put with a definite article: Is there *the* God? For I should have known at once that the question was elliptical in form, and that some indicated context would serve to define and specify the nature of the object referred to. It might be the God of Abraham, Isaac and Jacob; of the Aristotelian metaphysics; of the Homeric Olympus; of the Athanasian Creed; of Islam; of St. Thomas Aquinas; of Spinoza's Ethics, of Rousseau's Savoyard Vicar; of Kant's Critique of Practical Reason, to mention a few of the many possibilities. In every such case, there would still be difficulty in arriving at a satisfactory answer. There would be difficulty in determining even the criteria for deciding whether a particular answer was satisfactory or not. We would be prepared to come to the discussion

[First published in *Christian Century* 50 (8 February 1933): 193–96. For Wieman's and Macintosh's reply to this review, see this volume, Appendix 3, and for Dewey's rejoinder, see this volume, pp. 223–28.]

with the expectation that different individuals and different schools would give opposed answers because they use different logics—that is to say, depend upon different rules of evidence and canons of proof. But at least the meaning of the question would be definite. It might not be completely specified down to the last detail, but the nature of the object into whose existence inquiry was made would be at least sufficiently indicated so that the subject of discourse would remain before us with reasonable unambiguity.

The question of whether *a* God exists seems to me to be at the opposite pole; to be, indeed, a question which by the very terms of its formulation invites to mental confusion. I cannot think it, therefore, an accident that so much of the discussion shifts about from one question to another. One of the two questions concerns the issue: What is the *nature* of God; what is or what must be God, in case he or it exists? And the other question, supposing an answer to the first question has been reached by way of fixation of the theme of discourse, is: Is there any being or object in existence which answers the description? The question whether *a* God exists, seems to me to invite by its very nature an undesirable scrambling together of these two very different questions.

In what has just been said I appear to be doing injustice to the position and argument of Mr. Macintosh. We are not left in doubt as to what he affirms when he affirms the being of a God. It is a "superhuman spiritual being, an essentially personal cosmic power, an intelligent loving moral mind and will," one standing in a definitely favorable relation to specifiable interests of mankind. The being indicated is not as definite as the God of Israel, but it is sufficiently close to one of the historic religious traditions to provide a reasonably unambiguous subject for discussion. There are plenty of difficulties in the way of arriving at a definite answer as to whether such a being exists. But at least we have a working idea of what we are thinking and talking about, and similarly we know what Mr. Otto intends when he expresses an "affirmative faith" in the non-existence of such a cosmic personal being.

As far as form is concerned, then, it would seem fairer to bring my charge against Mr. Wieman. It is he who insists that he wants to "formulate the idea of God so that the question of God's existence becomes a dead issue"; that he wants to prove existence only by definition; that the "question of God's existence is not a question to debate." Mr. Wieman's insistence that the only genuine question is what meaning is to be given to the term God and that it is possible to find a meaning such that existence cannot be intelligibly denied upon the whole sets the pace of the whole discussion.

I shall have to say something later concerning Mr. Wieman's particular views. But there is a general point involved in the transformation from discussion of *the* God of a particular nation, creed, confession, church, or thinker to *a* God in general, which seems to be more fundamental and more important than all the other issues put together. As the transformation affects Mr. Macintosh's position as well as Mr. Wieman's special views, I shall speak of this general point first. I suppose of all *the* gods mentioned, that of Abraham, Isaac and Jacob, is the most exactly identifiable, with the possible exception of his Moslem counterpart. Other Gods, however, have shared something of the exclusiveness which characterized the God who was a jealous God, who would not permit any other God to come before him in honor and obedience, and who selected a chosen people from among all the nations of the earth to stand for him. No one in the European religious tradition can possibly escape all memory and all effect of this unique and exclusive being and some image of him comes to mind when *a* God is spoken of. About *his* singular individuality there can be no doubt. All other Gods are false Gods; they are worse than non-existent for they deceive mankind and lead to destruction. The exclusiveness of the elect people or the church or body of believers is the visible symbol of the all-embracing jealousy of the God in question.

What the moral effect upon mankind has been of belief in this God—and descendants like him in exclusiveness of inherent rightful exactions—I shall not go into, though personally I agree with Mr. Otto that its beneficent effects have been, to put it mildly, much exaggerated. But one thing is clear. The existence or non-existence of such a God is something to get excited about. Existence makes a difference to every aspect and phase of life. Orthodox Christianity emphasized the difference thus made by projecting it into that between an everlasting state of unalloyed bliss and one of eternal damnation and suffering.

Now I seem to find a contradiction inhering in the position of those who have broken with the traditional religious machinery and landscape, and who yet insist upon the peculiar importance of belief in *a* God, and a unique importance attached to particular attitudes of worship and dependence; to special kinds of experience which are alone regarded by them as religious, because alone having to do with the unique objects which can evoke true religious attitudes. The contradiction lies in the fact that while the idea of the exclusiveness attached to traditional gods has been surrendered, while indeed the persons in question go to the opposite pole of asserting the inclusiveness and universality of God, they yet continue to envisage and to demand that limitation of human response and attitude which was appropriate to the exclusive and jealous God of Israel. They still insist upon a particular being or object, *a* God, and particular methods and channels of approach.

The reason why liberalists or modernists in religion have been forced to change their conception of God from something exclusive to something inclusive needs no extensive mention. They are those who, as Mr. Morrison indicates in his Introduction, have felt the need of coming to terms with modern secular knowledge, with science. The latter has forced a movement from the idea of a tight confined universe of which the world is the centre and crown to belief in indefinite multitudes not merely of solar systems but of universes. The exclusive and self-centered history of man on this planet with the unique importance of the drama of sin and redemption has been broadened to include an endless sweep of developments among which the story of man on this planet is but an inconsiderable incident, not the culmination of the meaning of the whole. There are, of course, millions of devoted believers in whom both conceptions still exist side by side. But anyone who has faced the full intellectual scope and depth of the change in the idea of the universe and of man's history, has no alternative but surrender of the older conception of God or else a broadening out of it to meet the change in the conception of the universe and history to which the God believed in is related. History and anthropology have moreover made clear the tribal origin and status of the exclusive God.

There is a curious change in the liberalist conception of religion which corresponds to the change just mentioned. There was a time, and not so very long ago, when *other* religions were referred to only by way of contrast with the true religion. In accord with the idea of intense jealousy and exclusiveness, these other religions were heathenish, products of the sinful will of man, and signs of his alienation from the true God. A striking trait of present liberal apologetics is the reversal which has taken place. The universality of religion, the presence among all peoples, *even* the most degraded "heathen," of some form of religious worship and belief, is now dwelt upon. As far as this broadening leads to greater tolerance and humaneness, it is of course to the good. But intellectually, it falls in with the change from *the* God to *a* God; it chimes with the use of the most colorless and indefinite word in the English language, and with the thinning down and rarifying of the meaning of the object to which the term refers.

The case of Mr. Macintosh is especially significant here, because he remains the nearest of the two theistic participants to the tradition of the western Christian world. The search for a universal inclusive foundation is marked in him, as it must be in any thinker who wishes to keep his religious faith in connection with the chief intellectual movements of modern philosophy and science. Without derogating from his originality (and most certainly not from his sincerity) it may be said he builds upon that fact which Kant found to be so comprehensive, so little exclusive, that it could be made the foundation of a rational faith in a God: the imperatives of the moral life, and the alleged rational necessity that their ultimate triumph be cosmically guaranteed. He proceeds along lines similar to those of Kant (although free from the latter's overburdened technique) to argue that our best scientific knowledge leaves us with the *permissible* idea of a cosmic personal power who is concerned in the moral development of mankind and the ultimate victory of moral ideals. And so he argues that if "moral optimism is justified, the God we need exists." From this "moral right to believe in God," Mr. Macintosh goes on to argue that "religious experience"—like the experience of the scientist with *his* realm of objects—verifies this rational and moral faith.

I am not concerned here to criticize the details of Mr. Macintosh's argument, which of course I have only roughly indicated. What I want to point out is again the enormous transformation which it marks in traditional religious faith—a change, it seems to me, not merely in content but in foundation and aim, and which therefore implies, intellectually, the necessity of going on to a totally different point of view. The first thing I would especially call attention to is the reversal involved in basing faith in God upon a fact of human existence, no matter how universal—the imperatives of the moral life and the need of faith in their ultimate triumph. I am not asking whether the facts are as universal as they are alleged to be. I am saying that the court of ultimate appeal is so changed from that of the exclusiveness of the religious tradition that one who starts to walk this road must be prepared totally to surrender old foundations and old goals. If you appeal to the moral life for your basis and direction, you must be content to derive your conceptions of religion and of God wholly from the implications of the moral life. *The question whether there is some physical or metaphysical, some existential, extraneous power working for the realization of moral demands and ideals, is totally irrelevant.* To appeal to the supremacy of moral ideals as the ground for the content of religious ideas, including that of God, and then to insist upon a God to give moral ideals external and independent support involves an inherent contradiction.

The second point is similar. After appealing to a universal fact of human life, moral obligation, Mr. Macintosh appeals to a definitely limited channel and organ of experience, denominated "religious." I cannot go into detail here, but I ask anyone to read Mr. Macintosh's "sixth cycle" and ask whether the "*right* religious adjustment" (which is said to give experimental proof of the existence of the kind of God he has asserted) is conceivable except in terms of the limited experience of the western Christian tradition—and upon the whole the still more limited Protestant evangelical version of this tradition. The "right religious adjustment" of devout Parsee, Islamite, Buddhist, Vedantist, etc., would yield other "empirical evidence." I cite the argument here as another illustration of the contradiction I find so common among religious modernists, that between an asserted universality on one hand and a definite survival on the other hand of an earlier exclusive tradition and cult. It is this contradiction which renders the position of the religious liberal one of intrinsic unstable equilibrium.

The contradiction is even more evident in the case of Mr.

Wieman. It is more evident, because he presses further in the direction of *a* God, wishing as we have already seen to institute a conception of God such that there can be no question as to existence. Mr. Wieman objects in effect to Mr. Macintosh that the latter uses God merely as a hypothesis to support and justify man's moral idealism. Mr. Macintosh might justly reply, I think, that reference to moral idealism is used as *ratio cognoscendi*, not as *ratio essendi*—that it is used as rational approach to the idea of God's existence, not as defining God's inherent nature. But however this may be, the gravamen of Mr. Wieman's charge seems to me to rebound heavily against himself. For what does he start from? The alleged need of man for something to love, adore: "the hunger in the hearts of men for something to love which is of such incomparable and unchanging worth that it becomes the glory of all human living to offer up every sacrifice and devotion in its service and adoration." This is *his* universal fact upon which rests an automatic surety of God's existence beyond all need and possibility of argument. Mr. Macintosh wants a cosmic guarantee for our moral idealism and optimism. Mr. Wieman wants an objective counterpart for human love and devotion. Of the two, the latter seems the much more subjective.

If I stopped at this point I should be rightly chargeable with doing Mr. Wieman an injustice. For Mr. Wieman insists that there is something objective which generates, supports and constitutes good; that this is the undeniable reality which we *find* in our conduct and that this something is precisely what is meant by God. But right here is where the shift in Mr. Wieman's position comes in, a shift between something altogether too universal and inclusive to be identified with any historic religion and conception of God, and something sufficiently exclusive to be linked with, say, some phase of Christian theism. The shift is between the fact that men find conditions and forces in existence which generate and sustain the goods of living, and the assertion that these things constitute a unified and single object which "*rightly* demands the supreme devotion of all human living." An intellectual self-preservative instinct makes Mr. Wieman add that by God he does "not mean merely the supreme good. I mean that but I mean more. I mean that which has a certain function in human life, namely of *commanding* this supreme devotion that is passionate, fiery and tragic." So the "most distinctive function of God is the one to adore supremely, to serve and fail, and die for," etc.

Now what I am here implying is that there is here a shift from something which we may be said intelligibly to find in experience, namely, forces making for the production and extension of goods, to something which we do *not* find: a power which *rightfully* commands the supreme and exclusive adoration, from the very human fact of love, care and service to some devotion and love of all human beings. Yet without making that shift I do not see that there is a shred of theism in Mr. Wieman's position. And to repeat once more my main point, the shift is from something too universal and inclusive in human experience to be identified with any historic religious tradition whatever, to say nothing of Christian theism, to something sufficiently "jealous" and exclusive to be an emotional carrier of one strain of traditional religious belief.

Mr. Wieman remarks that "God is a word of love and adoration and dedication. *It is not a descriptive term.*" (Italics mine.) I hope I am not placing undue dependence upon a single passage when I say that this passage contains in gist the fundamental shift and contradiction. What we find is surely the fact of objects, persons and causes which elicit devotion and dedication. But *without* God as a descriptive and identifying term there is no transition from this fact to a being (whether personal or impersonal) who is intrinsically worthful of all consuming, exclusive, jealous, love and worship. I can but think that Mr. Wieman's God rests upon hypostatization of an undeniable fact, experience of things, persons, causes, found to be good and worth cherishing, into a single objective existence, *a* God.

For the sake of brevity, my argument is undeniably abstract and formal. It can be brought to a concrete focus. Let us admit that there are in existence conditions and forces which, apart from human desire and intent, bring about enjoyed and enjoyable goods, and that the security and extension of goods are promoted by attention to and service of these conditions. Does this admitted fact throw any light whatever upon the unity and singleness of the forces and factors which make for good? If not, Mr. Wieman's argument would seem to me to amount simply to a plea that in a time of transition and disturbance many persons will find it helpful and consoling to continue to use the *word* "God" to designate what actually are a collection of forces, unified only in their functional effect: the furtherance of goods in human life. This is an intelligible position; intelligent and honest persons will differ among themselves as to the desirability of carrying over the *term*, God. Preference in this matter will depend upon many factors, temperament, education, environment, etc. But it will be plain in any case that the word is used simply to designate a multitude of factors and forces which are brought together simply with respect to their coincidence in producing one undesigned effect—the furtherance of good in human life.

If so much is agreed upon, then there may also be persons who get an added ecstasy from an emotional hypostasis, that is, by concentrating and intensifying emotion in some especial way. But it should be clear that this is a personal idiosyncracy, a personal and private privilege of enjoyment, if you will, like a capacity for peculiar enjoyment of some kinds of music or poetry on the part of some persons, but containing in it nothing authoritative or obligatory for others, containing, that is, none of the limitations as to organs, channels and objects which is characteristic of traditional religions. To put the matter from the other and positive side, those who chose *distribution* of objects of devotion, service and affection rather than hypostatic concentration of times, seasons, objects are wholly within their intellectual and moral rights. To which I would add that experience seems to me to demonstrate that for the great majority of persons this is much the saner course to follow. Ecstasy has a place, but a place which often exceeds its bounds. The result of excess on one side is the insincerity which attends all inflation beyond bounds of human measure, and on the other side it is the deprivation of moral attitudes and relationships of life of their full meed of meaning.

As far as I can see and judge, the real meaning of growth of a secularized humanism lies here. It has been influenced, of course, by the growth of new beliefs based on scientific inquiry. But the more significant thing is the expansion and distribution of valid meanings and goods through large ranges of experiences. It is impossible to confine any longer what is regarded by religionists as of authoritative value to limited and exclusive organs, channels and objects. To my mind, Mr. Wieman is one who recognizes that fact, but who is held back from realizing its full implications because in the end he is overmastered by emotional overtones derived from the earlier conception of an exclusive and jealous God.

Those who have followed to its completion the generalization of earlier ideas of the divine enjoy in countless multitudes of ways within the normal processes of living and human relationships all the goods which the theist, no matter how liberal, is still striving to confine to special types of experience and to particular objects and systems of objects. We can only invite those who are still tied down to the possession of the larger peace to be found in variety of distributed goods of experience.

Dr. Dewey Replies

Editor the *Christian Century*:

Sir: Before coming to a discussion of the replies of Drs. Wieman and Macintosh to my review of their portions of the book, *Is There a God?* I want to express my surprise at finding two things that are contained in their articles, one in each. That of Mr. Macintosh is to the effect that my attitude toward Christianity is probably colored by some untoward happening in my own early personal history. I am surprised because I thought the discussion was supposed to be a philosophical one. Since however Mr. Macintosh has introduced the matter, I will state that nothing untoward happened, and that my present attitude toward theology, various creeds and various philosophies of religion developed slowly and *pari passu* with the general maturing of my philosophic ideas.

The thing that surprises me in Mr. Wieman's article is his statement that I held that he rests his "whole case for belief in existence of God on the fact that man needs something to love, adore," and then when he finds (and in the very next paragraph) a statement which attributes to him another ground for that belief, that I am engaged in a half-hearted retraction. The simple fact is that I was so far from holding that he rests his whole case on the need of man, that I began the paragraph after the one in which I quoted Mr. Wieman on the point of man's need with the statement that if I left the matter there, I should be doing him a great injustice, while the great bulk of my article is addressed precisely to his other ground. (I shall show below however, that the second ground is more closely connected with the first than

[First published in *Christian Century* 50 (22 March 1933): 394–95. For Wieman's and Macintosh's reply, to which this is a rejoinder, see this volume, Appendix 3, and for Dewey's review, see this volume, pp. 213–22.]

Mr. Wieman realizes, as well as more than I tried to bring out in my original review.)

I shall begin in an area remote from the immediate controversy since I take it we are all more concerned with clearing up the situation than with making points against one another. Separating the matter of religious experience from the question of the existence of God (as for example those as far apart from one another as the Buddhists and the Comtean Positivists have done), I have found—and there are many who will corroborate my experience by their own—that all of the things which traditional religionists prize and which they connect exclusively with their own conception of God can be had equally well in the ordinary course of human experience in our relations to the natural world and to one another as human beings related in the family, friendship, industry, art, science, and citizenship. *Either then the concept of God can be dropped out as far as genuinely religious experience is concerned, or it must be framed wholly in terms of natural and human relationship involved in our straightaway human experience.* It was from this standpoint that I wrote my review, and my difficulty with Mr. Wieman's chapters was that his general tenor seemed to commit him so nearly to the second alternative, while (especially marking his position off from that of Mr. Otto) he kept introducing another external factor to which he gave the name God.

I continue my discussion by references to this latter point which I omitted from my review for lack of space. Mr. Wieman regularly interprets humanism in general and that of Mr. Otto in particular as if a humanist must mean that man is completely isolated from everything objective to his own skin and feelings. He thus took Mr. Otto's reference to man's "social and natural environment" as an *admission* that man is not sufficient unto himself. I cannot speak of course for Mr. Otto, but does Mr. Wieman really suppose that there is any humanist who is not aware that man *is man in* his relations to nature and society and not in isolation? Of course health is a good and of course health is not something which man apart from nature and from his parents and friends deliberately invents and procures for himself; the same may be said for friendships as good, for language, science, art, and the other values which we cherish.

Man in conscious and haughty isolation did not originate the state nor the family, though he does much in remaking them to better their values. In that sense Mr. Wieman of course is quite right in saying that objective forces produce our values. As Shakespeare said some time ago, "Nature is made better by no mean but nature makes that mean." Now Mr. Wieman says that recognition of this fact—along of course with some development of what is here stated too baldly—commits us to a belief in God, at least in God as he interprets him. Well, we say—at least I do—that the important thing is the fact, the reality, namely, that certain objective forces, of a great variety of kinds, actually promote human wellbeing, that the efficacy of these forces is increased by human attention to and care for the working of these forces, so that if Mr. Wieman or any one else gets contentment and energy by naming them God as they function to promote welfare, let him do so—*provided* it is clear *what* it is to which is given the name God. Now if this is what Mr. Wieman means, I am happy to know it; I shall not refuse to congratulate him, for the sake of keeping up a possible difference about a name.

There are, however, at least two reasons why I hesitate to attribute this position to Mr. Wieman, much as I should like to do so. One is his frequently repeated reference to God as "*The* power which," etc. (Of course, I think it would conduce to understanding and clearness if Mr. Wieman would turn his sentences around so that they would read, "The power that makes for greatest good is God.") And this mode of statement does not seem to be merely verbal; it seems to agree with a general tendency to make the force in question a *singular* being—which, and nothing emotional, is what I was getting at in my references to the historic "jealous God." But if I am wrong in my interpretation, Mr. Wieman has only to say so.

The more important thing which gives me hesitation is Mr. Wieman's shift between God as the power which *makes* for the greatest good and God as the Greatest Good. Now passing over a certain chariness on my part as to superlatives, like "greatest," let me point out that that which *makes* for good, whether it be singular or collective, demands care, attention, watchfulness, from man in order that it (or they) may do its (their) work most effectively and surely. But there is nothing about it or them particularly to demand love and adoration. I can love a healthy person in a way that is enhanced by that person's health, and I can feel a grateful affection for the *person* who brings me greater health. I do not know just what love (or adoration) of the chemico-physical processes that basically determine health would be, though of course I understand the need of thoughtful cooperation with their workings.

Now as I understand Mr. Wieman—and I am writing to get more light—the transition from the causal conditions that *make* for good to the Good itself is constituted by the activities which bring about integration, an organic, vital, unity among these causal conditions. This vital unity is then the thing supremely worthy. But this is something, as far as I can possibly see, in which human thought and action intervene. It is something which *should* exist, or as far as it is already exemplified in existence, it is something effected through the mediation of past generations of human devotion and energy. Again if any one wishes to give this humanly mediated ideal and fact (as far as it is a fact) the *name* God, I do not see how anyone can say him nay—provided once more that to which the name is given is made clear.

Now the basic trouble with Mr. Wieman's position is that his entire logic seems to commit him to the conclusion just stated. But in that case there is an absolutely indispensable connection between "God," so defined, and human desire and devotion—and yet this is what Mr. Wieman denies and reproaches me for having attributed to him. For the transformation of objective forces which *make* for good into the Good itself is unqualifiedly dependent upon human desire, loyalty, devotion.

Let me quote *in extenso* a passage from the book itself (p. 15): "What right have I for saying that what I have described is God? First, because it generates, sustains, promotes and constitutes the greatest good that ever was, is or can be. Second, because it functions with human conscious purpose to bring forth values over and above all human power of control and conscious intent. Third, because it is that which men can love and adore above all else. . . . Fourth, because it responds to prayer and is precisely what answers prayer. . . . Fifth, because in God so conceived suffering love finds its sovereignty," etc. Note that the first of these clauses (barring an ambiguity in the word "constitutes") has to do with causative power; the other four all involve human cooperation and intervention. And Mr. Wieman's last article seems to point even more definitely in the same direction. "This unity or organization which makes us and our activities and interests functioning members one of another, and which is always operative in our midst to some degree as long as we are human, is the reality to which, called by whatever name, we must give ourselves." That is a fine *ethical* statement, and if religion is "morality touched with emotion" a fine religious one. I should agree—provided once more it is clearly understood that *organization* exists in and through the means and modes of our human institutions, arrangements, relationships. If this is what Mr. Wieman intends, I do not see how a humanist can quarrel with him, nor he with a humanist—after he has corrected the strange idea that a humanist is one who separates man both from nature and from himself—or the social environment.

I have used up most of my space in dealing with Mr. Wieman. This is because I have a feeling that perhaps or probably Mr. Wieman is headed toward a position not especially distinguishable, save maybe in words, from that of Mr. Otto and myself, while there is wide gulf in any case between the position of Mr. Macintosh and my own. As to the relation between God and the ethical ideal, I do not think I misunderstood Mr. Macintosh's position though my language may not always have been precise. I did not intend to impute to him the idea that God is the *author* of the absolute moral ideal. I understand that Mr. Macintosh regards God as subject to this ideal. The point I tried to make—and would repeat—is that it is a "contradiction" to make the ideal absolute and then insist upon the necessity of some existent Being in order to ensure its triumph. *If* the ideal be absolute, then it takes care of itself, existential triumph or not. In my own mind, the second point he makes is covered by my opening remarks that more and more persons find a completely satisfactory religious experience, and an empirically self-verifying one, in objects and interests that have no connection with the sanctions and realities which Mr. Macintosh sets up. And I would add for what it may be worth my personal conviction that many more persons than do at present would "enjoy" religious experience had not professional religionists taught them that, because of lack of certain beliefs, they surely are *ir*-religious.

As to the third point, I do not of course deny the logical possibility of the existence of a personal will which is causative and directive of the universe and which is devoted to the promotion of moral ends. The question of the evidences which would justify a working belief in the actuality of this possibility is not one to discuss in a brief article. I must, unfortunately, terminate with a statement of a position which perhaps will seem wrong-headed if not wrong-hearted to Mr. Macintosh: If the future of religion is bound up with really finding such justificatory evidence, I fear for the future of religion. But, then, I do not think its future is thus bound up. In so far at least I have common ground with Mr. Wieman.

JOHN DEWEY

Social Stresses and Strains

Recent Social Trends in the United States: Report of the President's Research Committee on Social Trends. New York and London: McGraw-Hill Book Co., 1933.

There is no unanimity among students of morals as to the relation between social conditions and the problems of right and wrong, good and evil, which come home to individual persons. To many of us, it seems as if moralists upon the whole have tremendously exaggerated the purely personal phase of the origin and nature of moral problems. Such persons will undoubtedly find a mine of information and a wealth of suggestions in these monumental volumes dealing with social trends in the United States. But fortunately it is not necessary to limit the value of the volumes for the student of ethics to this particular side of the matter. For no one denies that the moral problems uppermost at a particular time have some connection with the way in which social currents are running or denies that times in which old institutions are decaying and old customs are disintegrating are especially charged with moral perplexities.

Of course, the main purpose of those who prepared the various studies which form the chapters of the two volumes was not with the student of morals, nor indeed with morals as such. The study is primarily sociological and economic, and the twenty-nine different inquiries and reports which form its contents are composed from the standpoint of specialists in as many fields. Naturally, then, one approaching the volumes with an ethical interest will find different chapters of unequal interest and will not write of the volumes as he would if he were attempting a comprehensive review. Selection is determined in part by the nature of the subject. One will not expect to find as much material for the moralists in the section dealing with problems of "physical heritage" as in that dealing with problems of "biological heritage," nor in that as in the section (containing many more studies) on "social heritage." And within the latter chapters there is a difference connected with the respective method of approach used by the various writers. Some are more factual. They give informational material which the moralist may draw upon in making his own generalizations. Others engage more in interpretation and supply the student of ethics with generalizations that will give definite direction to his thinking. The chapters on "Shifting Occupational Patterns," "Education," "Crime and Punishment," "Law," for example, are of the former type. The chapters dealing with "Inventions," "The Family," "Consumers," and "Government" are rather of the second-named sort. Of course the distinction drawn here is not exclusive. All writers give basic factual material, and all of them engage in a certain amount of generalization. But there is a difference of tendency which does not seem to be definitely connected with the nature of the subject treated.

At all events, the chapters which engage in relatively the greater amount of generalization and interpretation must give the cue to a reviewer, even if only on the score of brevity. And in this matter the general review of Committee findings, prefixed to the special chapters, demands primary attention. I do not think I do any injustice to the spirit of this prefatory interpretation if I say that the chief impression left upon the editors of the volumes by reports on special trends is that we are undergoing a great disturbance of social equilibrium, and that the present great social problem, affecting all lines of social activity, is the problem of coordination and integration. There is nothing startlingly new in this conclusion. I suppose that every serious student of social phenomena has arrived at a similar conclusion. But none the less to have assembled the material from every facet of our many-sided social life which supports in detail the generalization, to have given the only comprehensive picture of the resulting confusion, and clear-cut depiction of the whole problem is a great service. And to my mind the value of the service is not lessened because of the conservative, or at least sober, tone of the statements made, and the limited scope of recommendations made: much less radical, one may suppose, than many of the writers would have indulged in were they writing on their personal account. The moderation of the volumes adds to their weight of impartiality and objectivity.

There is a certain irony in the fact that the necessity of transferring attention from particularistic and largely competitive lines of activity and interest over to the problem of integration, by means of increase of social planning and control, should have come to be urged upon us through the agency of the pleading representative of rugged individualism. For, if the consensus of judgment represented in the volumes is correct, our present problems are the consequences of an epoch of unrelated growths which have indeed developed remarkable energy and extraordinary speed but which have left society as a whole and in its various constituents in a condition of extreme unbalance.

Let me quote a few statements from the Committee's own summary:

> The Committee does not exaggerate the bewildering confusion of problems; it has merely uncovered the situation as it is. . . . Along with this amazing mobility and complexity there has run a marked indifference to the interrelation among the parts of our huge social system. . . . The outstanding problem might be stated as that of bringing about a realization of the interdependence of the factors of our complicated social structure. . . . Under the heterogeneous features of modern life, a vast amount of disorganization has been possible in our economic, political and social affairs. . . . It is the express purpose of this review . . . to direct attention to the importance of balance among the factors of change. A nation advances not only by dynamic power, but by and through the maintenance of some degree of equilibrium among the moving forces.

And the following may be cited as a summary of the spirit of the whole:

> If, then, the report reveals, as it must, confusion and complexity in American life during recent years, striking inequality in the rates of change, uneven advances in inventions, institutions, attitudes and ideals, dangerous *tensions and torsions* in our social arrangements, we may hold steadily to the importance of viewing social situations as a whole in terms of the interrelation and interdependence of our national life. [Italics mine.]

It will be noted that the statements quoted emphasize not only existing disturbances of equilibrium and the need of attention to their interrelations, but also suggest the cause of our disequilibration, namely, the inequalities in the rate of development of various lines of activity. The widest generalization which is offered is precisely that this lack of synchronization in rates of change is the source of social maladjustments. The most rapid rate of change is found in technological matters; spiritual values are the slowest in changing to meet altered conditions. Between the two stand the great historic institutions, family, government, business, schools, and church, which are intermediate in rate of change. But just as technological changes do not proceed uniformly among themselves, neither do institutions change at the same rate. The economic institution adjusts itself most rapidly, being in closest contact with technological change and science; the government is next rapid in readjustment, while the church and family have actually declined in social significance, though not in human values. Since the latter two institutions are those which connect most directly with what the editors call "spiritual values," the relative immobility of the latter gets enhanced importance. And when one modifies the statement of the editors about change in political institutions to include what seems to me the undoubted fact, namely, that the fundamental legal conceptions and practices connected with the older scheme of values have hardly changed at all, one has a sufficient challenge to the student of morals.

The generalizations of the introductory chapter are well borne out by the material of the twenty-nine special reports, even when no comprehensive interpretations are ventured upon. Some confirmation may be cited, taken almost at random from the successive chapters. Thus in the one on "Inventions" we read that "the fact that the different parts of a highly integrated society are changing at unequal rates of speed means that there is lack of harmony, frequently a grievous maladjustment, and always a failure to make the most out of a possible development." The section on economic organization points out that since the World War the economic pace has been so tremendously accelerated that serious maladjustments have taken place. For example, increase in plant and equipment has far outrun the capacity of the ultimate consumer to buy, and while manufacturing industry was increasing rapidly, agricultural industry actually declined—a disparity that finally, of course, reacted on factory production. There was a constant tendency to increasing disparity of price among the main groups of commodities. The present crisis cannot be understood apart from these disparities. Obviously with great inequality in the services and commodities of different major groups and corresponding inequality in the purchasing power of each group, social maladjustment on a large scale was bound to result.

The chapter on "The Family" points out that of the two main functions of the family, the institutional (the economic and the educational, by way of example) and the personality function—the mutual personal adjustments of parents and children with one another—the former has declined, thus rendering the service performed, or unperformed, by the personality function of increased importance. And while there is no express statement to that effect, I think it is reasonable to infer that the decrease in extent and importance of the institutional functions is one great cause for much greater strain being put upon the members of the family in their personal relations to one another. For institutional functions served as objective and impersonal mediators. As they disappear, individuals are thrown into more immediate personal relations with one another and the sources of friction are multiplied and intensified. Moreover, this occurs in a situation in which there has been no previous training to generate skill and art in personal adjustment. Important problems are set to both psychology and morals by this fact. Increase in divorce can hardly be separated, I think, from this source of strain. Then the instability which attends this increase tends to remove one of the chief forces of training for personality relationships. Here, as in so many other matters, we find ourselves caught in a vicious circle.

The chapter on "The Child" is a natural pendant to that on "The Family." In the summary it is stated that "the outstanding development is the growing belief in the possibility of directing and controlling social life through the care and nurture of children." There can be no doubt as to the correctness of this statement. Yet at the very time in which scientific studies (well described in the chapter) are both enforcing this lesson and contributing techniques for realization of the possibility, the stability and efficacy of the home, through which to so large an extent the operation must take effect, are in a state of decline approaching disintegration. And here too even on the positive side of the field we have the centrifugal effect of independent and uncoordinated movements. "There is indifference or reluctance to coordinate the knowledge, techniques and practices of child care into an integrated plan of treatment or nurture"; the same fact is found in the organization and administration of agencies dealing with child care—each tends to go its own way without either using the knowledge gained in the experience of other agencies or any mutual correlation of activities.

Perhaps among the different reports that on trends in government is the frankest in its exposure of the fundamental discrepancy and conflict that now exist between ultimate cultural values—as I should wish to translate the "spiritual values" of the Introduction—and institutional habits and procedures. In politics,

> the prevailing attitude has been non-theoretical and intolerant toward other systems than our own, and non-experimental in the field of government structure, especially if constitutional change were involved. In business and mechanical enterprise the general attitude has been that of free and welcome experiment, but the opposite has been true in governmental affairs, where the weight of traditions has been more heavily felt and where proposals for change have been identified with treason to the state.

And here, too, and in an independent way, the cause of the inertia and of the opposition to the very idea of change as well as to special proposed changes is located in the economic area. It is declared to be

> not merely the result of preoccupation with expansive interests or a special American type of mentality, but grows largely out of the identification of the present industrial situation with the preservation of the status quo in constitutional arrangements, and the fear that change might jeopardize existing property interests. The same situation helps explain the extensive business boycott of government except where special favors are concerned, and the theory that the worst government is the best.

In the treatment of governmental changes I seem to find brought out the basic underlying cause of the tensions effected through disparity in the rate of different social trends. The business institution is that which changes most rapidly in its own inner processes and techniques. But it is the most resistant to changes in other institutions, especially law and politics (and I should also say in church and school), lest changes there should modify the character of the economic territory within which technical changes are welcomed. There is more than a paradox here. There is basic contradiction and conflict. Then President Hoover in his Foreword remarks that "since the task assigned to the Committee was to inquire into changing trends, the result is emphasis on elements of instability rather than stability in our social structure." But the studies reveal, and the one under consideration with especial clearness, that the difficulties in our situation result from the fact that the unstable features are invading and undermining the older stable ones, and are doing so the more effectually because of the identification in politics of stability with hostility to any structural modification. It is difficult to see more than two alternatives with respect to the contradiction between the power of the economic group to accelerate change in their own field and its power to resist change in law and government. One is surrender of hostility to political, including constitutional, change. The other is the smash-up of our present political system.

In touching upon only one theme, in commenting upon one single line of texts, I have of course put the material of the volumes as a whole in a false perspective. But not, I venture to think, for students of present society who approach their study in the interest of ethics. I have seen criticisms of these volumes on the ground that they are timid in proposing specific changes and reforms, and backward in setting forth a comprehensive social philosophy from whose standpoint the whole situation should be surveyed. I do not agree with the criticisms. I believe the enduring influence of the report will be increased by its reserves in these two respects. I think that in the long run the interests which those who make the criticisms have at heart will be best served by the style of treatment adopted. I have often been impatient with methods of mere "fact-finding" used by so-called social and political science. But in these volumes we have something more than *mere* fact-finding. The facts are presented—sometimes only implicitly, sometimes explicitly—so as to make *problems* stand out, and that, in my judgment, is the proper function of statement of facts. Hence the volumes are an arsenal. And I would rather have an arsenal of authoritative knowledge than such a premature firing-off of guns as would make a lot of noise and emit great amounts of smoke.

While emphasizing the value of these volumes to the student of morals, while laying stress upon the fact that this exposition of social tensions and torsions is a challenge to the thinker on ethical subjects, I would also say that, in my mind, it issues a challenge to contemporary American philosophy. What is the matter, at a time when there are so many deep and thought-provoking general problems to deal with, that American philosophers, to judge from their public output, are so largely occupied with merely technical and formal questions so that we are threatened with a new kind of scholasticism that lacks the vitality of classic scholasticism? Not long ago, literary folk seemed to be correspondingly self-conscious in their preoccupation with questions of literary form and of "pure" literature for the sake of its purity—as literature, of course, and not as morality. Many of them have had a tremendous jounce and jolt through the recent course of social events. Possibly they are in danger of going to an opposite extreme which will submerge literature as art in social propaganda. But I should like to see our philosophical students and teachers moving in the direction in which dramatists and novelists and even poets are moving. I do not think there is any danger of their being overwhelmed in the process.

Mr. Justice Brandeis, edited by Felix Frankfurter with an Introduction by Oliver Wendell Holmes. New Haven: Yale University Press, 1932.

This book consists, besides the brief introduction by former Justice Holmes, of six essays called forth by the seventy-fifth birthday of Justice Brandeis, and first published in three legal periodicals. The one by Justice Hughes is brief—practically another introduction—but in a way it strikes the keynote of the volume when it says that "Mr. Justice Brandeis writes for students, both for those who are beginning and for those who are mature." In all there is expressed the greatest respect for the workmanship of Justice Brandeis as a legal technician, coupled with the recognition that what nevertheless gives the subject of these essays his distinction is that his knowledge and juristic skill are controlled by a deeply felt scheme of social values—by what in a true sense is a social philosophy. Yet it is not one of that formal kind which Justice Brandeis repudiated when he asserted that he had "no rigid social philosophy: I have been too intent on concrete problems of practical justice."

The great contribution of Justice Brandeis is brought out by all the essayists. It is contained in his own citation of the old maxim *ex facto jus oritur*, with his comment that only on this basis can law be kept "living." His technique was foreshadowed in his famous brief in *Muller v. Oregon* framed before he came to the bench. Mr. Max Lerner in his essay on "The Social Thought of Mr. Justice Brandeis" brings out with particular force the admirable way in which his earlier experience fitted him, on the bench, for his service in bringing the law into more realistic connection with the facts of modern economic and industrial life. Justice Brandeis had had close and intimate contact in practice with the problems of trade unions, public utilities in electric

[First published in *Columbia Law Review* 33 (January 1933): 175–76.]

lighting and street traction, railways, insurance, conservation of natural resources, *etc.*; his method in each case was not only to master the factual detail but to proffer a plan for constructive action often fruitful of thought and endeavor along new lines. This trait, and his emphasis upon the necessity of attention to what Mr. Lerner well calls the "contextual situation" may well have been the ground of his denial that he had any social philosophy. But at all events strict adherence to this policy of reference to factual context is one of the great contributions to legal thought in the last generation. Nor can I imagine any sound social or ethical philosophy in which this idea is not fundamental. I have to refer to the book itself for an adequate statement of the thoroughgoing way in which Mr. Brandeis has lived up to this principle since his elevation to the Supreme Court. If he has not completely won victory for it, it is because vested interests are fearful of the results of resort to factual material.

Justice Brandeis' ethical ideal is controlled by his substantial faith in the American ideals of democracy and individual liberty. While his conviction on this subject is implied in all his important opinions, it is made explicit in some extra-judicial opinions. "The development of the individual is both a necessary means and the end sought. For our objective is the making of men and women who shall be free, self-respecting members of a democracy—and who shall be worthy of respect." This ideal, it will be noted, has to do with the development, the *making*, of individuals; it does not assume their ready-made existence. Hence it offers a criterion for criticism of economic institutions and measures. Many things which have been justified on the basis of "rugged individualism" are to be condemned as hostile to the *development* of free individuals. The constant opposition of Justice Brandeis to what he calls the "curse of bigness" is explicable on this ground. It also explains his belief in the necessity of industrial democracy. Workers must assume responsibility for the conduct of business if they are to be free to develop. Both the negative and the positive aspects of his social philosophy are indicated in his hostility to all measures calculated "to endow property with active militant power which would make it dominant over men."

I have only sketched the general tenor of what is fully developed in the essays themselves. Whether or not conditions will allow the continuance of the type of individualism for which Justice Brandeis has consistently stood, and which has given solidity and unity to his treatment of a great number of varied themes and problems, the value of his work as an indispensable guide to students remains.

Santayana's Orthodoxy

Some Turns of Thought in Modern Philosophy: Five Essays, by George Santayana. New York: Charles Scribner's Sons, 1934.

In the first of these five essays, Mr. Santayana remarks that although all philosophies are frail, since they are products of the "reactive, spontaneous and volatile" human mind, yet there are certain comparatively steady principles. "These principles form a sort of orthodox reason which may become the current grammar of mankind." The two great representatives of this orthodoxy are, in Mr. Santayana's mind, Aristotle and Spinoza; and one need not confine oneself to the present work to find evidence that he likes to think of himself as one of the relatively few among modern philosophers with the sanity and simple candor to adhere to orthodoxy. Nor need the fact that in his recent metaphysical excursions Mr. Santayana seems to have transferred his spiritual allegiance to Indian thought be seriously disturbing, since one aspect at least of the Greek view of the universe is congenial to an elevation of the supremely real beyond nature and hence beyond science as well as beyond experience.

Fortunately and unfortunately, Mr. Santayana's own orthodoxy is extremely heretical. Fortunately, because his departures confer upon him an originality lacking in the orthodox who are strict in their orthodoxy. Unfortunately, because—in spite of the charm and piquancy with which his deviations from the correct line are set forth—he often seems to take back in one paragraph what he has said in another, so that one is at times not quite certain how much of his genial irony may be directed at himself.

His first essay, from which I have already quoted, deals with "Locke and the Frontiers of Common Sense." Here Locke is depicted as the embodiment of two opposing tendencies. On the one hand he represents the essential common-sense position:

[First published in *New Republic* 78 (28 February 1934): 79–80.]

that, although our contact with reality is only through the medium of ideas (of whose nature we have an immediate intuition), yet the practical demands of our being, rooted in our animal and material nature, force upon us an unwavering faith in the existence of a substantial material world that is the ground of our own existence and the only object of knowledge (as distinct from the enjoyable immediate intuition of essences). Mr. Santayana's first objection to this side of Locke's philosophy is that he took scientific ideas a little too seriously, not seeing that such conceptions as space and atoms were themselves as human and graphic as our sensations of sound and color, and that they require, just as do the latter, animal faith for connection with existence. His other objection is that Locke did not take with sufficient seriousness the realm of intuitions—on their own account and in their own content—since his puritan predilections hindered his perception of their value as material for art, for fiction and music. "A good God, he murmurs, would not have made us poets against our will."

But on the other side of Locke's philosophy, Mr. Santayana finds him to be the source of what he has elsewhere called "malicious psychology"—the resolution of ideas into states of consciousness, until states of mind form the whole of the known and knowable universe. As against this conception Mr. Santayana refers to a conception of his own, that neither of the two kinds of legitimate psychology, scientific and literary, is concerned with "disembodied mental states." Scientific psychology is biological, and falls within the province of physical science, while literary psychology is animated by interest in human nature—the interest which Santayana justly calls "moral"—and describes experience in terms that are imaginative, while always retaining the sense of the material world as the setting in which human experience—pleasures and pains, emotions and images—go on.

I have given an undue amount of space to what I hope may pass for a summary of the first essay. But I have done so because I think Mr. Santayana's treatment of Locke illustrates his heretical departure from the orthodoxy he admires. The dualism of mind and matter which he regards as Locke's essential record of common sense is as far from Aristotle as was Descartes himself— whether Spinoza can be forced into it or not. And this dualism runs through every essay in the volume. On the one hand, Mr. Santayana is a materialist *à l'outrance*, holding that matter is the only existence having causal efficacy, while he suspects that Democritus with his atoms and Newton with his absolute space and time are truer guides in this realm than contemporary physics with its relativity and quanta. On the other hand, he believes that there is nothing of value save the poetic and moral realm, the realm of ideas and feelings. Since it is the source of all value, the idealistic philosophy, which is scientifically false, has at least the merit of being an exploration of this realm, which the prosaic and scientific mind tends to neglect. Science, on the contrary, is but a symbolic rendering of a world unknown in itself, a transcript valuable because it is a necessity of our organic and practical nature. Few commentators seem to have grasped that Santayana's view of science justifies it only as a "pragmatic" escape from that enclosure within our own images and feelings which, on purely theoretical grounds, is completely justified. I cannot regard this rather thrilling mode of escape from thoroughgoing cognitive skepticism as other than an interesting and highly personal heresy. Santayana is even more Lockean than Locke.

The essay on "Revolutions in Science," the third in order, seems to indicate double-mindedness even more strikingly. On the one hand, he finds in the latest outgivings of science a virtual acknowledgment—even if one not as yet recognized by the leaders in the revolution of science—that science does not pretend that it is "laying bare the intrinsic nature of things." It yields "practical assurances couched in symbolic terms, but no ultimate insight." This achievement is a great gain, for it emancipates science so that it can deal with the territory in which it is most at home, the intuition of mathematical essences. For, as he says, "intelligence is never gayer, never surer, than when it is strictly formal." But afterwards he concludes that this revolution takes science farther away from experience and that it is allied to a faith in private perspectives which implies the substitution of intellectual anarchy for the good old faith of classical physics in substantial atoms and absolute space and time. If Mr. Santayana confined his doubts to those interpreters, like Eddington and Jeans, who are turning scientific findings into a mystical metaphysics, I could understand his doubts. But he seems to be turning his earlier blessing into a distrust, if not a cursing, of the tendencies of modern science itself.

I cannot indicate how the other two essays, one on Freud's discovery of the principle of inertia, or habit, after his earlier exclusive celebrations of the principles of pleasure and pain, and the other on Benda's enthusiasm—in its literal sense—for the realm of infinite and nonexistent and undefined possibilities, bear upon Mr. Santayana's heretical version of the "orthodox" tradition. The first contains, however, such a charming statement of Mr. Santayana's personal position that I shall quote it in full:

> The ineptitude of our aesthetic minds to unravel the nature of mechanism does not deprive these minds of their own clearness and euphony. Besides sounding their various musical notes, they have the cognitive function of indicating the hour and catching the echoes of distant events or of maturing inward dispositions.

Here in two sentences are his fundamental skepticism, his purely practical justification of knowledge, and his unfailing sense of the significance of the poetic and moral. Why should this deeply original personal vision be offered us as a contemporary restatement of Aristotle and Spinoza?

Acquiescence and Activity in Communism

A Philosophic Approach to Communism, by Theodore B. H. Brameld. Chicago: University of Chicago Press, 1933.

Dr. Brameld proposes, he says, to examine the philosophical basis of the doctrine of Lenin and Marx mainly in the light of one concept, that of acquiescence. The problem of the book is to determine whether the underlying philosophy of communism is essentially that of an automatic historical evolution or whether this philosophy permits and demands activistic efforts put forth by individuals to shape the course, especially the future course, of history. Dr. Brameld's own treatment is somewhat dialectical—in the Hegelian sense. He regards compliance with the trend of social relations as the thesis, its negation by individual effort as the antithesis, and the classless state as the ultimate synthesis. In the latter, individuality has free play according to the inherent capacities of each person, instead of being a struggle against others—the class war—while sociality is so complete "as to unite the individual within the objective mass."

The value of the book does not, however, depend upon acceptance of Dr. Brameld's own dialectical treatment. It contains a very large amount of concrete material drawn from Marx, Engels and Lenin. While the material is organized with reference to matters that are of special interest within the communist faith, it also provides the non-communist with material highly valuable in understanding both communist theory and practice.

It occurs to me that part of the various incompatible interpretations of Marx and Lenin among both communists and non-communists is due to the fact that interpreters and critics are wont to suppose that practically everything said by one who professes a philosophy must be deduced from his fundamental philosophic position. But philosophers like everybody else are first of all human beings, and the human element exceeds the philosophical. In dealing with special questions, even a thinker gives his mind considerable free play in view of the special conditions approached from a particular temporal angle.

More fundamentally, it is true, I think, that both Marx and Lenin may be interpreted, with respect to their Hegelian element, in both the acquiescent and the activist manner. If one takes the broad sweep, there is a historical movement. But individuals are within the historic process as its constituents. One who is engaged in emphasizing total process will, with respect to that emphasis, be interpreted as upholding the concept of compliance. But when he is concerned with particular phases of the process, he will inevitably concentrate upon the active role of individuals *in* the historic process. One who regards revolution as inevitable will surely emphasize the role of activity of individuals in the revolutionary period. It seems altogether likely that one reason the Hegelian dialectic appealed to European communist thinkers was that it enabled them to make a synthesis of a necessary social process with the "negative" protesting and revolutionary efforts of individuals. Whether or not the synthesis that Dr. Brameld attempts of acquiescence and activity is philosophically and historically sound, it seems to me to throw much light on the psychology of the intellectual strategy of communist leaders.

People's Lobby Bulletin

Unemployed and Underpaid Consumers Should Not Pay Billion Dollar Subsidy to Speculators

The so-called farm allotment plan owes its present popularity to widespread sympathy for farmers, and while farmers should share, with the unemployed, the relief funds of Federal and State Governments, the allotment plan must not be permitted to block constructive measures to remedy the agricultural situation.

The following measures are essential to make agriculture a going concern:

Writing down farmers' debts one-third to one-half, and reducing their interest rates similarly.

Transferring taxes from farmers, and others, as producers, to farmers and others as land speculators, and profit makers.

Creating a government marketing corporation empowered not only to buy farm products but to process them, and to distribute them to consumers, as provided in the Norris-Sinclair bill introduced in Congress a decade ago.

Ridding farmers of Old-Man-of-the-Sea-Tariff.

Unification of the nation's transportation to serve producers.

Such organization of agricultural production as will enable it to meet the needs of American consumers and supply our share of world markets currently, without being forced to dump during recurrent, but always temporary world surpluses.

The plea for allotment subsidies at the expense of over twenty million consumer families in American cities and towns, most with incomes of less than $1,200 a year, of whom millions have less than $1,000, is at least ill advised.

The avowed purpose of the proponents of the various farm allotment schemes, now before Congress, to help working farmers, must be subjected to a realistic analysis.

Capping tariffs on farm products, now so high as in many cases to constitute an embargo, with a bounty at the expense of millions in cities, in quite as dire straits as the alleged farmer beneficiaries of such tariffs and bounties, cannot in either the long, or the short, run benefit farmers.

The chief factors in the stupidly high costs of production of farm products in the United States are speculative prices for farm lands, and mortgages pyramided upon those speculative prices as exorbitant interest rates; high taxes due to the farmers' own failure to tax land speculators, and the similar unearned income of others; and to high prices charged farmers for what they buy, because farmers, or at least their official spokesmen have exchanged support for tariffs on farm products, for support for tariffs on manufactures, and have secured exemption from anti-trust laws for farm products, instead of opposing tariff-patent-price-fixing-association created trusts, for manufactured products.

High costs of distribution of farm products are primarily due to competitive railroading of which farmers are, and have been with Wall Street, the chief protagonists, and to chaotic wasteful and obsolete marketing systems, fully exposed a decade ago by the Congressional Committee which investigated Agriculture, and fully condoned ever since, by official spokesmen for farm organizations.

Nearly four times as large a proportion of farmers gainfully employed, are members of the National Grange, the Farmers' Union and the American Farm Bureau Federation, as the proportion of the non-agricultural gainful workers who are members of the American Federation of Labor.

All city workers, however, particularly in a period of distress which would be seriously aggravated by higher prices for essential foods, would register at the earliest election their verdict upon being compelled by Congressional action to pay for agriculture's mistakes and having charged to them the failure of Congress to act intelligently.

The allotment plan is an evasion, and not a solution, of the farm problem.

Naturally farmers and their families, as well as the unemployed, are entitled to Federal relief while we are working out of our economic morass, but that relief will be paid by those able to pay.

Robbing bankrupt Peter Consumer, to pay bankrupt Paul Producer is the reverse of economic statesmanship.

Relief Is Vital

Business Week recently reported that in November, 1932, 15,252,000 people were unemployed, that is 31.2 per cent, nearly one-third, of those who were gainfully employed in April, 1930. It says:
"Taking the accepted average of 1½ dependents for each worker, that means 37½ million men, women and children directly and immediately affected by unemployment this winter."

This conservative McGraw-Hill publication states that 2,057,000 were unemployed in the building trades, or 80.3 per cent of the number gainfully employed in April, 1930, and 1,078,000 were unemployed in the iron and steel industry, or 45.2 per cent of those gainfully employed in April, 1930, while the total number unemployed in all manufacturing and mechanical industry was 6,618,000, that is 46.2 per cent of those gainfully employed in April, 1930.

William Green, President of the American Federation of Labor, estimates that the loss of wages and salaries for 1930 and 1931, compared with 1929, amounted to $36,667,000,000.

In 1932, wages and salaries were at least $14,000,000,000, and possibly $15,000,000,000 less than in 1929.

In spite of the fact that 1929 was regarded as a peak prosperity period *Business Week* also reports that the 45,337,000 persons having that year incomes of $3,000 or less, spent $8,229,000,000 more than their income of $70,401,000,000. Their reported savings of $3,746,000,000, were actually less than half of the amount by which their expenditures exceeded their income.

That the figures on unemployment do not tell the whole story of deprivation, is shown by the statement of Mr. Walter C. Teagle, Chairman of the Share-the-Work Committee, that but for the

[First published in *People's Lobby Bulletin* 2 (February 1933): 1–2.]

general adoption of shorter working schedules by industries, 5,000,000 more men and women would be unemployed.

In many, if not most cases, work sharing is wage paring, if not wage sharing.

Such a "Share a job—Cut a Wage" policy is working havoc with family budgets and standards of living.

There is no substitute for relief—direct and immediate. America's delay in meeting the unemployment situation is one of the darkest pages in our national history.

Access to land, the basic source of subsistence, is blocked by our tax system, even were any large number of the unemployed trained to raise vegetables and other foodstuffs.

A large-scale housing program cannot be started in time to help the situation materially before fall.

Road building, and the much needed program of public works, including school houses, are held up by taxpayers' strikes.

Most cities, counties and states are reducing, instead of increasing, their public works and roads appropriations.

Most cities, counties and states also have exhausted their funds for relief.

The $500,000,000 provided by the Costigan-La Follette Relief Bill for direct relief, and relief work during the present year is woefully inadequate.

The People's Lobby and the Joint Committee on Unemployment have asked that $1,000,000,000 be appropriated.

The $500,000,000 of the Costigan-La Follette Bill means less than $35.00 per unemployed person.

The balance available for relief in the Reconstruction Finance Corporation, would bring the average up to only about $50.00.

The Wagner substitute for the Costigan-La Follette Relief Bill making $300,000,000 more available to the Reconstruction Finance Corporation for loans to states and cities for direct relief and relief work means that the average per unemployed person is dropped to about $34.

This is utterly inadequate.

It should be spent within the next three or four months.

The Banking Crisis

Irresponsible speculation with other people's money, as well as with one's own, inevitably brings a reaction. It does not necessarily bring a collapse, but does require adjustment on a large scale.

That adjustment, railroads, industries, banks, and other financial institutions refused to make voluntarily, and Governments, Federal and State, failed to compel them to make.

The revelations of the financial transactions of Charles E. Mitchell as President of the National City Bank, made in the closing days of the past Congress, may have been an occasion of the raids on the banks, which caused the President to declare a banking moratorium, but the causes of the trouble go further back than even speculative use of other people's money.

The chief causes of the conditions which finally resulted in a nation-wide run on banks were the failure of Government, Federal, State and municipal, to provide work or relief for the unemployed; failure to arrange in an orderly but positive way for writing down debts, Government and non-Government, and interest rates thereon, and failure to arrange for wiping out the fictitious capitalization amounting to many billions of dollars, of commercial, transportation, and financial institutions.

One would be inclined to add Government's failure to effect a redistribution of the national income through taxation, for that sin of omission is chiefly responsible for unemployment and human suffering. People skimp and put their starvation savings in savings and other fiduciary institutions, to protect themselves and their children.

It seems that we are not to have the "inflation" which bankers opposed, but the "expansion" which will relieve their difficulties.

[First published in *People's Lobby Bulletin* 2 (March 1933): 1–2.]

The issue of two or three billion dollars of additional currency may ease the situation. It is not, however, practical or desirable to attempt to raise prices to the peak of 1929, and such action would be necessary to validate many of the loans made by banks and trust companies.

Although the farm mortgage indebtedness has been reduced nearly a billion dollars since 1929—chiefly through foreclosure—it would be foolish to attempt to increase prices of farm products sufficiently to bring the land values of farms carrying such mortgages, up to the inflated prices on which these loans were placed.

This is largely true of the nearly thirty-five billion dollars of urban mortgages. Increasing rents (even were this possible), to maintain urban land values at a level to justify mortgages now outstanding, would place a paralyzing burden on production, and indefinitely postpone business improvement.

The People's Lobby has been urging for many months that the Federal Government under emergency powers write down debts, and interest rates.

Such action seems inevitable in the near future, although the announced program of the Administration to deal with the situation does not include any such plan.

The basic factor in the situation is that a large part of non-Government loans have been made on valuations which should not, and probably cannot be recovered.

Equity demands that losses sustained from writing down losses due to excessive valuation of securities, as distinguished from chicanery and fraud, should be proportioned to the investment.

With sixty-eight million life insurance policies in force, and over fifty million accounts in savings and fiduciary institutions, such an adjustment will not be easy.

The alternative method, which has been tried so long—withdrawal of currency, gold coin or bullion for hoarding, has proven disastrous.

Even official Washington recognizes, however, that the demand that banking and the issuing of credit be made a Federal non-profit monopoly is increasing.

Making the President a banking dictator in a crisis is not a solution—it is merely a postponement of the inevitable remaking of our profiteering banking system.

Congress Faces Its Test on Taxation

A succession of palliatives and stop gaps have been proposed, since the bubble of false prosperity broke in 1929.

The statement on another page, on the need for a drastic redistribution of the national income through taxation, signed by scores of our leading economists, publicists, social workers and church and labor leaders emphasizes what is rapidly coming to be considered as the real test of Congress, and also of the Democratic Administration.

That statement refers to Federal taxation.

Of almost equal importance, though complicated by the diverse practices of forty-eight states and hundreds of municipal and county governments, is the method of obtaining state and local revenues.

No permanent improvement in employment, and no genuine prosperity can be achieved, until state and local governments and particularly municipal governments, abandon their short-sighted taxing policies, and raise at least the major part of their budgets by taxing land values, so enabling them to exempt from taxation buildings, other labor products, machinery and stocks of goods, and personal property.

The advocates of panaceas for the disaster which we have brought upon ourselves, deserve short shrift, but no less do the optimists of ignorance, who ignore the basic importance of our land policy.

This is no less true of agriculture than of other industries.

The farm mortgage debt amounting in 1929 to about nine and a half billion dollars, and since reduced nearly a billion dollars largely by foreclosures, is an evidence not so much of the hard luck of farmers, as of their orgy of speculation in farm lands.

[First published in *People's Lobby Bulletin* 2 (April 1933): 1–2.]

A generation ago, a large mortgage on a farm, or increasing a farm mortgage year after year, was regarded as proof of inefficiency, or at least of bad management.

In spite of the fact that the selling price of farm lands more than doubled the first decade of this century, and nearly doubled the second decade, the actual selling price of farm lands today is probably only about two-fifths of the selling price of urban land.

Any form of price fixing for farm products, or reduction of interest rates on farm mortgage and commercial debt, will tend to start another orgy of speculation in farm lands and defeat the avowed purpose of such farm relief legislation, unless all labor products are exempted from taxation and the revenue hitherto derived from such sources, obtained by taxing land values more heavily. This is the only practical method also, of insuring that writing down of the principal of farm debts, inures to the benefit of producing farmers, instead of farm land speculators.

With tragic insouciance, most of the vocal and professional pleaders for farm relief ignore this basic fact.

The total income of agriculture in 1932, about $5,000,000,000, inadequate as it was to meet farmers' fixed charges and living costs, would, with what farmers raised themselves, have afforded them a much better standard of living than most labor but highly paid city workers enjoyed—except for taxes and debt payments which amounted to about $1,500,000,000.

Farmers' debt and hence debt service is largely their own fault, while under even a semi-intelligent tax system, the selling price, or sales value, of farm lands would be next to nothing, their taxes thereon negligible, and the rest of their possessions, as well as their consumption, would be exempt from taxation. In other words, farmers would not have to pay either principal, nor interest on debt, nor much taxes.

It is not a coincidence that the mortgage debt on taxable real estate in New York City is about eight billion dollars, or practically the selling price now, of taxable land in that city.

That debt is about equal to the entire farm mortgage debt. That selling price of taxable land in New York City is due to the city's failure to tax land values sufficiently, as also to deliberately stimulated speculation. It is about half the sum which all farm lands in the United States, exclusive of improvements, would probably bring today.

The present selling price of most farm lands and most city lands is now highly inflated.

All relief and all construction credits will tend to increase still further the speculative selling price of farm and city lands. This must be prevented to avoid a repetition of our present situation. It can be effectively prevented only by transferring taxes from improvements to land values.

The Real Test of the "New Deal"

The real test of the "New Deal" is revising the Revenue Act.

The funds for the relief bill—appropriating $500,000,000—are to be raised by a bond issue.

For every $500,000,000 bond issue at 4 per cent, running for twenty-five years, the creditor class—that is those with means—will receive $500,000,000 in interest—probably tax-exempt.

As Dr. Joseph McGoldrick, Professor of Public Law at Columbia University, stated about the financing of unemployment relief and construction:

> A bond sale is not the answer. If people can buy bonds they can pay taxes. Our present imperious need is for a huge national fund to provide employment and create purchasing power.

We could increase purchasing power almost as much, by repealing four or five billion dollars of consumption taxes now paid by those with incomes under $1,500.

Congress should raise $2,550,000,000 additional revenue as follows:

$1,000,000,000 by the personal income tax.

$1,000,000,000 by taxing surpluses and undivided profits of large corporations.

$300,000,000 by increasing estate taxes.

$250,000,000 by taxing income from government securities.

This program of taxation would greatly reduce the amount of bonds the Federal Government would issue—and so maintain its credit.

It would enable the Federal Government to pay its share of the

[First published in *People's Lobby Bulletin* 3 (May 1933): 1.]

cost of maintaining the unemployed and their dependents, by current taxation.

Write the President and Hon. Robert L. Doughton, Chairman, the Ways and Means Committee, Washington, D.C., asking them to initiate revision of the Revenue Act, now.

The Democratic Platform states:

> We favor maintenance of the national credit by a federal budget annually balanced on the basis of accurate executive estimates within revenues, raised by a system of taxation levied on the principle of ability to pay.

Superficial Treatment Must Fail

Superficial treatment of the basic causes which have produced a depression, not only in the United States, but throughout the world, will not end the depression. It may help some of the victims—but at best only temporarily.

Emergency measures imply that they are directed to meet an emergency, but the present world-wide chaos is not a condition from which the world can emerge on a basis of assured and general prosperity, without fundamental changes in the economic systems of every major nation, except Russia.

America's problems cannot be settled on a narrow nationalistic basis. Every major economic issue of every nation is international, and cannot be settled upon a strictly legalistic basis, nor upon standards of international ethics which have hitherto passed muster.

Practical international cooperation must be substituted for international rivalry. This means adjustment of international debts, of loans from capital export to capital import countries, of titles to natural resources, and of concessions held by foreigners, as well as adjustment of tariffs and other barriers to freedom of exchange.

Obviously our immediate problem in America is to secure a redistribution of the national income not merely in numbers of dollars, but in actual purchasing power. We cannot do this merely by taxing incomes, estates and corporation surpluses, essential as these are. Debts and interest rates must be written down and utility charges reduced.

It is still true that so long as cities and States tax buildings and other labor products, instead of obtaining the major part of their income from the taxation of land values, the land owner will be the residual beneficiary of expenditures by Federal Governments

[First published in *People's Lobby Bulletin* 3 (June 1933): 1–3.]

for relief and for made work, as well as the beneficiary of public improvements and other ordinary municipal and State expenditures, which increase the selling price of land.

Hitherto the major part of responsibility for unemployment has been attributed to the Federal Government. It has its part.

State and municipal governments, however, have their responsibility no less urgent and no less important. Despite the aggressiveness of certain farm leaders, it is still true that American farmers have been and are in large measure today, land value animals—and not land animals as are the peasants of other countries.

In large measure, small home owners in our cities also look forward to selling their homes and obtaining additional income, through the increase in the selling price of the site of their home—to more than offset the depreciation in the value of their building.

Housing reformers have for some reason almost entirely neglected this fundamental factor in the housing problem. It is worth while to repeat the statement of Mr. William Stanley Parker, Fellow of the American Institute of Architects, as Chairman of Mayor Curley's Committee making an architectural survey of Boston:

> Reconstruction Finance Corporation funds constitute a new opportunity to accomplish slum clearance. The local legislation needed will, perhaps, develop opposition, but that will be the easiest part of the problem to solve.
>
> The real problem will be to obtain the slum areas at any price that will permit demolition of the existing structures and the construction of new housing of the required low-cost units with a density per acre not exceeding what the surrounding local conditions will determine to be reasonable.
>
> There's the rub. Until this underlying land cost problem is solved, consideration of the details and costs of the contemplated new housing units is somewhat academic. Concentration on this problem should be, I believe, the first concern of the organized study of slum clearance and low-cost housing here and elsewhere.

The late Herbert Quick, one of the farmers' best friends, who was for years one of the Federal Land Bank Commissioners in Washington, analyzed the farm situation in America, with cogency and logic which has not been surpassed. He said:

> What will cure agriculture of its diseases is a state of things in which good land will be once more cheap, so that a poor man can own it, and in which everything done by, or for the farmers will not at once curse them with high land values and increased rents.
>
> The first necessary of life is land. It comes before even such things as food and shelter, for we can not have either of these without access to land. The grossest error of mankind is the thought that high land values mean good to man. We fall into that destructive mistake, because with land monopolized all good to man is reflected in increasing land values. The high price of our land, however, comes from the good to humanity and not the good to humanity from the land values. This is a fundamental distinction.
>
> We shall go on from bad to worse if we can not make land cheap once more. Our good cheap land is gone. Our problem is to get it back again, in city and country. We shall get it back if society is destroyed, but it will do nobody any good in that case. Mesopotamia must once have had high land values; but when the hordes of Central Asia overwhelmed it they destroyed the land values with the society which built them up.

Among the social advantages of exempting improvements from taxation and covering most of ground rents into public treasuries, may be noted the following:

Reducing taxes paid by small home owners by one-half to three-fifths, and making ownership of homes and farms easier.

Reducing rents by at least one-third to one-half.

Making slum clearance practical, instead of a bonus to land speculators.

Reducing municipal and state expenditures to care for people who contract sickness from bad housing, and for detection and prevention of crime attributable to bad housing.

Reducing Federal, State and local expenditures for land for public purposes, to a negligible sum.

Reducing the net worth capitalization of railroads and all public utilities, and so the rates which they may legally charge.

Increasing the consuming power of the masses of the people by most of the net $5,000,000,000 to $6,000,000,000 which goes to land owners every year, and so materially increasing employment.

Greatly facilitating acquisition of natural resources by the government, because it will reduce the amount the owners can get allowed by the Courts as payment.

In every major city from 5 to 10 per cent of the people collect most of the ground rent. There is not such concentration with respect to farm lands.

It has been carefully estimated, however, that less than 10 per cent of the families of America collect and retain the major part of the five to six billion dollars of net ground rents which today go to land owners in America.

Until States and cities meet their share of the responsibility for present economic conditions, Federal subvention of unemployment insurance, Federal relief, and Federal conscription of income will fail to achieve its full purpose of relieving unemployment, and opening up employment. There must be active cooperation by State and municipal legislative bodies with the Federal Government in meeting the disaster, of which unemployment is merely a register and not a cause.

Inflationary Measures Injure the Masses

(Letter to President Roosevelt early in May)

The effects of inflationary anticipations have probably been fully discounted in the stock market, and the first beneficiaries thereof have already cashed in heavily.

Real estate dealers in New York City, which has often been described as the "Paradise of Land Speculators," are hailing inflationary measures as certain to bring a rapid and large increase in the selling price of land.

Landlords will be the next beneficiaries, as rents increase.

Middlemen and retailers also will participate in the profits of an upswing in prices of commodities.

Wages and salaries, however, have generally been cut, and admittedly will not be increased voluntarily, nor soon, to offset the rise in the cost of living.

Even in 1929, the year of highest wage rates, and largest national income, the 45,337,000 persons receiving incomes of $3,000 or less, spent $8,213,000,000 more than their income.

Unless there is a marked gain in the purchasing power of the masses of the people from current income, any prosperity from inflation would be at best temporary.

Inflation does not increase the purchasing power of the masses.

The major policies which you have sponsored, will benefit chiefly, and almost exclusively property owners, and largely at the expense of those who earn their meagre living as producing farmers, and as wage and salary earners. Since four per cent of the people own about four-fifths of the national wealth, and a very large proportion, probably a third, own no property or less than $1,000 worth, it is obvious that the program you advocate,

[First published in *People's Lobby Bulletin* 3 (July 1933): 1–2.]

will produce an even greater concentration of wealth, and of income, than at present.

The proposed industry control bill cannot effect any appreciable improvement in the economic status of the masses of the American people, unless it is accompanied by legislation to prevent increased selling prices of land, and consequently, increased rents, and living costs.

The proposed limitation of output of factories which produce goods of permanent value and general demand, is unwise, and means reducing the standard of living, for which there is no excuse, with the national income what it is now. The effective demand for such goods at a reasonable price can be greatly increased, perhaps doubled, within three to six months, with such a redistribution of the national income, as can be effected by September 1st, through immediate practical revision of our tax system.

Any effort to keep consumers' prices near present levels, will, of course, be nullified if inflationary policies are carried into full effect, and prices of raw materials are thereby increased appreciably.

Factories which produce luxuries can be closed, by emergency authority.

The effect of your policies to date, is to compel the American people to carry the burden of excessive land values and consequent heavy debts, and to pay more taxes which the wealthy should pay,—through curtailing consumption, and so further deepening the depression.

The Constitution proscribes direct Federal taxation of land values, but as an emergency measure this would probably be upheld by the Supreme Court.

We earnestly request, therefore, that you recommend that Congress impose an annual tax of at least 1 per cent upon the full assessed value of all taxable land in the United States, exclusive of sub-soil wealth, or improvements on and in land.

Such a tax would prevent much speculation in farm and city land, reduce rents for farms and tenements, modify such rapid increase in the cost of living as any appreciable inflation will induce, and yield a revenue of between $850,000,000 and $900,000,000 to the Federal Government, so making possible the repeal of most burdensome consumption taxes.

Wild Inflation Would Paralyze Nation

Inflation is the most volatile of all nostrums, and as difficult to control as escaping gas. It is difficult to believe that the nearly one-fifth of the American families now in degrading poverty, and a fifth only slightly above such poverty, with at best no prospect of appreciable increase in their dollar incomes, will quietly submit to the increase of one-quarter to one-third in the cost of living, which even a moderate and "controlled" inflation would almost inevitably produce.

Much legislation enacted by Congress since March 4th, has failed to recognize that the basic causes of our depression are maldistribution of the national income between various classes, especially the inequitable distribution of the national income between property and producers.

The Bureau of Internal Revenue reports that in 1931 about one and one-half per cent of the families received nearly one-fifth of the national income, and there is every reason to believe that there was a similar concentration of income in 1932, while the National Bureau of Economic Research has shown that in 1928, about four-ninths of the national income went to property and only about five-ninths went to the 47,000,000 persons gainfully employed, as pay for work.

Nearly two-thirds of the income of the one and one-half per cent of the families receiving one-fifth of the national income is from ownership or control of property. Dividend and interest charges are still maintained on a scale out of all proportion to salary and wages.

It is extremely doubtful whether the purchasing power of the masses of the American people is much, if any, greater now than on March 4th, in spite of the two million or more who have been

[First published in *People's Lobby Bulletin* 3 (September 1933): 1–2.]

employed since that date, and in spite of some increases in wages, because of the increase in the cost of living, and hundreds of millions of dollars of additional sales taxes and other consumption taxes levied by the Federal and State Governments.

There is much more certainty that living costs will soar from inflation, than that even such slight gains as have already taken place, will endure.

Among the classes who suffer from inflation are all those on fixed incomes, whether from property or on salaries, including all teachers, and all employees of governments, Federal, State and local—all veterans and other pensioners. All insurance policies will be depreciated in value.

Freight rates will naturally have to be boosted and regulating bodies will be flooded with applications for permission to increase charges.

The contemplated inflation of a third to a half in prices will make it necessary for the Federal Government to appropriate at least $500,000,000 more for relief to afford the same standard as with the price level of last March, while it will increase the general budget of all governments, Federal, State and local, by three billion to four billion dollars a year.

Inflation benefits, not producers on farms, and in factories, mines and in transportation, but property owners.

As four per cent of the people own nearly four-fifths of the wealth of the nation, the ultimate benefit of inflation will go to land speculators, monopolizers of natural resources, and holders of stocks, rather than to the farmers and other producers, on behalf of whom it is urged.

Admittedly, the American people cannot and should not pay the full burden of nearly two hundred and fifty billion dollars of government and non-government debt, but this should be adjusted and written down, by sane methods, instead of by an orgy of passing the buck, through inflation.

Naturally the middle classes, now victims of the tug-of-war between capitalists,—industrial, financial and agricultural,—and labor, will pay a large share of the cost of debt adjustment by inflation.

Such inflation would be the last goad to drive these middle classes into effective economic and political action, to save themselves from the tragedy of insane economic policies.

Lobby Asks Special Session on Debts

(Letter of President Dewey to the President)

The general opposition to currency inflation, which we share fully, cannot obliterate the fact that it is not practical to ask the debtors of the nation to pay even in the dollars of today, either interest or principal in full on the nearly $250,000,000,000 of government and non-government debt—long term and commercial.

Refraining from currency inflation, does not increase the paying capacity of debtors.

There is little reason to think that a moratorium on interest and principal payments for two or three years, would help the situation materially, for it is doubtful whether the distribution of the national income after that time will be such as to make renewal of current payments and arrears practical or equitable.

Government loans to farmers to hold reduced crops for a higher price, loans to distressed banks to carry frozen assets, and loans to employers to pay wages, are segments of a vicious circle of debt which is almost certain to end in the same bog as international loans.

During the decade 1920 to 1930, the valuation of farm lands (exclusive of improvements thereon) dropped from $54,829,563,000 to $34,929,994,000—a reduction of $19,899,569,000, or 36.3 per cent. Most of this reduction came in the first half of that decade.

A similar reduction in the selling price of urban land would be highly beneficial.

It is manifestly inequitable, however, that the burden of mortgage debt should remain on either farm or urban land, or buildings either, after such a reduction in the selling price, and the

[First published in *People's Lobby Bulletin* 3 (October 1933): 1.]

reduced selling price of land is a distinct help in lowering costs of production, and increasing the power of the American people to consume goods.

A reduction in mortgage debts and interest rates somewhat proportionate to the reduction in prices of farm lands seems imperatively needed. This should of course be accompanied by measures to prevent increase in the selling price of land, farm and urban.

The farmers of the nation had what amounts to a capital levy of about $17,100,000,000 from 1920 to 1925, in this reduction of the fictitious valuation of farm lands.

The complaint is frequently made that city real estate is being taxed too heavily, but the real difficulty is that owners are pressed to meet the carrying charges on mortgage indebtedness which amounts to about $27,500,000,000 on urban property.

With the rapid increase in the cost of living, and continued widespread unemployment, carrying charges on mortgage debts will be increasingly difficult to meet.

The sentiment of a large number of the members of both branches of Congress, is growing, for adjustment of debts.

To postpone intelligent action on this matter until Congress meets in January, will invite erratic action then.

Will you, therefore, call Congress in special session early in November, and present to it legislation authorizing a reduction in principal and interest rates on private mortgage indebtedness now amounting to about $36,000,000,000, and creating Debt Revaluation Boards, to adjust both long term and commercial debts?

Unemployment Committee Asks Adequate Relief

The Joint Committee on Unemployment, Through John Dewey, Chairman, Dr. Sidney E. Goldstein, Chairman of the Executive Committee, and Mary Fox, Secretary, Have Written Relief Administrator Hopkins Asking Adequate Relief and Representation of the Unemployed on Relief Boards; Their Reasons are Compelling.

The reports that we have received from the different States and local communities indicate clearly that relief standards in many sections are unbelievably and outrageously low.

The Hearings recently held in New York City by the Citizens Jury on Unemployment, have accumulated evidence that can leave no doubt in the mind of impartial men and women as to the pitifully low allowances now being made in New York to the families under the care of the city. The food allowance in itself is confessedly insufficient to maintain the children and parents on a level of health; the rent policy is such as to lead to a constant and haunting fear of being dispossessed, and to a tremendous increase in evictions from month to month; and no provision whatever, we have learned, is being made for other items, such items for example as medical and nursing care. What is revealed in these Hearings in New York is duplicated again and again through reports we have received from other cities in the country.

As Administrator of Relief for the Federal Government you may not have, it is true, the legal authority to insist upon what we all know to be a reasonable level of relief. But your position and authority and power are such as to permit you to require adequate standards as a condition of Federal subsidy in cities and States. In permitting the States and smaller communities to force the unemployed into the state of utter desperation in which

[First published in *People's Lobby Bulletin* 3 (October 1933): 5–6.]

we find them today, the Federal Government convicts itself of connivance.

In order that the unemployed may not continue to suffer on this worse than disaster level of relief, we urge you to estimate now the number of families that will probably require aid during the rest of this year and the first six months of 1934. This we believe can be done on the basis of the present trend in employment and relief reports. It would then be possible to calculate roughly at least the amount that would be required from Congress for the first half of 1934. Our own estimate is that you will need at least $500,000,000 for the first six months of 1934 and Congress must be informed in time and prepared to meet this need.

Another matter that we desire urgently to bring to your attention is the composition of the Relief Boards in the different States. We are informed that these Boards are as a rule composed chiefly of employers and contain no representatives of the unemployed. We are emphatically of the opinion that every Relief Board, State and local, should include representatives of the unemployed groups. This we believe is in the spirit of fairness to the groups that know their own needs best, and that must be served. The unemployed better than any other group understand what they require and the way in which the work should be done.

Farm Processing and Other Consumption Taxes Must Be Repealed

Letter to President Roosevelt

Several months' experience with the processing taxes on farm products has shown that they have directly reduced consumption of farm products, and reduced the consuming power of the masses to buy manufactured products. They have not, as recent events attest, solved nor apparently materially improved the status of farmers.

Even most of the short-sighted advocates of a general sales tax, drew the line on sales taxes on food stuffs, and farm products consumed by the masses, such as cotton.

Leaders of the three general farm organizations, the American Farm Bureau Federation, the National Grange, and the Farmers' National Educational and Cooperative Union, opposed a general sales tax, as did the American Federation of Labor, and civic and social service organizations.

Probably in the belief that economic laws could be suspended by Congress, on behalf of distressed agriculture, some farm leaders officially approved the processing taxes on farm products, sponsored by the Administration.

The cost to consumers, of farm processing taxes levied, or contemplated, will be at least $600,000,000 to $650,000,000 a year.

On behalf of the consumers of America, the restoration of whose purchasing power is prerequisite to prosperity, we earnestly urge you to call Congress to meet two weeks before the scheduled date, to repeal all processing taxes on farm products, and at least a billion dollars of other consumption taxes.

Such repeal will obviously increase the purchasing power of

[First published in *People's Lobby Bulletin* 3 (November 1933): 1.]

the masses, farmers, wage earners, and small salaried people, by at least $1,600,000,000 a year.

It is the most important repeal.

It involves revision of the entire Revenue Act, and the raising of essential Federal revenues by a system of taxation based upon the principle of ability to pay.

Increased surtaxes will yield $1,600,000,000.

In 1931, 34,677 persons with net incomes of $25,000 received an aggregate net income of $2,088,624,962, and after paying all surtaxes and other taxes, had left $1,897,689,233—an average of $54,468.

In 1931, the 521,443 persons with net incomes of $5,000 to $25,000, received an aggregate net income of $4,591,727,080, and after paying all surtaxes and other taxes had left $4,548,729,934, an average of $8,723.

The first class paid only $190,935,729 in Federal income taxes and surtaxes. They could easily have paid at least $800,000,000 more.

The second class paid only $42,997,146 in Federal income taxes and surtaxes. They could easily have paid at least $800,000,000 more—a total for both classes of $1,600,000,000.

Most of the $1,600,000,000 of processing taxes on farm products, and of consumption taxes, we ask to have repealed, is paid by the masses—those with incomes below $3,000.

Farm products processing taxes—if needed—should be paid directly out of the Federal Treasury.

The Next Session and the People's Lobby

The next session of Congress will be the most important as well as the liveliest for many years. Special groups will be urging legislation in their own interests. Some will demand an inflation that will in the end further depress the wages of labor and will practically ruin teachers, clerks and all on a fixed salary, and seriously injure all who are insured and who have moderate savings banks deposits. Chambers of Commerce and bankers and "Wall Street" are urging as the only alternative a return to putting the control of money in their hands and stimulation of money speculation by re-establishment of unrestricted foreign exchange. The program of the People's Lobby stands for the public welfare.

Wage-earners and the middle classes have everything to gain by ending special privilege and securing public welfare legislation. It can be done without injury to the producers, the farmers, and to their ultimate benefit. The producing farmer has nothing to gain in the long run by lowering the purchasing power of the great mass of the urban population. Only those more interested in selling their land than in farming it, have anything to gain by starting land booms and promoting land speculation. Many of the present troubles of the farmer are the product of similar speculation in the past. Progress and prosperity will not be had by swapping old debts for new. Constructive measures are needed.

Demand for paper-money inflation will run wild, unless interest on long term debts can be written down. The unemployed and the workers who are insecure may join the cry, unless a program of extensive works puts in their hands the money needed to buy food, clothes, and pay rent.

[First published in *People's Lobby Bulletin* 3 (December 1933): 1.]

Even with a fair measure of recovery, depression and collapse will be just around the corner unless the national income is more justly distributed. Unconsumed profits will destroy our economic system if they continue to pile up.

Since changes in political party and control, and in individual membership in Congress always accompany economic discontent, members of Congress will be more than usually ready to pay attention to demands from constituents. Special groups are organized in their special lobbies.

The People's Lobby represents the public welfare. Its domestic program for the next Congress follows. Let every member of the Lobby write his and her Representative in the House and Senate and demand support for it.

Socialization of income through taxation.

Writing down interest on long term debts.

A Government Marketing Corporation.

Large Federal credits for public works and public housing.

Federal responsibility for adequate relief.

President's Policies Help Property Owners Chiefly

(Open Letter from President Dewey to the President)

You have recognized the futility of the policy of your predecessor who believed that if only finance and industry were stimulated at the top, prosperity would under the beneficent hands of overlords gradually trickle down to the masses. You have recognized in theory that there can be no enduring prosperity without increase of the consuming power of the masses, brought about by increase of purchasing power.

At the same time, Mr. President, you are continuing in practice the policies of President Hoover and the Republican Administration, that did nothing to lift the American people from the depression. Loans of billions are made to banks, railways and insurance corporations, adding to the debt structure of the country and to the burden of interest that must be paid through taxation. Loans and gifts at the top have, in spite of your declared policies, outweighed help at the bottom in the ratio of seven to one.

You have tried to stem the tide of deflation as your predecessor did not. You have announced as your goal the restoration of the price level to that of 1926. But the methods by which this end is being sought are such that the chief effect is to assist those in least need of help, those who are already the beneficiaries of our inequitable system.

The effect is to make solvent speculative land values, and to bolster the mortgage debts and rates of interest based thereon; to validate the impossible burdensome capitalization of railways, public utilities, mining and manufacturing corporations. How-

[First published in *People's Lobby Bulletin* 3 (January 1934): 1–2.]

ever good your intentions, your policies are in their consequences a continuation of the favors extended to organized and speculative wealth by your predecessor.

Mr. President, I am convinced in common with the great majority of our fellow citizens, that you do not desire to see our farmers reduced to a state of peasantry, and the wage earners to a condition a little above that of serfdom. But what is the end to be, when along with the increase of debts through large expenditures, taxes still continue to be piled upon the consumer, and the cost of living of the mass rises more rapidly than wages and salaries?

When five per cent of the people own and control four-fifths of the wealth of the country, nothing but a continuation of the evil causes that have produced the present situation can be expected from policies that put the burden of debt and increased cost of living upon those least able to stand it, while refusing to use power to tax higher incomes and estates, to secure that equalization of income which will alone guarantee mass consumption, to take care of mass production.

With a fair distribution of national incomes, and with reasonable prices for goods, we could consume every year for a number of years to come, from one to one and a half billion more bales of cotton than at present; could construct two million more homes, consume almost two billion more gallons of milk, and increase vastly the production and use of furniture, household and dress goods. Such an increase would of necessity create a demand also for capital expenditures.

There is but one way open to recovery which is anything more than a temporary hectic fever. That way is not being taken. It is simple and direct. It is on one side, the use of taxation to achieve an adequate, equitable distribution of consuming and purchasing power, and on the other side, the use of government authority and power to relieve the suffering that is due to unemployment, and to raise the standard of living and of economic demand by an adequate program of housing, and of social services in health, education and all things where individuals are dependent upon the community.

A beginning has been made in the latter direction, and we desire to give you full credit for that beginning. But we ask you,

Mr. President, to compare your own figures of expenditures in this direction for what is being done to aid the wealthy who live by investment and not by work, to see how one-sided are present policies and how sure they are to end in disaster.

New Deal Program Must Be Appraised

(Open Letter to Members of Congress)

An appraisal of the real effectiveness of the legislation and measures known as the "New Deal" must be made at once by Congress, in order that Congress, still a coordinate branch of government, may know what new legislation is needed to prevent disaster.

Congress, which gave the President more unlimited powers than have ever before been conferred upon a peace-time President, cannot continue to remain in abeyance. It has the same right now, to appraise the real and possible benefits of the measures the President sponsored, urged, and defends, as the constituents of Congress have, and will exercise at the polls in ten months.

Constituents will judge members of both branches of Congress not so much upon the results of the Roosevelt policies to date, as upon the results of those policies during the next ten months, and the passive acquiescence of Congress in the continuation of those policies.

Specifically, Congress should ascertain what has been the success and methods of the National Recovery Administration under General Johnson, who has been responsible only to the President.

Has its operation increased the consuming power of the masses of non-agricultural workers? It will be difficult to claim this, since payrolls during the first nine months of 1933 were 3.2 less than during the same period in 1932, and have not increased much during the last quarter of the year.

What possibility is there that increases in employment and in wages can be achieved under the present set-up, to offset or even

[First published in *People's Lobby Bulletin* 3 (January 1934): 5.]

keep up to that increase in the cost of living, implicit in the Administration's effort to restore the 1926 price level?

Has the organization of self-determining labor unions been encouraged, or discouraged under General Johnson?

Why have consumers, upon whose pocketbooks revival depends, been ignored in the Administration's plans for revival?

Has General Johnson's practical prohibition of strikes been due to reluctance to interrupt production, or to knowledge that most recent strikes were due to unfair working conditions, and inadequate wages?

Since the purchasing power of the masses is determined by their real wages, can the N.R.A. succeed in creating a sufficient surplus of producers' purchasing income, after fixed charges as interest, profits, and rents, are met?

What is being done to protect consumers and small producers to correspond to protection to large producers in dropping the Sherman Anti-Trust Law?

What reason has the Administration to think that conditions will improve sufficiently to justify its policy of postponed payments, and incurring a debt of $4,000,000,000 for current outlays? Why not tax swollen wealth now, instead of incurring a burden the future cannot carry?

These are some of the questions Congress should ask in a thorough investigation of the N.R.A.

A Real Test of the Administration

The Revenue Bill constitutes a real and inescapable test of the sincerity of the Administration.

It will show whether many of the measures that have been put into operation are actually calculated to secure a more equitable distribution of the national income, or while creating the impression that a new system is in the making, enable the beneficiaries of government up to date, to continue their prerogative of being the chief financial beneficiaries of government. The intent of many of the measures which have been put into operation since March 4th—nearly a year ago—may be in question; their effect has been to increase concentration not only of control, but of profits, and to place upon the common people of America—farmers, wage earners, and small professional people generally—a heavy burden which they are unable to bear.

Taxation based upon the principle of ability to pay and service rendered by Government does not require any Constitutional Amendment, nor is it contingent upon approval by the Supreme Court of the United States. Here is an immediate issue which cannot be ignored, and the responsibility for which cannot be evaded by pointing out that Cabinet Members and high government officials under the preceding Administration used public office for improper purposes—including their own enrichment.

Any government official and any member of Congress who advocates increased consumption taxes, keeping income tax rates down, sparing the vast liquid surpluses of corporations from taxation, and increasing consumption taxes on the masses in order to prevent increasing taxes upon his own income, is in effect ethically though not legally, in the same class with gov-

[First published in *People's Lobby Bulletin* 3 (February 1934): 1–2.]

ernment officials who use their public position to feather their own nests.

When the only function of the Federal Government was to maintain judges as a last court of resort in conflicts between states, to run the post office, and advise farmers how to make two blades of grass grow where one had been growing; to compile statistics as to the conditions of labor, and of women and children in industry, and to maintain an army and navy to defend this nation against aggression and defend aggressive American citizens abroad who have impinged upon the rights of people in other countries—the question of Federal sources of revenue was not so important. Even in the days when a billion dollar Federal budget seemed extravagant, systems of revenue raising for the Federal Government were not so vital because that billion dollar budget was only about four or five per cent of the national income.

The Federal budget for the year ending June 30th next, nearly $10,000,000,000 is approximately twenty-five per cent of the national income for the year.

The Federal Government has been obliged to abandon its role of interstate policeman, statistics gatherer, and protector of American citizens against real or imaginary enemies abroad.

The Federal Government has now admitted its responsibility to provide work or maintenance for every American citizen who cannot obtain work or maintenance in ordinary commercial undertakings. Despite the optimistic fore-cast of the Secretary of Commerce that a large proportion of the 10,000,000 unemployed will shortly be re-absorbed into productive commercial employment, it is probable that we shall have permanently an army of unemployed, or unemployable by private industry, of four to six million men and women. The Federal Government's admission of responsibility for these people cannot be abandoned lightly. Such abandonment would mean disaster, chaos, and probably wide-spread violence. To meet the responsibilities it has admitted, the Federal Government must spend billions a year for years to come. The nearly $10,000,000,000 budget for the year ending in less than five months, can be raised in three ways: taxation, loans, or a combination of taxation and loans.

Every billion dollars borrowed by twenty-five year bonds at

four per cent interest, means a payment of a billion dollars in interest alone, plus amortization charges. It is obvious that until America taxes incomes and corporations as heavily as other countries, we cannot claim to have exhausted the possibilities of taxation.

During the fiscal year ending March, 1932, England with roughly one-third of the population of the United States obtained from the individual and corporation tax, the vast sum of $1,781,500,000, while the United States during our fiscal year 1932 raised from these taxes only $1,056,757,000. Obviously we could have raised from these two taxes, considering our wealth and population, at least four and a half, to five billion dollars. The Administration has not indicated any intention to urge a different revenue bill than the thoroughly inequitable bill reported by the House Ways and Means Committee, which makes practically no increase in individual income taxes or in taxation of corporations.

Under present plans, the masses of the American people will pay at least four and a half billion dollars in interest alone, to the investing classes, for whose benefit the government is this year incurring a deficit of approximately $6,631,000,000.

The only hope for obtaining a fair revenue bill to tax privilege instead of poverty, is in the Senate. Every reader of the *People's Lobby Bulletin* and citizens generally, should write both their United States Senators, demanding that the major part of government expenditures for this year, be met through taxation of privilege and wealth. A personal letter with such demand to both United States Senators is the best investment any citizen can make.

America's Public Ownership Program

(Speech at Conference of People's Lobby in Washington)

The present chaos in production and distribution is largely responsible for the continuation of the depression. It bears down most heavily upon consumers and wage earners. The latter have to stand it at both ends. They suffer from insecurity and from the burden that falls on all consumers. Farmers suffer from lack of secure markets, from high costs of transportation, from bad distribution, and from the taxes they pay as consumers, on all manufactured goods. Their inability to purchase, reacts on production and the wage-earner.

This vicious circle cannot be broken by patchwork measures. It requires organization to get us out of the chaos.

The Government as the representative of the whole people is the sole agency that is capable of taking the necessary measures. The obvious beginning is for the people through their government to take over the basic agencies upon which industry and commerce depend. Modern production and business are carried on by credit.

Bankers have failed disgracefully because they are more concerned to make profits for themselves, than to perform their indispensable social function.

Private means of transportation stand like a stone wall between producer and consumer, and yet are the only ways by which these two can get together. The gross income of railroads, and public utility corporations for last year was about ten billion dollars—a tax on the producing and consuming public. Yet

[First published in *People's Lobby Bulletin* 3 (March 1934): 1.]

the Government has turned over to these private corporations through the Reconstruction Finance Corporation and the Public Works Administration at least half a billion dollars that has not been repaid.

We live in a power age. Electricity is no longer a domestic convenience but a necessity for manufacturing and producing. Governor Pinchot has stated that light and power companies have overcharged the public half a billion dollars a year. This money that has gone into private pockets would not only relieve the consumer, but would give the agencies of production a great stimulus and increase employment, if they were relieved of the tax upon them, now collected by private persons, who lack public responsibility.

Under a proper system, mines and oil wells being a part of the land would never have fallen into private hands to exploit for their own advantage. Society that creates their wealth would have taken by taxation the value society creates. Their gross profit of nearly two billions can still go to the people as a whole if the Government takes them over, and at the same time there would be elimination of waste and conservation of natural resources.

The one great question before the American public is whether it is going to trust to various measures of hocus-pocus to ensure against an even more tragic return of our present abominable and unnecessary calamities, or whether it has the intelligence and courage to take over the basic agencies of public welfare and manage them for the welfare of all the people.

Facing the Era of Realities

"The emergency acts are coming home to roost and the time is rapidly approaching when the realities must be considered and dealt with. . . . For nearly a year the President and his advisers postponed facing these realities."

In these words Mr. Arthur Krock, head of the Washington Bureau of the *New York Times*,—very friendly to the Administration, recently summarized the situation.

This view is generally held in Washington—unofficially.

The fate of the automobile workers, the fight over wage cuts for railway employees, the crisis in the soft coal fields, the demobilizations of hundreds of thousands of C.W.A. workers, many of them being shifted to relief rolls at $7.20 to $10.00 a week, and the failure of the public works program, have forced reconsideration of the efficacy of measures tried for a year to increase mass purchasing power, recognized as essential to permanent improvement in the economic status of the masses.

The report by a careful economist of the Department of Agriculture that on the basis of present production, several million more acres of crop lands than are now under cultivation would be used to supply the domestic requirements of a moderate standard of consumption of farm products, plus present exports, has challenged the program of "plowing under" or curtailing essential raw material for food and clothing.

The recent report of the National Bureau of Economic Research on national income from 1929 to 1932, shows that reliance upon maintaining mass consumption by skimpy allowances to labor out of the total value of production is doomed.

In 1929, property income was nearly one-third of labor income, and in 1932 was still close to one-third. In 1932, about

[First published in *People's Lobby Bulletin* 3 (April 1934): 1–2.]

340,000 people got three-eighths of the property income, while in 1930, 810,000 people got less than two-thirds of the property income.

Concentration of income from property into fewer and fewer hands has been going on apparently continuously since the stock market collapse of 1929, although there are probably between ten and eleven million stockholders in the country. The vital question is what shift in policies will be adopted by the Administration, now that the program of restricting production and consumption to maintain property income has been tried and found wanting.

The enormous vote by which the President's veto of the bill providing veterans compensation and increasing pay of Federal employees was overridden in the House, and the vote in the Senate, reveals the widespread discontent with the results of policies to date. The next six to eight months will probably see the Administration committed to a direct swing to the right or to the left. Which the swing shall be depends in large measure upon the aggressiveness with which liberals and radicals urge their programs. Politics hates a vacuum as much as nature.

The successful fight for Stock Exchange Control which the Senate Committee on Banking and Currency, under the Chairmanship of Senator Fletcher of Florida, and with the active cooperation of Senators Costigan and Couzens, have made against overwhelming opposition by the financiers of the nation is keenly encouraging. Even should this bill be defeated in either branch of Congress at this session, such legislation to prevent gambling on a nation-wide scale on the prior claim of property to values produced, must be checked and controlled in the near future. Nationalization of banking and of credit is the logical sequence to the enactment of stock exchange control legislation.

Redistribution of the national income through taxation is the imperative duty of Congress at this session. Failure of agencies hitherto set up to effect such a redistribution through ordinary channels of production, makes this more than ever imperative.

No Half-Way House for America

Conceding the high purpose of the President to succor the forgotten man, the methods used to this end are doomed to failure.

Wishful worship of social justice cannot right a single wrong.

Despite the criticism of business leaders, for a year and a half legislation and administrative effort have been directed largely to trying to save the profit system from itself, thereby in the end restoring the conditions responsible for the collapse of 1929, and for the depression.

There is no half-way house for America.

Invoking the profit motive to provide employment is a confession of impotency, since the quest for profits—as rent, interest and gains on invested capital—is the cause of unemployment and poverty.

There is no way out for America, except to recognize that labor has prior claims upon production which take precedence of current return upon property, even when property ownership is due to investment of savings from labor income.

A return to the conditions of alleged prosperity of 1929, when only a thirteenth of our people had a comfort income or better, an eighth were in moderate circumstances, about a third were in minimum comfort, and over two-fifths were on a bare subsistence level or in stark poverty, is unthinkable.

Yet that is precisely the goal of dominant industrial and financial, and of certain landed urban and agricultural interests.

We cannot achieve a decent standard of living for more than a fraction of the American people, by any other method than that to which the British Labor Party and the Social Democratic Parties of Europe are committed—the socialization of all natural

[First published in *People's Lobby Bulletin* 4 (November 1934): 1.]

resources and natural monopolies, of ground rent, and of basic industries.

Classification as Democrat or Republican means nothing in America today—the only vital distinction is on such socialization.

Public ownership has greater difficulties in America because of our long era of frenzied finance, watered capitalization, and inflated land values, and of the relatively large number of people holding evidences of title to a share in profits, but this can be overcome in a very few years through the British system of taxation; and socialization of ground rent means elimination of much fictitious capitalization.

Only elimination of profits through socialization, will prevent eventual chaos.

Miscellany

Religions and the "Religious"

Sir: Mr. Norbert Guterman says in his notice of my book, *A Common Faith* [the *New Republic*, February 20], that I ascribe "the diminishing influence of religions on our life to their intellectual inadequacies"; that I neglect their inadequacy with respect to their social function, and that consequently what I would put in their place "is a mere state of mind."

I do not know whether Mr. Guterman did not read my book, or whether his eyes having fallen upon its pages, he suffers from never having been able to learn to read. More space is devoted in my book to the inadequacies of religions in their social bearings than to their intellectual inadequacies, and the former are said to be more serious and more injurious. One-third of my short volume is expressly devoted to the social implications of what I would put in place of religions. Mr. Guterman's review is a good example of "a state of mind" substituted for objective fact.

JOHN DEWEY

[First published in *New Republic* 82 (13 March 1935): 132. For Guterman's review to which this is a reply, see this volume, Appendix 4.]

Reply to Aubrey and Wieman in "Is John Dewey a Theist?"

Editor the *Christian Century*:

Sir: Having had the opportunity to read both Mr. Aubrey's communication and the comment of Mr. Wieman, I wish to say that the latter does not in any way modify my previous complete approval of Mr. Aubrey's statement of my position. In fact, Mr. Wieman's reply has only made it clearer to me that he *has* read his own position into his interpretation of mine.

There is a fundamental difference between that to which I said, with some reservations, the *name* God might be applied and Mr. Wieman's attribution to me of something "that holds the actual and ideal together." What I said was that the union of ideals with *some* natural forces that generate and sustain them, accomplished in human imagination and to be realized through human choice and action, is that to which the name God might be applied, with of course the understanding that that is just what is meant by the word. I thought the *word* might be used because it seems to me that it is this union which has actually functioned in human experience in its religious dimension.

A philosophic polytheist, using Mr. Wieman's logic, might attribute to me a belief in polytheism, since I said that there were many different natural forces and conditions that generate and sustain our ideal ends. The *unification* of these, was, I said, the work of human imagination and will.

The passage which Mr. Wieman quotes in his comment upon Mr. Aubrey's letter is found in a chapter which is entitled "The *Human* Abode of the Religious Function." There is nothing in its

[First published in *Christian Century* 51 (5 December 1934): 1551–52. For letters by Edwin Ewart Aubrey and Henry Nelson Wieman, to which this is a reply, see this volume, Appendixes 6 and 7, and for Wieman's review see this volume, Appendix 5.]

context about God. The tone and purpose of the passage may be indicated by such neighboring phrases as "transfer of idealizing imagination, thought and emotion to natural human relations"; "we who now live are parts of a humanity that extends into the remote past, a humanity that has *interacted* with nature." The "causes and consequences" mentioned in the passage refer to the work of intelligence in discovering them and to the need of transferring to intelligence some of the zeal and devotion that in historic religions have been expended upon the supernatural. And it never occurred to me that anyone could suppose that when I stated that the human community is the best "symbol of the mysterious totality of being the imagination calls the universe," anyone would suppose I was identifying the universe with God. Even at that, I repeat here what was explicitly stated before, that "universe" is a term of the imagination—a poetic rather than a cognitive term. To say that the human community in its total scope is "the matrix within which our ideal aspirations are born and bred" does not mean, I hasten to add, that I regard this community as something to be worshiped.

It is quite true that in my whole philosophy I regard man as part of nature. But Mr. Wieman when he says that "this matrix" (referring to my passage as quoted) is "what holds ideal and actual 'together'" slips from the human community over to all nature as embracing man. When we come to nature as this larger, inclusive matrix, I supposed I had made it clear that I regarded nature in this sense as the matrix in which bad human impulses and habits are also "born and bred." I supposed I had made it clear that the "actual" to which I referred was something *selected* by human thought and action out of the totality. From my point of view Mr. Wieman in assimilating my thought to his has thus fallen into a double confusion.

Mr. Wieman's review was so sympathetic in intent that I should have preferred to keep silent. But that very sympathetic quality is all the more reason that I should make my own position clear. For an adverse tone might possibly have put readers more on their guard as to his interpretation of my book, *A Common Faith*.

JOHN DEWEY

Introduction to
Challenge to the New Deal

When future historians come to look back upon the first part of the Roosevelt Administration, it is quite possible that they will find it the most important epoch in our history since the "critical period" following the establishment of the Republic. To an increasing number of people it has meant the bankruptcy of a system and the last attempt to solve the contradictions of that system through peaceful reform. Now, at a time when the whole New Deal is everywhere being called in question, a review of the last year and a half is more than timely. This book, by as able an array of talent as could be assembled, is such a review.

The brief period covered in this book has been crammed with drama. Following the election of Roosevelt, the very bottom began to drop out of things: panic and hysteria and doubt were the order of the day. Technocracy had swept the country like a new religion as the fourth winter of an unparalleled depression drove Americans for the first time to seek a drastic way out of their plight. With Roosevelt, "action," the New Deal and its new hope, the drama went on at a heightening speed. Then came a consolidation period. During the winter and spring of 1934 people were still waiting for the New Deal to bring prosperity, but there began to dawn an increasing realization that it could not. And now in its second summer, the Roosevelt experiment is being generally admitted a failure. More than ever perspective and vision are necessary, as talk of "revolution" is again in the air.

This month to month drama of strikes, farm revolts, silent suffering, and the desperate measures of industrial and monetary reform that culminated in a flood of billions of dollars of Federal

[First published in Alfred Mitchell Bingham and Selden Rodman, eds., *Challenge to the New Deal* (New York: Falcon Press, 1934), pp. v–vii.]

money to keep the machine running, cannot be adequately told by any single volume of history. There is probably no better way to survey the picture and learn its lessons than through the pages of an intelligent periodical—especially if such a periodical can draw on the best brains in the field of social and political writing.

Neither this book nor the magazine from which it grew has attempted to present a balanced "liberal" view of all sides of the great questions which we face. Such a book is unthinkable today. Two years ago there was much discussion of the fact that "the intellectuals are turning left." But there is no longer such a discussion: the intellectuals *are* left. In this collection of the writings of some of our leading thinkers, there is obviously no question of their "leftness." The only question is how far left they have gone. For this reason the book brings out in sharp relief the problems of radicalism in America.

Particularly *in America*. For there is here little emphasis on the international nature of the problems besetting the world. Americans are increasingly becoming aware of the solution inherent in the vast natural plenty and industrial development of their country. At the same time American radicalism is turning away from European models and philosophies in an increasingly intelligent attempt to solve its own problems in its own way. The Technocracy movement was an indication of this trend. The growth of the Farmer-Labor or "third party" movement in the Middle West is another. The NRA and the whole New Deal are American phenomena, bearing ominous analogies to Fascism abroad, it is true, but still in their inception and in the criticism which they evoke, calling for an American analysis.

This volume, therefore, depicts American radicalism finding itself. As it becomes increasingly obvious to American intelligence that the present system is nearing dissolution, great problems in social engineering arise. How can a world be brought through collapse to a better social order?

The subject falls naturally into three parts. The first is largely descriptive of the collapse of the system as it appeared at the end of the Hoover administration: panic, bewilderment and misery followed by the New Deal "answer." The gigantic Roosevelt experiment of "relief, reform and recovery" showed a definitely new bias, to a controlled and humanized capitalism as contrasted with the brutality of *laissez faire*. But the necessary conclusion seems to be that no such compromise with a decaying system is possible.

The second part goes back to analyze the fundamental flaws in the capitalist economy, and the promise of an intelligent economy, whether seen from the perspective of machine values or human values.

In the last part some definite conclusions begin to emerge. Political action, political power for an economic transformation, a mass political party militantly opposed to the two old parties of privilege—these are essential. The patent failure of the existing radical movement is confronted by the patent increase of American radical thought. A genuine American revolt is developing both in the Farmer-Labor movement of the Middle West and in the unconventional drive of American youth. In the opinion of the writers who conclude this book there is something like a second American Revolution looming ahead. And while it may not be "*the* Revolution" to the disciples of Marx, it should none the less allow no truckling to capitalism.

In an argument of this kind, coming from a group of writers with differing points of view, there might seem to be little consistency. Some of the writers may privately avow a belief in Fascism, others a belief in Communism. Few of them, perhaps, would accept the implications of the complete argument as here presented. They include agrarian liberals and city radicals, intellectuals and active organizers. Yet by and large they represent as able brains as can be mustered to tackle the main problem. And by and large they *do* present a coherent argument, logically developed from step to step.

That this should be so is due to the fact that they have all had a part in a publication that kept to a consistent editorial policy. The articles (and drawings) herein contained all appeared in the pages of *Common Sense*. The two young men who started this magazine in December, 1932, hoped for just such a logical development of an American radical philosophy—a philosophy that would work. And the fact that they went back to the title of Thomas Paine's revolutionary pamphlet of 1776 was merely symbolic of their hope that America might once more become a leader in human progress as she did at the time of the *first* American Revolution.

Foreword to
The Philosophy of Henry George

The life history of Henry George is typically American even though it has few parallels in this country. There are many instances of rise from poverty and obscurity to wealth or fame or both in the realms of business and politics, and there have been many self-made thinkers in various fields. But Henry George stands almost alone in our history as an example of a man who, without a scholastic background, succeeded by sheer force of observation and thinking that were dictated by human sympathy, and who left an indelible impress on not only his own generation and country but on the world and the future. He is an outstanding example of something of which we hear a good deal, but mainly in the way of unjustified boasting, since the quality in question is more marked in talk than evident in conduct: Practical Idealism. He is an example of what may be accomplished by unswerving devotion and self-sacrifice to a dominating idea. He was, we might say, a man of a single idea, but the statement would be misleading unless we also said that he broadened this one idea until it included a vast range of social phenomena and became a comprehensive social philosophy.

Henry George is typically American not only in his career but in the practical bent of his mind, in his desire to *do* something about the phenomena he studied and not to be content with a theoretic study. Of course he was not unique in this respect. The same desire has been shared by many British economists. John Stuart Mill's theoretical writings were ultimately inspired by interest in social reform. But there is something distinctive in the ardent crusade which George carried on. His ideas were always of the nature of a challenge to action and a call to action. The "science" of politi-

[First published in George Raymond Geiger, *The Philosophy of Henry George* (New York: Macmillan Co., 1933), pp. ix–xiii.]

cal economy was to him a body of principles to provide the basis of policies to be executed, measures to be carried out, not just ideas to be intellectually entertained, plus a faint hope that they might sometime affect action. His ideas were intrinsically "plans of action."

Unfortunately, in some respects, the American public was practical-minded in a much narrower sense and shorter range than was Henry George himself. It is perfectly true that the culmination and indeed the meaning of his social philosophy is to be found in his proposals regarding taxation. It is also true that many persons accept and are justified in accepting his taxation scheme without having knowledge of or interest in the background of principles and aims with which this scheme was organically associated in the mind of Henry George himself. But nevertheless the connection between the theoretical part and the practical part was vital in the thought of George himself. Something vital in acquaintance with his thought is lost when the connection is broken. One may understand the plan of tax reform by itself but one comes far short in that case of understanding the idea which inspired Henry George.

In spite, therefore, of the immense circulation of George's writings, especially of *Progress and Poverty* (which I suppose has had a wider distribution than almost all other books on political economy put together), the full sweep of George's ideas is not at all adequately grasped by the American public, not even by that part which has experienced what we call a higher education. Henry George is one of a small number of definitely original social philosophers that the world has produced. Hence this lack of knowledge of the wider and deeper aspects of his thinking marks a great intellectual loss. In saying this, I am not speaking of acceptance of his ideas but of acquaintance with them, the kind of acquaintance that is expected as a matter of course of cultivated persons with other great social thinkers, irrespective of adoption or nonadoption of their policies.

I should hesitate to write in this way, lest I might be thought to depreciate the practical importance of his plan of social action were it not for two things. One of these things is the fact which I have already stated. His theoretical conceptions and his program of social action are so closely united that knowledge of the first will inevitably lead on to a better understanding of the second.

The other reason is more immediately applicable. Actual social conditions (like those for example of the present) are bound to raise the problem of reform and revision of methods of taxation and public finance. The practical side of George's program is bound in any case to come forward for increased attention. It is impossible to conceive any scheme of permanent tax reform which does not include at least *some* part of George's appropriation by society for social purposes of rental value of land. For instance, we are just beginning to understand how large a part unregulated speculation has played in bringing about the present crisis. And I cannot imagine any informed student of social economy denying that land speculation is basic in the general wild orgy, or that this speculation would have been averted by social appropriation, through taxation, of rent. To a large extent, then, some knowledge of the directly practical side of George's thought is bound, in the long run, to result from the movement of social forces. A corresponding knowledge of George's theory of the importance of land—in the broad sense in which he uses the word—in social development, of the causes of moral progress and deterioration, cannot be secured, however, without an understanding of his underlying philosophy.

The importance of a knowledge of this underlying philosophy is urged in spite of the fact that the present writer does not believe in the conceptions of nature and natural rights which at first sight seem to be fundamental in the social philosophy of Henry George. For, as I see the matter, these conceptions are symbols, expressed in the temporary vocabulary of a certain stage of human history of a truth which can be stated in other language without any serious injury to the general philosophy implied. It has repeatedly been pointed out that the real issue in the "natural rights" conception is the relation of moral aims and criteria to legal and political phenomena. Personally, I have little difficulty in translating a considerable part of what George says on nature over into an assertion that economic phenomena, as well as legal and political, cannot be understood nor regulated apart from consideration of consequences upon human values, upon human good: that is, apart from moral considerations. The question whether a "science" of industry and finance, of wealth, or of law and the State, can exist in abstraction from ethical aims and principles is a much more fundamental one than is the adequacy of certain historical concepts of "nature" which George adopted as a means of expressing the supremacy of ethical concepts, and on this fundamental question I think George was in the right.

This statement brings me to the connection which exists between the foregoing remarks and the work of Dr. Geiger to which the remarks are introductory. In connection with every topic he discusses, Dr. Geiger makes it clear that a vital connection between ends, human values, and economic means is at the basis of George's distinctive treatment. This fact alone gives a distinctive and timely color to this book. Moreover, the significance of Dr. Geiger's treatment does not stop at this point. There is no phase of the work and the influence of Henry George which is not considered. The account of his life and development forms a personal thread which binds all the parts together. Dr. Geiger has given us a book which meets the contemporary demand for an adequate interpretation of the thought and activity of Henry George regarded as a vital whole and not as an aggregate of isolated parts. It will enable the reader to obtain a clear and comprehensive view of one of the world's great social philosophers, certainly the greatest which this country has produced.

Meaning, Assertion and Proposal

Sir: The reading of Dr. Carnap's article "On the Character of Philosophic Problems" has left me with two questions. It is possible that others besides myself would have their attitude toward the general system of Logical Positivism clarified by further discussion of these questions.

1. The view taken as to the relation between formal and connotative (inhaltlich) consideration is not clear to me beyond a certain point. The main thesis maintained is that "it is possible . . . from a viewpoint in which one does not reckon with the meaning, finally to arrive to the answering of all those questions which are formulated as connotative questions" (p. 9). But later on (p. 12) it is stated that "all statements of fact are synthetic"; while on p. 17, it is stated that "mathematical concepts attain their meaning by the fact that the rules of their application in empirical science are given," and on p. 19 the more general statement is made that "what induces us to prefer certain forms of language is the recourse to the empirical material which scientific investigation furnishes."

My question concerns the meaning of connotative or inhaltlich in the contrast drawn; or, putting the question the other way around, what relation, if any, is there between Inhalt and the "empirical material" mentioned in the last two quotations. I get the feeling, possibly quite wrongly, that in the more general thesis as stated "formal" denotes "without reference to meaning or Inhalt"; from later portions I derive rather the impression that "formal" denotes an accurate symbolic statement of Inhalt. ["Fundamentally really there is no difference between the two approaches" (p. 13). And certainly in some of the instances that

[First published in *Philosophy of Science* 1 (April 1934): 237–38.]

are given of the two modes of speech, what is given as "connotative" is a vague or ambiguous statement even from the side of meaning, while the formal mode is a precise rendering of meaning.]

2. Dr. Carnap distinguishes, clearly and justly, between propositions that are assertions and those that are proposals. How far can this distinction, which seems basic, be treated as propositional in character and how far is reference to "assertion" and "proposal" extra-propositional? I am not implying, even in an indirect manner, that we have here a reference to anything psychological, but I should like more light on the exact relation of assertion and proposal to propositions. Of course, we can make the proposition that such and such a proposition is a proposal, not an assertion. But the question then arises: Is *this* proposition an assertion or a proposal? and so on and on.

JOHN DEWEY

To Save the Rand School

To the Editors of the *Nation*:

The Rand School of Social Science is in the midst of a campaign to raise $17,000 in order to continue its work after twenty-seven years of existence. It would be a calamity if the Rand School were compelled to close its doors. It would be a calamity for the thousand and more students, men and women, old and young, who, laboring through the day, depend on the services of the school for enlightenment and refreshment. It would be a calamity to the civic life of the community, since the headquarters of the school also house a large number of offices of organized labor and other agencies whose activities reach out into the life of the city, and even, by means of correspondence courses and extension work and summer camps, into the life of State and nation.

It would be a calamity to intelligent, untrammeled thought and speech everywhere. The Rand School has been one of the foremost agencies in the country for the promotion of economic literacy and political understanding. The joy that reactionary forces would take in its closing is a measure of its usefulness and its standing. Its friends and the friends of enlightenment and sound adult education must see to it that its great work is not brought to a close for lack of funds.

The $17,000 required to save the Rand School and the People's House, if raised, will save the Rand Bookstore, the Rand School Press, the Labor Research Department, the Debs Auditorium, the Workers' Theater, the Meyer London Memorial Library, the Rand School extension and correspondence courses, and

[First published in *Nation* 137 (12 July 1933): 47.]

the home of the Workmen's Circle Children's School, the *New Leader*, the New York Socialist Party, and a host of trade-union organizations.

Readers of the *Nation* are urged to send their contributions to Mrs. Bertha H. Mailly, Chairman, Special Committee, 7 East Fifteenth Street, New York City.

JOHN DEWEY

The Drive against Hunger

Sir: Americans or scavengers, which shall it be? Over 30 million children, women and men, families of the unemployed in our nation, through no fault of their own are being placed upon the most degrading, cruel dole system. Our large cities are giving on the average one dollar per week, per person, for relief. A large majority of cities give nothing for rent, light and heat.

Self-respecting Americans are taking the place of rats as they scavenge from garbage cans to live. Only misery is being shared by the "share-the-work" campaign. Wages are being cut everywhere, the total loss to workers being over forty billion dollars during the depression.

Farmers are losing their farms by the tens of thousands and as a result peasantry is being established in the United States. Cities and states are going bankrupt. Nothing adequate to meet this desperate situation is being proposed by either of the old parties.

The League for Independent Political Action proposes to do something about it. In May the League will assemble a national congress in Washington, D.C., to organize a united New Party. You are aware of the tremendous significance of this step.

Earnestly, I invite you to join us. The national situation calls for action, *now*, by courageous and clear-thinking citizens. Our spring congress will necessitate funds and the strengthening of our membership. We cannot carry this through unless we have the means. We urgently beg of you to send us a contribution, whatever its size.

To create and distribute wealth so as to make it a stable and continuous blessing for the whole people is the cornerstone of

[First published in *New Republic* 74 (29 March 1933): 190.]

our program. As a member you will help shape our action, and share in the greatest task of this generation. Won't you send us your membership application today? Headquarters are at 112 East Nineteenth Street, New York City.

JOHN DEWEY, Chairman

Radio's Influence on the Mind

The radio is the most powerful instrument of social education the world has ever seen. The eye is superior to the ear with respect to the understanding of physical and technical matters. But in all social matters the mass of people are guided through hearing rather than by sight. The progress of democracy has been greatly hindered by the fact that modern means of exchange of physical things has advanced far beyond the means for exchange of knowledge and ideas. The radio brings us the possibility of redressing the balance.

It is only a possibility, not as yet an accomplished fact. The radio lends itself to propaganda in behalf of special interests. It can be used to distort facts and mislead the public mind. In my opinion, the question as to whether it is to be employed for this end or for the social public interest is one of the most crucial problems of the present. Upon the way in which it is practically answered depends to a larger extent than we yet realize the formation of that enlightened and fair-minded public opinion and sentiment that are necessary for the success of democracy. The radio even when in private hands is affected with a profound public interest. For this reason every attempt at genuine education of the millions who daily listen in is of greatest concern. That is one reason, and a great one, why I welcome the endeavors of Station WEVD to conduct the University of the Air. May it succeed and may its influence spread till every broadcasting organization follows its example.

[First published in *School and Society* 60 (15 December 1934): 805, from a 8 December 1934 radio address over the WEVD University of the Air.]

Preface to the English Edition of *Terror in Cuba*

Terror reigns in a beautiful island along the coast of the United States, in a country that the United States, acting as a responsible nation, helped liberate. The expression "reign of terror" is not an empty literary phrase; it describes exactly the way the assassin Machado stays in power. We in the United States feel justifiable indignation about events in Germany and far-off India. But do we recognize that at our very doorstep, in a country with which we are directly involved, atrocities are occurring that make those in more distant countries pale?

Why are we so indifferent to what is happening in Cuba? Why are our people not impelled by a spirit of outrage to take some action to stop the crimes done against humanity within reach of our own shores? Surely we do not lack information. Surely there is no longer any doubt about the authenticity of the information we have about this tyrant's bloody regime in Cuba. The *New York Times* sent one of its best reporters to make on-the-spot observations. Here is an extract from his report:

> Under the Machado régime, however, assassination has risen to the dignity of a political art. Official killings began in 1925.... Politicians, labor leaders and editors opposed to the government were mysteriously killed—the murderers went unpunished.... Having emerged victorious from the 1931 revolution, President Machado embarked upon a policy of complete ruthlessness in an effort to wipe out all opposition to his government.... The secret police and *porra*, or strong-arm squads, were ordered to break up meetings and to

[First published in Comité de jeunes révolutionnaires cubains, *La terreur à Cuba* (Paris: Courbevoie, la Cootypographie, 1933), pp. 9–10. First published in English in *School and Society* 96 (23 November 1968): 444–45, translated by Jo Ann Boydston.]

arrest the conspirators. Homes and offices were invaded; suspects were sent to prison by military courts or held incommunicado in military fortresses without trial; and finally the bodies of political prisoners began to be found in the streets, shot to death after being beaten and tortured.[1]

It is appropriate that the touching and eloquent appeal in the following pages should come from an organization of Cuban students. These students have been heroic leaders in the Cuban fight against a bloodthirsty and unscrupulous dictatorship. University students have been in the forefront of all attempts to defend civil liberties, attempts that led to the closing of the University three years ago. When younger boys and girls then became involved in the fight, lycées and Normal Schools were also closed. A number of professors were outlawed, obliged to hide, and finally, to go into exile. More than sixty were killed—most of them found dead in the streets with unmistakable marks of beating or torture. Most recently (I am writing in April), New York newspapers have reported the discovery of a student's body in the streets of Havana on Good Friday; the death of four others marked the eve of Easter. In no case was there any semblance of a trial, not even by military tribunals.

I consider it a great honor to have been invited to present to my fellow citizens a brief appeal from these students who, even though they escaped the death that befell their companions and friends, are now suffering the martyrdom of exile and the agony of their national tragedy. They ask nothing for themselves, only for a universal cause—for independence and national dignity, for common liberty, for the support of education and culture. I cannot believe that our hearts are so hardened as not to respond to their appeal.

1. Translator's note: The quotation is from Russell Porter, "Cuba Under President Machado," *Current History*, 38:29–30, April, 1933. Porter's six articles written for the *New York Times* appeared Feb. 4–9, 1933.

Statement on Technocracy

Response to three questions proposed by Common Sense: *Can the capitalistic system meet the scientific criticism of Technocracy? Is their prophecy of the immediate collapse of Capitalism exaggerated? Has Technocracy possibilities as a political movement?*

I have no doubt the capitalist system will disappear in time as have other socio-economic systems. I see no signs of its immediate total collapse, in the sense of its being replaced by a definitely different system. It has many roots and bulwarks and I expect to see these disappear or be taken over one by one and not in a sensational wholesale way. This is not an expression of my hopes but of the situation as I see it. Unless Technocracy changes its present purpose quite radically I see no political future for it. It will undoubtedly have some indirect political effect but whether toward Fascism or in a socialistic direction I do not know.

[First published in *Common Sense* 1 (2 February 1933): 9.]

Reports and Interview

On the Grievance Committee's Report

Let me say first, quoting words that were said a good many years ago, that it is a condition and not a theory which confronts the Union. It is that condition, not theory and not even the charges, but the fact which the sessions of the Grievance Committee brought out,—the fact which was stated over and over again,—more by the defendants and their witnesses even than by the witnesses against them, of the seriousness of the situation within the Union, that is responsible for the recommendations of the Grievance Committee concerning the action it regarded as advisable.

As for the need of a Delegate Assembly, the membership is growing. It would soon be so large, in any case, that some kind of representative organization would be necessary. At the very most, as far as that point is concerned, the recommendation in the report of the Grievance Committee that a Delegate Assembly be established merely hastens by a short time action which would have been inevitable. Everybody who will view this matter impartially knows that a representative organization elected by schools and districts will enlist the interest of the members of the organization more completely than any other course. The Assembly will be able to do business and carry on the purposes of the organization, much more effectively than anything else.

As far as some of the other recommendations are concerned, they very definitely come from the condition. That condition, I repeat, by the evidence before the committee is the state of affairs that has been produced by the leaders of the two organized minority groups. I am sorry for the lack of sportsmanship which

[First published in *Union Teacher* 10 (May 1933): 2–4, from a stenographic report of an address to the Teachers Union, Local 5, on 29 April 1933 at the High School of Commerce in New York City.]

the defendants and their witnesses showed. They absolutely ignored the fact that charges of all kinds, charges against the honor, the honesty, the integrity, the leadership of members of the "Administration" had finally exasperated not only these persons, but brought the Union itself to a condition where something had to be done. Then, after the minority members absolutely ignored how their own conduct, their own previous activity in making charges, had brought about the situation, they resorted to, what in all honesty can only be called the "baby act"—they whined; they complained. They said that a smoke screen of "red-baiting" had been sent forth. The authors of baiting ought to be the authorities on baiting, but in this case they do not seem to be so. They claim to have become mere victims, as if these charges against them were made in a vacuum, or descended out of the blue sky, instead of being logically and inevitably the consequences of the tactics which they themselves had pursued.

I could take a long time in going over misrepresentation, actual misrepresentation, in this left-wing "literature" which has been distributed today. I take but one example. It says in this literature that the Committee "admitted" that the leaders said that they did not wish to come into control of the Union excepting on the *platform* that they propose. That statement is made out of whole cloth! The statement they made before the Committee and the statement the Committee made was that the minority groups did not want to come into power except on the basis of the ideology which they represented. It is the difference between their indirect and concealed ideology and their actual platform that constitutes in large measure the backbone of the general report of the Grievance Committee.

The only explanation I know of the tactics of the organized minority groups—I refer to their leaders—is that they have some end in view which they did not hold it expedient to avow publicly, and moreover that they regard that end as so important as to justify any means of misrepresentation and abuse that can be employed to further their ultimate end.

Again, their document mentions five points in the minority platform. It wants to know if these points are grounds for disqualification. Of course they are not. They are definite proposals such that if they had been advanced in good faith and without accompanying abuse and misrepresentation could have been discussed amicably and could have been settled one way or another without any disruption whatsoever. The whole point of the situation as it came out (and I repeat the important basis is in the evidence of the defendants and their supporters), is that they had surrounded these propositions with such an atmosphere of insinuation, imputing bad motives to their opponents, that it became impossible to consider even reasonable propositions on their merit because of the poison that had been injected.

The atmosphere of emotionalism that has developed in the Union amounts in some cases almost to hysteria. I should not even refer to an "open letter" addressed to me except that I find it has been printed and circulated. Perhaps that is sufficient justification for making some reference to it. It asks:

> Do you, a prominent Union member, who has advised Teachers Union members that they must give leadership to the American Labor movement, approve of the changes in the structure of the Union, which are proposed on the strength of your report? Do you approve of the amendments designed to completely stifle initiative on the part of the general membership, rule out all opposition thought and activity, not only prohibit decisive action by the general membership on any particular problem, but even limit the possibilities of discussion? Dr. Dewey, are you ready to say that dissenting opinions are healthy, but that their expression must be stifled? Are you ready to lead the teachers away from "Democracy in Education, Education or Democracy"? As one of the most prominent members of our profession, are you ready to assume the responsibility for setting an example, to the educational authorities and to the entire labor movement, in administrative dictatorship and in the suppression of all opposition?

Now, wouldn't that be terrible—if only anybody had ever thought of it! What is the object of circulating such a statement except to leave in the minds of those who have not read the Report or have not analyzed the situation, an absolutely misleading, and false representation of both the purport and the fact? "*Eliminating the membership,*" when the members annually with proportional representation elect not merely the Executive Board but also the Assembly! "*Limiting the participation,*" when the Union is simply asking to introduce into the conduct of its own affairs representative action which has been found to be most successful everywhere in conducting large organizations!

Of course I believe in democracy! And it is because I believe in democracy that I believe in this principle of just representation, especially when it is backed up by proportional representation that gives the minority its full voice.

My friends, this sort of misrepresentation in order to arouse prejudice in the minds of those who have not followed the development of the situation was the sort of thing that we of the Grievance Committee listened to from the defendants and their chief witness day after day. It is for this reason that I, who claim to have come to this task with a fair mind, an open mind, not only was glad to sign the report, but also took the personal responsibility of drafting a large part of it.

Now let me say one thing more on one point—the fundamental point. We do not want suppression. We want frank and open discussion. One of the difficulties in the situation has been precisely that ulterior purposes have been kept under cover and not brought out into the open.

We believe in opposition. I might possibly become a member of the opposition, if it set forth its hopes and its aims frankly and candidly and tried to get them adopted by the Union by fair and open and above-board discussion, not permeated by misrepresentation, insinuation, and false attribution of unworthy methods of the kind that have been engaged in.

We do not want fixation. It is true that times change. It is true that the activities and the aims of the Union must change from time to time instead of being fixated. But again my friends, Fellow Members of the Union, it has been the very attacks of these representatives of the minority groups that have tended to fixate things and to create divisions that will hamper the growth of the Teachers Union, Local No. 5, of the American Federation of Teachers.

Personally—I am speaking now for myself—I do not pretend now to speak for the other members of the Committee—I am one of those who believe that the Teachers Union in the future, because of the economic development, because of the crisis we are facing, must not occupy itself exclusively with professional questions, but must take more and more into account the general labor movement. It must express itself sympathetically not only with workers in the profession, but also with all oppressed labor. I would like to see the Union move forward in that direction. And again I tell you, my friends, that the greatest difficulty and the greatest obstruction in the way of the Union resides in the tactics of the leaders in these organized minority groups.

If there are others who agree with me in liking to see the Teachers Union and other unions move to the left in political and economic matters, let me say that this is something that cannot be accomplished as long as these minority groups persist in the tactics in which they have engaged. It is for that reason that I have given all the intelligence and the honesty of thought of which I am capable to the analysis of this situation, and have drawn up and am signing the report, of which I now have the honor to move the adoption.

The Report of the
Special Grievance Committee
of the Teachers Union

I. Introduction

ORGANIZATION OF GRIEVANCE COMMITTEE

The Grievance Committee was elected by the membership at a meeting of the Teachers Union on October 27, 1932. It consisted of Mrs. Esther S. Gross, Mr. Max Kline, Mr. John Dewey, Mr. Raphael Philipson, Mr. Charles J. Hendley (alternate, who took the place of Miss Ruth G. Hardy who retired in his favor). The defendants against whom charges were brought were Miss Clara Rieber, Mr. Abraham Zitron, Mr. Isidore Begun, Mr. Joseph Leboit, Mr. Bertram D. Wolfe, Miss Alice Citron. The case of the last defendant was not heard because her physician presented a statement that she was not able to engage in any activities for at least six months, except the minimum of school work.

The committee organized by electing Mr. John Dewey, Chairman, and Mr. Raphael Philipson, Secretary. It held twenty-four meetings of from two to three hours each. Five of these were executive meetings for the consideration of matters presented by the defendants and for the preparation of the report. The transcript of the evidence consists of 721 closely typewritten or printed pages of evidence and minutes. Of these 181 pages were presented to the Grievance Committee by the Joint Committee before the hearings commenced. Up to date the total expense for postage, stenographer, typewriting, printing and office work has been $700.00. Sixty-three witnesses were heard in behalf of the

[First published as an eight-page report by the Teachers Union, Local 5, American Federation of Teachers (New York: Meadowbrook Press, 1933).]

charges brought by the Joint Committee against the defendants. Forty-six witnesses were introduced by the defendants, a total of one hundred nine.

METHOD OF PROCEDURE

At the meeting when the Committee completed its organization it decided to emphasize the concluding section of the Joint Committee report of October 27, 1932 which stated:

> This Committee is unanimous in thinking that a work basis has not yet been found for securing cooperation with the members of the Left Wing groups. We are leaving the solution of this vexed question in the hands of the members.

Because of this decision to inquire into the general situation rather than to confine its inquiries to specific charges against specific individuals, the Committee decided not to appoint anyone as prosecuting counsel.

At the preliminary meeting held with the defendants on November 15, 1932, the Chairman explained to the defendants that the main purpose of the Committee was to try to understand the broader phases of the situation in the Union as well as to hear evidence on the charges against individuals. All the defendants except Miss Rieber agreed to cooperate from this point of view with the Committee. Miss Rieber objected by saying:

> I want the Committee to hear the charges brought against me. To some degree it may be necessary to go into the broader aspects, but to the extent it can be limited I stand on that.

The Chairman answered:

> In Miss Rieber's case we will carry out the procedure of sticking to the letter of the law.

Each defendant had the right to be represented by counsel. Mrs. Royce appeared for Miss Rieber; Mr. Davidson for Mr. Wolfe; and Mr. Kirshner for Mr. Begun.

Since the Committee considered itself investigators and judges rather than prosecutors, it gave witnesses on both sides very wide latitude. Hearings were also necessarily informal because the Committee had no power to compel attendance of witnesses nor to enforce answers from witnesses when they declined to respond. A good deal of testimony was introduced on both sides that, strictly speaking, was irrelevant. It served the purposes, however, of communicating to the Committee the temper and the atmosphere of the situation in the Union and of helping the Committee to understand the divergent points of policy at issue.

The hearings were somewhat prolonged by the intervention of vacations, holidays, and the illness of the Chairman.

Since the Committee was charged with unfairness to the defendants by the counsel for Mr. Begun in his final summing up, the Committee regards it as desirable to state the facts. The charge of Mr. Kirshner was that the Committee allowed "the widest latitude" to the prosecution while restricting the witnesses for the defense. His statement was, "When the defense wished to introduce witnesses who could testify as to the prejudiced atmosphere at Union meetings indicated by numerous provocative acts and illustrations of red-baiting by Administration leaders at Union meetings, the defense was told to stick to the specific charges and bring charges against the Administration leaders if they desired redress."

As a matter of fact, the record is full of charges made against various members of the Administration by defendants and their witnesses bearing on precisely the points mentioned. Moreover, the record shows that four witnesses testified, some of them at considerable length, as to the "prejudicial atmosphere" that was alleged to have accompanied the meeting of October 27, 1932. At one session, however, Mr. Begun and counsel wished to introduce a number of additional witnesses to testify solely on the conduct of the meeting of October 27th. The Chairman then ruled that any appeal on that score should go to the general membership, as it was obviously absurd to ask the Committee to pass upon the body which elected it. The further statement that the defense was told that it must stick to "*specific* charges" is false. The defense had the same latitude given it as had the prosecution, illustrated for example by the fact that Mr. Begun's defense occupied four entire meetings or over eight hours, about twice as much as was taken by the prosecution in his case.

II. Analysis of the Situation

FACTIONAL ALIGNMENT IN THE UNION

The Committee finds that the immediate source of trouble in the Union is the activities of two organized groups that regard the Administration and the Executive Board as merely another faction like their own, except that, as will appear below, the Administration Group is regarded by the others as simply a "clique" interested in keeping power by any means. Nothing was more convincing to the Committee about the attitude of the leaders of the opposition groups, than their uniform disregard of the fact that no administration could gain and hold power except with the support of the Union as a whole.

Originally there was but one organized opposition group. Part of the members of this group seceded and formed a new group, calling themselves the Rank and File, while the original group is known as the Progressives. The causes of the split were not made entirely clear in the testimony. It was stated, however, that those who took the lead in forming the new group did not regard the leaders of the old Progressive Group as sufficiently radical in their policies, nor sufficiently militant in their tactics. The charges that are brought by the two groups against each other agree with this statement. The Rank and File charges the Progressives with being only a pseudo-opposition and in reality an ally of the Administration. The Progressive Group charges the Rank and File with the purpose of ultimately "splitting" the Union.

Each group, according to the testimony of their leaders, has both a loose organization that holds open meetings and a directing body called either the Executive Board or else made up of those who are entitled to attend executive sessions. Each faction has a secretary and possibly other officers, holds frequent meetings of the open and closed types, and is at considerable expense for rent of halls, printing, mimeographing, postage, etc. The immediate situation then is that the Union is confronted with two organized factions that are hostile both to each other and to the Administration, each one of the two uniformly treating the elected officers of the Board as constituting another faction but lacking their own high principles and purposes.

DANGER IN FACTIONAL STRIFE

The Committee sees no reason why opposition should not arise from time to time to the views of administrative officers and no reason why such opposition should not be helpful. When, however, minorities are permanently organized with their own leaders and officials and become permanent opposition factions, there is, to say the least, a danger that standing and ever-growing antagonisms will be fostered and that these will seriously hamper the effectiveness of the Union. The Committee finds that this danger point has been reached and exceeded in the condition which now confronts the Union. At a critical time when unity is imperatively needed, a condition exists which threatens not only the usefulness of the Union, but its very existence.

This situation is more serious because the great body of the membership is not organized in any group, whether the Administration, so-called, the Progressive, or the Rank and File. Testimony amply shows that members are confused and bewildered, while they tend to be made doubtful as to the efficacy of the Union, and so resentful of conditions that they find prevailing in the meetings of the Union that they are unwilling to attend. Evidence was presented which showed that the existing division and antagonism operate to prevent many teachers from joining the Union.

The larger unorganized body of teachers in the Union finds itself the passive victim of angry disputes, and has little influence on policies. If matters continue as they have been going the tendency will be for these members themselves to organize new groups in order to have a voice in the conduct of the Union. Thus, the fractionization tendency will go still further.

The Committee accordingly finds this a convenient place in which to state its views upon a point presented for its consideration by the Rank and File Group. The latter requested that "such minority groups as may exist at any time in relation to various issues" should be recognized through preallotment of definite amounts of time for discussion in Union meetings, and should be given proportionate space in the *Union Teacher*. While the Committee is of the opinion that any special arrangements which will promote order in debate, are desirable, it is unanimously of the opinion that it would be very unfair to the great body of unorganized members, if official recognition were given to factions that are organized. Such a course would either deprive the unorganized members of a chance to get an adequate hearing or else force them into the undesirable procedure of forming new factional groups.

SERIOUSNESS OF THE SITUATION

The Committee regards it, therefore, as its first duty to report to the Union that the situation which exists is most serious. It wishes particularly to impress upon the membership that while personal antagonisms have been aroused and while some members of the Executive Board have been provoked by false and injurious charges into responding by the use of provocative language, the seriousness of the situation far transcends all personal differences and animosities. It grows out of differences of policies, and these differences are declared by leaders of the minority groups to be fundamental. Moreover, they are enthusiastically certain that their own policies constitute the "correct line," while elected officers of the Union are said to have either wrong policies or else no policy at all excepting opportunistic drift.

ACCUSATIONS AGAINST THE ADMINISTRATION

The minority factions, especially the leaders of the Rank and File, accuse the Administration officers of being undemocratic, arbitrary, dictatorial, oppressive; with going to the limit in using measures of coercion so as to keep themselves in power; with being bureaucratic, mechanical, and apathetic; with either failing to lead the membership or with misleading them; with fawning on 59th Street in order to get favors, so much so that a struggle against the Administration is the same thing as a struggle against 59th Street. The Administration is charged with winning whatever successes the Union has gained not by adhering to definite policies, but by catering to their superiors in office; with maintaining the interests of the higher paid "aristocracy of labor," instead of the interests of the mass of teachers; with using the referendum (which is admitted to be in principle a democratic measure) simply to induce the membership to support their own reactionary policies, thus making the Union, in the words of Mr. Begun, "a mail order Union." The Administration was charged with gratuitously employing red-baiting tactics in order to prejudice the membership of the Union against the leaders of the opposition groups, this being said to be part of their tactics for keeping themselves in power. Every one of the phrases used in the previous statements is a literal transcript from the testimony of the defendants and their witnesses. The charges were repeatedly summed up in the statement that the officers of the Union, Dr. Linville and Dr. Lefkowitz in particular, were engaged in "betraying the Union."

It is obvious that even if such charges were purely personal in nature, they are so serious that they have a tendency to disrupt the Union or at least to reduce greatly its efficiency. But the testimony, especially as coming from the defendants themselves, showed that these charges are not merely personal, but are integral parts of a deliberately adopted procedure of so discrediting the Administration as to bring about a thorough change in the basic policies, aims and methods of the Union. While personal feelings have been aroused on both sides and crimination and recrimination were freely aired before the Committee, the Committee wishes to record its firm and unanimous conviction that the basic cause of the crisis goes far beyond any personal difference.

DEFENDANTS' JUSTIFICATION FOR ACCUSATIONS

One of the matters that was most instructive to the Committee was the reply of the defendants to the charge brought against them that they engaged in continuous misrepresentation of the Administration and its policies. The defense proffered by the defendants was justification for their charges against the Administration. The reasons they gave in justifying their cause brought out very clearly the nature of their objection to the policies of the Administration and the nature of the fundamental change of policies which they desire. Examples are given below:

1. Motions introduced by leaders of the minority factions under conditions that led to their being ruled out of order for parliamentary reasons were made the basis for asserting that the Executive Board was opposed to the cause involved. This misrepresentation was repeatedly made about matters on which the Administration was already actively on record in behalf of the cause in question. Flagrant instances of this procedure are found in connection with the Mooney Case, the Scottsboro boys, insurance for the unemployed, and such general issues as disarmament and the recognition of Soviet Russia. The fact that there was opposition to the exclusive endorsement of a particular agency such as the International Labor Defense, the legal arm of the Communist Party, was made the basis of the charge that the Administration objected to the cause itself.
2. The use of parliamentary regulations without which any deliberate body cannot do business, such as having a quorum, introduction of substitute motions, etc., is made the basis of the charge that the Administration will go the limit for the suppression of minorities, that the Administration desires, to quote the statement of leaders of the Rank and File, "to eliminate entirely any participation of the membership." Such unblushing misrepresentations like the violent accusations already noted can be explained only on the ground that leaders of the factional groups, especially the Rank and File, regard all opposition to their policies as inherently vicious.

The failure of the Administration to approve the ulterior aims and tactics of the minority groups is, the Committee finds, the sole basis of the charge that the elected officials of the Union are betraying the Union and the labor movement. Thus, the policies and aims of the minority groups are, in the minds of their leaders, the sole standard for measuring loyalty. Because the testimony revealed so clearly the nature of the situation, the Committee became less concerned with the evidence introduced to prove the charge of misrepresentation and sabotage brought against the defendants than in the justification which the defendants themselves offered for adopting their uncompromising course of opposition.

DETAILS OF CHARGES AGAINST ADMINISTRATION

The Committee believes that that portion of the Union which has not been committed to any faction, and indeed many individuals who have been more or less regular adherents of one or the other of the minority groups, will gain an appreciation of what is involved in the counter charges brought against the Administration, by considering a number of these counter charges in some detail.

1. The Administration is attacked because it uses methods of legislation and general publicity instead of those of mass action.
2. It is attacked on the alleged ground that the wage cuts which have occurred and others which may take place in the future are entirely the result of the policy of the Administration. It was asserted that if certain resolutions offered by the minority leaders had been adopted these cuts would not have occurred.
3. It is attacked on the ground that a difference of opinion as to the best method to be pursued in dealing with a particular issue indicates a deliberate betrayal of the cause involved. A good illustration of these tactics of attack against the Administration is found in the way in which the latter dealt with the matter of the so-called voluntary contributions to the School Relief Fund. The leaders of the Rank and File Group asserted that when the contributions were opposed on the ground of "coercion" instead of on the ground of being a "salary reduction," the Administration deliberately failed to oppose the reduction of salaries, and thus helped to bring on cuts later.
4. Not content with their local charge, the leaders of the Rank and File faction extended their policy of attack to include the Chicago unions, claiming that the policy of these unions was the cause of the salary troubles in which Chicago teachers were involved. It was asserted that policies in Local 5, New York, similar to those of the Chicago unions were leading to results like those that have happened in Chicago. When asked for justification of the pub-

lic charges of the Rank and File Group against the Chicago unions, Mr. Begun pleaded ignorance of the Chicago situation as a reason for inability to supply any facts whatever. It was characteristic of his tactics in defense that he went on to blame the Executive Board for his being ignorant of the Chicago situation—although, in fact, articles explaining it have been repeatedly printed in the organ of the American Federation of Teachers, the *American Teacher*.
5. The attacks on the Administration and on the Union itself were extended to include misrepresentation of their policies and their acts in formal charges addressed to the Sixteenth Annual Convention of the American Federation of Teachers of June, 1932.
6. The Administration is attacked for complete indifference to the interests of the substitute teachers and the unemployed teachers, because it proposed and followed out different methods for dealing with them than those desired by the minority groups.
7. The Administration was attacked on the ground that an expression, even if it came from merely one of its members, of a desire for discipline of leaders of the minority groups, proved the existence merely of resentment against those who exposed the bureaucratic methods and lack of leadership of the officers of the Union. Although it is self-evident that power to expel destructive elements must always be in any organization a measure of final resort, a suggestion that expulsion should take place under any conditions was used as proof of the coercive and arbitrary nature of the Administration in a desire to suppress all criticism.

The Committee wishes at this point to emphasize again the statement that it is not now so much concerned with the truth or falsity of particular charges and counter-charges, as it is with the fact that the charges are so constant, multiplied, accumulative, and acrimonious, as to prove beyond a shadow of doubt that the Union is faced not with a matter of personal controversy, but with differences of policy that are fundamental to its existence. For the defendants justify their attacks on the Administration on the ground that the attacks themselves grow out of basic differences as to the proper policies of the Union. Unless this point is clearly understood, many members of the Union will remain confused, bewildered and wavering in their loyalty to the Union because they do not understand what the troubles are about.

DIFFERENCES ARE FUNDAMENTAL

Differences of opinion and frank discussion are helpful in any large organization, but a campaign that aims to destroy the confidence of the members of an organization in the officers it has chosen, that subjects to constant ridicule and misrepresentation the measures and aims which the Union has itself established and followed for many years, creates the necessity for a full and candid consideration of aims, tactics, and probable consequences. The necessity for this full consideration cannot be avoided by the desire of those conducting the campaign to shelter their movements from examination behind the cry of "red-baiting." We repeat that specific charges and counter charges cannot be understood of themselves, but only when placed in the light of that conflict of policies which the leading defendants have themselves declared to be fundamental. For this reason the Committee decided that the chief service it could render to the Union was to put before the membership the conclusions it has reached regarding the nature of this conflict.

III. Causes of the Conflict

MINOR CAUSES

We return, therefore, from a statement of the outer symptoms of the conflict to an analysis of the causes that have created it. The testimony given before the Committee disclosed a number of minor causes and one major cause. The minor ones may be listed as follows:

1. There is a certain amount of cleavage between older members who feel that they understand best the traditions of the Union and members who have come in recently who

incline to the idea that new conditions require new methods and that the older membership is imbued with too much conservatism.
2. There is a certain amount of cleavage between older and younger teachers, the former feeling that they have the wisdom of maturity and the latter feeling that age tends to become conservative and that youth brings in new vigor and fresh blood for more energetic and vital activity. This difference was evident in the fact that the very things, friction, dispute, bickering, etc., that repelled many members from attendance at the Union meetings, were remarked upon by a smaller number as signs of increasing vitality.
3. There are, as is inevitable in any large organization, differences of personal temperament. These psychological differences have reached an acute pitch in the case of a number of members of the Union. They account for some, although not all, of the charges of obstreperous and unseemly manners brought against the defendants and also their counter charges that witnesses against them had been guilty of equally bad manners and unnecessary provocation—a counter charge that the Committee believes to contain a certain amount of truth.
4. There is some evidence of a difference of attitude between those members of the Union who respectively hold the lower salaried and the higher salaried positions in the schools.
5. There are differences due to unlike cultural backgrounds of earlier surroundings and of academic traditions. It is natural that the distinctively educational features of the Union should appeal more strongly to some teachers, and that the industrial phases and the need of cooperation with oppressed labor should appeal more strongly to others.

In listing these sources of divergence, the Committee does not imply that the right lies with one tendency or the other. On the contrary, the Committee holds that such differences as these may be made sources of increased strength to the Union, if they are exhibited in a genuinely cooperative spirit in behalf of a common end.

THE MAJOR CAUSE OF CONFLICT

In any case these differences are not the real cause of present troubles. They would hardly produce more than a passing friction if they had not become bound up, in the minds of many persons, with the main cause. This main cause is the existence of a conception as to the proper functions and objectives of the Union that goes contrary to policies established and approved in the past. The leaders of the minority groups conceive that the proper purpose of the Union is to join the class war in order to promote the cause of workers against employers. Employers of teachers as well as of all other workers use their power, in the minds of these minority leaders, to oppress the workers. In the case of teachers, the Board of Education and other high authorities in the school system represent the employing and oppressive class. Accordingly, the Union must not only join in the class war in order to "fight with the working class for their economic and political demands," but must also fight the people above them, from the Board of Education through the Superintendents down to principals and supervisors. Any let-up in this struggle, to say nothing of cooperation with supervisors even for educational purposes, is "betrayal" of the workers' cause.

While immediate demands relating to wages, conditions of work, etc., must be made, and while individual teachers must be vigorously protected when their rights are threatened, these operations are not ends in themselves, but are means of carrying on the class struggle. As long as the mass of the membership and the majority of the Administration fail to take this view, that the sole fundamental aim of the Union is to promote "the political and economic demands of the workers in the class struggle," conflict in the Union is inevitable and irrepressible. Moreover, the conflict is made more acute because some of the leaders of the minority factions feel it necessary to conceal their ultimate aims while carrying on the tactics which in their view will conduce ultimately to their realization. The Committee is of the opinion that the ultimate ends have been so concealed from the sight of many individuals, that even many members of the minority groups are not themselves aware of them, but take the view that the conflict is merely on special points where differences of judgment are wholly legitimate.

CRISIS IN THE GENERAL LABOR MOVEMENT

Because of the Committee's conviction that the basic cause of the troubles in the Union comes from this difference as to the proper function and methods of the Union, we feel that a brief discussion of the situation in which organized labor in general now finds itself, will lead to a better understanding of the situation in the Union itself. The existence in the United States of twelve to fifteen millions of unemployed workers, the part-time employment of millions of others, the drastic reduction in the wages of workers, necessarily have a profound influence on the lives and consequently on the ideas and emotions of workers. It is equally inevitable that radical differences of opinion should arise, and that there be great emotional excitement over what is to be done in the face of the apparent collapse of the present capitalistic economy.

This divergence of opinion and feeling in the labor unions at large is reflected in violent internal strife, in great decline of membership in many unions, in the split-up of some unions, in the disappearance of others, and in the rise of new unions. These results have definitely weakened the power of the labor movement in this country, and have given a correspondingly greater advantage to the already powerful employing class. Thus, labor is divided and without effective power in the face of the greatest need for solidarity in its whole history.

Division in the trade unions is due of course to many causes. There is an evident conflict between old-line craft unionism, which has been rendered archaic by technological development, and the newer principle of industrial unionism which is a conflict between elements innately conservative and those which are militant. There is a danger in every union of excessive growth of conservatism and consequently a failure to recognize that new conditions may require new methods. Differences in political and economic philosophies manifest themselves in practically all unions. The differences range from anarchism and syndicalism on one side to the most reactionary capitalistic policies on the other extreme. Unions may be classified as radical, reformist, and reactionary. But these are relative terms. Consequently, much of the classification that is made reflects only the temperament of the classifier. For example, the Teachers Union is reputed to be radical, reformist, and reactionary, depending on the point of view of the observer.

It was probably humanly inevitable that these forces which are operating throughout the whole labor movement should find their way to some extent into our Local 5. The Committee does not believe that these differences are inherently bad. It does not believe that those individuals who hold even extreme radical economic and political views do not have a proper place in the Union, nor that they might not contribute an element of strength and growth to it. This statement, however, does not apply to the matter of tactics which have been steadily pursued in promoting the desired realignment of policies.

The Committee was much impressed with the fact that leaders of the minority groups, especially of the Rank and File, openly expressed the conviction that all sincere believers in any particular political movement would necessarily attempt to use the Union as an instrumentality for promoting their special views.

WRECKING OF ESTABLISHED UNIONS

One method of union procedure that the Committee has had to take into account is the method for destroying old unions to make way for new ones which would presumably be better suited to the times. It is argued that conservative and reactionary unions stand in the way of the advance of the working class. It is then argued that all unions which do not definitely ally themselves with the class struggle of workers are conservative and reactionary. A conclusion is thus drawn that they are either to be destroyed by frontal attacks or that they should be captured and transformed, by boring from within, into entirely new organizations with new objectives and new tactics. When operating in unions that do not accept this policy, minority factions, in order to operate as a wrecking crew, must camouflage their objective of either splitting or capturing the organization. Hence, a familiar tactic in the American labor movement is to exploit the weaknesses of any union that is not pursuing what is considered the "correct line," not for the purpose of correcting the weaknesses, but for the purpose of confusing and dividing the membership. Examples of disastrous work of this kind are seen in the wrecking of the Furriers' Union and the crippling of the textile and the garment workers' unions.

In this connection it is interesting to know that one of the defendants who is a leader of the Progressive Group, has charged in a printed pamphlet that it has been the policy of some extreme left-wing movements to send a handful of workers into one or another American Federation of Labor union, not to seek to rebuild or transform the old unions, but to undermine and disrupt them, and to make new and more successful splits. (Wolfe—*What Is the Communist Opposition?* page 25.)

THE ISSUE OF DUAL UNIONISM

Dual unionism is, therefore, such a fact in the labor movement that the Committee was compelled to take seriously the charges made on this score and to go into that subject. The defendants replied to the charge brought against them by claiming that the attempt to discipline them is itself creating dual unionism. In fact, they charged the Administration with being the chief promoters of dual unionism in the Teachers Union. The Committee found that the term is used not merely to describe unions organized under separate names, and unions outside of the American Federation of Labor paralleling unions within the latter, as in the case of the clothing trades, but also in the sense of an organized combination within a union. Technically, the factional groups in the Teachers Union do not now constitute dual unions. But the Committee is strongly of the opinion that the strategy and tactics of the leaders of these two groups tend definitely in the direction of dual unionism.

The Progressive Group charges the Rank and File Group with deliberately working to split the Union. On behalf of the Progressive Group Mr. Wolfe introduced facts showing that the Communist Opposition believes in capturing unions rather than in dividing them, and that this difference of policy is one of the points at issue between the Communist Opposition and the official Communist Party. The Committee accepts this evidence. Leaders of the Progressive Group, however, did not seem to realize that tactics used with the view of capturing the Union might be just as disruptive as those employed in splitting it. Leaders of the

Rank and File Group asserted their loyalty to the Union in case it adopts the principles for which they stand. While proclaiming the principle of "united front," they strongly asserted that this united front could be had only on the basis of "the correct line" which they alone represented.

THE TACTIC OF CONSTANT ATTACK

There is undoubted difficulty in determining the exact point at which organized opposition to the policies which have prevailed for many years in an organization become disruptive. But there could be no doubt of the preposterousness of the claim of the Rank and File leaders that they have the right to continue with impunity a constant barrage of attacks upon that portion of the Union that is unwilling to accept their program. They must know that such attacks provoke counter attacks. These counter attacks are then used by them as if they had originated gratuitously in the Administration itself. By circulating these counter attacks with no reference to the conditions under which they arose, they have succeeded in misleading some of the passive members of the Union into a belief that they are being violently and falsely attacked merely for expressing disapproval of policies on particular points. The continuance of such performances is bewildering, as well as repellant and tiresome, to many members. The testimony given to the Committee indicates that too much of the discussion in the Union has degenerated into mere bickering which has bred mutual hostility and contempt.

We have been unable to discover constructive results coming from the organized opposition. The latter has put its emphasis on struggle as a means of progress with little or no regard for the character of the struggle. Although it urges that struggle is a manifestation of life, it is clear that chaotic struggle leads to frustration of purpose and is a symptom and cause of decline. Recent growth in the Union membership was pointed to by the opposition groups as a sign that they were pursuing the correct line. The fact seems to be that the economic crisis has brought about the increase in membership in spite of internal strife, and not because of it. The Committee feels that if the opposition groups showed as much concern about factionalism in the Union as they claim to have on the subject of dual unionism, there would be much less danger of the latter becoming a reality. Their seemingly entire lack of concern for the bad consequences of factionalism throws grave doubt upon their profession of desire for unity.

Members of both groups asserted that the condition of struggle indicated a healthy state of affairs. Mr. Begun, for example, stated, "The Union can grow only on struggle or fight." This type of statement was repeated by him a number of times. In general, reckless denunciation was justified as a necessary part of development of the internal fight which is said to be a sign of a healthy condition.

The denunciation was condoned much as politicians condone it in the heat of campaign. Leaders and witnesses for the defendants made light of the suggestion coming from members of the Committee that reckless charges of betrayal, arbitrary conduct, reactionism, dishonesty, if continually repeated, might injure the persons attacked and injure the Union, in spite of the fact that the charges may be false.

FACTIONAL ANIMOSITIES AND LOYALTIES

During the long discussions that have taken place since the beginning of the hearings of the Grievance Committee, we have been impressed by the rigidity of attitudes taken by leaders of the opposition groups. None of them seemed willing to have the identity of the group merged with the interests of the Union as a whole. We have had exhibitions of factional animosities from both defendants and some of the prosecuting witnesses. They indicate factional loyalties which apparently have been permanently crystallized. Moreover, the Rank and File and Progressive Groups criticize each other and oppose each other as severely and vehemently as they oppose the rest of the Union.

Unless all factions obtain an orientation to a common cause larger than that of the objectives of separate groups, we fear the Union is doomed to be split into two or three competing unions. Extremely disastrous as such a division would be, it may be urged, and with much force, that it would not be so bad as a continuance of the present factional alignment. In dual unionism there is at least a frank recognition of fundamental differences in objectives and tactics. In such strife as now exists not only are real issues beclouded but also ultimate purposes are deliberately concealed and the energies of the Union are diverted from purposeful activity.

Nothing was more instructive to the members of the Committee than the assertion of the leaders of both opposition groups that although they expect finally to come into control of the Union, they do not desire to do so excepting on the basis of the ideologies which they respectively hold. The present officers, and inferentially the members who elected them, were criticized on the ground that the officers were not chosen on the basis of definite political economic ideology. We do not question the sincerity of the defendants' belief in their own ideologies. We do point out, however, and as emphatically as possible, that the more sincerely their belief as to the proper function of the Union is held, the more dangerous it is when it is pressed immoderately as the only criterion by which to judge present policies and the officers who are chosen to carry them out. If the membership of the Union is to be brought over to a change in the conception of the proper activity of the Union, it can be done consistently with the effectiveness of the Union, only by a process of education and frank and open discussion. Concealment of the ultimate desire to convert the Union into an organization for carrying on the class war, and the attempt to lead the membership to think that the sole difference is on matters of isolated items of immediate policy, conjoined to the tactics of unscrupulous attack, can lead only to the bitterness, friction, crimination and recrimination that now exist.

THE ISSUE OF COMMUNISM

While, therefore, it might be personally agreeable to the Committee to avoid any reference to Communism, it is not possible to do so, for the special aims and tactics on particular issues of the opposition groups cannot be understood or put in their proper context without frank discussion of this topic. Preliminary to the discussion, however, the Committee wishes to state definitely that no evidence was presented that a majority of the members of either group belong to any of the various factions of the Communist faith. Moreover, the testimony is far from showing that it is the conscious intention of the bulk of those affiliated with these opposition groups to use the Union as a tool of any particular economic political creed. It is quite likely that a large number of the members of both minority groups regard questions under dispute as isolated special points. To the leaders, however, these matters are inter-connected details of tactics in the general strategy of bringing about a radical change in the purpose and function of the Union. So frank were some of the leaders of the groups in stating this fact that the Committee does not think that they will publicly deny it, nor can the bitterness of their attacks be explained in any other way. The Committee finds that these leaders are systematically striving to subordinate the Union to their own special ends.

Before the Committee, as well as at other times and places, the defendants used any reference to the topic of Communism to support a claim that they were being subjected to "red-baiting" merely in order to weaken their influence with the membership. The Committee therefore is bound to state as positively as possible, that it has no concern with the political and economic faith as such, of any member of the Union; that it made no attempt to ascertain the political affiliations of any of the defendants; and that it does not believe that the Union should or does question the right of any teacher, whether in or out of the Union, to hold such economical or political views as seem to him to be justified. But if there were evidence that a Republican, Democratic or Socialist group, or any faction representing a religious body or sect, were striving to use the Union as an instrumentality to carry out the policies of that outside organization, every intelligent person would recognize the disruptive evidence of such a policy. The Committee would be unmindful of the weight of evidence submitted to it (largely by the defendants themselves) if it did not record its conviction that this is the sort of thing that is now going on within the Union. The Committee suggested a number of times to the defendants that there is a real distinction between economic and political beliefs on one hand, and the use on the other hand of such organized tactics as they employ in order to control trade union policy in behalf of these beliefs. The defendants declined to accept the distinction. Their failure is perhaps accounted for by the statement of one of the defendants that it is impossible to separate faith in Communist principles from the use of the tactics that are endorsed by that party. In general, he expressed the conviction that any sincere adherent of any political economic view must naturally use the Union to promote the interests of his own cause.

Much evidence was presented as to similarities between procedure of the leaders of the Rank and File Group and that of the official Communist Party, and of the Progressive Group and one branch of the Communist Opposition. The Committee believes that no one in studying this evidence could emerge with the belief that the similarities are mere coincidence. We do not believe that it is merely a coincidence that we have in the Teachers Union a Rank and File Group and a Progressive Group corresponding practically point by point to Communist Groups of the same names in many trade unions throughout the country. We do not think it a mere coincidence that our own Rank and File Group and the Progressive Group criticize each other in identically the same way in which the official Party and the Opposition criticize each other. Communist literature abounds in the discussion of strategies and tactics to be employed in trade unions. In view of the Communists' great interest in unions it would be indeed strange if they were to overlook the Teachers Union. The strenuous efforts of defendants to make light of the various coincidences, to dismiss them as having no significance whatsoever, to decline to view them as anything but further evidence of "red-baiting," appears to us to be evidence that there *is* significance in the points of identity. The charge that the Committee was engaged in "red-baiting" because it ventured to bring up the subject, comes in any case with poor grace from those who have been strenuous and persistent in attacks upon the majority of the Union officials as reactionaries and traitors to the cause of the teachers.

WHY MENTION COMMUNISM?

The Committee does not question the right of the defendants to raise the question which they brought up, "Is it within the province of the Grievance Committee to question the propriety of the defendants' tactics because of any similarity to Communist tactics?" followed with the query—"What of it even if the tactics of our groups and of the Communists are alike?" We think it was wholly within the province of the Committee to do so for at least three reasons.

In the first place and fundamentally, the cause of the trouble in the Union cannot be understood apart from the desire of some individuals at any cost to use the Union as an instrument in militant war to overthrow the existing economic system,

In the second place, the Union has much to gain from an open and above-board exploration of all Union policies including those of Communists and other radical groups. Instead of the Union's being scandalized by such an exploration and discussion, it might obtain by this means a new and beneficial orientation in regard to the whole labor movement in relation to existing social and economic trends. To ignore the issue of Communism is to encourage deception and concealment within our ranks and to protect from exposure bugaboos which exist because of the fear of Communism. A courageous, frank meeting of all issues is the surest way to defeat any "red-baiters" that may exist, namely persons who would exploit the prejudice against Communists for some ulterior purpose of their own. The principle of democracy demands that within our own ranks we speak openly of all that vitally concerns the Union,

In the third place, comparison between the tactics of opposition groups with the trade union tactics employed by the Communists supports the charge that the opposition groups have employed disruptive methods.

We cite particular instances of material found in the *Education Worker* for January, March, May, July and December 1932. This publication is issued by the Education Workers League of New York, which is affiliated with the Trade Union Unity League and the Educational Workers International—Communist organizations.

The *Education Worker* of three of these dates contains the same bitter criticisms of the Teachers Union and its officials as those made by the Rank and File leaders, both in their public statements and in their testimony given to the Committee. For example, the January, 1932, issue discusses the revision of the Union's Constitution in the following words:

> The day is done. The constitution has been uplifted another inch or two. Some plucky teachers "want to save the union." They will not let the old dame die. They want to rejuvenate it. Vain hope! Lefkowitz and his cronies carry her

in their pockets. She will rot there unless they trade her to 59th Street for principalships and superintendencies. When this becomes quite clear the Education Workers League will grow even faster than it is now.

It is evident that this secret League has teachers in its membership, that it definitely considers itself to be a dual union and a rival of the Teachers Union, and as an organization that is bound to grow through the splitting of the Teachers Union. To ignore the similarity of this view with the accusations brought by the Rank and File Group against the Administration in connection with a revision of the constitution is to engage in the silly policy of shutting one's eyes to the facts. In this connection it should be noted that the Communists denounce all progressive and radical labor unions that do not identify themselves with the "correct line" of the Communists with much greater severity than they attack reactionaries. The latter are regarded as merely living up to their bourgeois prejudices while the former are traitors. Thus the attacks of the Rank and File Group against the officers of the Union agree almost verbally with the denunciations that are brought in Communist literature generally against so-called "reformist unions," the latter being those that have a somewhat socialistic outlook, but do not go the whole way with the Communist movement. The "Progressives," the name belonging to one of the groups opposed to the official party, desires, in the words of its representatives, to "eliminate reformist influences."

IV. Remedies Proposed

AN ELECTED ASSEMBLY

As far as the general situation is concerned, the Committee is therefore, unanimously of the opinion that certain changes in the conduct of the Teachers Union are necessary in order to moderate the use of disruptive tactics and bickering procedures that tend to disgust large numbers of members. We propose, therefore, such action by Constitutional amendment and otherwise as will effect the following:

(1) The creation of an Assembly whose delegates will be elected to represent the members in their respective schools.

This assembly will have the powers—deliberative and voting—now exercised at business meetings.
(2) Business meetings of the membership to discuss, deliberate, and suggest to the Assembly, but not to commit the Union to any policy.
(3) Cultural and social meetings of the membership.

The Committee recommends the above because it feels the Union membership too large to be able to deliberate adequately at meetings. It feels that an Assembly of delegates would represent more adequately the majority of the members than does a meeting of 200 or 300 members at present.
(4) The referendum to be retained to ensure a membership check upon its delegates in cases of importance.

DISCIPLINE OF MEMBERS

(1) The Chairman should have the power to suspend from any meeting any member guilty of improper conduct at that meeting.
(2) Any member or group of members spreading false or libelous statements or charges against any other member or group of members, using obstructive tactics, or showing repeated insubordination to the Chairman at meetings, may be suspended, after a hearing, by the Executive Board for a period not exceeding six months.

The Committee hopes that the adoption of the above suggestions will insure orderly meetings, do away with violent, undisciplined charges and counter-charges, and bring back to the Union the unity in a common cause at present being corroded by the basically opposed groups.

The Committee believes that action along the lines recommended is essential to the preservation of the effectiveness and probably of the existence of the Union as a united body. At the same time we record our conviction that formal rules are not sufficient in themselves.

THE SPIRIT OF COOPERATION

The main requirement is for the Union as a whole to understand the situation, a willingness on the part of all to recognize the need for frankness in stating ulterior purposes; and the pressing need for mutual respect, personal forbearance, the cessation of personal attacks and misrepresentations, and a spirit of cooperation for common ends—considerations that should be easy to accept by those who proclaim that the essential contest is not personal, but is one of fundamental principles. However, the Committee has seen and heard too much of the tactics that have come into use, to be under any illusion as to the probable effect of our appeal upon some of the leaders of the factions. We do believe, however, that it is possible for the mass of the membership, including very large numbers of those who are loosely affiliated with the two opposition groups, by the pressure of public opinion and sentiment, to render the Union practically immune to the poison of the germs of disruption that have been introduced.

BASIS FOR DEMOCRATIC PROCEDURE

The Committee is unanimously committed to the principle of democratic procedure in the Union, and assumes that the organization is definitely committed to this as one of its fundamentals. We wish, therefore, to emphasize certain elementary principles of psychology that are the basis of democracy. First, it rests on an abiding faith in the integrity and inherent wisdom of the mass of the Union membership. There can be no democracy resting on cynical contempt for the average membership or on a general suspicion concerning the motives of fellow members whose opinions differ. Democracy does not consist merely of the machinery for registering the opinions of the membership, as in frequent elections, proportional representation, free discussion, etc. These mechanics of democracy can function only when there is a clear understanding of the community of interest that the membership has, and likewise a deep, sympathetic understanding of one another's weaknesses, shortcomings, and proneness to error.

Secondly, to effect a change of policy in any democratic organization, as the defendants clearly wish to do in the Teachers Union, requires a patient process of education. Such changes must come as a matter of growth and development, if it is to be done democratically, rather than through a fight resulting in victory for one side and conquest of the other. We who teach ought to be able to see the educational principles involved.

The Committee feels that it must warn those who have appeared as witnesses against the defendants that forbearance must be mutual, and that a certain flexibility in attitudes is absolutely necessary for the salvation of the Union. The great crisis in our general social and economic environment is putting democratic principles to the severest test. We wish to reiterate that we regard differences of opinion that arise concerning fundamental principles of unionism as not necessarily the cause for weakness or division but rather the opposite. If our organization can make a demonstration of how these differences can be used to develop greater power, it will make a most valuable contribution to the history of organized labor.

The report of the Committee on specific charges against individuals will be presented at the general meeting called for April 29, 1933. Copies of that report will be sent to the defendants and their counsel in season to allow plenty of time for their consideration and for preparation of such defense as they may wish to make.

The Committee has requested that this Report be printed and sent to all members.

ESTHER S. GROSS
CHARLES J. HENDLEY
MAX KLINE
RAPHAEL PHILIPSON, *Secretary*
JOHN DEWEY, *Chairman*

New York and the Seabury Investigation

The Government of New York City

Most of us, if we were asked to describe the government of New York City, would mention the Board of Estimate and Apportionment, the Board of Aldermen, the Mayor and the many heads of departments appointed by him, the Controller, the five Borough Presidents, and the various grades of courts. This description would be correct as far as it went but it would be superficial; it would leave out the actual governing powers. For side by side with the government provided for in the city charter is another government, an unofficial government, controlled by a group of men who, although they, for the most part, hold no official positions, have greater power than the regularly elected officials. These men are the political leaders, the party bosses. Mr. Curry of Manhattan, Mr. McCooey of Brooklyn, Mr. Flynn of the Bronx, Mr. Theofel of Queens, and Mr. Rendt of Richmond are the men who really decide the vital questions which affect New York City.

What is the source of the power of these men? They get their power from their ability to control enough votes to win the primaries and the elections. They are able to control votes because of their control of the party organization, the machine as it is commonly called. Starting with the five boroughs or counties the party organization extends down through the aldermanic districts (the assembly districts are practically the same as the aldermanic districts) to the election districts or precincts.

[First published by the City Affairs Committee (New York, 1933), 48 pp.]

How the Party Organization Works

The privates in the army of the political organization are the precinct leaders, the "captains" of the election districts. It is they who are responsible for getting out the vote. It is their business to know the voters of their districts, to get acquainted with new people who move into the districts. It is they to whom the voters of the district turn for advice, for help in time of trouble, for special favors from the city departments or city officials. The precinct captain advises the immigrant in his district how to go about getting his naturalization papers, how to get his sick wife into a hospital, how to get working papers for his son, how, perhaps, to get a job for himself. It is the captain who goes to see the district leader (that is, the aldermanic or assembly district leader) when one of his constituents wants to get excused from jury duty, or wants to get a "ticket" for speeding or a summons for illegal parking killed, or wants a transfer to an easier job for his son who is on the police force. It is the captain who carries to the district leader requests for the privilege of evading the health regulations, or the tenement house law, or the building regulations.

Ruling over the precinct captains is the district leader, usually himself a former precinct captain who has risen from the ranks by virtue of his ability to win favors for his friends, his ability to mix well with his neighbors and his fellow captains, and above all his ability to deliver the votes when they are needed. The headquarters of the district leader is the club house. Here he holds court, meeting the precinct captains and citizens who are important enough to go to him directly with their troubles and their requests for favors. Some of these requests he has power to grant himself; for others he has to go to the county leader, "the big boss."

The county or borough leaders—Curry, McCooey, Flynn, Theofel, and Rendt are elected by the district leaders in their respective counties. It is they to whom the district leaders go with their problems and to whom the more powerful seekers for favors and privileges—public utility officials looking for franchises, bankers looking for city deposits, manufacturers with goods to sell to the city, those who want office high or low—go directly. The county leaders in conference with their district leaders select the party candidates for office both elective and appointive from alderman to mayor, from city magistrate to Judge of the Supreme Court. How political bosses choose Supreme Court judges was described before Judge Seabury by John Theofel.

> Q. Now, Mr. Theofel, you know that during the last session of the Legislature a law was enacted increasing the number of justices of the Supreme Court in the Second Judicial District?
> A. Yes, sir.
> Q. Also increasing the number of County Court Judges, was it not?
> A. One judge.
> Q. In your county?
> A. Yes.
> Q. And increasing the number of City Court judges?
> A. Two.
> Q. Two. And how about Municipal Court?
> A. Two.
> Q. All right. Now, you understand that some of those were to go to one county, others to another, didn't you?
> A. Yes, sir.
> Q. And there was nothing in the law about what county the Justices should come from, was there?
> A. No, sir.
> Q. If that was to be determined in advance, then it had to be a determination arrived at by the leaders, didn't it?
> A. I should imagine so.
> Q. Well, now, before this law was enacted, do you remember a meeting in the spring in Brooklyn?
> A. Yes, sir.
> Q. When was it that you held that meeting—in the early spring?
> A. I think it was, Judge.
> Q. And before the bill was enacted into law?
> A. Yes, sir.
> Q. And who was present at that meeting?
> A. Mr. McCooey, Mr. Rendt, Mr. Krug, Mr. Rasquin and myself. (County leaders.)
> Q. And where was that conference held?

A. In Mr. McCooey's office.
Q. Was it a private office or a public office?
A. Political office.
Q. Political?
A. It is the building owned by the organization.
Q. By what organization?
A. The Democratic Organization of Kings County.
Q. And who called the conference?
A. Why, I was telephoned and invited down.
Q. That was a conference of all the Democratic leaders in the Second Judicial District?
A. Yes, sir.
Q. Now, taking into account (the) grave perils that resulted from the law's delay, did those who were assembled there arrive at any conclusion as to the method by which they could remedy these grave abuses?
A. The only way to remedy it was to get more Judges.
Q. Well, how could those who were assembled there, every one of them Democrats, get more Judges?
A. I don't know.
Q. They couldn't, could they?
A. Not without the assistance of somebody. . . .
Q. And then did anyone suggest how many more Judges might be provided for?
A. Well, they said, somebody said, or they discussed the matter that it couldn't, that we couldn't get more Judges unless the Republicans put them through.
Q. That is in the Legislature?
A. Yes, sir.
Q. Well, now, Mr. Theofel, didn't somebody say that the Republicans wouldn't put it through and create more Judgeships, because if they did the Democrats would elect them all?
A. I wish they had of put them through, Judge.
Q. Well, they wouldn't, would they?
A. They didn't.
Q. And didn't someone say the reason why they wouldn't was because the Democrats would elect them all?
A. I think the Democrats would have elected the whole twelve.
Q. The whole twelve?

A. Yes, sir.
Q. No matter who they put up or on the ticket?
A. I think so. That is only my opinion. I may be wrong.
Q. At any rate, you statesmen who were there assembled (laughter, gavel). . . .
A. Thank you.
Q. Recognizing the difficulties, you were there to devise a method for relief for the Supreme Court calendar, weren't you?
A. Well, we were looking to get more Judges; also to help the calendar.
Q. And was the net result of that conference that it was agreed that the gentlemen who were assembled there representing the Democratic leaders in the Second District, should enter into a deal with the Republican leaders, if they could get a bill through creating more Judges? Was that the understanding in words and effect?
A. Well, I don't know whether they should enter in or the Republican enter in with us. I don't know which it was. . . .
Q. Wasn't that, in substance and effect, the result of this conference of Democratic leaders?
A. Along those lines.
Q. You wouldn't say that my statement of it was inaccurate in any substantial respect, would you?
A. No.
Q. Was the manner in which those places should be allocated to counties after the bill became a law, discussed?
A. Well, they talked about so many for Brooklyn, and so many for Queens. I was trying to get as many as I could for Queens.
Q. You, as a loyal Queens leader, wanted as many as you could?
A. I would like to have gotten the whole 12 if I could.
Q. You would have taken the whole 12 (laughter—gavel). You could have used them there, couldn't you?
A. I believe so.
Q. How many did they cut you down to?
A. Three.
Q. That is, they cut your county down to three?

A. Yes.
Q. You had to make provision for the Republicans in that three, didn't you?
A. Well, it is up to me to get away with three Democrats, if I could.
Q. If you could. Well, now you never expected if three were to be allocated to Queens County, that you would be able to get away with the whole three?
A. I tried hard enough, Judge, but the Republicans wouldn't let me.
Q. You had to give up one didn't you?
A. Yes, sir.
Q. And how many did Mr. McCooey want allocated to him?
A. Well, I guess he got five?
Q. Five. Whatever you could get in Queens County, you were to name, and whatever he could get in Kings County, he was to name?
A. Yes, sir.
Q. And he got five in this conference, didn't he?
A. Yes, sir.
Q. Well, now, how much did Rendt get for Richmond?
A. He got one, Judge.
Q. One. How was he going to meet his Republican situation? (Laughter—gavel.) With only one Judge.
A. That was a tough job.
Q. It was a tough job. Well, why didn't they make it thirteen Judges and give two to Richmond?
A. I don't know.
Q. Well, now, all this apportionment was determined upon, as I understand it, in the spring of this year, before the bill was enacted into law?
A. Yes, sir.
Q. And was anything said as to how many of the twelve they would have to give the Republicans for passing the legislation?
A. I don't know. I believe it was up to you to get away with as many as you could.
Q. It was up to them to get away with as many as they could?
A. Yes, sir. If I could have got away with the three, I would

have grabbed the three for Queens, but as I said, my Republican leader would not stand for it.
Q. No. Well, it was tentatively understood, was it not, that with reasonable skill the Democrats ought to be able to hold seven out of the 12?
A. Well, that was the general opinion.
Q. General opinion. It was not thought fair that they should give the Republicans more than five just for passing the bill?
A. Well, it was a Democratic district, Judge.
Q. Exactly.
A. And the vote would show that if the Republicans passed the legislation without doing business with the Democrats, that the Democrats could go out and nominate 12 Democrats and elect 12.
Q. Therefore there had to be some kind of a gentleman's agreement, didn't there?
A. Yes, sir.
Q. That if the Republicans would create the judgeships the Democrats would not grab them all but would give five to the Republicans and take seven to themselves?
A. Yes, sir.
Q. And that is the way, in the ordinary course of human events, the thing finally worked out, wasn't it?
A. About the way, yes, sir.
Q. And then it came down to selecting the number that had been allocated to Queens?
A. Yes, sir.
Q. You didn't assume to dictate to Mr. McCooey whom he should select in Kings, did you?
A. No, sir.
Q. And Mr. McCooey did not assume to dictate to you whom you should take in Queens?
A. Well, he didn't dictate.
Q. Well, did he suggest?
A. No.
Q. That was a matter for you to fight out with your Republican colleague, wasn't it?
A. Yes, sir.

Q. And who was the Republican partner in Queens?
A. Mr. Ashmead.
Q. Mr. Ashmead. He represented the Republicans?
A. Yes, sir.
Q. And you represented the Democrats?
A. Yes, sir.
Q. Well, did you gentlemen confer on how many you should get and how many Mr. Ashmead should get and whether or not Mr. Ashmead would endorse your two and whether or not you would endorse his one?
A. Yes, we did.
Q. And as the result of the conference between you and Mr. Ashmead it was understood between you and Mr. Ashmead, was it not, that you should name two Judges in Queens and that he should name one?
A. Yes, but Mr. Ashmead would have taken the two if I would have let him get away with it.
Q. He was perfectly willing to take the two and give you one?
A. Yes, sir.
Q. You wouldn't let him get away with that?
A. Not if I could help it. I tried to get the three.
Q. You tried to get the three but he wouldn't let you get away with that, would he?
A. No, sir.
Q. So that as the result of these meetings between you and Mr. Ashmead it was finally agreed that you should have two and that he should have one?
A. Yes, sir.

At times in the past there has been a city boss—Richard Croker for example—a county leader powerful enough to control the other county leaders. At present there is no absolute boss, although John F. Curry is chief county leader. Each county leader has considerable independent power in his own county. Acting together they divide the spoils and make the decisions that affect the city as a whole. The Democratic organization in Manhattan is popularly known as Tammany Hall. In theory Tammany Hall, the Democratic organization is distinct from the

Tammany Society, a private fraternal and social organization. Practically, the two organizations are identical, the same men being in control of both.

It is obvious that it takes a great deal of work to keep the party organization functioning. Why are party workers—precinct captains, district leaders, county bosses—willing to give so freely of their time without pay? The answer is that their work is not without pay. There are no salaries attached to their positions but there are incidental rewards—large rewards for the district leaders and more powerful bosses, small rewards for the less important party workers. Doubtless many people work for their party because of loyalty to its principles and desire to be of service. The great majority of professional politicians, however, are in politics for what they can get out of it. Little bosses do favors for big bosses because they expect favors in return. Big bosses do favors for little bosses for the same reason, and these favors are at the expense of the citizen and taxpayer. As Boss Croker testified in 1889 in answer to the question, "Then you are working for your own pocket, are you not?" "All the time, the same as you." The Seabury Reports show that this was as true in New York City in 1932 as it was in 1889. Completely dissociated from this privileged inner circle of the Tammany regime is the (in the main) meritorious army of civil service workers who do the most basic and important work in our community, and who, as step-children of the city administration, have received salary cuts out of proportion to the services rendered.

The Seabury Investigations Disclose What Makes the Political Machine Function

Following charges of abuses in the magistrates' courts of New York City the Appellate Division of the Supreme Court of the State of New York, First Judicial Department, in August, 1930, appointed Samuel Seabury as referee to conduct an investigation into the Magistrates' Courts of the First Judicial Department (Manhattan and The Bronx). In March, 1931, following charges by the City Club of New York City against Thomas C. T.

Crain, District Attorney of New York County, Governor Roosevelt appointed Mr. Seabury Commissioner to investigate and report on these charges. In April, 1931, Mr. Seabury was appointed Counsel to the Joint Committee of the Senate and Assembly of the State of New York created to investigate the various departments of government of the City of New York. With staffs of able assistants Mr. Seabury conducted the three investigations. The facts related below have been, except where otherwise noted, culled from the testimony taken at these investigations and the reports of Mr. Seabury.

Mr. Seabury had power merely to investigate and report. He had no power to indict anyone, to try anyone, to convict anyone, or to remove anyone from office. It should be remembered, therefore, that many of the persons whom he accuses in his reports have not been convicted by a jury, nor have the facts been proven in a court of law. The interpretation of facts in the reports is Mr. Seabury's, but the circumstantial evidence in most cases is so strong as to make any other interpretation seem silly. Even more damning than the evidence brought out in the investigations was the attitude of the Democratic organization toward the investigations, especially that of the Tammany members of the Legislative Committee. They charged, which is obviously true, that the Republicans in the legislature were looking for partisan advantage when they established the committee. But once the investigation had started, instead of cooperating to bring out the truth in regard to the city government they used every means in their power to block the inquiry. City officials while protesting that they had nothing to conceal were constantly obstructive in their attitude. They and other Tammany witnesses made use of every possible legal technicality to prevent the truth from coming out; they evaded questions; they destroyed records they consistently failed to remember.

Incomes of District Leaders

The three Seabury investigations combine to give an illuminating picture of how the extra-legal government of New York City functions. They show the power of the district and county leaders and also why they want power. The district leaders themselves hold many important offices. In 1932 the Civil Service Reform Association published a list of 106 district leaders, mostly Democrats, and relatives of district leaders who held positions on the city payroll for which the combined salaries totalled $715,000 a year. Practically all these positions were appointive positions exempt from civil service regulations.

The generous salaries which the leaders receive from the city are, however, but a small part of their income. The record of Thomas M. Farley, leader of the 14th Assembly District, Manhattan, as disclosed by the Seabury investigation is interesting. Farley was an alderman from 1916 to 1922, from 1922 to 1928 he was Deputy County Clerk, in 1929 he was County Clerk and from 1930 he was Sheriff of New York County until his removal in 1932 by Governor Roosevelt as a result of the Seabury disclosures. From January 1, 1925, to September 22, 1931, he deposited in various banks $360,660.34 although his salary and other income of which he could give any reasonable account, amounted to less than $90,000 for the period. Mr. Farley's explanation of these deposits was that at an earlier period of his life, when he was business agent for a union he had accumulated more than $100,000 in cash which he kept in a tin box in his home, and that it was from this "wonderful box" that the money came to make the deposits from time to time.

Harry C. Perry, Chief Clerk of the City Court of the City of New York, leader of the Second Assembly District, Manhattan, banked $135,000 in four years on a salary of less than $50,000 for the period. Michael J. Cruise, City Clerk of the City of New York and Democratic Leader of the Twelfth Assembly District, Manhattan, banked $80,000 in excess of his salary in six years. Charles W. Culkin, formerly Sheriff of New York County and co-Leader of the Third Assembly District, Manhattan, deposited salary checks of $54,000 and other checks and cash to a total of $1,929,759.00 in a period of seven years. A part of Culkin's deposits represented interest kept by him on monies impounded with him as sheriff. Another part was his income as an official of the Monroe Lamp and Equipment Co., a firm which had great success in selling electric bulbs to hotels, theatres, and business houses who desired special favors from the city government. Mr. Culkin was not examined in a public hearing because he refused to waive immunity completely.

James J. McCormick, Leader of the 22nd Assembly District, Manhattan, and since 1921 Deputy City Clerk performing marriage ceremonies at the City Hall, deposited between 1925 and 1931 $384,788. Mr. McCormick could make no accounting for over $150,000 of these but admitted that the balance came from gifts or tips given him by couples for whom he performed the marriage ceremony. This was the duty he was paid by the city to perform; couples were practically forced to pay the "gifts." As a result of the Seabury disclosures McCormick was indicted for failure to pay federal income tax on his income from tips, was convicted, and resigned from his position as Deputy City Clerk and also as District Leader.

The account by James A. McQuade, Leader of the 15th Assembly District, Brooklyn, then Register of Kings County, and now Sheriff, of how he was able to deposit $520,000 in six years on a total salary for these years of less than $50,000 was one of the comedy features of the investigation.

Q. Now it appears, Mr. Register, that in the year 1925, you deposited in the Kings County Trust Company your salary checks for the amount of $9,365.40. That is in accord with your recollection?

A. Yes, sir.

Q. It also appears in that year you deposited in cash, not other checks, there were other checks, too, but deposited in cash $55,833.07; that you deposited other checks in addition to your salary checks for fourteen odd thousand dollars, and that your total deposits for that year in the Kings County Trust Company amounted to $80,058.41. Now bearing in mind what you have told us about not having any other gainful pursuits than your public office, will you be good enough to tell me where you got the seventy odd thousand dollars in 1925, which you deposited, $55,000 of which was in cash?

A. Money that I borrowed. If you want me to get to the start of it, I will have to take and go over the family in its entirety, without feeling that I am humiliated in the least or am not humiliating the other 33 McQuades. If this Committee can take the time, it can take the time to listen, and you can, and the public in general, I will go over it from the start.

I unfortunately went into politics. I say that cautiously.
Q. You don't base that on that deposit, do you?
A. I am going to get to that deposit, if you will let me. If you will let me. I bailed a man out who stole off McQuade Brothers $260,000, which necessitated the folding up of the McQuade Bros. firm, selling eight seats they had in the Exchange for $6,000 apiece, that afterwards brought $225,000. After they liquidated, the 34 McQuades were placed on my back, I being the only breadwinner, so to speak, and after that it was necessary to keep life in their body, sustenance, to go out and borrow money.

After they paid up all they could, I took over their responsibilities. It was not necessary; I felt it my duty, being that they were my flesh and blood, part and parcel of me, to help them. I am getting along in fairly good shape, when my mother, Lord have mercy on her, in 1925 dropped dead. I am going along nicely, when my brother, Lord have mercy on him, in 1926 or 1927 dropped dead. But doing nicely when I have two other brothers, and when my brother died he willed me his family, which I am still taking care of, thank God. Two other brothers, who have been very sick, and are sick, so much so that when your Committee notified me, I was waiting for one of them to die.

They have 24 children that I am trying to keep fed, clothed and educated, which means that I must borrow money. The extra money that you see in this year or any year from that year on has been money that I borrowed,—not ashamed of it—
Q. Now, Mr. Register,—
A. If the Lord lets me live, I intend to pay it all. And I borrowed more in 1926, 1927, 1928 and 1929, and in the last month alone, I think, I borrowed $10,000 to keep the roof over their homes.
Q. Well, now, Mr. Register, will you be good enough to indicate from whom you borrowed this money?
A. O, Judge, offhand I could not. I borrowed, which you ought to remember. I was introduced to you, Judge, in the Pennsylvania Railroad depot by the late Judge McCall, who said to you at that time, "This is my friend, Jim McQuade, Judge Seabury, and he is in need and I am

going to help him." I don't know whether you remember or not.

Q. I am sorry; I don't recall it, Mr. Register.

A. I was standing right beside you, and the Judge asked me if I would ride down with him, and I told him I couldn't. The next day he gave me $5,000. That was the start of my trying to keep the McQuade family together.

Q. Well, now, Mr. McQuade, you understand, I take it, that you were accorded a full opportunity to make any statement that you wanted to make in private, and that you declined. You understand that, don't you?

A. Yes. I haven't the faintest idea what it was. I am not ashamed of anything that I am testifying here.

Q. Now, you have told us this story, which from your version of it, shows the great charity and benevolence that actuated you in reference to the members of the McQuade family, to whom you have made reference. That all relates, as I understand it, to money that you paid out from time to time?

A. That is right.

Q. Doesn't it?

A. You see, in these deposits, Judge—

Q. Doesn't it relate to money that you paid out?

A. From time to time for them.

Q. Well, now, my question, Mr. Register, I wasn't interested at all in what you did with the money. I am quite ready to assume that you made charitable and benevolent dispositions of the money. Let us assume that, for the sake of argument. My question is: How, in the year 1925, with your salary of $9,365.40, you deposited $80,000-odd?

A. I would, for instance, borrow $1,000 off John Brown. In two weeks' time John wanted that $1,000, and I would borrow $1,000 off John Jones. Another, maybe two weeks or less, he would want that. I would get it off John Smith, where in reality there would be possibly $10,000 deposited for the $1,000 that was actually working.

Q. I see—just over and over again using the same $1,000?

A. That is it, trying to keep my—

Q. Can you give the names of the persons from whom you borrowed this money that brought your total deposits of that year up to $80,000?

A. I can't offhand, Judge, remember that far back. I had troubles enough to—
Q. Have you any data or writing that will enable you to designate the persons from whom you borrowed these sums?
A. As the money was paid, it was off my mind, and I thanked God for it and destroyed anything that I might have.
Q. Destroyed everything you might have?
A. After I paid it, it was no good to me.
Q. Why do you give thanks to Divine Providence?
A. I give thanks to Divine Providence for permitting me to pay those people who were kind enough to loan me the money.

An interesting example of how leaders use their political power to promote their private business is John Theofel's connection with an automobile agency. Mr. Theofel is Democratic boss of Queens. We quote from Judge Seabury's report, dated January, 1932:

Theofel has been interested in Wilson Bros., Inc., since its inception. The stockholders are himself, his son-in-law, Dudley Wilson, and his son-in-law's brother. Theofel is also a director and the treasurer, and the largest individual stockholder. The corporation conducts a Pierce-Arrow Sales Agency.

The County Clerk of Queens County bought his car from Wilson Bros., Inc.; the District Attorney of Queens County bought his car from Wilson Bros., Inc.; the Borough President of Queens bought his car from Wilson Bros., Inc.; Magistrate Marvin of Queens County bought his car from Wilson Bros., Inc.; Park Commissioner Benninger of Queens County bought his car from Wilson Bros., Inc.; Assistant District Attorney Loscalzo of Queens County bought his car from Wilson Bros., Inc.; and Sheriff Burden of Queens County bought his car from Wilson Bros., Inc. Some of these cars were "Official" cars, purchased by the City for the official use of the public officer; others were purchased by the officials individually.

The following testimony of Sheriff Burden indicates the relations between the purchase of automobiles by public officials in Queens County from Wilson Bros., Inc., and the fact that the Democratic Leader of Queens County has a large interest therein:

Q. When was that (a Pierce-Arrow automobile) purchased for you?
A. Purchased about April or May, 1930.
Q. Where was it purchased?
A. From Wilson Bros., Inc., in Flushing.
Q. Do you know either of the Wilson brothers?
A. I know one of them, Dudley.
Q. Dudley?
A. Yes.
Q. He is the son-in-law to John Theofel?
A. Yes.
Q. Did Dudley Wilson ask you for that order?
A. Yes. I went to another fellow by the name of Adam Bayer—
Q. You know Adam Bayer?
A. I know of him. I don't know—he spoke to me about it also.
Q. Is Bayer over with Wilson Bros.?
A. No, sir, he has an agency of his own.
Q. Where?
A. Astoria.
Q. Pierce-Arrow Agency?
A. Yes; and I wanted to give it to him because he lived in my district, but Wilson Bros. was in the automobile business and I gave it to them, son-in-law of the boss, you know, the usual procedure.

From 1924 to 1930 Theofel's regular income from salary and other sources did not exceed $11,500 a year but his net worth increased from $28,650 to $201,000.

Board of Standards and Appeals as a Source of Political Profit

District leaders are not, unfortunately, the only ones to use their political power and their city offices to promote their own ends. The system extends to many city officials, high and low, and to a host of friends. One of the main sources of special favors seems to have been the Board of Standards and Appeals which has the power to modify the building zone regulations of the City of New York. The building zone regulations divide the city into residential, business, and factory districts and also govern the height and type of buildings permitted. These regulations not only protect the value of property in residential districts but are also important safeguards for the health and safety of the people. The Seabury investigations show that the Board of Standards and Appeals, made up of political appointees, used its power to grant special favors and promote the private interests of a favored few politicians who brought cases before it.

While George W. Olvany was leader of Tammany Hall the law firm of which he was a member received nearly $200,000 for acting as attorneys for applicants for changes in regulations before the Board of Standards and Appeals. The interest of the Olvany firm in the proceedings was hidden by having some other lawyer act as attorney of record and turn over a large part of the fees to it. It seems to have been understood that those who wanted modifications in the regulations must retain Olvany's or one or two other favored firms in order to get them.

Olvany's profits, however, seem petty compared to those of William F. Doyle. Dr. Doyle, formerly a veterinary surgeon and a member of the Bureau of Fire Prevention of the City of New York, in 1917 began practice before the Board of Standards and Appeals. So successful was he that in a few years he deposited more than $1,000,000. Doyle admitted that he split his fees but declared that he never bribed any public official. Even after eighteen days in jail for contempt for refusing to answer Seabury's questions he refused to state with whom his fees had been split. The high fees paid to Doyle and Olvany were obviously not merely for legal services before the Board, but because through their political connections they were able to get special favors. These fees, of course, were added to the cost of the buildings and passed on to the tenants in higher rents.

The Activities of William J. Flynn, Commissioner of Public Works of The Bronx

It was brought out in the investigations that William J. Flynn used the Board of Standards and Appeals as well as other departments of the city government to further his own interests in his long struggle with Louis H. Willard. This struggle finally ended tragically in the suicide of Willard's wife in 1930, and his own suicide in 1933. In 1923 Willard bought a parcel of real estate in the Bronx and applied to the Board of Standards and Appeals for permission to erect a garage on it. In a letter to the Board over his official signature as Acting Borough President of The Bronx, Flynn opposed the grant and the Board denied the application. In 1925 Flynn, acting through a dummy, bought land immediately across the street from Willard's land. For two years this land was left unused while the application of a neighbor of Flynn's for a public garage in the neighborhood was carried through the courts to the Appellate Division of the Supreme Court, where it was finally denied. Then Flynn, convinced that he would not be allowed to erect a public garage on the property, decided to build 27 small garages each housing five cars. Shortly after this a resolution was introduced into the Board of Estimate and Apportionment prohibiting such small garages on contiguous plots. This resolution was referred to the Committee on City Planning of the Board and at a meeting of this committee over which Flynn presided (acting as the representative of the Bronx Borough President), he introduced and secured the passage of the following amendment: "This provision shall in no way interfere with carrying out of plans approved prior to the date of the passage of this resolution." After he had introduced this amendment but before the resolution as amended had been adopted he filed his plans for his 27 garage units. In this way he secured what amounted to a public garage directly across the street from where he had prevented Willard from building a garage. Incidentally Flynn was the only person in the city who benefited from his amendment.

Meanwhile Willard to get some return from his property had built stores and a public meeting hall upon it, but was unable to rent them. On three different occasions he made application to Flynn as Commissioner of Public Works for a curb cut twelve feet wide to meet the demands of prospective tenants, who refused to rent unless they secured the curb cut. Flynn denied all three of these applications although his own property directly across the street had four curb cuts each twenty feet wide for which no permission had ever been granted.

In 1929 Willard again applied to the Board of Standards and

Appeals for permission to erect a garage on his property. Flynn with an attorney appeared before the board in opposition. Although one of the Commissioners declared to Flynn, "You are running a public garage, purely and simple, and taking a very selfish attitude," the application was again denied. Following this the mortgage on Willard's property was foreclosed, he lost his own home, and his wife committed suicide.

Flynn became enraged with Willard for his testimony before the Seabury Committee and was instrumental in having him indicted for perjury by the Grand Jury of New York County. Willard was acquitted but shortly after, evidently worn out by the long strain to which he had been subjected, he committed suicide. Flynn brought suit against the *New York World-Telegram* for $1,000,000 for an editorial in which the newspaper asserted that Flynn was responsible for Willard's death.

One more instance from the many in which Flynn has used his official position for his own selfish ends will help to explain how his bank deposits in thirteen years amounted to $650,000 and his equities in real estate increased to nearly $400,000 during the same period. In 1924 Flynn was one of the signers to a petition to have the city purchase land for a park directly across from an apartment house which he owned. The city bought this land and the Board of Estimate and Apportionment voted that 25 percent of the cost of the park be raised by a special assessment on adjoining property. Flynn's assessment was $13,000. Flynn then used his influence to have the Board of Estimate change its ruling and have the city bear the entire cost of the park. In this way he helped to get the park which greatly increased the value of his apartment house without having to pay any special assessment at all.

The Case of Ex-Mayor Walker

Of all the persons drawn into the net of the Seabury investigations none was more conspicuous than Mayor James J. Walker. This was due not only to his importance as head of the government of the greatest city in the western world but also due to international reputation as a "good fellow" and "wisecracking" man about town. The evidence in Mayor Walker's case shows clearly the demoralizing influence on city government of private business looking to officials to grant them special favors.

With the congestion in city streets due to automobile traffic buses have largely displaced street cars as a means of transporting passengers. The right to operate buses in the streets of New York is one that is worth many millions to the company or companies that secure it. In his campaign for election in 1925 Mayor Walker promised a speedy solution of the bus problem. Soon after Walker's nomination State Senator John A. Hastings, a political associate and an intimate friend of the mayor, organized a group of bus and tire manufacturers in Ohio to form a company for the purpose of securing a franchise to operate buses in New York City. Immediately after Walker's election this group formed the Equitable Coach Company and applied for a city-wide bus franchise in New York. Hastings was given a block of the common stock and was also retained as "political contact man" at a salary of $1,000 per month. Mayor Walker sponsored the resolution favoring the Equitable grant before the Board of Estimate, and repeatedly urged it in opposition to the application of the Service Bus Company which offered a much better bargain to the city and which had sounder financial backing than the Equitable.

After long negotiations and much wrangling in the Board of Estimate the application was modified to allow separate franchises for bus operation in the boroughs of The Bronx and Richmond. This won the votes of the Presidents of those boroughs for the Equitable, and on July 28, 1927, the Equitable franchise was awarded by the Board of Estimate. Mayor Walker signed the contract on August 10 and on the same day sailed for Europe with a letter of credit for $10,000 which had been purchased for cash from the Equitable Trust Co. by J. Allan Smith, one of the leading promoters of the Equitable Bus Co. Later in Europe Mayor Walker made an overdraft of $3,000 on this letter of credit which was paid by the same J. Allan Smith. Mayor Walker's explanation of this transaction was that the letter of credit was paid for by funds raised by the late Senator Downing to which all members of the party contributed, that he himself contributed $3,000 in cash which covered all that he spent.

Before the Equitable Co. could start operations it had to get a "Certificate of Convenience and Necessity" from the State Transit Commission. Although the Mayor interested himself in getting financial backing for the company it was unable to get sufficient support to satisfy the State Transit Commission and was refused a certificate, thus making its franchise worthless.

In April, 1930, Mayor Walker appointed a commission to study the taxicab situation in New York City and, following its report, the Mayor was instrumental in having passed by the Municipal Assembly a bill creating a Board of Taxicab Control, consisting of five members to be appointed by the mayor, with power to regulate the licensing and control of all taxicabs in the city. The avowed purpose of the Board was to limit the number of taxicabs. Such limitation would obviously work to the advantage of the companies already in the field, especially the large companies. We are not concerned here with the wisdom of this action but with why Mayor Walker was interested in it. Mr. Seabury brought out the fact that shortly before the appointment of the commission to investigate the taxicab situation Mayor Walker received from J. A. Sisto, a stock broker, $26,000 in bonds of various companies. The Sisto Company was heavily interested in the Parmelee Transportation Company, a holding company which controlled several taxicab companies, and was selling agent for the stocks and bonds of the company. Mayor Walker declared that the $26,000 was his share in the profits of a stock pool. No convincing evidence of the existence of such a pool was presented and Mr. Sisto testified that the $26,000 was a gift to the mayor made because of personal admiration. It was also brought out that Samuel Ungerleider and Co., another brokerage firm interested in the Parmelee Transportation Co., had in May, 1930, bought from Russell T. Sherwood, the mayor's financial agent, stocks for which they paid him $22,000 more than the market price. The money from these stocks went into a bank account of Sherwood's from which he paid obligations of the mayor. Mayor Walker denied any knowledge of this transaction and Mr. Ungerleider testified that the excess price paid for the stocks was due to an oral agreement made at the time that the stocks had been purchased to buy them back if they fell in value. Mr. Ungerleider admitted that this sort of an agreement was usually made only with a favored customer and that Sherwood had never had any other dealings with the firm.

Mayor Walker's relations with Sherwood remain one of the

mysteries of the investigation. For several years before 1930 Sherwood had been employed as bookkeeper by the law firm with which Mayor Walker was formerly associated, at an annual salary of $3,000. He supplemented his salary by doing accounting work for other people and performed various personal services for Mr. Walker both before and after he became mayor. From January 1, 1926, when Mayor Walker took office until Sherwood's disappearance in August, 1931, Sherwood had deposited in various banks and brokerage accounts sums approximating $960,000 of which $730,000 was in cash. Mayor Walker denied that this or any part of it was his money, or that he knew anything about it. He declared that it was Sherwood's own money which he had made by the business he transacted outside of his regular employment. An obvious answer to this is that in 1930 Sherwood was glad to get a full-time position with the Bank of Manhattan Company at $10,000 per year, which salary would hardly seem attractive to a person who was able to make such large sums as he deposited.

Mr. Seabury introduced a great deal of testimony to show that a large part of the funds deposited by Sherwood could have come from no one else than Mayor Walker and summed up their relations as follows:

> He was admittedly the Mayor's agent for many purposes. He kept the Mayor's check book; he made the Mayor's bank deposits; he made the Mayor's bank withdrawals; he handled the Mayor's finances; he maintained substantial bank and brokerage accounts which, as we shall show, were the Mayor's; he took delivery of stock purchased by the Mayor and he delivered the cash consideration therefor; he procured letters of credit for the Mayor's wife and for Betty Compton; he paid the expenses of a yacht used by Mrs. Walker, including salaries and maintenance charges, drawing checks therefor on the bank account kept in his name; he paid an allowance which the Mayor made periodically to his sister, drawing checks therefor on an account which he kept in his name; he paid the rental of the joint safe deposit box with the Mayor. It was to Sherwood that accountings were made for fees owing to the Mayor for legal services. It was to Sherwood that the Mayor, the day before he took office, assigned

certain bank stock, his impression at the time being that as Mayor he should not hold such stock. Sherwood came frequently to City Hall in reference to the Mayor's personal financial matters and those of his family.

One of the most damning facts in the whole affair is that when Sherwood was subpoenaed to appear before the Legislative Committee he disappeared and stayed away until long after the inquiry was ended—June, 1933. Mayor Walker asserted that he was anxious to have Sherwood appear before the committee and that he did all that he could to have him appear. Walker failed, however, to specify a single step that he did take to bring Sherwood back. To quote Mr. Seabury again:

> If these transactions were not the Mayor's, why should Sherwood have fled, giving out originally the false statement that he was leaving the City only to go on a honeymoon but, as subsequent facts have shown, leaving the City to stay away for a period which has already reached almost a year and which undoubtedly will continue until after the Joint Legislative Committee is discharged? There is no suggestion that Sherwood acted for any other public official. He would therefore have had nothing to conceal in any transactions he may have conducted as agent for others; indeed, he would not even be subject to interrogation by the Committee with respect to them. What man leaves his home, his job and his friends, goes into hiding, and subjects himself to an adjudication of contempt and a fine of $50,000, as Sherwood has, unless he has something to conceal? Has there been any suggestion from anyone that Sherwood has anything to conceal except his relations with the Mayor?

Another charge of the many brought by Mr. Seabury against Mayor Walker was that he permitted the Corporation Counsel to appoint on city compensation cases, doctors who split their fees with the Mayor's brother, Dr. W. H. Walker. Testimony was introduced to show that Dr. Walker, who already held two city positions—Medical Examiner to the City Pension Retirement Board and Medical Examiner to the Department of Education—shared offices and maintained joint bank accounts with certain doctors who had been designated by the Corporation Counsel to act on behalf of the city in workmen's compensation cases involving city employees. The bills presented by these doctors were paid without any thorough check as to the services rendered or the fairness of the charges. Dr. Walker admitted that he had received sums of money from each of these doctors, but denied, except in the case of one of them, that this money represented split fees on compensation cases. He explained the fact that the sums he had received were exactly equal to one-half the sums received by the doctors in certain compensation cases as a "coincidence." Dr. Walker later lost his job with the Board of Education, and the doctors associated with him were no longer employed by the city in compensation cases, but they were acquitted of fraud charges by the State Medical Grievance Committee.

Governor Roosevelt submitted the Seabury specifications to Mayor Walker and requested an answer. After the Mayor had filed his answer and Seabury had filed his reply to the answer hearings were begun by Governor Roosevelt to determine whether the facts warranted the removal of the Mayor. In the course of the hearings the Mayor's counsel applied to Justice Staley of the Supreme Court for an order restraining the Governor from going on with the removal proceedings. Justice Staley admitted that he had no jurisdiction to act, but he incorporated in his opinion statements condemning part of the procedure. Mayor Walker, declaring that the opinion showed that he could not receive a fair hearing under the circumstances, resigned, asserting that he would stand for reelection as a vindication. The right to stand for reelection was denied him by the county leaders—which in itself is a commentary on their opinion of the strength of the Mayor's case.

The issues in the Walker case are bigger than Mayor Walker or any other individual. Walker was a machine-made mayor. He owed his nomination and his election to Tammany Hall, a debt which he freely acknowledged. When charges were brought against him Tammany and its cohorts rallied to his defense, not anxious to determine whether he had been a good mayor, anxious only that his misdeeds, if there were any, should be hid so that the organization might not be harmed. So long as there seemed to be hope of blocking the investigation Tammany supported him; when his case seemed hopeless it dropped him. Walker has gone but Tammany remains. The struggle for good government in New York City has only begun. So long as the present system of control by county and district leaders lasts, so long as officials from mayor down are nominated for services rendered and favors promised we can expect to see those officials put allegiance to party bosses above allegiance to the common welfare, we can expect to see those officials conspire with business interests to mulct the city for their mutual interests.

The Magistrates' Courts

The investigation of the Magistrates' Courts conducted by Mr. Seabury disclosed shocking conditions. The investigation showed, moreover, that the evils were due to the same cause that produced inefficiency and corruption in the administrative departments, that the courts as well as the other departments were conducted as parts of a political spoils system. The Magistrates' Courts are in fact a most important part of the system; they furnish a large number of jobs as rewards for party workers, and through their control of the courts the leaders are able to secure favors for a host of friends. To quote from Mr. Seabury's report:

> It (the Inferior Criminal Courts Act of 1910 which reorganized the Magistrates' Courts) left the Magistrates to be appointed by a political agency, the Mayor, upon the recommendation of the district leaders within his political party— and these men, as we know, have regarded the places to be filled as plums to be distributed as rewards for services rendered by faithful party workers. The Courts are directed by these Magistrates in co-operation with the Court clerks, who are not Civil Service employees and who are appointed without the slightest regard to fitness or qualification, but solely through political agencies and because of political influences. The assistant clerks and attendants, though nominally taken from the Civil Service List, are still, in almost all instances, faithful party workers who, despite Civil Service provisions, have secured their places through political influence as a recompense for services performed for the Party. The insidious auspices under which the Magistrates, the clerks, the assistant clerks and the attendants are appointed are bad

enough; the conditions under which they retain their appointments are infinitely worse, because they involve the subserviency in office to district leaders and other politicians. It is a by-word in the corridors of the Magistrates' Courts of the City of New York that intervention of a friend in the district political club is much more potent in the disposition of cases than the merits of the cause or the services of the best lawyer and, unfortunately, the truth of the statement alone prevents it from being a slander upon the good name of the City.

Much, if not all, of the hideous caricature which parades as justice in these courts is avoidable; complaisancy, unconcern and corruption are alone responsible for it—and these causes, in turn, are the product of the system which permits what was intended to be a great instrument of justice to remain a part of a political system, the purpose of which is to retain and control the jobs and perquisites relating to government.

The testimony of the Magistrates themselves shows the dominant influence which the district leaders have over the appointments. Eight Magistrates testified that district leaders aided them in getting their appointments. Another, Jean Norris, was a co-leader herself. The testimony of Magistrate Brodsky is typical:

> Magistrate Brodsky testified that a couple of months before his appointment he spoke to his District Leader, James J. Hagan, about his desire to hold a public office.
>
>> I spoke to Mr. Hagan and I mentioned the fact that I had rendered services to the organization and that I felt that I ought to get some recognition, that up to that time I had received none, that I had worked hard, and he said that if I waited a while, the first opportunity he would get, he felt I was entitled to it by reason of my experience at the Bar and the work that I had done, that I had earned some recognition, and that is the substance of the conversation we had. . . .
>>
>> Later on I understood there was to be a vacancy, a temporary vacancy, and Mr. Hagan said to me, "Louis, there is to be a temporary vacancy; how would you like to take it?"
>
> Q. Temporary vacancy where?

A. For a Magistrate. The Judge then sitting on the Bench was sick and there was to be this vacancy. I said I thought I would like to take it temporarily and he said that he would urge my appointment to the party. . . . I meant by that that he would urge it to the party, to the powers is what I really meant. . . . And then he did urge it and eventually I was appointed a temporary magistrate. . . .
Q. What do you know about his urging?
A. Excepting that he told me so.
Q. What did he tell you?
A. He told me he had presented my name.
Q. To whom?
A. To the leaders of Tammany Hall; to the leader of Tammany Hall.

Magistrate Brodsky was then appointed for two successive thirty-day terms.

Q. Now, then, you have told us about your original appointment. Coming now to your reappointment last year, what did you do in order to get that appointment?
A. I continued—substantially nothing.
Q. Substantially nothing?
A. Excepting to talk to Mr. Marsh Ingram.
Q. Who is he?
A. He is the present leader who succeeded Mr. James J. Hagan.
Q. You mean in the district where you reside?
A. In the district where I reside.
Q. Well, what did he do?
A. I assume he presented my name to the leader of Tammany Hall.
Q. Did he tell you that he would?
A. Yes, he said he would.

The testimony of Magistrate Silbermann is also interesting:

Magistrate Silbermann testified that some years prior to his appointment, when a vacancy was created by the elevation of Magistrate Schulz to the Surrogate's Court
I asked Mr. Murphy (Arthur H. Murphy, Democratic County Leader of Bronx County) whether he would assist me in getting his unexpired term.

Q. What did Mr. Murphy say to that?
A. He said he couldn't.
Q. What?
A. He said he could not.
Q. He could not assist you?
A. Right.
Q. Did he give any reason for his inability to do so?
A. No.
Q. Well, did you do anything else towards getting this unexpired term of Surrogate Schulz?
A. I did not.
Q. You dropped it?
A. I did.
Q. Did you drop it because you realized that without Mr. Murphy's support you could not get it?
A. That is right.

Magistrate Silbermann was appointed in 1920:
> After my appointment . . . I learned that the Mayor decided to appoint a Hebrew from the Bronx and he communicated with Mr. Murphy and asked him to suggest a name of some Hebrew.

Q. That is, Arthur Murphy?
A. Yes, Arthur H. Murphy.
Q. Yes, we are talking about Mr. Arthur H. Murphy.
A. That he should suggest some Hebrew from the Bronx as a temporary magistrate in place of the late Magistrate Matthew B. Breen, who then was ill and who was a Bronx resident at that time. . . .
Q. Now, Judge Silbermann, what I am anxious to have you state, if you will, and if you know, is just why you, Jesse Silbermann, were selected to be magistrate up there rather than some other Hebrew up there in the Bronx who was a member of the bar in good standing.
A. I have stated the reasons. I was active in the party; I was chairman of the Law Committee of the Democratic party up there prior to my appointment; I was active in politics.

Political control of the Magistrates' Courts is also assured through the Court Clerks, Assistant Clerks and Attendants. The position of Clerk is exempt from civil service; practically all the clerks are active party workers and receive their positions as a reward for their political services. As the Seabury report says: "Sixteen clerks . . . admitted upon examination that they were active politically; their appointments were rewards for service within their political organization. The great majority of them had no previous experience or actual knowledge of court procedure or any form of preparation for the duties which they were called upon to perform." And again: "Nothing could be more clear from the investigation than that the court clerk is in the main a politician and only secondarily an administrative officer serving the machinery of justice." Several clerks admitted that it was the practice of party leaders to call upon them to intercede for favored persons.

The assistant clerks and court attendants are appointed from civil service lists, but the testimony showed that ways were found to evade the civil service law to secure the appointment of party workers. One of the main duties of the assistant clerk is to make out complaints against defendants. One form—O-14—is supposed to be used where there is doubt whether the facts warrant holding the defendant. Political leaders often got the clerks to draw up form O-14 for their henchmen. Joseph Wolfman, a pseudo lawyer who had studied law in a correspondence school and had never been admitted to the bar, practiced for three years in the 7th District Court. He testified before the Referee that by splitting his fee with the clerk he was able to get form O-14 drawn up for his clients. The Magistrates practically always dismissed a case where an O-14 was drawn. Wolfman also testified that he had an understanding with several court attendants whereby they turned cases over to him in return for half the fee he collected.

There are 9 Deputy Assistant District Attorneys assigned to Magistrates' Courts to represent the city in the trial of offenders. The Seabury investigation showed that the men assigned were usually inexperienced, incompetent and often corrupt in addition, and that they received so little supervision from the District Attorney's office that most of them did not even bother to make reports. John C. Weston, Deputy Assistant District Attorney assigned to the Women's Court for seven years, admitted that he had accepted bribes to allow some 600 cases to be thrown out, making at least $20,000 by doing so. "Any time one of my cases goes out I will see that you get $25," was the bargain Weston admitted 21 different lawyers had made with him.

One result of the control of Magistrates' Courts by politicians is that offenders who have a pull get off; we have one law for friends of the machine and another for other citizens. An even more serious result is that it leaves the way open for all sorts of rackets to rob the innocent. One of the most disgusting rings was uncovered in the Women's Court in which crooked policemen of the vice squad combined with crooked lawyers, crooked bondsmen, and "fixers" to prey on innocent and guilty alike. The policemen usually worked through stool pigeons, that is, men who induce people to commit crimes so that they may be arrested or get innocent persons into situations where they may plausibly be accused of crimes and then have them arrested. The Seabury report shows how the ring worked:

> In some cases they would make arrests and immediately offer to sell immunity without requiring the prisoner even to go to the Police Station. If the money was paid, the matter was ended then and there. If the money was not paid, the person arrested was arraigned in the Police Station. Here a bondsman, whose virtue is extolled by the policeman, is quickly provided, the prisoner having previously been refused permission to communicate by telephone or otherwise with anyone else. The prisoner, unfamiliar with legal processes, wonders at the magic which unlocks the door of the cell, but unlocked it is. The prisoner is taken by the bondsman, as his pawn, to the bondsman's office, usually nearby, where further inquiry as to the prisoner's financial status is made. Here the bondsman learns that the prisoner has a savings bank account. The prisoner is put into the bondsman's automobile and taken home, where the bank book is delivered and assigned to the bondsman. The next morning the bondsman, having the bank book and its assignment in his pocket, takes the prisoner to the bank, where sufficient money is drawn out to pay what is supposed to pave the way to freedom, and this is given to the bondsman. This amount includes an exorbitant charge for the bail bond, rarely less than twice the legal fee, and an additional sum, which the bondsman ad-

vises is to be used to pay for a lawyer, whom he will provide to represent the prisoner, and to "fix" the case, by bribing the officers to testify so as to make the proof insufficient to hold the defendant, and the representative of the District Attorney, to "go easy." Where the bondsman has discovered that the person arrested has additional funds, the victim is held up for additional amounts, on the ground that alleged complications have intervened, requiring the payment of larger amounts than were originally contemplated. When the defendant has been mulcted of all the money possible, the play proceeds; the case comes to trial, the officers testify to a state of facts insufficient to make out a case, the representative of the District Attorney stands mute, and the defendant is discharged.

If the money demanded by the bondsman is not paid, the officers testify to a complete case. Being officers of the law, as one Magistrate put it, their testimony is presumed to be true, and the defendant is convicted, no matter what the defendant may say, the theory being, as another Magistrate put it, that the person arrested would naturally give evidence consistent only with innocence.

The procedure was the same, whether the person arrested was guilty or whether the arrest was a pure frame-up.

The conditions disclosed in the Magistrates' Courts by the Seabury investigation are a disgrace to New York City and to the citizens who allow them to exist. Moreover they are a menace to the fundamentals of democratic government itself. In 1930 alone more than 500,000 persons were arraigned in Magistrates' Courts. These 500,000 are not the rich and powerful but for the most part the poor, helpless, and the ignorant. For many of them their contact with the Magistrates' Courts is the only contact they have with government. What ideas of justice can people have who know only the travesty on justice that is handed out by these courts? What loyalty to democracy can we expect from people who see only government by the bosses for the benefit of the faithful few?

Two magistrates resigned as a result of the scandals which led to the Seabury investigation. Three others resigned pending their public hearing before the Referee; two were removed by the Appellate Division as a result of charges. Six policemen were convicted of crimes; thirteen others were removed from the police force or resigned. Two lawyers were disbarred and one other was reprimanded. This is one of the results of the Seabury investigation.

Among the most important recommendations made by Mr. Seabury for reform of the Magistrates' Courts are: (1) For the purpose of efficiency and economy, the consolidation of the Magistrates' Courts, the Children's Court, and the Court of Special Sessions into a new Court of Special Sessions. (2) The appointment of the judges of this new court by the Appellate Division of the Supreme Court. (3) The centralization of courts in one building. (4) Requiring that all court clerks be appointed from lists made up by civil service examinations open to all qualified persons and cutting down drastically the number of assistant clerks and court attendants. (5) Eliminating the graft in the bail bond business by establishing a central bail bond bureau and reducing the bail required in petty cases to from $10 to $25 to be paid largely in cash. (6) In order to eliminate the opportunity for fixing cases and for the third degree by policemen requiring that all persons arrested be arraigned immediately before a magistrate instead of being booked at a police station. (7) To free defendants from being preyed upon by unscrupulous and incompetent lawyers to have the Appellate Division name a list of lawyers to represent defendants and to have these lawyers paid by the city.

These reforms are important and necessary. They would still leave, however, the fundamental evil of the courts—that they are handled as part of a political spoils system. The system itself must be crushed before we can expect our lower courts to function as agencies of justice.

The Significance of the Seabury Disclosures

What is the significance of the Seabury disclosures? What do the conditions revealed really mean to the citizens of New York City? In the first place they mean that, since many city positions are filled by political appointees who have neither training nor qualifications for their jobs, many persons in the city service are inefficient and incompetent. As Assemblyman Cuvillier said at a hearing:

> I have seen commissioners come on this stand, getting $10,000 or $15,000 a year; on the outside they could not make $1,500 a year. And they know no more about their departments than a boy in the street. . . .

Theofel, County Leader of Queens and Chief Clerk of the Queens County Surrogate's Court since July, 1930, at a salary of $8,000 per year was not even able to tell Mr. Seabury what departments there were in his office.

In the second place, there is a tremendous waste of the taxpayer's money—in the great number of useless positions created and maintained for political henchmen, in the needless duplication of activities of different departments, in the excessive price paid for land condemned for city purposes, in the high prices paid to favored contractors for city work, in the general extravagance in many city offices.

Typical of this extravagance is the fact that on February 23, 1932, there were 835 passenger automobiles provided by the city for departments other than the Fire and Police. These automobiles cost the city more than one million dollars and the city paid 509 chauffeurs annual salaries amounting to another million to operate them. Fifteen department heads and one assistant had two chauffeurs each. This extravagance has brought about a situation where the richest city in the world is unable to pay its unemployed families enough to live on under conditions even approaching decency, where important educational and social services have to be curtailed, where the city has to pay excessive rates of interest on its bonds, where it has to go, hat in hand, to the bankers to find out what activities it will be permitted to carry on.

Thirdly, and perhaps most important of all, the great power of the dominant political machine and the way its influence extends to all branches of the city government have developed in many people a feeling of indifference and cynicism. Why work for good government when it is so much easier to accept what the machine has to give? Why vote for reform candidates? Why bother to vote at all when your vote will probably not be counted? Why worry about justice when it is so much easier to cultivate the favor of a party leader?

Mr. Seabury sums up the situation well when he says:

> In a very large measure the affairs of the City of New York are conducted, not with a view to the benefits which can be conferred upon the residents of our City, but for the profit which the dominant political organization in the City and its satellites can make out of the running of it. The consequence is that widespread inefficiency and sloth are tolerated in politically appointed and protected city employees, and every subterfuge is availed of to furnish excuses for the spending of money, not because the spending thereof is necessary, or even desirable, in the public interest, but because of the opportunities for graft incident thereto.

The Seabury reports give a dark picture of the government of New York City. It is not true, however, that these conditions are peculiar to New York. Relatively they can be duplicated in every city and town in the country where a political machine has undisputed power. Tammany is no worse than other political organizations; it merely has more power and a wider field of activities. There is no evidence that the regular Republican organization of New York City would be better if it were in power. In many cases the Republican leaders have worked hand in glove with the Democratic leaders for their mutual advantage. The trials of election officials for irregularities in the election of 1932 show that many Republican officials conspired with Democrats to falsify the returns. In the list of district leaders who hold important offices in the city government there are several Republicans who apparently work smoothly with their Democratic associates. Mr. Harvey, Borough President of Queens, the lone Republican on the Board of Estimate and Apportionment, has voted for most of Tammany's pet measures; he introduced the resolution increasing the salaries of members of the Board by amounts varying from 100 to 166 percent.

One of the best examples of the way the two machines work together is the notorious deal on Supreme Court Judges in the Second Judicial District which was described in the testimony of John Theofel, which has already been quoted. In this deal the leaders of each party agreed to nominate only the number of judges assigned to it, and to endorse the candidates of the other party. The deal went through as planned and the twelve judges nominated by the two organizations were elected in spite of the attempt of indignant citizens to elect independent candidates. One of the Democratic-Republican judges elected in Kings County was John McCooey, Jr., the 31-year-old son of Boss McCooey of Brooklyn.

Recommendations for Reform

In his report submitting recommendations for reform Mr. Seabury, after pointing out that mere prohibitions and penalties will accomplish nothing, continues:

> This, in my opinion, leads to the irresistible conclusion that no substantial improvement in the processes of our City government can reasonably be anticipated unless a radical change be made in the legislative and money-spending agencies of our government, so as to insure full and open discussion and wide publicity of its activities. I know of no more effective way of accomplishing this end than by fair and equitable representation of minorities in the group constituting this agency. Our government is founded upon the principle that it should be representative of all the people. This is a wise political economy. The complete and absolute control of the vital agency of government in New York City by a single party prevents the operation of that principle in the place where we need it most, the place from which flows the money that the City spends. I labor under no delusion that minority representation will be the panacea of all our governmental ills. I am completely persuaded, however, that there is every reasonable ground to believe it will result in a tremendous improvement.

Mr. Seabury's chief recommendations are:

> The election of a single legislative chamber, or council, to succeed to the powers of the Board of Estimate and Apportionment, the Board of Aldermen and the Commissioners of the Sinking Fund;

That the members of the Council shall be elected by Boroughs, upon a non-partisan ballot, without party designation or party emblems and under a system of proportional representation, the result of which would be that every group sufficiently strong to be entitled thereto would be represented in the Council, each according to its relative strength;

That the Borough Presidents' offices should be abolished and their duties vested in a Commissioner of Public Works, to be appointed by the Mayor;

That there be ten specified departments, exclusive of education, by which shall be performed the various executive and administrative functions now performed by the various city departments;

There should be a non-partisan, not a bi-partisan, Municipal Civil Service Commission, the members of which should be selected from a list furnished by the presidents of certain educational and cultural institutions;

That persons in the administrative service of the city should take no active part in municipal elections, and that it be the duty of the Commissioner of Inquiry and the Municipal Civil Service Commission to see that these provisions are properly enforced.

In support of his first recommendation Mr. Seabury points out that the tendency in American cities has been to do away with two-chambered legislative bodies, and that the present Board of Aldermen which has been costing the city $714,930.00 annually is practically worthless, being a mere rubber stamp for the Board of Estimate. A single chamber of about 25 members would be small enough to promote efficiency and at the same time large enough to insure representation of minorities.

Members of the Council would be elected not by single-member districts but by the borough as a whole, each borough having one member for every 50,000 votes cast. The system of proportional representation proposed for the election of the Council is that known as the single transferable vote. The system is designed to give representation to every group of 50,000. The voter indicates his first choice by a figure 1, his second choice by a figure 2, and so on, showing as many choices as he pleases. If his first choice does not receive sufficient votes to be elected his second choice is counted, if his second choice is not elected his third choice is counted, and so on till one of his choices is elected, or all of them defeated. The system is based on the principle that each voter is entitled to one representative only but that he is always entitled to that one representative unless all of his choices are for candidates whom less than 50,000 other voters want.

The system has been opposed as being too complicated. Voting is simple enough; the count is somewhat complicated but offers no real difficulties once the principle is understood. Briefly the system of counting is as follows. All the ballots cast in a borough are counted in one central place. The first step is to count the first choices indicated on the ballots. As soon as a candidate receives 50,000 first choices he is declared elected and thereafter ballots which indicate him for first choice are credited to the candidate for whom they indicate second choice. After all ballots have been counted in this way the candidate with the lowest number of first choices is dropped and his ballots are given to the candidate for whom second choice is indicated—in case the second choice is already elected they are given to the third choice and so on. This process is continued until every candidate has either been elected or dropped. It seems obvious that the benefits derived from this system outweigh the difficulties of the count.

Some system which will give minority representation on the Council is particularly important. Much of the inefficiency and corruption in the present city government would be eliminated, even if Tammany had a majority in the Board of Estimate and the Board of Aldermen, if there were in these two bodies an alert and fearless minority which could call attention to what was going on there-by keeping public opinion informed. The unfairness of the system of electing a board by single-member districts is well illustrated in the present Board of Aldermen. In the Aldermanic election of 1931 the Democratic candidates received 66 per cent of the votes, the Republicans 25, and the Socialists 9. The Democrats, however, elected 64 out of 65 members or more than 98 per cent, the Republicans one, and the Socialists none.

Mr. Seabury favors retaining the Mayor as the head of the city government rather than adopting the city manager plan on the ground that the people are accustomed to focusing attention on the choice of a mayor in municipal elections and that it is "probably easier to arouse public interest in the election of an able and honest man to the post of mayor than it is to bring about the election of a high-grade governing board" which would appoint and control the city manager. Under the plan proposed the mayor and comptroller would be elected by the voters of the entire city under a system of preferential voting.

One measure favored by Mr. Seabury has already been adopted by Mayor O'Brien's administration, that is the executive budget.

On the principle that responsibility cannot be secured without power the mayor would be given even more power than he has at present. Under Mr. Seabury's plan he would have much the same power over the budget that the Governor of New York State has over the state budget. Under this plan the mayor is entirely responsible for preparing the budget for submission to the Board of Estimate.

The proposal that the offices of the Borough Presidents be abolished and their duties performed by a Commissioner of Public Works appointed by the Mayor has three arguments in its favor. Centralizing this work under one official would result in greater efficiency and economy. It would prevent the log rolling that now goes on among the Borough Presidents with each President trying to get all that he can for his own borough. It would help break the hold of the county leaders who now use the patronage of the Borough Presidents' offices to strengthen their local machines.

At present the administrative functions of the city are distributed among a multitude of departments, bureaus, commissions, and boards over which the mayor has varying kinds and amounts of control. This situation is partly due to accident. As the city has assumed new functions they have been assigned to existing agencies to perform, or new agencies have been created with no logical plan. There is little doubt also that some of these agencies were created for the sake of making more jobs for the party in power. The ten departments, exclusive of Education, which is controlled by state law, suggested by Mr. Seabury are: Executive, Fire, Health, Inspection and Licenses, Law, Police, Public Works, Social Welfare, Taxes and Assessment, and Transportation and Commerce. Under his plan the actual assignment of functions to these ten departments would be made after a careful scientific study. The creation of these ten departments would result in greater efficiency and economy by eliminating many overlapping agencies and would result in greater centralization of responsibility.

The Seabury investigations disclosed various abuses in the

civil service and various evasions of the civil service laws. Instead of being a bulwark against the spoils system the Municipal Civil Service Commission, appointed by the mayor, has been a part of the machine, or at least it has allowed the machine to debauch the civil service laws. A stringent enforcement of the merit system of appointments is necessary if the power of the political organization is to be broken and Mr. Seabury therefore recommends that the appointment of the Civil Service Commission be taken from the mayor and given to the Council. As a further safeguard the Council is to make appointments only from a list of nominees made by a board made up of the presidents of the colleges and universities in the city.

To the final proposal of Mr. Seabury that persons in the administrative service of the city be prohibited from taking any part in municipal elections except as voters a great deal of opposition has developed among municipal employees. They contend that this action would deprive them of civil rights and that a strict enforcement of civil service regulations would make such a provision unnecessary; they contend that city employees are as much interested in good government as other citizens and should have the same right to work for it. Mr. Seabury's reasons for making this recommendation are as follows:

> Persons in the administrative service of the City should be made to realize that the continuity of their employment depends upon merit and merit alone; their tenure should not depend on subservience to any particular party or upon the continuance in power of any particular party.

The Seabury recommendations, if adopted, will go far toward giving New York City an honest and efficient government. One way of judging the value of proposals is by the enemies they make. The Seabury recommendations have had the most bitter opposition from the Democratic organization. Aided by the lukewarm attitude of the regular Republican politicians Tammany has been able, so far, to block all steps in the legislature toward their adoption. The citizens of New York must show more interest, more determination to have good government if the Seabury investigations are to come to anything.

It is true that good government is not merely a matter of machinery and good laws; constitutions, charters, and laws are a means toward good government; they do not in themselves make good government. The best form of government will be futile unless the voters know what good government is, insist that they have it, and be willing to make sacrifices in order to get it.

If the majority of New York City's voters want Tammany in power, or are too ignorant, too indifferent, or too hopeless to care who is in power, Tammany will remain.

It will doubtless seem to many that the Seabury proposals do not go far enough, that they do not go to the real roots of the trouble. Time and again during the investigations it was brought out that the cause of corruption was private business looking for special favors. No politician can be bribed if no one wants to bribe him. There would have been no Equitable Bus scandal if there had been no Equitable Bus Company looking for a franchise. If the City of New York owned and operated its own bus lines, its own subways, its own gas and electric plants, it is true that a host of new administrative problems would rise, but the main source of corruption would be removed. Moreover, much of the indifference of New Yorkers toward their government is doubtless due to the feeling that the government is relatively unimportant in their lives; if the city government performed vital services for its citizens would it not go far to rouse them from their lethargy and lead them to insist that the city government do its job well?

Tomorrow May Be Too Late: Save the Schools Now

This is a dark hour for education in this country, but it need not be a zero hour. It may even be an educational opportunity for a big step forward if the forces are mobilized to deal with the situation hopefully and constructively.

The most significant thing that has happened in our national life in the past twenty years has been the expansion of education to include all ages and all members of our social group. Before the depression, grandmothers as well as children were going to school. Education was trying to make a place for every one who needed or wanted it, and there was a tremendous, growing faith in the power of education. It is at that faith, which is our greatest hope for a continuing civilization, that the present situation is striking.

It is hard to believe that we can not find adequate means to support our schools. The whole cost of public education is only a little more than a third of what we spend a year for tobacco, jewelry, cosmetics, sporting goods, and toys. We pay five times as much for our automobiles every year as we do for our schools. It would seem that with judicious readjustment of our scale of social values we can meet the situation.

If we had been fair to our schools, not a dollar of the $368,000,000 would have been cut from their budgets, and not a teacher removed. You might question that statement in the face of the fact that all prices of equipment and school supplies as well as the cost of living generally have gone down. But these have not gone down in proportion to the increased demands on the schools.

The number of pupils in our public schools has rapidly in-

[First published in *Good Housekeeping* 98 (March 1934): 20–21, 222–27, from an interview with Katherine Glover.]

creased since the depression. In the period between 1930 and 1932 our school population increased by the size of the population of the entire State of Montana. This increase represents more than the number of all the pupils enrolled in our public high schools in 1900.

All of us have rejoiced in the great victory of the NRA in abolishing child labor, which has liberated from shop and factory and office an estimated 100,000 youths and delivered them back to the schools of the country. Under existing conditions, what can the schools do with these liberated youths? Already they are spilling over. There are not desks and chairs enough to take care of the students who have come back begging for more schooling. And this increased enrollment is in the high schools, where education is most costly. In 1930 the average amount necessary to educate a high-school child was $136, while for an elementary pupil, the cost was $65.

It is in the face of this increased need for schooling that operating expenses have been so indiscriminately slashed. A policy that would be considered madness in a clothing factory, a grocery store, or a steel mill is considered good enough for our schools, *whose output is the citizen of tomorrow.*

In the fall of 1931 there was an infantile paralysis epidemic which left in its wake several thousand crippled children. Our schools took these children in. Special classes were provided for them as well as for other handicapped children. It is a comparatively expensive form of education, requiring trained teachers and a different kind of teaching equipment. This special education is being cut out of many of our schools in the program of economy. It is classed as one of the "frills" of modern education. Yet educating these children to be useful members of society is much less costly than taking care of them later on as adults in benevolent institutions, even if we did not consider the happiness of the individuals.

It is in such items as these that schools are "saving." Health care is being cut down. Vocational training is being eliminated in many places, kindergartens done away with, school terms shortened, the number of teachers reduced, and the size of classes increased. The situation in regard to textbooks is so acute that Dr. George Zook, Commissioner of Education, recently called a conference in Washington at which it was revealed that in some schools textbooks published eleven years ago, and later discarded, have been brought back into use. Books, unsightly, unsanitary, with pages missing, are being used by as many as six classes a day in some schools, and in many schools throughout the country classes are trying to carry on their work with wholly inadequate materials.

Many a leading business man, member of a local school board, who has willingly signed the NRA code for his business, has cheerfully voted for a 20 percent cut in teachers' salaries and a reduction in the number of teachers. He has approved a budget cut that means a serious curtailing of the school program. He feels as virtuous in taking teachers off the school payroll to add to the unemployed as he does in adding new employees to the payroll of his store.

He does not realize that a lowering of school standards will eventually affect his business, yet whenever he calls in his secretary for dictation, she brings him the benefit of more than a thousand dollar investment in elementary and high-school education; his manager gives him the results of twelve years of public school and four years of college. His employees bring him a total of training that is one of the chief assets of his business. If that training were lessened, his business would soon suffer.

Good education costs more than poor education. It is like good plumbing, good clothing, good furniture. If we want shoddy material, we can get it at a cheaper price. But if we want quality, we can not expect to get it at the bargain, marked-down rate to which education has been reduced in many parts of the country. Taking a long-range view of the situation, we should compare the cost of educating a child at an average of $91 a year, and the cost of keeping a man in prison at $300 a year. In cutting down our costs for education we are almost certain to run up our bill for crime.

Where economy logically should strike is at the fundamentals, such as more economical school districting, centralization in the purchase of supplies, school buildings designed for maximum usefulness rather than to flatter community pride, sound and efficient management instead of political control.

The methods of economy of many school boards might be compared to skimming the icing off a cake. They have simply taken off what was added last and what they denounce as frills and fluff. These subjects are not frills and fluff but are the ones most in key with life today, which have been added in an attempt to adapt our schools to our changing world.

About 40 years ago, a new idea dawned in education. Educators began to see that education should parallel life, that the school should reproduce the child's world. In this new type of education the child instead of the curriculum became the centre of interest, and since the child is active, changing, creative, education ceased to be static, became dynamic and creative in response to the needs of the child. Many things were added to schools which before had been considered out of their province. These changes have come very slowly and unevenly and are still far from being generally accepted.

In a survey of secondary education in this country made by the Federal Office of Education recently, it was found that the number of courses offered by schools has practically doubled in recent years. And in some schools non-academic subjects have come to claim from one-third to two-fifths of the time of all pupils. What does this mean? Simply that the modern school offers to the pupils what the school of earlier days gave them, plus much that the home used to teach. As the nature of the home has changed and as all our life has become more complex, due to the contributions of science and machinery, the child can not depend upon home opportunities and tasks for his training.

When girls used to learn the fine arts of cooking and sewing under the tutelage of their mothers and their grandmothers, it was not considered a "frill" or useless knowledge. Now the teaching of sewing and cooking, together with the chemistry of foods and a good deal more, is transferred to the school under the name of home economics. Boys, instead of going into shops or businesses of their fathers as apprentices, have their training in the high school. It is wiser economy, and it fits in better with our whole scheme of living.

The change from healthy country living to cramped city life has been met by physical education and health work. Music, art, and dancing, which children used to get in their home and community life, are woven into the school's activities. Civics, athletics, out-of-classroom interests give training in cooperative group living made necessary in our present complex civilization. Science, manual training, and the crafts should play a larger part in the schools and should begin in the elementary grades if children are to adjust themselves satisfactorily to a technological age.

We do not need fewer of these subjects; we need more. A reorganization of our courses of study is needed which will make them as fundamental a part of education as the well-known three R's. Reading and writing need not be isolated subjects. Even very young children can read and write *about something*; for instance, about their work in arithmetic, nature study, or what happens on the playground. The fundamentals of arithmetic can be more economically and just as thoroughly taught if they are linked up with shop work, domestic science, and geography. The three subjects, geography, history, and civics, are, in some schools, being replaced by one subject—social studies—which gives pupils the information on which they can build up an understanding of social, economic, and political institutions today.

Giving up the old-fashioned recitation where one pupil stands and tells the teacher what he has learned while the rest of the class sit idle and bored, has proved a practical way of getting more time to teach other things. A rearranging of subjects and methods in the light of a new philosophy which sees education as a total experience, exactly as life is a total experience, would provide economy in time, materials, and cost, that would be a far more sensible proceeding than setting our schools backward by lopping off the activities and courses that have been pointing the way toward a new deal in education.

When the panic of 1837 struck the country, public education was just gaining a foothold, especially in Massachusetts and New York. Before that, education was considered a privilege, paid for in tuition by those who could afford it. Horace Mann, a rising young lawyer in Massachusetts, gave up his practice and for a beggarly sum became secretary of the State Board of Education. In that capacity he preached the doctrine of education for all children and proposed that schools be supported by taxation.

It was from that crusade, following on the heels of a depression such as we are going through now, that public education had its first real impetus in this country. The infant that grew under the encouragement of Mann in Massachusetts and of Henry Barnard in Connecticut, has grown tremendously, but it is still being supported by methods of a century ago. The property tax was the logical means of support when Horace Mann preached his crusade of tax-supported schools. In those days nearly every one owned his home and place of business, and life was individual and simple. Education reflected that simplicity, and, logically, education took on the tinge of the local life and habits. There was no such concentration of wealth in certain areas of the country, due to the concentration of business and industry, as now exists.

We can not determine clearly what can be done to save our schools without first facing the question of the foundation of support on which they rest. It is the cause of most if not all of the inequalities which exist in our educational system. If we wait for reform, state by state, and in all of our 130,000 separate school districts, it will be at the price of the sacrifice of educational opportunity for hundreds of thousands of American children to whom that sacrifice can never be made up.

Why should a child benefit by being born in New York State, Delaware, or California, where the schools, because of great wealth and an intelligent use of that wealth for education, have weathered the depression, or suffer for being born in Arkansas or Alabama, where there is no such wealth nor a satisfactory subsidy for education? In New York, the poorest schools are spending $78 a year per pupil; in Arkansas, the poorest schools have only $12 a year per pupil. And even if all the wealth of the State of Arkansas were taxed through property, income, and other possible taxes, it could yield only $24 a year for each pupil instead of $12.

In Alabama for the past two years about 275,000 school children have had their school term shortened. In some places the teachers have taught without pay in order to stretch out the term a little longer. They have lived in the schoolhouses and cooked their meals on the heating stove, the children bringing them food from the farms. In Lamar County, Alabama, the schools closed the middle of December, both this year and last. This year the children will again have three and a quarter months of school, instead of the eight full months they should have.

Across an invisible line, in Lowndes County, Mississippi, the children went to school a full term last year and will again this year. The difference between what happens on one side of that invisible line and the other is the difference between the tax system of the two states. The schools of Alabama are still limping along on an old and unsatisfactory method of taxation. In Mississippi, which is the most rural of the forty-eight states and as hard hit by the depression as any in the Union, the support of the schools is taken care of by an emergency sales tax which was passed in 1932 when the schools were about to close.

Equal opportunity for an education for the children of this nation rests upon the fortuitous circumstance of the kind of taxation that state or community may have. The country boy does not have the same opportunity as the boy in the city. There is a wide range of inequalities between states, between counties in the same state, even between neighboring townships. On the average the city child goes to school more than five weeks longer each term than the boy or girl who lives in the country; the total time—or education—a country boy thus loses during the grammar grades is equivalent to a whole school year. Only one-fourth of the rural children between fifteen and eighteen years of age go to high school, compared with three-fourths of city children. In one state the richest school district is 275 times better able to support its schools than the poorest district.

These inequalities existed even in normal times. The depression merely shows up the contrast in sharper outlines. They are not facts that come under codes, nor has any NRA been organized to deal with the situation, grave though it is.

In those states where education has suffered least during the depression some means of support for the schools other than sole dependence upon the property tax has been found. There has been a healthy progression from local to state support. A common school fund, or an equalization fund as it is sometimes called, has been established, with gratifying results, in a number of the states.

The next logical step should be equalization in all of the forty-eight states through some form of Federal aid. This would insure a square deal to education not by states or by sections, but for the nation as a whole. In other words, education has outgrown its purely local character which it had in the days of Horace Mann, and is tending toward nationalization. We are no longer an isolated, pioneer people; we have become homogeneous. Without losing our local flavor we should secure the benefits to education of national unity.

If the citizens of any state stayed within the state, the rest of the country might look with unconcern upon the denial of educational opportunities to its children, but inescapably bound together as we are, and traveling and moving as freely as we do, the whole country has a vital interest in the whole educational setup. The uneducated boy of any state may become the pauper citizen of any other; the educational problems of one state are the concern of all the others.

Since education is the keystone of democracy, education should be truly democratic. The facts which have been cited show that as education exists in America today it is not democratic, and probably can not be unless we establish some centralization of education in the government.

The time seems ripe to urge again a Federal Department of Education with a Secretary of Education in the President's cabinet. England, France, Germany, Italy—in fact, nearly all of the large countries of the world except the United States—have departments of education in their governments. Our Federal Office of Education, as it now exists, is mainly an advisory and factfinding bureau with no power to help education out of its present dilemma. This office, just one of a number of bureaus in the Department of the Interior, with an appropriation of $270,000, makes an interesting contrast with the Department of Agriculture with its appropriation of more than $370,000,000, and its vast activities and powers operating at the moment to pull farmers out of the red.

Education, which deals with the future of American citizens, has reached its present grave crisis with no national program of recovery. As some one has tersely put it, children are not getting a new deal, they are getting a raw deal.

Under the recovery program, a small beginning recently has been made for the aid of schools, which gives help in repair and reconstruction of schools and in reopening schools that are closed. Some teachers are being reemployed, and over the country at large two million dollars a month are being allocated for emergency educational programs, chiefly for adult education and nursery-school projects. Though a move in the right direction, this hand held out to the biggest of our public services, the schools, is pathetically small in comparison to the aid given to forests, post offices, highways, and bridges.

A Federal Department of Education would not mean, as many

seem to fear, a standardized system of education any more than the Department of Agriculture means standardized farming, unsuited to local conditions. It would mean a fair deal for American children just as the Department of Agriculture is trying to give the farmer a fair deal. This fair dealing would be further safeguarded if the new Federal Department were not confined to education alone, but were given authority over every phase of child welfare and protection. Then the activities now carried on with such splendid results by the Children's Bureau could be coordinated with education, and the whole administered as an effective unit.

It is significant that in those countries of Europe which have governmental supervision of education, the schools have not buckled under the depression as ours have, even though the economic situation has been more acute than with us. It is said that in forty other countries the educational front has held better than ours has under the attack of world-wide economic depression.

If educational supervision were passed over into the hands of the government, we would have Uncle Sam collecting taxes for the benefit of the schools and returning it to the states to supplement local taxes. In this case such contrasts as that between Alabama and her neighbor state could not exist. By setting up a Federal Department of Education we would not be weakening the local educational structure, but rather strengthening it by having for the first time a machinery which could wipe out undemocratic inequalities.

One can not believe that the American people will stand by and see their system of public education go bankrupt; that the same energy and initiative which are being roused for the revision of industry can not be stirred in defense of the schools. The schools of America are the real laboratories in which any new deal can be permanently and successfully inaugurated.

Some such national planning as our financial institutions are undergoing is needed for education. The very desperateness of the school situation may serve as the fuel to start a conflagration in their behalf. The starting point is in the local school district, where the leadership may lie in the Parent-Teacher Association, in the League of Women Voters, or the Civic Club, in the Rotary or the Kiwanis. The communities should begin with the thing closest at hand, study the changes being made in their schools, the tax system on which they are dependent. Then, if necessary, help should be asked of the state educational authorities, and Federal aid urged through the representatives in Washington. A sufficiently aroused public opinion can command what it will.

The hunger for education in this country is as great as, if not far greater than, the hunger for food. There are bread lines at the doors of our schools which it is as dangerous to turn away as the bread lines at the doors of our welfare agencies. We need not less, but more, education for our children, and not alone for our children, but for our adults, released to new leisure.

If there should sweep over us a concern for education which sees it as essential to the "longer pull" of any far-reaching recovery plan, we may bring about a reconstruction of our entire system of education which will be the culmination of that impulse begun forty years ago to bring education into line with the life of today and tomorrow. The result of that reconstruction would be to justify, as we must admit it has not been justified in the past, the hope over the doorways of our schools, "An equal opportunity for an education for every American child."

Appendixes

Appendix 1
After Capitalism—What?
By Reinhold Niebuhr

The following analysis of American social and political conditions is written on the assumption that capitalism is dying and with the conviction that it ought to die. It is dying because it is a contracting economy which is unable to support the necessities of an industrial system that requires mass production for its maintenance, and because it disturbs the relations of an international economic system with the anarchy of nationalistic politics. It ought to die because it is unable to make the wealth created by modern technology available to all who participate in the productive process on terms of justice.

The conviction that capitalism is dying and that it ought to die gives us no clue to the method of its passing. Will it perish in another world war? Or in the collapse of the credit structure through which it manipulates its various functions? Will it, perhaps, give way to a new social order created by the political power of those who have been disinherited by it? Or will it be destroyed by a revolution? These questions are difficult to answer for any portion of Western civilization, and they are particularly puzzling when directed to the American scene. We may believe that the basic forces moving in modern industrial society are roughly similar in all nations. Yet we cannot evade the fact that various nations reveal a wide variety of unique social and economic characteristics and that our own nation is particularly unique in some of the aspects of its political and economic life. Our wealth has been greater than that of any modern nation, the ideals of a pioneer democracy have retarded the formation of definite classes, the frontier spirit belongs to so recent a past that its individualism is not yet dissipated, and the complete pre-

[First published in *World Tomorrow* 16 (1 March 1933): 203–5. For Dewey's reply, see this volume, pp. 71–75.]

occupation of the nation with its engineering task to the exclusion of political and social problems makes us singularly incompetent as a people in the field of politics. All these factors, and some others which might be mentioned, warn the prophet to be circumspect in applying generalizations, derived from European conditions to our situation. It is therefore advisable to divide our problem of analysis by considering first those aspects of the situation about which generalizations equally applicable to Europe and America can be made; the uniquely American aspects may then be seen in clearer light.

The most generally applicable judgment which can be made is that capitalism will not reform itself from within. There is nothing in history to support the thesis that a dominant class ever yields its position or privileges in society because its rule has been convicted of ineptness or injustices. Those who still regard this as possible are rationalists and moralists who have only a slight understanding of the stubborn inertia and blindness of collective egoism.

Politically this judgment implies that liberalism in politics is a spent force. In so far as liberalism is based upon confidence in the ability and willingness of rational and moral individuals to change the basis of society, it has suffered disillusion in every modern nation. As the social struggle becomes more sharply defined, the confused liberals drift reluctantly into the camp of reaction and the minority of clear-sighted intellectuals and idealists are forced either to espouse the cause of radicalism or to escape to the bleachers and become disinterested observers. The liberal middle ground has been almost completely wiped out in Germany. It is held today only by the Catholic party, a unique phenomenon in Western politics. In England only the free-trade liberals who managed to extricate themselves from the Tory embrace and the quite lonely and slightly pathetic Mr. Lloyd George stand in the liberal position. The English liberals who interpreted their position as a championship of the community of consumers against warring camps of producers have had to learn that the stakes which men have in the productive process outweigh their interests as consumers. Mr. Roosevelt's effort at, or pretension to, liberalizing the Democratic Party may be regarded as a belated American effort to do what Europe has proved to be impossible.

Equally futile will be the efforts of liberals who stand to the left of Mr. Roosevelt and who hope to organize a party which will give the feverish American patient pills of diluted socialism coated with liberalism, in the hope that his aversion to bitter pills will thus be circumvented.

All this does not mean that intellectual and moral idealism are futile. They are needed to bring decency and fairness into any system of society; for no basic reorganization of society will ever guarantee the preservation of humaneness if good men do not preserve it. Furthermore, the intelligence of a dominant group will determine in what measure it will yield in time under pressure or to what degree it will defend its entrenched positions so uncompromisingly that an orderly retreat becomes impossible and a disorderly rout envelops the whole of society in chaos. That ought to be high enough stake for those of us to play for who are engaged in the task of education and moral suasion among the privileged. If such conclusions seem unduly cynical they will seem so only because the moral idealists of the past century, both religious and rational, have been unduly sentimental in their estimates of human nature. Perhaps it will be permitted the writer to add, by way of parenthesis, that he has been greatly instructed by the number of letters which have come to him in late months complaining that a religious radical ought not to give up his faith in human nature so completely lest he betray thereby his lack of faith in the divine. Classical religion has always spoken rather unequivocally of the depravity of human nature, a conclusion at which it arrived by looking at human nature from the perspective of the divine. It is one of the strange phenomena of our culture that an optimistic estimate of human nature has been made the basis of theistic theologies.

Next to the futility of liberalism we may set down the inevitability of fascism as a practical certainty in every Western nation. A disintegrating social system will try to save itself by closing ranks and eliminating the anarchy within itself. It will thus undoubtedly be able to perpetuate itself for several decades. It will not finally succeed because it will have no way of curing the two basic defects of capitalism, inequality of consumption and international anarchy. It will probably succeed longer in Italy and Germany than in America, because fascism in those countries derives its strength from a combination of the military and capitalistic castes. The military caste has a greater interest in avoiding revolution than in preserving the privileges of the capitalists. It may therefore be counted upon to circumscribe these privileges more rigorously than will be the case in America, where such a caste does not exist and where military men lack social prestige. A von Schleicher can always be counted on to build a more stable fascism than a "committee of public safety" consisting of Owen Youngs, et al., to whom the fascist task will undoubtedly be entrusted in America.

The certainty that dominant social groups which now control society will not easily yield and that their rule is nevertheless doomed raises interesting problems of strategy for those who desire a new social order. In America these problems are complicated by the fact that there is no real proletarian class in this country. All but the most disinherited workers still belong to the middle class, and they will not be united in a strong political party of their own for some years to come. Distressing social experience will finally produce radical convictions among them, but experience without education and an adequate political philosophy will merely result in sporadic violence. We are literally in the midst of a disintegrating economic empire with no receiver in bankruptcy in sight to assume responsibility for the defunct institution. All this probably means that capitalism has many a decade to run in this country, particularly if it should find momentary relief from present difficulties through some inflationary movement. The sooner a strong political labor movement, expressing itself in socialist terms develops, the greater is the probability of achieving essential change without undue violence or social chaos.

One of the difficulties of the situation is that America may have to go through a period of purely parliamentary socialism even after Europe has proved that a socialism which makes a fetish of parliamentarism will not be able to press through to its goal. Though we will probably have to go through the experience of parliamentarism, we may be able to qualify our faith in it sufficiently to be pragmatic and experimental in the choice of our radical techniques. To disavow pure parliamentarism does not mean to espouse revolution. Any modern industrial civilization has a natural and justified instinctive avoidance of revolution. It rightly fears that revolution may result in suicide for the whole civilization. When European nations are unable to achieve a bare Socialist majority in their legislative bodies, it is hardly probable that in America we will ever have such a preponderance of Socialist conviction that Socialist amendments to the constitution could be enacted. But revolution is equally unthinkable. There is no possibility of a purely revolutionary movement establishing order on this continent without years of internecine strife. For this reason it is important that parliamentary socialism seek to enact as much of its program as possible within the present constitutional framework during the next decades, without hoping, however, that socialism itself can be established in this manner. The final struggle between socialism and fascism will probably be a long and drawn-out conflict in which it is possible that fascism will finally capitulate without a military or revolutionary venture being initiated against it. It will capitulate simply because the inexorable logic of history plus the determined opposition of the labor group will finally destroy it. The final transfer of power may come through the use of a general strike or some similar technique.

Prediction at long range may seem idle and useless. But it is important to recognize that neither the parliamentary nor the revolutionary course offers modern society an easy way to the mastery of a technological civilization. If this is the case, it becomes very important to develop such forms of resistance and mass coercion as will disturb the intricacies of an industrial civilization as little as possible, and as will preserve the temper of mutual respect within the area of social conflict. Political realists have become cynical about moral and religious idealism in politics chiefly because so frequently it is expressed in terms of confusion which hide the basic facts of the social struggle. Once the realities of this struggle are freely admitted, there is every possibility of introducing very important ethical elements into the struggle in the way, for instance, that Gandhi introduces them in India.

The inability of religious and intellectual idealists to gauge properly the course of historical events results from their constant over-estimate of idealistic and unselfish factors in political life. They think that an entire nation can be educated toward a new social ideal when all the testimony of history proves that new societies are born out of social struggle, in which the positions of the various social groups are determined by their economic interests.

Those who wish to participate in such a struggle creatively, to help history toward a goal of justice and to eliminate as much confusion, chaos and conflict in the attainment of the goal as possible, will accomplish this result only if they do not permit their own comparative emancipation from the determining and conditioning economic factors to obscure the fact that these factors are generally determining. No amount of education or religious idealism will ever persuade a social class to espouse a cause or seek a goal which is counter to its economic interest. Social intelligence can have a part in guiding social impulse only if it does not commit the error of assuming that intelligence has destroyed and sublimated impulse to such a degree that impulse is no longer potent. This is the real issue between liberalism and political realism. The liberal is an idealist who imagines that his particular type of education or his special kind of religious idealism will accomplish what history has never before revealed: the complete sublimation of the natural impulse of a social group.

Dominant groups will always have the impulse to hold on to their power as long as possible. In the interest of a progressive justice they must be dislodged, and this will be done least painfully and with least confusion if the social group which has the future in its hands becomes conscious of its destiny as soon as possible, is disciplined and self-confident in the knowledge of its destiny and gradually acquires all the heights of prestige and power in society which it is possible to acquire without a struggle. When the inevitable struggle comes (for all contests of power must finally issue in a crisis) there is always the possibility that the old will capitulate and the new assume social direction without internecine conflict. That is why an adequate political realism will ultimately make for more peace in society than a liberalism which does not read the facts of human nature and human history aright, and which is betrayed by these errors into erroneous historical calculations which prolong the death agonies of the old order and postpone the coming of the new.

It may be important to say in conclusion that educational and religious idealists shrink from the conclusions to which a realistic analysis of history forces the careful student, partly because they live in the false hope that the impulses of nature in man can be sublimated by mind and conscience to a larger degree than is actually possible, and partly because their own personal idealism shrinks from the "brutalities" of the social struggle which a realistic theory envisages. But this idealism is full of confusion. It does not recognize that everyone but the ascetic is a participant in the brutalities of the social struggle now. The only question of importance is on what side of the struggle they are. Think of all the kind souls who stand in horror of a social conflict who are at this moment benefiting from, and living comfortable lives at the expense of, a social system which condemns 13 million men to misery and semi-starvation. Failure to recognize this covert brutality of the social struggle is probably the greatest weakness of middle-class liberals, and it lends a note of hypocrisy and self-deception to every moral pretension which seeks to eliminate violence in the social struggle.

The relation of the sensitive conscience to the brutal realities of man's collective behavior will always create its own problem—a problem in the solution of which orthodox religion has frequently been more shrewd than liberalism because it did not over-estimate the virtue of human society, but rather recognized the "sinful" character of man's collective life. This problem has its own difficulties, and they ought not to be confused with the problem of achieving an adequate social and political strategy for the attainment of a just society or for the attainment of a higher approximation of justice than a decadent capitalism grants.

Appendix 2
Shall We Abolish School "Frills"? Yes
By H. L. Mencken

Whenever anyone ventures to say that the public schools of the United States are too expensive, or that some of the things commonly taught in them are useless and silly, or that they turn out multitudes of pupils who are ignorant of what every civilized human being should know, the learned and haughty "experts" who are in charge of them usually answer by charging that the critic is a brutal foe of the poor school children, and wants to see them grow up in Egyptian darkness.

This charge, until a year or so ago, struck the majority of right-thinking Americans as very plausible, and in consequence all criticism of the schools tended to be timorous and ineffective. But of late the bitter needs of the time have forced people in all parts of the country to give a stricter heed than formerly to what becomes of their tax money, and there is now in progress, North, East, South, and West a somewhat uneasy and even suspicious reëxamination of all the chief agencies of government, including, of course, the public schools.

The result appears to be a fast-growing conviction that the "experts" have run them both extravagantly and foolishly, and out of it flows a demand that they be reformed. That demand, it becomes plainer every day, does not really come from misanthropes who hate children, and wish to do them evil. On the contrary, it comes very largely from parents, and for the rest it comes from persons who are quite as eager for the welfare and happiness of the children as any of the "experts."

As everyone knows, those experts came into power among us as the politicians went out. A generation ago the public schools of the average American town were still the sport of corrupt poli-

[First published in *Rotarian* 42 (May 1933): 16–17, 48. For Dewey's response to the question, see this volume, pp. 141–46.]

tics, and most of them stood on a low level. To be sure, there were some excellent teachers in them, even at the worst, but the principals and superintendents were mainly political appointees, and not many of them had any professional conscience or dignity. In due time there was a revolt against this unhappy state of affairs, and nearly all the more enlightened communities of the country attempted reforms. One of them put teaching on a civil-service basis, and sought to protect the competent teacher against political interference. Another set up standards for principals and superintendents, and tried to confine their work to persons who really knew something about it. A third attempted to provide better school buildings and equipment, so that the children should be housed in a sanitary and comfortable manner, and have the proper tools for both study and play.

There can be no doubt that these reforms were urged in perfect good faith, and that they were all worth while. The first of them, by liberating the schoolma'm from the politicians, gave her a feeling of professional autonomy, and encouraged her to improve skill and diligence. The second, by clearing out a great many half-literate quacks, opened the way for a new race of very serious young pedagogues, all of them determined to make pedagogy something resembling a learned profession. And the third made going to school much pleasanter than it had ever been before, and incited a great number of children to continue far beyond the grades that had contented their parents.

Unfortunately, some evils came in with these goods, as is apparently inevitable in human affairs. For one thing, the schoolma'ms, once they had begun to feel professional, began to demand professional salaries, and before long they were getting so much more than they had got in the past that the cost of maintaining them became a heavy burden on the taxpayer. For another thing, the building of new schoolhouses and reëquipment of old ones went on so fast, and on so lavish a scale, that great debts were piled up, and the taxpayer began to stagger under the interest and amortization. And for a third thing, and perhaps most importantly, the new pedagogues, having got a free hand to do pretty much as they pleased, at once proceeded to overhaul the traditional scheme of elementary education, and to convert it into something so strange, so complicated, and so costly that large numbers of people could not understand it at all, and many of those who could understand it came to have grave doubts that it was wise.

These doubts, when they were first heard, were expressed with sufficient modesty. Some people, undoubtedly friendly to the schools, began to say that the New Pedagogy, while it plainly had many good points, seemed to lay too much stress upon what were essentially play activities—manual training, music, games, and so on—and too little upon the immemorial fundamentals—reading, writing and arithmetic. And others, quite as friendly, began to say that, while all these new activities might be plausibly defended on the ground that they were pleasant for the children, and hence likely to stimulate their interest, it was impossible to escape the fact that they were enormously and perhaps even prohibitively expensive to the taxpayer.

These doubts and dubieties, as I have said, were put forward in a very moderate way, and mainly by persons who believed in the schools and were eager to see them flourish. But the pedagogues did not condescend to answer their critics politely. On the contrary, they undertook to dispose of them by denouncing them as implacable enemies of all education, and indeed of all children, and by setting up the dogma that they themselves, the pedagogues alone, were competent to decide what ought to be taught in the schools, or how and by whom, or at what expense. This effort still goes on, but the steam in it, I believe, is beginning to diminish.

In part, at least, it probably had its origin in a fear that the politicians, disguised as taxpayers and even as parents, were trying to sneak back into the schools. Whether or not this fear had any justification I do not pretend to say; perhaps it did. But whether it was well grounded or not, it did not move the pedagogues half as powerfully as something else, and that was their new professional vanity. They resented being brought to book by laymen just as lawyers or medical men would have resented it. They believed that they were the sole owners and proprietors of a novel and inspired arcanum that was quite beyond the grasp of the lay mind, and so they regarded any questioning of it, however well intended, as a sort of insult to their dignity.

But was this arcanum real? Did it have any overt and palpable existence? I have given some attention to the question, seeking light and leading from the standard pedagogical literature, and I find myself unhappily in doubt. The New Pedagogy, in fact, was mainly buncombe. There was, of course some admixture of sense in it, but not very much. In large part it was simply a kind of Brummagem magic. The psychological data upon which it was based were absurd, and the miracles that it was supposed to achieve were imaginary.

Children came out of the new pedagogical Taj Mahals no better prepared for life than their parents had come out of the little red schoolhouse, and the new Model A pedagogue, with his polychrome graphs and bold hypotheses, turned out to be scarcely as competent as the Model T ma'm of the last generation, with her dog's-eared speller and her ready rattan.

In brief, all the learned rumble-bumble emanating from Teachers College, Columbia, and other such shrines of the new evangel could not conceal the massive fact that teaching children the elements is essentially a simple and lowly craft, and that a person who is bursting with bogus psychology is much less likely to practice it successfully than a simple soul who really loves it. The old-time pedagogue, whether male or female, saw spelling as a great adventure and penmanship as a noble art, and that enthusiasm had a way of being contagious. But the new "expert," soaring higher, only too often left the children far behind, and even forgot them altogether.

This Golden Age of the New Pedagogy was marked by a staggering series of new techniques, all of them designed to glorify and make mysterious the simple business of the teacher. There was a school which maintained that children should not be taught anything at all, but allowed to pick up what they ought to know by following their own devices. There was another which treated them like guinea pigs in a laboratory, forgetting altogether that they were human beings. There was a third which argued stoutly that it was absurd to teach the multiplication table, and a fourth which sneered at spelling, and a fifth which had no use for grammar, and so on almost *ad infinitum*. Some of these novelties were so grotesque that even the more rational of the New Pedagogues bucked at them, and in the literature of the movement you will find many bitter debates over them, one saying one thing and one another.

With them there flourished the doctrine that children ought to be kept in school as long as possible, regardless of their tastes or capacities, and that those who were obviously too stupid to master the common branches should be entertained by various forms of play, most of them requiring expensive equipment and more expensive "experts." Every country town was induced to put up a grandiose high-school, and in it the future husbandmen of the vicinage were instructed in scoutcraft, football, and parliamentary law, and their future wives were taught to make beds, decorate rooms, and prepare canapés in the style of Park Avenue. Instruction in music was provided for all, and not only in music but also in military tactics and the art of dress.

Some of the more advanced pedagogues went even further. They began to think of themselves, not only as scientists of a novel and subtle sort, but also as prophets. Their job, they announced boldly, was to regenerate the nation. They began to dose their charges with idealism of a dozen varieties. Pedagogy thus became a kind of theology and was presently seen to be strongly evangelistic in doctrine. For one thing, it threw itself ardently into the Prohibition movement, and became an eager agent of the Anti-Saloon League. For another, it began to rub in briskly the kind of patriotism patronized by those who went on the theory that the national treasury ought to be ready, on demand, to pay every true lover of the flag whatever he wants.

The chief prophets of the movement, in those gaudy days, went to great lengths. They built larger and larger schoolhouses, with fewer and fewer classrooms and more and more gymnasia, laboratories, *ateliers*, and shops. They invented multitudinous new species of "experts" and put them gloriously to work. They sweated the poor schoolma'ms during the hot summers with interminable courses in quack "sciences." They called for larger and larger contributions from the taxpayer, and damned him boldly whenever he cried for quarter. And in their topmost ranks they dreamed voluptuously of adding a secretary of education to the cabinet, and of centralizing the whole romantic business of uplifting the nation in one grand Camorra of pedagogical politicians.

All this went on until the depression struck the country, and budgets began to go unbalanced. There ensued a somewhat bilious inquiry into the whole pedagogical hocus-pocus. It was found that the brethren were getting away with nearly three billions annually (or maybe even four billions: the figures are not easily come by), and that they were planning to demand much more. It was found that the cost of "educating" a pupil a year, which had been $15.00 in 1880, had soared to nearly $100, and that it was still going up. It was found that this vast outpouring of money had already reduced hundreds of American counties and towns to bankruptcy, and was seriously imperilling the solvency of whole states.

So there came a reconsideration, still going on. So far it has damaged only the poor teachers, whose salaries are everywhere much reduced, in some places to nothing. The bogus experts and tinpot idealists have escaped as yet, and some of them still dream of that place in the cabinet. But I suspect that their turn will come presently.

Appendix 3
Mr. Wieman and Mr. Macintosh "Converse" with Mr. Dewey

Editor the *Christian Century*:

Sir: Many points raised by Mr. Dewey I should like to discuss in replying to his criticism of my part in the Conversation about God. But my space is strictly limited so I must concentrate on the main issue he raises.

One flagrant error of his, however, I must immediately correct. He says that I rest my whole case for belief in existence of God on the fact that man needs something to love, adore. I gave considerable part of my discussion to showing that man's need of God has nothing to do with the question of God's existence. Otto and Macintosh, however, made so much of it, and their statement of man's need of God seemed to me to be so incorrect, that I made my own statement. But I explicitly denied that man's need was valid ground for man's belief. Indeed, Mr. Dewey in the very next paragraph retracts his first interpretation of my argument, although in a rather half-hearted way. In his retraction he writes, "Mr. Wieman insists that there is something objective which generates, supports and constitutes good," etc.

But now to the main issue Mr. Dewey raises.

First, it should be noted that Mr. Dewey fully grants one-half of my main contention in the conversation. He grants "that there are in existence conditions and forces which, *apart from human desire and intent*, (italics mine) bring about enjoyed and enjoyable goods, and that the security and extension of goods are promoted by attention to and service of these conditions." He makes this statement not only once but three times. Prior to the statement just quoted he writes: "Men find conditions and forces in

[First published in *Christian Century* 50 (1 March 1933): 299–302. For Dewey's review to which this is a reply, see this volume, pp. 213–22, and for Dewey's rejoinder, see this volume, pp. 223–28.]

existence which generate and sustain the goods of living." Still again he writes, "We may be said intelligently to find in experience forces making for the production and extension of goods."

That, then, is settled so far as Mr. Dewey is concerned. There *are* conditions and forces in existence which make for good over and above the conscious purpose and effort of men, upon which we are dependent and which we should serve. That is a great step in the argument. There remains the one great criticism he makes of my position. It is that these "conditions and forces" do not have enough unity to constitute a unitary object of devotion and so cannot be considered God.

I shall endeavor to show that according to Mr. Dewey's own principles, set forth in many writings, these conditions and forces do constitute a unitary object which does command our supreme devotion. But the remarkable fact is that when Mr. Dewey turns to discuss the idea of God he no longer keeps true to those principles. He seems to show that very "shift and contradiction" in his thinking which he attributes to me. When he makes the astounding claim that the idea of God must not be allowed to develop beyond the boundaries set up by various historical groups—especially the ideas of God that dominated his own youth—he seems to show that he, rather than I, "is overmastered by emotional overtones derived from the earlier conception of an exclusive and jealous God." The only idea of God you can "get excited about," he writes, is that exclusive and jealous God. Note "the emotional overtones"!

Plainly, all that can ever command our highest devotion is what has greatest value, whether it be actual or possible or partly both. I take it to be self-evident that greatest value should be worthy of our highest devotion; for greatest value means precisely to be so worthy. No matter how limited the highest value may be, a greater measure of devotion cannot be rightly given to anything else.

But what constitutes value? More particularly, what constitutes greatest value?

According to many writings of Mr. Dewey, the conditions and forces which bring about enjoyed and enjoyable goods have all the value of those goods. Indeed, according to him value lies exactly in this unity between enjoyed or enjoyable goods, and their conditions and consequences. Goods enjoyed without regard to conditions and consequences have no value, according to Mr. Dewey. In that claim he goes even a little farther than I would. But let that pass. His error, if error it be, is on the side of the angels. Not only must the conditions and forces be connected by meaning and value with the enjoyable goods they bring forth, but this connectedness constitutes the value. But Mr. Dewey goes still farther. The enjoyable goods must be functionally connected with still other goods in such a way as to constitute a meaningful system in which the enjoyment of each situation sustains and promotes the others. In any high value a chief part of the enjoyment must be consciousness of the meaning of what I do, that is to say, consciousness that what I now enjoy has this function of sustaining and promoting a whole system of mutually sustaining conditions, forces and enjoyable goods. Such is the teaching of Mr. Dewey about value.

A simple illustration of value according to this view is the case of a woman sweeping her floor who finds value in the sweeping because she knows it fills a needed function in that total unitary system made up of home, children, husband, love, neighborhood and prevailing culture.

What, then, constitutes greatest value according to these principles advocated by Mr. Dewey in many writings throughout the past forty years? Plainly, greatest value lies in whatsoever unity there is now, or ever can be, among all the conditions, forces and enjoyable goods that are ever to be had in the present and future of this world's existence. This unity does not mean uniformity. It does not diminish variety and diversity, but requires these. To illustrate, heart and lungs, eye and hand, are functional members one of another, yet they are very different and their respective functions in this unity require this diversity and variety. So likewise the unity of conditions and forces and enjoyable goods which constitutes high value requires great variety.

Let us summarize our argument. Whatsoever is of greatest value should ipso facto command our supreme devotion. Whatsoever unity there is, or may come to be, among all the conditions, forces and enjoyable goods which are to be found in the present actual world, and its future possible development, constitutes greatest value. Such value and such unity, and it only, is the rightful object of supreme religious devotion, no matter how incompletely realized it may be in our present state of existence, and no matter how limited and weak or vast and mighty it is.

Let me state the argument in still another way. Highest value is found in organic unity. By organic unity we mean such connectedness and organization among diverse activities and situations of life that when we undertake any activity or enter any situation we shall find in it the dignity and value of serving some needed function in this total unit of life. Such organic unity is a matter of degree. To the degree that it prevails, every activity and situation will carry the meaning of being a functional member in the total organization of life.

Such an organization of activities and situations is what constitutes culture in a noble, sociological sense. A people has a worthy culture, and so finds a great value in life, in so far as its world is organized in this way.

Civilization is not the same as culture. Civilization means the efficiency of our techniques for doing. Culture means the meaning and value of our doings by reason of the way they are functionally related to one another. Such culture cannot be constructed or manufactured by human intelligence. It must grow. All men can do is to provide conditions most favorable for its growth. The process of its growth is that of integrative interaction between individuals, groups and successive generations, a great part of which is unconscious and unintended. This organic unity which constitutes greatest value, grows in our midst, when favorable conditions are provided.

Since organic unity in this sense can alone constitute highest value, it alone should receive our highest devotion. It alone can rightfully command it. If this is true, three religious views are possible. One is that of absolute idealism which asserts that since organic unity does have highest value, the total universe must be such a unity and can be rationally demonstrated so to be. That is not my claim. The second view is that since organic unity has highest value we can hold the faith that the total universe is such a unit, although we cannot know it to be. That is not my claim. I make no assertion about the total universe. To identify the whole universe with value is absurd, I claim. But I hold the third view. The third view is that whatever organic unity there is in the universe, actual or possible, is worthy our highest devotion, understanding organic unity in the sense above indicated. To this unity, actual and possible, we should give our utmost reverence and service, for no other reason than that it constitutes greatest value. Such value and such devotion belong to this unity regardless of what limitations or scope it may have; and our religious devotion should be given to it without allowing our needs, desires or tradition to lead us to believe concerning it what is not supported by observation, reason and experiment. Indeed, one of the major requirements of a true devotion is that we do not allow our beliefs to depart from the tested findings.

So we conclude that the only objection Mr. Dewey makes against our claim that there is a God is shown to be invalid; and its invalidity is demonstrated by his own principles of what constitutes value. In saying, as he does in his criticism of me, that the unity, actual and possible, in conditions, forces and enjoyable goods of this world, is not of supreme value, and is not what calls for our highest devotion, he has almost betrayed the holy cause for which he has given the greater part of his life in devoted service.

Even should I have misinterpreted Mr. Dewey's theory of value (I do not think I have, for I have studied it very carefully), my argument stands just the same. For I do not hold this view of value merely because I happen to think it is the view held by Mr. Dewey. I am quite ready to defend it on its own merits, regardless of what Mr. Dewey may think about value. My view of value is not identical with his throughout, but the points in his theory which I have emphasized, I also hold as my own.

Whatever may be done with the *word* God, we cannot without disaster ignore the reality which I am here trying to indicate by means of it. What is that reality? It is the growth in our midst of that organic unity wherein the activities and situations which engage us acquire maximum value by reason of fulfilling a worthy function in that total system of mutually sustaining activities and situations which should include as much of human life as possible. It is that for which all human life should be lived.

The present perilous state of our civilization and culture calls for such religious devotion with an urgency that is terrible. Our state is perilous because the techniques of efficient doing, which constitute our civilization, have changed and complicated our life so rapidly, that the organizing unity which makes us functional members one of another has not kept up. We must turn with all our powers of devotion and service, sensitivity and intelligence, to this unity in our midst which makes us functional members one of another, and which is capable of growth if we give ourselves to it with sufficient devotion. If we cannot call this functioning unity God, then let us give it another name. But it alone can save us. This unity or organization which makes us and our activities and interests functioning members one of another, and which is always operative in our midst to some degree as long as we are human, is the reality to which, called by whatever name, we must give ourselves. If a sufficient number of us would yield to this functioning unity our ideals and programs and policies, our institutions and needs and hopes, to be reconstructed by its requirements, we should be lifted, molded and renewed, and our civilization would pass triumphantly beyond the disasters that now threaten it.

HENRY NELSON WIEMAN

Editor the *Christian Century*:

Sir: In his review of our book, *Is There a God?* Mr. Dewey makes four principal criticisms, two of which are directed mainly against my position and two against Mr. Wieman's. The charge of ambiguity, particularly as against Mr. Wieman's use of the term "God," is one with which I so largely sympathize that I am content to leave it to Mr. Wieman to make the reply. But the other criticism directed mainly against Mr. Wieman, that the factors and forces making for human well-being are many rather than a single divine being, affects my argument also, so that I shall have to give it consideration. Before doing so, however, I must take up Mr. Dewey's challenge that in my position there are two "inherent contradictions."

Mr. Dewey finds a contradiction in appealing to "the supremacy of moral ideals as the ground for the content of religious ideas, including that of God," and then insisting upon a God "to give moral ideals external and independent support." Now if I am not misinterpreting my critic here, he has surely misinterpreted me. The criticism would have had much justification if I had first tried to *prove* the existence of a moral God from the objectivity and absoluteness of moral values and then had based the absoluteness of the moral law on its being the will of an existent absolute sovereign and law-giver. But I have been careful to avoid just this mistake. I believe that when the moral ideal is stated in terms of the greatest ultimate good, moral, intellectual, esthetic and social, of all persons concerned and the conduct necessary to realize that ultimate good, it is absolutely valid for all persons everywhere and always; that if there be a personal God, this ideal is absolutely valid for him also; but that it is valid anyway and needs no external law-giver to make it unconditionally imperative.

At the same time, it can be said that reality as a whole must be such as is consistent with this absoluteness of moral values. An absolutely binding moral obligation rests on us; and reality, internal and external, must be such as to put this absolute obligation upon us. Furthermore, the natural surmise that there is a superhuman cosmic Being whose will for man coincides with the true moral ideal readily enters as a constituent of what seems to me, in the light of certain cosmic facts and tendencies and spiritual experiences, to be an essentially reasonable religious faith. And if there be such a superhuman moral cosmic Being, presumably his activity will be directed toward the production and conservation of those same absolutely valid values of the moral life.

But throughout the Conversation I avoided and even explicitly repudiated any attempt to *demonstrate* the existence of a *personal* God, above all by argument. What I argued for was the initial reasonableness of adopting as a sort of working hypothesis for life the morally optimistic faith which fits in with ethical theism, subjecting it however to critical reexamination in the light of further experience, and particularly in the face of such seemingly adverse facts as suggest the "problem of evil." Is it not ironical that I should be called upon to defend this essentially empirical procedure in religion against the rather *a priori* objections of one who has been considered the outstanding living exponent of empiricism, and that I should have to be at pains to point out that my empirical realism in religion is quite independent of the old-time speculative, *a priori* "proofs"?

The other supposed contradiction in my position—and it is one to which Mr. Dewey refers several times—is even more closely related to my advocacy of the adoption in religion of the inductive methods which Mr. Dewey himself esteems so highly for their results in the recognized empirical sciences. Religious liberalism is in unstable equilibrium, he says, because of the contradiction between its assertion of the universality of its ideas and values and its exclusive emphasis upon the ideas and experiences of a particular traditional religion, namely, those of Christianity, or even of evangelical Protestantism.

Here again, if I mistake not, Mr. Dewey has missed the point. There are religious liberals, I have no doubt, whose position lies open to the criticism Mr. Dewey offers. There is contradiction, or something like it, in first maintaining that the different ideas of God are the necessary and appropriate expressions of the different kinds of religious feeling characteristic of different historic religions, and then attempting to change a people's idea of God by mere argument and without dealing at all with the roots of their religious feeling. And there would be contradiction in advocating a religion of rational demonstration and at the same time shielding one's own traditional faith from rational criticism. But the procedure I advocate is definitely designed to avoid just such contradictions.

In calling attention once more to the objective empirical approach to the problem of religious knowledge, may I begin by reminding Mr. Dewey that there is no *necessary* contradiction between "an asserted universality" and "the survival of an earlier exclusive tradition"? Most universal scientific truths were at first the exclusive discovery and possession of a particular historic person or group. No one complains of an "inherent contradiction" between the asserted universal validity of a heliocentric astronomy and the "definite survival" of a Copernican traditionalism, or between the universal and permanent validity of the discovery of America and the annual celebration of Columbus day. What I claim is that in religion as in other phases of life it is possible for pioneers to make discoveries which may not at once be universally accepted but which are universally valid and thus fitted to win ultimate worldwide acceptance.

It is in this objective, essentially scientific sense that I have used the much misunderstood term, "the right religious adjustment." A religious adjustment is not right because it "feels right" subjectively. It is right for the same reason that any adjustment in any applied science is right, namely, that it takes right account of dependable process and thus dependably conditions desired results. Now it so happens that it is in the realm of spiritual and particularly of moral experience (in promoting the development of the good will), and not in the external physical realm (in the control of the weather, for instance) that the religious adjustment I have described and identified as the "right" one has direct, dependable, desirable results. And so I conclude that the *right* religious adjustment is of this specific spiritual type. Furthermore, since I seem to discover this type of adjustment and the ensuing experience on the whole more fully and more frequently in the "western Christian tradition" and especially in the "Protestant evangelical version of this tradition" than elsewhere, I frankly avow the belief that with all due allowance for the universal significance of religious discoveries which may have been made outside of historic Christianity, there is something in evangelical Christianity at its most vital and best which is so essentially "right," both scientifically and in its spiritual value, that it is worth while for those who know about it to do what they can to share it with the rest of the world. But in any case, the test suggested as to the *rightness* of any religious adjustment is no merely subjective test, but one thoroughly objective and essentially scientific.

The third critical remark of Mr. Dewey on which I wish to comment is the statement that what we discover is "a multitude of factors and forces" which coincide in producing the furtherance of the good life, and not any single, unitary divine Being. This is very much like what the mechanistic philosopher says about human behavior, no matter how purposive it may be. He sees the minute details but not the grand strategy of the movement. But the chemical and mechanical "factors and forces" which enter into human conduct are not its *adequate cause* without the directive factor of mind, transcending all purely physical factors but immanent in their operation as it uses them as instruments.

Similarly it seems to me not unreasonable to posit in the cosmos a directive Factor analogous to mind and will in the human organism, especially if we are interested to discover the *adequate cause* of (1) the rational order of the cosmos, even if we do not try to account for primordial becoming (cf. Whitehead); (2) the emergent evolution of new and higher kinds of existence (first consciousness, for instance), and the "orthogenetic" evolution culminating in the appearance of man as a rational and spiritual being with his unfathomed capacities for further progress; (3) the production in human history, of values so universally, eternally, and absolutely valid as to be appropriately rated as "divine," qualitatively speaking; and (4) the dependable, desirable result of what I have felt warranted in calling the *right* religious adjustment. To interpret the *adequate cause* of this ordered, evolving, personality-producing, personality-educating, personality-regenerating process as ultimately a mere accidental coincidence of blind, mechanical factors and forces seems to me almost on a par, for reasonableness, with the theory which would eliminate directive mind and will from the adequate causation of the words and works of man.

Mr. Dewey seems almost surprised at the "enormous transformation in traditional religious faith" indicated by the details of my argument. If the changes have been great, perhaps they are no greater than were to have been expected from the application of empirical tests to the constructions of traditional religious thought. One could wish that Mr. Dewey himself had given to the problems of religion throughout the years the sympathetic and consequently understanding thought which, from his empirical point of view, he has bestowed upon the problems of education, social ethics, and government. If he had, I feel sure he would have arrived at a result more constructive, more humane, and at the same time certainly no less respectable intellectually than the "secularized humanism" to which he lends his adherence and the prestige of his name and for the development of which in its American form he is in considerable measure responsible. One hesitates to bring against so great a man, so urbane and, in social relations, so Christian a gentleman, and so candid a thinker, the charge of prejudice, and still more to resort to the current, all-solvent explanation of a "complex"; but one cannot but wonder whether something untoward may not have happened in his early religious history which has unduly colored all his later thinking on the subject and partially blinded him to the undeniable values and possibilities for good of religion and particularly of our western Christianity in its Protestant evangelical form. It is something at least that has unfortunately happened in the experience of many others, and while Mr. Dewey's philosophical autobiography (in *Contemporary American Phi-*

losophy, Macmillan, 1930), with its record of reaction against such influences as those of theological institutionalism and Butler's *Analogy*, throws considerable light on his present position, the explanation it gives is perhaps incomplete. I seem to remember reading or hearing of his making the statement that he had had too much religion in his youth. Perhaps he was taught religion, or rather the dogmas and other externals of religion, not wisely and *not* too well. Anyway, it's a pity. Still, I could wish and would even venture to hope that on second thought he may at least withdraw the charge of a twofold "inherent contradiction" in the modest experimental religious realism which I venture to defend.

DOUGLAS CLYDE MACINTOSH

Appendix 4
John Dewey's Credo
By Norbert Guterman

A Common Faith, by John Dewey. New Haven: Yale University Press, 1934.

In this small book, John Dewey undertakes to offer us "the naturalistic foundations and bearings of religion." He conceives of his work as have many other philosophers before him, that is, as a critique of religion aimed at purifying and upholding religious values. Dewey thinks that these religious values are obscured and thwarted by the traditional dogmas. He advances an original and weighty argument against their acceptance: by attempting to found the authority of moral ideals on some prior embodiment in an ontological realm, the various creeds only undermine the strength of those ideals, make useless an active faith directed toward their realization. The doctrine of revealed truth is not only contrary to our ideals of scientific knowledge; it is also opposed to the ethical ideals preached by the churches.

Thus religions in the traditional meaning of this word are rejected. But Dewey is not an atheist. He finds in experience an "irreducible" religious element, and this he proposes to maintain. Dewey names it "the religious"—an adjective as opposed to "religion," the noun. "The religious" is defined by its function. It has a triple role: to unify the self by an all-inclusive ideal of action, to unify man with the universe by a feeling of pious communion with nature, and to unify the individual with society and mankind. In this construction God does not disappear, but is redefined as the "active relation between ideal and actual." Dewey has no difficulty in showing that these unifying functions can be

[First published in *New Republic* 82 (20 February 1935): 53. For Dewey's reply, see this volume, p. 293.]

accomplished without "the necessity of resort to apologetics." He believes that the existing churches can survive their present crisis if they abandon all scientific claims and preach instead a faith of individual and social reformism, "a faith that shall not be confined to sect, class or race."

A Common Faith touches upon many interesting philosophical and sociological problems. A thorough discussion of this book would carry us beyond the limits of a review, but I should like to attempt a brief analysis of one fundamental issue that Dewey raises.

He ascribes the diminishing influence of religions on our life to their intellectual inadequacies. In order to disprove this absolute diagnosis, it should be enough to recall how many advanced scientists have recently seemed to go "back" to religion. The real cause of the disease should be looked for in the social role of religions, in their function. But contrary to what he does for "the religious," which is defined in functional terms, Dewey neglects to examine religions from the same functional point of view. Had he done so, he surely would not have to declare that, between religious values as he conceives of them and religion, there is an opposition "not to be bridged." For religions, too, perform a unifying function—of a special, religious sort. The serf and the lord, the worker and the capitalist, the poor and the rich, are spiritually united in God. Religious unity may be presented as an end in itself; in fact its function is to conceal real oppositions. Religion masks the social conflicts, consoles the slave by the promise of a transcendent compensation, justifies the master by superficial rites and attitudes.

One has no right to speak of "unity" without qualifying it. Otherwise it remains an abstract, metaphysical concept, an empty form. The unification accomplished by Dewey's "religious" is not essentially different from that accomplished by religions. It is a mere state of mind, a spiritual attitude. Dewey speaks of unification without analyzing the causes of division, as if division of man within himself and his separation from society and nature were not relative to a given social order, but something inherent and everlasting. There is a goal nobler and more inclusive of the highest ideals of mankind than the creation of spiritual oases in the midst of real struggles: this goal is the real unification of man in a classless society, and it can be attained only by practical revolutionary activity. The revolutionary will excludes religion, because instead of real unity it accomplishes only a pretense of unity, because it preaches a faith above classes, when, in order to bring about real unity, it is necessary to fight against one of the classes, the ruling class. And substituting "the religious" for religion does not change the situation.

Appendix 5
John Dewey's Common Faith
By Henry Nelson Wieman

John Dewey has served the world richly in many walks of life. Now at last in the ripeness of his years he turns to religion, and his service here is equal to any he has given. Some of us have known for a long time that he was a deeply religious man. Furthermore, many of us have seen in all his writings the implicit outline of a noble religion. But he never made it explicit. You had to get it between the lines. It was like invisible ink, waiting to be made plain for all to see. Now at last he has stated it. We are not disappointed.

In his latest book, *A Common Faith*, he touches on most of the matters that concern the religious person. He discusses religious experience, making certain important and clarifying distinctions (pp. 10–11 [page numbers refer to this volume]). He does not use the word "conversion," but he describes that transformation of the will, that redirection of "the organic plenitude of our being," which most of us recognize to be conversion, and declares that it is necessary to enter the religious way of living (pp. 13, 23–24). He sets forth the nature of religious living and the place of faith in it, and distinguishes the kind of faith that is essential to religious living from faith that is mere intellectual assent (pp. 16–17, 23–24). He shows the importance and value of mystical experience and distinguishes its misuses from its true importance (pp. 25–26). He pronounces non-theistic humanism as futile and mistaken and thus clearly separates himself from that movement with which many have identified him

[First published in *Christian Century* 51 (14 November 1934): 1450–52. For comment by Aubrey and Wieman, see this volume, Appendixes 6 and 7, and for Dewey's reply, see this volume, pp. 294–95.]

(pp. 36–37). Above all, he declares his knowledge of God and devotion to God.

This knowledge of God for Dewey is not merely a belief which may or may not be true, on which one "bets his life." Dewey is convinced, and we share the conviction, that religion has been degraded and weakened by clinging to beliefs for which we have no assured evidence.

A Vision and a Proposal

Dewey comes to religion with a vision and a constructive proposal. The vision is of what the religious function in life has been and should be. The proposal is to bring it back to the high place it once had.

For three hundred years the religious functioning of life has been dragged down to the second, to the third, to the fourth place amid the functions of human living. This dethronement of the religious function began about the time of the renaissance and has been increasing ever since. Dewey calls it "the greatest revolution that has taken place in religion during the thousands of years that man has been upon this earth." It is a radical change in the social place and function of religion.

Once religion gave character, meaning, direction, dignity to the total social process, the collective life of the group. It was the utmost outreach and glory of the life of man so far as the individual could imaginatively compass that life. One did not join a church as a separate and special function and institution. One was born into a group whose life was overarched and horizoned by an ultimate outreach after the Highest. The priesthood and the ceremonies did not represent a church as merely one part and one institution within the group life, an institution furthermore which is today often ignored and shouldered to one side by other interests. The priesthood, the prophets, the ceremonies expressed the highest loyalty of all human living so far as the individuals of this group could apprehend it. To be sure, the individual members did not always yield their undivided loyalty. Far from it. But they all recognized the rightful place and function of religion as sovereign over life.

Modern Religion as a Special Interest

This elevated status of religion is so alien to our present way of living that it is almost inconceivable to the modern mind. Religion today is a special interest competing with other interests. Generally, it is in the keeping of a special institution called the church. One today has other interests alongside that of religion, such as the economic, political, social, familial, and these others demand more and more of his thought and energy, meet more and more of his needs, while less and less is left for religion. The problem would not be solved even though church membership increased by leaps and bounds, much more rapidly than the population, so that at last almost everyone belonged to some church and almost everyone attended church on Sunday. No matter how much time and energy is given to religious activities, the problem will not be solved as long as the religious interest is one among a great number of competing interests, rather than being their wellspring and inclusive ideal. It is a matter neither of church membership and attendance nor of allotment of interest to religion. It is a matter of the vital "social place and function of religion." This subordinate, competitive status of religion would have been inconceivable in the days when religion functioned normally.

What is the trouble? Dewey suggests a diagnosis and a cure. First the diagnosis, locating the cause of the trouble. The religious attitude—that is, the vital functioning of religion in the life of man—has been caught, cramped, confined and cribbed by a set of beliefs which head up in the supernatural. Religion is socially recognized as that part of human life which is concerned with the supernatural. There may be individuals who recognize their own religion to be more than that. But the established tradition connects religion with the supernatural and leaves it there. The overwhelming mass of people, whether professing religion or not, think of it as man's concern with the supernatural, particularly with a supernatural God and immortality.

Now there was a time when the line of division between the natural and the supernatural, according to man's thinking, was a horizontal line, not a vertical one, as it is now. That is to say, the supernatural overarched the natural. Here below were the natural interests of man; there above was the supernatural. The rightful goal of all natural interests was to lead up toward the supernatural.

Natural and Supernatural

But today the line of division is vertical. In order to traffic with the supernatural you must turn aside from other matters. These other interests do not pour into the supernatural as a river into the sea. We may declare in theory that they do, but in the actual thought and practice of men they do not and they cannot. In our thinking and practice today, nature has no fixed and known boundaries. Activities going on in nature lead on to still further activities and these on and on without limit. We may say that somewhere beyond the scope of our comprehension they lead into the supernatural. Men may hold that as a theory but it cannot exercise the coercive control of an observable fact.

The consequences of such a situation are inevitable. When the natural and supernatural are so conceived, a religion that is concerned with the supernatural will be shoved more and more to one side while the practical, urgent matters of daily living will command more and more of the attention of men. Men may reserve a certain time for church and for expressing their devotion to the supernatural, when other more urgent matters do not demand their attention. They may do this in increasing numbers. But this is a caricature of the religious attitude.

So much for the diagnosis. Now for the cure. The religious attitude must be released from this diverting, perverting obsession with the supernatural. But first, what is this religious attitude Dewey talks about? It is devotion to an ideal reality which exercises control over one's conduct. It is loyalty in service and adoration to what one holds to be supremely worthful, not only for himself alone, but for all human living. This attitude must be released from bondage to certain fixed, traditional beliefs which confine all its questing to such narrow bounds. It must be free to range far and wide and high to find what truly is most worthy of the sovereign loyalty of all human living.

Diagnosis and Cure

If the religious attitude can be freed from the prison house that now confines it, says Dewey, it will again take the high place in human life that belongs to it. To be sure, even now it is not wholly confined. You cannot keep Pegasus in the pound. But wherever it has broken out beyond the imprisoning walls of fixed beliefs about the supremacy of the supernatural, it is not recognized as religious, because these fixed beliefs claim to hold a monopoly on the religious. Therefore, where it has broken free, it cannot function socially because it is not socially recognized. When it travels incognito, its sovereignty is eclipsed. When the religious attitude is thus furtive and unconscious of itself it cannot propagate itself. It cannot organize and direct the life of the group. It cannot pervade and dominate.

Here then is the cure: to release the religious attitude from the prison walls of belief about the supernatural and do this openly and publicly. The religious attitude must no longer be compelled, when it does escape from these imprisoning beliefs, to wander in a sort of dream state, unconscious of its own identity and unrecognized by man.

But what is the object of this religious loyalty we have been discussing? It is God. None other but God can rightfully command the highest loyalty of all human living, says John Dewey. We ask the reader to turn to the book and read what Dewey himself says about God. The pages are 32 to 37, and 56 to 57. On the last two pages he does not use the word God but he is there discussing again what he presents in the earlier pages, where he does use the word. He is discussing the reality which is the rightful object of man's supreme devotion.

God the Object of Loyalty

Dewey speaks much of ideals in connection with God. But God is not merely our ideals. Our ideals are simply our conscious, imaginative apprehension of possibilities which are rooted in the existing world. God is not merely something in this existing world. Neither is God merely the possibilities of great value.

But God is that operative reality in this existing world which carries these possibilities. Read Dewey's own statement of his idea of God:

"We are in the presence neither of ideals completely embodied in existence nor yet of ideals that are mere rootless ideals, fantasies, utopias. For there are forces in nature and society that generate and support the ideals."

The last sentence quoted should be especially pondered. Notice he does not say merely "in society," but "in nature and society." Again he writes: "It is this *active* relation between ideal and actual to which I would give the name of God." God is what holds the actual and the ideal together. Not that the actual is the ideal, nor the ideal the actual. That is the mistake of idealism. But the two are connected and the activity which connects them is God.

This activity which unites the actual and the ideal is not merely the conscious, intelligent effort of men. It is an interaction between the aim of conscious intelligent effort and those existent conditions that are relevant to that aim. This interaction progressively transforms the aim of man as much as the aim transforms the conditions. Therefore the controlling power is not the aim, for the aim is itself continuously remade. The controlling power is the interaction. But the interaction is not only between the aim and certain non-human conditions. It is also an interaction between the aims of different individuals, groups and generations.

Here is an operative reality which brings into dynamic, creative unity many different activities, so that the criticism of one stimulates the thought of the other, so that the buffetings of fortune develop meaning and value and noble purpose in human history, so that the activity of one carries on to larger fulfilment the activities of the other, and the existing things of nature are transformed from brute fact into bearers of meaning and value.

Let Dewey describe this operative reality of God in his own words: "The community of causes and consequences in which we, together with those not born, are enmeshed . . . is the matrix within which our ideal aspirations are born and bred. It is the source of the values that the moral imagination projects as directive criteria and as shaping purposes."

A Creed that Cannot Be Shaken

Think on that for a while; then read the next statement. "The continuing life of this comprehensive community of beings includes all the significant achievement of men in science and art and all the kindly offices of intercourse and communication. It holds within its content all the material that gives verifiable intellectual support to our ideal faiths. A 'creed' founded on this material will change and grow, but it cannot be shaken."

We must take these sentences one by one if we are to get their full import. "What it [this faith] surrenders it gives up gladly because of new light and not as a reluctant concession. What it adds, it adds because new knowledge gives further insight into the conditions that bear upon the formation and execution of our life purposes. . . . The unification of what is known at any given time, not upon an impossible eternal and abstract basis but upon that of its bearing upon the unification of human desire and purpose, furnishes a sufficient creed for human acceptance, one that would provide a religious release and reinforcement of knowledge."

This unification of human desire and purpose, enmeshed in a system of causes and consequences, human and non-human, is a reality that can grow when human attitudes are rightly disposed in reverence and devotion to it, and utmost human effort is given to providing conditions most favorable to it. It is the growth in this world of what is supremely worthful. It is the growing good. It is progressive integration. God, as an operative reality in which our practical daily lives are constantly involved, is this growing good. If the religious attitude can be released from its present bondage and turned in service and devotion to this, the beneficent results will be incalculable, says Dewey.

We can put Dewey's idea of God into a single summarizing sentence: God is the activity which connects the ideal with the actual.

More than Human

This activity is not supernatural, but it is superhuman. It is not superhuman in the sense that it excludes the human. On the contrary it works in and with the human. It is not superhuman in the sense that it has a mind, intelligence or personality that is superior to man. But it is superhuman because it is more than personality, mind or intelligence. It is superhuman on five counts.

First, this activity sustains and promotes the highest values with scope and power greater than any single personality possibly could, no matter how greatly magnified. Therefore God understood in this way is higher above the human than a mere personality could possibly be, no matter how glorified.

Second, this activity is superhuman because it carries possibilities of value far beyond what men can sense or imagine except as the values emerge in existence or human consciousness, and as man's capacity is developed to appreciate them.

Third, this activity is superhuman because it generates, develops and brings to highest fulfilment human personality. Man does not make it. It makes men. Human personality is dependent on this mesh of interaction for the very breath of its existence and all its highest development. Hence God is superhuman because he cradles human personality as a higher personality could not do.

Fourth, this activity is superhuman because it exercises the might of gentleness as no human could do. Its might is the might of growth, and growth is always gentle beyond any of the works of man.

Fifth, it is superhuman because man must be mastered by it in order to receive the sustenance, development and high fulfilment that it can bring. In so far as man tries to master it, he loses the values which it pours into human life.

Sovereign Authority

This activity is neither omnipotent nor omniscient. It has none of the "omnies," so far as we know. But it is God because it exercises rightful sovereign authority over every impulse and habit, institution and practice, dream and desire of man. However, this authority is not that of brute force. It is that of commanding our highest loyalty by reason of supreme worthfulness.

This activity is God because it answers prayer when prayer is understood to be adjustment of human personality to it. Dewey makes no reference to prayer, so this is my own claim, not his. In answer to prayer, understood not as contractions of the larynx causing vibrations of the air supposed to reach a superhuman tympanum, but understood as right adjustment of personality to this activity of interaction, God changes the physical world for good in ways that human intelligence could not otherwise do.

This activity which is God comforts and sustains in time of trouble and disaster, if warm fellowship of sympathetic hearts is solace, for it is this activity which unites us in bonds of brotherhood. Even when human companionship is not available, it is comforting to know there is an activity that forever works to draw the world and men into closer bonds of mutual support, and does fold the world about us with sustaining arms even when many forces work to destroy us.

The religious function will not come again to the earth to fill human life with passionate devotion to God until we discover God operating in the practical, everyday concerns of human living in some such way as Dewey indicates. We must leave the ossified forms, which Dewey calls religion, and recover the quickening spirit, which he calls the religious attitude. This quickening of the spirit can spread widely and mightily in human life only when we learn that God is natural, not supernatural.

Appendix 6
Is John Dewey a Theist?

Editor the *Christian Century*:

Sir: I have read with interest the review of John Dewey's *A Common Faith* by my esteemed colleague, Mr. Wieman. (The *Christian Century*, Nov. 14.) Because I am sure that many ministers will give three rousing cheers for the new convert to theism, I want to perform the ungracious task of questioning the interpretation offered of Mr. Dewey's new book.

That the great philosopher has now expressed a willingness to embody the letters G-O-D in his writings is the only matter of great moment—if it be momentous—in his book.

Mr. Wieman rejoices that Professor Dewey subscribes to the idea of God as "what holds the actual and the ideal together," and he lays great stress on Mr. Dewey's use of the phrase "forces in nature and society that generate and support the ideals." Now this phrase can be read two ways: either (following Whitehead's view) as affirming the existence of some more-than-human principle of progressive integration which is operative in the cosmos and partly in man; or (following Mr. Dewey's previous utterances) as affirming the power of corporate human intelligence to draw the actual given of nature and the projected ideals of the imagination together in a plan of directed activity.

A careful reading of *A Common Faith* fails to reveal that Mr. Dewey has gone beyond the second interpretation. Admittedly, the first position might be implied *on the basis of Mr. Wieman's own premises*; but that is not the same thing as imputing the views to Mr. Dewey. Mr. Wieman's wish is perhaps father to his

[First published in *Christian Century* 51 (5 December 1934): 1550. For Wieman's review of Dewey, on which Aubrey comments, see this volume, Appendix 5; for Wieman's comment see Appendix 7; and for Dewey's reply, see this volume, pp. 294–95.]

thought in this respect. There seems to be no warrant in the book for his declaration (presumably in exposition of Mr. Dewey) that "this activity which unites the actual and the ideal is not merely the conscious, intelligent effort of men"; and it is significant that no quotations are offered in support of this interpretation. Indeed, quotations might easily be ranged against such an interpretation.

There is a composing and harmonizing of the various elements of our being such that, in spite of changes in the special conditions that surround us, these conditions are also arranged, settled, in relation to us. This attitude includes a note of submission. *But it is voluntary, not externally imposed* . . . (pages 12–13, italics mine [page numbers refer to this volume]).

The fact that human destiny is so interwoven with forces beyond human control renders it unnecessary to suppose that dependence and the humility that accompanies it have to find the particular channel that is prescribed by traditional doctrines. . . . Natural piety . . . may rest upon a just sense of nature as the whole of which *we are parts . . . that are marked by intelligence and purpose,* having the capacity to strive by their aid to bring conditions into greater consonance with *what is humanly desirable* (page 18, italics mine).

Suppose for the moment that the word "God" means the ideal ends that at a given time and place one acknowledges as having authority over his volition and emotion, the values to which one is supremely devoted, as far as these ends, *through imagination,* take on unity (page 29, italics mine). . . . The unity signifies not a single Being, but the unity of loyalty and effort evoked by the fact that many ends are one in the power of their ideal, or imaginative, quality to stir and hold us (page 30).

Dependence upon an external power is the counterpart of surrender of human endeavor (pages 31–32).

. . . The ideal itself has its roots in natural conditions; it emerges when the imagination idealizes existence by laying hold of the possibilities offered to thought and action. . . . The idealizing imagination seizes upon the most precious things found in the climacteric moments of experience and projects them. We need *no external criterion and guarantee for their goodness* (page 33, italics mine).

The process [i.e., of interaction between actual and ideal] endures and advances with the life of humanity (page 34).
... Whether one gives the name "God" to this union, *operative in thought and action,* is a matter for individual decision (page 35, italics mine).

It would seem in the light of such statements as the above that the integrative power binding actual and ideal is still restricted, in Mr. Dewey's thought, to human imaginative intelligence. This interpretation is further reinforced by the third chapter of the volume in which, writing on the social implications of his position, the author insists that "all significant ends and all securities for stability and peace have grown up in the matrix of human relations" (page 47), and that they "assume concrete form in our understanding of our relations to one another and the values contained in these relations. We who now live are parts of a humanity that extends into the remote past, a humanity that has interacted with nature. The things in civilization we most prize are not of ourselves. They exist *by grace of the doings and sufferings of the continuous human community* in which we are a link" (page 57, italics mine). Whatever conclusions may be inferred by Mr. Dewey's readers, rightly or wrongly, from various statements in this book, Mr. Dewey is not yet talking of a God who is a trans-human power or principle of integration, as the review by Mr. Wieman seems to claim, but rather of a divinely creative human intelligence. And this is substantially the position which Mr. Dewey has expounded for years.

EDWIN EWART AUBREY

Appendix 7
Is John Dewey a Theist?

Editor the *Christian Century*:

Sir: When my friend and colleague, Mr. Aubrey, sent me his criticism of my survey of Dewey's Common Faith, I saw what I had not realized before, that my words about Dewey could be so greatly misunderstood. I do not identify Dewey's idea of God with that of Whitehead. I do not represent Dewey as a theist, if that means to believe in a God in whom all highest possibilities of value are actualized. It is very plain that Dewey repudiates such an idea, emphatically and consistently. Ideals and possibilities have no existence. They are to be brought into existence as fully as possible.

But Dewey's position does imply, and, if I understand his words at all, he states, that there are activities going on in nature which include intelligent human effort but are more than intelligence, because they constitute the matrix in which intelligence develops and in which it must function if it is to be effective.

> The community of causes and consequences in which we, together with those not born, are enmeshed is the widest and deepest symbol of the mysterious totality of being the imagination calls the universe. It is the embodiment for sense and thought of that encompassing scope of existence the intellect cannot grasp. It is the matrix within which our ideal aspirations are born and bred. It is the source of the values that the moral imagination projects as directive criteria and as shaping purposes.

[First published in *Christian Century* 51 (5 December 1934): 1550–51. For Wieman's review of Dewey's *A Common Faith*, see this volume, Appendix 5; for Aubrey's comment see Appendix 6; and for Dewey's reply, see this volume, pp. 294–95.]

This matrix is made up of causes and consequences which are not human activities but are connected with human activities. It also generates our ideals. It is not created by our ideal striving except in part. Further, it carries possibilities which men have not yet consciously apprehended.

It is this matrix, this community, this operative system, of inter-functioning activities with its possibilities, that holds the actual and the ideal together. I say "it holds them together," meaning that these possibilities of value would not be possibilities for this world without this system of actuating forces which is the matrix. It holds them together not in the sense that the ideals are already in existence in God or anywhere else. But without this actuating matrix these possibilities could not be held as ideals by intelligent human beings because they would not be either discoverable or workable. A careful reading of my review of Dewey's book should make plain that I attribute nothing else than this to him.

This community of interacting causes and consequences and human personalities with their ideals, and with the further possibilities of the total system, is the most worthful reality there is. To serve it and foster it and promote it to the end of actualizing its highest possibilities of value, is the supreme objective of human living. Hence it is this reality that rightfully commands the highest, sovereign loyalty of human life. In this sense, the name of God applies to it.

This community or matrix grows. It grows even when destructive forces tear it down faster than it grows. In this sense I have called it "progressive integration," and used that word in my review of Dewey's book, although he does not use this term. It may be an unfortunate expression that misleads.

The contents of thought which men have put into their ideas of God varied enormously, so much as to be mutually contradictory. No word has varied more in this respect. But its meaning in terms of human behavior has never varied when it was used sincerely. In terms of human behavior it has always meant what, by right of supreme importance, commands the most inclusive and sovereign loyalty of human living. This meaning in terms of human behavior is the most important meaning, and Dewey uses it, so I think, in this way.

Our knowledge of the reality which has this function of deity in human life is very limited. The manner of its formulation in human thought has varied from age to age according to the changing cultural context and the growth of understanding and insight. But nothing in life is more important than (1) that we give our highest loyalty to it and (2) that we recognize the fallibility of our judgments about it and seek earnestly and persistently to learn more about it.

Through all the débris of ancient patterns of thought one must seek this reality at the heart of human life, and reverently and loyally strive to fashion a pattern fitted to our time by which men may love and serve and give their all to it. The importance of *A Common Faith* is that it participates in this endeavor. However people may dispute about the content of Dewey's thought, his work has this significance. His search for the supremely worthful, stripped as it is of all traditional bias and wishful thinking, should be widely shared.

HENRY NELSON WIEMAN

Checklist of Dewey's References

This section gives full publication information for each work cited by Dewey. Books in Dewey's personal library (John Dewey Papers, Special Collections, Morris Library, Southern Illinois University at Carbondale) have been listed whenever possible. When Dewey gave page numbers for a reference, the edition has been identified by locating the citation; for other references, the edition listed here is his most likely source by reason of place or date of publication, general accessibility during the period, or evidence from correspondence and other materials.

Aubrey, Edwin Ewart. "Is John Dewey a Theist?" *Christian Century* 51 (5 December 1934): 1550. [*The Later Works of John Dewey, 1925–1953*, ed. Jo Ann Boydston, 9:435–37. Carbondale and Edwardsville: Southern Illinois University Press, 1986.]
Ayres, C. E. *Science: The False Messiah*. Indianapolis: Bobbs-Merrill Co., 1927.
Bellamy, Edward. *Equality*. New York: D. Appleton-Century Co., 1933.
———. *Looking Backward: 2000–1887*. Boston: Houghton Mifflin Co., 1926.
Brameld, Theodore B. H. *A Philosophic Approach to Communism*. Chicago: University of Chicago Press, 1933.
Breasted, James Henry. *The Dawn of Conscience*. New York: Charles Scribner's Sons, 1933.
Carnap, Rudolf. "On the Character of Philosophic Problems." *Philosophy of Science* 1 (January 1934): 5–19.
The Citizens Conference on the Crisis in Education. Washington, D.C.: American Council on Education, 1933.
"The Constitution Gets Revised." *Education Worker* 2 (January 1932): 4.
Counts, George S. *The American Road to Culture: A Social Interpretation of Education in the United States*. New York: John Day Co., 1930.
Dewey, John. *A Common Faith*. New Haven: Yale University Press, 1934. [*Later Works* 9:1–58.]

———. "Why I Am a Member of the Teachers Union." *American Teacher* 12 (January 1928): 3–6. [*Later Works* 3:269–75.]

Frankfurter, Felix, ed. *Mr. Justice Brandeis.* New Haven: Yale University Press, 1932.

George, Henry. *Progress and Poverty.* New York: D. Appleton and Co., 1880.

———. *Social Problems.* Garden City, N.Y.: Doubleday, Doran and Co., 1930.

Guterman, Norbert. "John Dewey's Credo." *New Republic* 82 (20 February 1935): 53. [*Later Works* 9:423–25.]

Hoover, Herbert. "The Proceedings of the Conference." In *The Citizens Conference on the Crisis in Education,* pp. 3–16. Washington, D.C.: American Council on Education, 1933.

"How Many Jobless?" *Business Week,* 18 January 1933, pp. 19–20.

Hume, David. *A Treatise of Human Nature: Being an Attempt to Introduce the Experimental Method of Reasoning into Moral Subjects.* Vol. 1, *Of the Understanding.* London: John Noon, 1739.

Kandel, I. L. "Mobilizing the Teacher." *Teachers College Record* 35 (March 1934): 473–79.

Krock, Arthur. "In Washington." *New York Times,* 22 March 1934, p. 20.

Lefèvre, Edwin. "Tax Blindness." *Saturday Evening Post* 205 (28 January 1933): 3–5, 57–58.

Locke, John. *The Philosophy of Locke in Extracts from the Essay concerning Human Understanding.* Arranged, with introductory notes, by John E. Russell. New York: Henry Holt and Co., 1891.

McGoldrick, Joseph. "Bankers Told They Shirk City Responsibility." *New York Herald Tribune,* 28 January 1933, p. 19.

Macintosh, Douglas Clyde, and Henry Nelson Wieman. "Mr. Wieman and Mr. Macintosh 'Converse' with Mr. Dewey." *Christian Century* 50 (1 March 1933): 299–302. [*Later Works* 9:412–22.]

Macintosh, Douglas Clyde, Henry Nelson Wieman, and Max Carl Otto. *Is There a God? A Conversation.* Chicago and New York: Willett, Clark and Co., 1932.

Mencken, H. L. "Shall We Abolish School 'Frills'? Yes." *Rotarian* 42 (May 1933): 16–17, 48. [*Later Works* 9:406–11.]

Morrison, Frank. "Points of View Presented, III." In *The Citizens Conference on the Crisis in Education,* pp. 29–31. Washington, D.C.: American Council on Education, 1933.

Mort, Paul R. "Shift of School Tax to States Is Urged." *New York Times,* 23 January 1933, p. 30.

New York (State). Legislature. Joint Committee on Affairs of the City of New York. *In the Matter of the Investigation of the Departments of* the Government of the City of New York, etc. Final Report. New York, December 27, 1932.

———. In the Matter of the Investigation of the Departments of the Government of the City of New York, etc. Intermediate Report. New York, January 25, 1932.

———. In the Matter of the Investigation of the Departments of the Government of the City of New York, etc. Second Intermediate Report. New York, December 19, 1932.

———. Supreme Court. Appellate Division. In the Matter of the Investigation of the Magistrates' Courts in the First Judicial Department and the Magistrates thereof, and of the Attorneys-at-law Practicing in said Courts. March 28, 1932. New York: Lawyers Press, 1932.

Niebuhr, Reinhold. Moral Man and Immoral Society: A Study in Ethics and Politics. New York: Charles Scribner's Sons, 1932.

———. "After Capitalism—What?" World Tomorrow 16 (1 March 1933): 203–5. [Later Works 9:399–405.]

Otto, Max Carl, Henry Nelson Wieman, and Douglas Clyde Macintosh. Is There a God? A Conversation. Chicago and New York: Willett, Clark and Co., 1932.

The Oxford English Dictionary. Vol. 8. Oxford: At the Clarendon Press, 1933.

Parker, William Stanley. "Weighs Slum Land Costs." New York Times, 27 October 1932, p. 37.

Porter, Russell. "Cuba under President Machado." Current History 38 (April 1933): 29–34.

Quick, Herbert. The Real Trouble with the Farmers. Indianapolis: Bobbs-Merrill Co., 1924.

Recent Social Trends in the United States: Report of the President's Research Committee on Social Trends. New York and London: McGraw-Hill Book Co., 1933.

Russell, Bertrand. "Why I Am Not a Communist." Modern Monthly 8 (April 1934): 133–34.

Santayana, George. Interpretations of Poetry and Religion. New York: Charles Scribner's Sons, 1927.

———. Some Turns of Thought in Modern Philosophy: Five Essays. New York: Charles Scribner's Sons, 1934.

Shakespeare, William. A Winter's Tale. The Temple Shakespeare. London: J. M. Dent, Aldine House, 1905.

Stevenson, Robert Louis. "Happy Thought." In A Child's Garden of Verses, p. 33. Boston: Herbert B. Turner and Co., 1906.

Thomas, Norman. As I See It. New York: Macmillan Co., 1932.

―――. "The Future of the Socialist Party." *Nation* 135 (14 December 1932): 584–86.

"Where Your Food Dollar Goes." *Consumers' Guide* 1 (9 April 1934): 12.

Wieman, Henry Nelson. "Is John Dewey a Theist?" *Christian Century* 51 (5 December 1934): 1550–51. [*Later Works* 9:438–40.]

―――. "John Dewey's Common Faith." *Christian Century* 51 (14 November 1934): 1450–52. [*Later Works* 9:426–34.]

Wieman, Henry Nelson, and Douglas Clyde Macintosh. "Mr. Wieman and Mr. Macintosh 'Converse' with Mr. Dewey." *Christian Century* 50 (1 March 1933): 299–302. [*Later Works* 9:412–22.]

Wieman, Henry Nelson, Douglas Clyde Macintosh, and Max Carl Otto. *Is There a God? A Conversation.* Chicago and New York: Willett, Clark and Co., 1932.

Wilbur, Ray Lyman. "The Proceedings of the Conference." In *The Citizens Conference on the Crisis in Education*, pp. 3–16. Washington, D.C.: American Council on Education, 1933.

Wolfe, Bertram D. *What Is the Communist Opposition?* New York: Workers Age Publishing Association, 1933.

Index

Activity: allied with God, 432–34, 436; concepts compared, 173–74; evaluated by tangible results, 171–72; as overt doing, 169–71; personal desire *vs.* social value in, 172–73; place in education of, 169, 173–74, 179

Actual: God as union of ideal and, xvi–xvii, 34–36, 435, 436, 437, 438, 439

Adams, George Plimpton, xii*n*

Adaptation: related to religion, 11–13, 14

Administration Group: charges against, 326–27, 328–30; in Teachers Union, 323–24, 325–26, 335, 336, 342. *See also* Grievance Committee

Adults: importance of education for, 100, 184–85, 191; role of, in utopian schools, 136–37

Agnosticism, xx, 57

Agricultural Adjustment Administration (AAA): report on dollar distribution, 83–84; report on parity prices, 84–85

Agriculture: need for organization in, 249. *See also* Farmers

Aid: federal, to education, 392–93

Allotment plan: for farmers, 249–50. *See also* Farmers

American Association of Teachers Colleges, 158*n*

American Civil Liberties Union, 87

American Farm Bureau Federation, 250, 273. *See also* Farmers

American Federation of Labor (AFL), 250, 252; and AFT, 123–24, 335; and crisis in education, 130*n*; educational statement of, 124–25; opposes sales taxes, 273. *See also* Teachers Union

American Federation of Teachers (AFT), 112 and *n*, 114; and AFL, 123–24, 335; Dewey on, 123–24; role of, in improving education, 122, 125–26; and Teachers Union, 318, 320*n*, 329. *See also* Grievance Committee

American Institute of Architects, 262

American Liberty League, 88–89

American Road to Culture, The (Counts), 177

American Teacher, 329

Analogy of Religion (Butler), xii, 422

Anthropology: related to religion, 3

Apologetics, 26, 27, 37, 217. *See also* Religion; Religions
Appellate Division: of New York State courts, 376–77. *See also* Seabury investigation
Aristotle, 240, 241, 243
Arnold, Matthew, 36–37; on Marcus Aurelius, xxxi–xxxii, xxxii*n*; on religious experience, xiv–xv, xv*n*, xvii–xviii, xviii*n*, xxiv–xxv, xxvii
Ashmead, Warren G., 353
As I See It (Thomas), 69
Asserted universality: Macintosh on, 419. *See also* Religion
Assertions: *vs.* proposals in philosophy of Carnap, 304
Atheism: aggressive, xvii, xxx, 36
Attitude: passive, in education, 159–60; religion *vs.* religious, xxvi, 12–13, 16–17, 19–20, 30–31, 56, 423–25, 429–30, 434, 436; scientific, 99–100; secular *vs.* religious, 44–45
Aubrey, Edwin Ewart, 294 and *n*, 426*n*, 438 and *n*; on Wieman's review of Dewey, 435–37
Augustine, Saint, 71
Autobiography (Mill), xxvi and *n*
Ayres, Clarence E.: on industrial revolution, 50

Baldwin, Roger, 206
Banks, 285; *vs.* congressional measures, 288; moratorium on, 254, 269; People's Lobby urges solution to crisis in, 254–55; problem of mortgages and, 255; programs urged by, 275; role of, in economic crisis, 114–115; Roosevelt and, 254, 255
Barnard, Henry, 167, 390

Bayer, Adam, 361
Beati possidentes: ideal of, 205
Begun, Isidore, 320, 321, 322, 329, 337. *See also* Grievance Committee; Teachers Union
Belief: compared with religions, 21–22, 23, 24–25; and intellectual content of religions, xv–xvi, 38–39, 40. *See also* Religion; Religions
Bellamy, Edward: compared with Marx, 103–4, 105; on view of new social order, 102–6
Benda, Julien, 243
Benninger, Albert C., 360
Bible: on morality, xxviii and *n*
Bingham, Alfred Mitchell, 296
Blake, William, 25
Board of Education, New York City: and Seabury investigation, 369; and Teachers Union, 332
Bolshevism, 76–77
Bosanquet, Bernard: on religious experience, xxv and *n*
Brameld, Theodore B. H.: on communism, 244–45
Brandeis, Louis Dembitz, 237–39
Breasted, James Henry: on man and the universe, 37–38
Breen, Matthew B., 373
British Labour party, 289
Brodsky, Louis B.: testimony of, 371–72. *See also* Seabury investigation
Burden, Samuel J., 360; testimony of, 361. *See also* Seabury investigation
Bus franchises: in New York City, 365–66, 385. *See also* Seabury investigation

INDEX   447

Business: influence of, on character, 193
Business Week: on unemployment, 252
Butler, Joseph, xii, 422

Capacity: native, in education, 197–99
Capitalism, 319; Bellamy on, 104–5; Dewey on Niebuhr's view of, 73; flaws in, 298; Niebuhr on state of, 399–405; and Roosevelt's policy, 297; social control of, 208
Carnap, Rudolf, 303, 304
Catholicism, Roman: *vs.* Protestantism in relation to God, 45–46. *See also* Religion; Religions
Cattell, James McKeen, 96*n*, 101
Challenge to the New Deal (Bingham and Rodman), 296
Character: influences affecting, 186–87, 188–89, 190–91, 192, 193, 203–4
Chicago, Ill.: teachers unions in, 328–29
Child care: effect on society of, 233–34
Children's Bureau, 394
Children's Court: in New York City, 377
Choice: related to religion, 6–7, 8
Choose Life (Mandelbaum), xxix*n*
Christian Century: religious discussions in, xxi and *n*, xxiii, 223, 294, 412, 417, 435, 438
Christianity, 22, 32, 215, 218, 219, 223, 419, 420, 421. *See also* Religion; Religions

Church: related to social issues, 46, 54–55
Citizens Conference on the Crisis in Education, 119, 120–21, 124–25, 129, 130*n*. *See also* Economics; Education
Citizenship: education for, 161, 163, 164
Citizens Jury on Unemployment: hearings by, 271
Citron, Alice, 320. *See also* Grievance Committee; Teachers Union
City Affairs Committee, 346*n*. *See also* Seabury investigation
City of God (St. Augustine), 71
Civilization: need to maintain values in, 57–58; Wieman on meaning of, 415, 416–17
Civil War, 176, 178; as national crisis, 77
Civil Works Administration (CWA), 287
Class: social, related to education, 114, 145, 202
Cohen, Marshall, xxi*n*
Collectivism, 207
College: progressive schools related to, 156
Committee on Social Trends, 133, 229, 230, 231, 235
Common Faith, A, xi–xxxii, 293, 295, 423, 424, 426, 435, 438*n*, 440
Common Sense, 298, 312
Common sense: Santayana on, 240–41
Communism, 76–77, 298; according to Bellamy, 103, 105; Brameld's view of, 244–45; comparison of Russian and Western, 91–94; reasons for

Communism (*continued*)
denouncing, 94–95; related to Teachers Union, 338–42
Communist Opposition: related to unions, 335–36, 340. *See also* Grievance Committee; Teachers Union
Communist party, 69, 327, 340
Community: place of schools in, 183–84, 185; relation of religion to, 40–41, 42, 57–58, 431
Compton, Betty, 367
Conference on the Educational Status of the Four- and Five-Year-Old Child, 136*n*
Conflict: causes of, in Teachers Union, 330–32. *See also* Grievance Committee
Conformity: in education, 197
Congress. *See* United States Congress
Consideration: formal *vs.* connotative, in Carnap, 303–4
Consumers, 249, 286; compared with producers, 64, 83–84, 85–86; effect of taxes on, 273–74, 278; in England, 400; purchasing power of, 277, 280, 281. *See also* Economics; Economy
Consumers' Guide, 83
Consumption: and capitalism, 401; of farm products, 287; *vs.* production, 232–33; and social planning, 134; and taxes, 259, 266, 268
Contemporary American Philosophy (Adams and Montague), xii and *n*, xiii*n*, 421–22
Conversion: Wieman on religious, 426
Cosmos: Macintosh relates man and, 214, 217, 420–21; Aubrey relates man and, 435. *See also* Religion; Religions
Costigan, Edward P., 288
Costigan-La Follette Relief Bill, 253
Counts, George S., 177
Courts: Appellate Division of New York State, 376–77; investigation of Magistrates', 370–77; judges in New York City, 348–53; political control of New York City, 370–77. *See also* Seabury investigation
Couzens, James, 288
Crain, Thomas C. T., 354–55
Creation: as result of imagination, 33–34. *See also* Religion; Religions
Creed: related to religion, 22, 28–29, 56–57, 432
Critique of Practical Reason (Kant), xxx
Critique of Pure Reason (Kant), xxx
Croker, Richard, 353, 354
Cruise, Michael J., 356
Cuba: political situation in, 310–11
"Cuba under President Machado" (Porter), 310–11, 311*n*
Culkin, Charles W., 356
Culture: and changing views of God, 439–40; and need for liberty, 89–90; related to religion, xv, 3, 6, 38; Wieman on, 415
Curiosity: need in education for, 180–81
Curley, James Michael, 262
Current History, 311*n*
Curriculum, 143, 145, 196–97, 388–90; adjusted to society,

151–52; effect on schools of changing, 179; historical changes in, 148–50; Mencken on, 408, 409; need for socially oriented, 167–68. *See also* Education
Curry, John F., 346, 347, 353
Cuvillier, Louis A., 378

Dawn of Conscience, The (Breasted), 37–38
Debts, 79, 278; compared with school taxes, 117; farmers', 249, 256–57; mortgage, 249, 250, 255, 256–57, 269–70, 277; national, 281; need to reduce, 261; People's Lobby on, 255, 269–70. *See also* Economics
Democracy: Bellamy's view of, 103; birth of, 76; in education, 393; need for interest in, 162–163; related to Brandeis, 238; related to Teachers Union, 317, 318, 341, 344–45
Democratic party, 66, 290; in New York City, 349–53, 356, 373, 379, 382, 384; role of, in economic crisis, 79; and Roosevelt, 400–401; on taxation, 260. *See also* Politics
Democritus, 242
Depression, 296; economic effects of, 267–68; effect of, on character, 190–91; People's Lobby on, 261–64. *See also* Economics; Economy
Descartes, René, 241
Development: stages in educational, 198–99; in traditional *vs.* new education, 200. *See also* Education
Devotion, 28, 219–20, 221, 225–26; Wieman on, 414–17, 427, 434. *See also* Religion; Religions
Discipline: in education, 176–77, 179; in Teachers Union, 343
Distribution: problems in, 232, 250, 285, 286
Diversity: in educational capacities, 196, 197–99
Divine, xvii, 32–33, 34–35, 36. *See also* God; Religion; Religions
"Dr. Dewey Replies," xxi*n*, xxii–xxiii, xxiii*n*
Doctrine: of Lenin, 244–45; in religions, xv, 18, 23–24, 436; scientific method opposed to, 27; and supernatural, 37
Dogberry [Prentice Mulford], 176
Doughton, Robert L., 260
Downing, Bernard, 365
Doyle, William F., 362
Dualism: according to Santayana, 241–42; related to religion, 49
Dual unionism, 335–37. *See also* Grievance Committee; Teachers Union
Du Pont, Irénée, 89. *See also* American Liberty League

Economics: allied with politics, 163; Bellamy's view of, 102–3, 104; and capitalism, 73; effect of education on, 183; effect of monopoly on, 63; effect of science on, 97–98; effect on character of, 190–91; function of family in, 233; George on, 61–65; influence of citizens' committees on, 112–13; international cooperation in, 261; *laissez faire* in, 206, 297; Niebuhr on, 399, 404; and

Economics (*continued*)
philosophy of history, 74–75; problems in, 61, 64, 77, 82–83; producer and consumer cooperation in, 85–86; regimentation of, 89–90, 206–7; related to educational crisis, 112–26, 128–29, 130, 141–45, 386–95; related to social conditions, 208, 229, 231, 232, 234–35, 312; related to Teachers Union, 318–19, 338, 339–40; role of Democratic party in, 79; role of unions in, 79–80; teacher study of, 183, 185

Economy: AAA reports on, 83–85; banks' role in crisis in, 113, 114–15; and emergency acts, 287; government responsibility for, 77, 264; need for redistribution of income in, 64, 82–83, 256, 261, 266, 288; related to unions, 333; role of Roosevelt in crisis in, 78–79, 277–79, 287, 288

Eddington, Sir Arthur Stanley, 242

Education: activity programs related to, 169, 173–74; for citizenship, 161, 163, 164; committees studying problems in, 167; compared in Europe and U.S., 393, 394; conformity in, 197; defined, 195; democracy in, 393; discipline in, 176–77, 179; economic crisis in, 112–26, 128–29, 130, 141–45, 386–95; environment and, 197, 200; equality of opportunity in, 392; federal aid to, 392–93; freedom in, 206–7; "frills" in, 141–46, 387, 388–89, 406–11; function of, in society, 132, 133; Grievance Committee and, 315–19, 320–45; historical changes in, 148–50, 175–76, 390–91; ideals in, 194–95, 196; importance of adult, 100, 184–85, 191; individuality in, 177–78, 179, 180, 183, 196, 198, 207; indoctrination as method in, 178, 179, 181–82; initiative in, 196–97, 205; Mencken criticizes, 406–11; Mort Committee and, 119–20, 129; need for curiosity in, 180–81; need for moral, 186–93; passive attitude in, 159–60; philosophy of, 194–204, 390; problems facing, 129; progressive, 151, 153–54, 155–57, 194; psychology related to, 150–51, 155, 179, 183, 191, 409; purposes of, 147–48, 194–95, 196; related to social affairs, 110–11, 127–28, 131–32, 133, 134–35, 159, 160–61, 167–68, 175, 180, 181, 182–83, 184–85, 206, 393–95; role of science in, 98–100, 195–96, 197–98; role of unions in improving, 125–26; social class related to, 114, 145, 202; social value as criterion of, 202–3; stages in development of, 198–99; for *status quo*, 181, 205, 206; study of evolution and, 161–62; subject-matter related to, 179, 181, 182, 184–85, 196, 199; success as motive for, 177–78, 179; taxes related to, 115–18, 119–20, 121–22, 394–95; in

utopian schools, 136–40; vacuum in, 127–28, 199–200; vocational, 145–46
Educational Workers International, 341
Education Worker, 341
Education Workers League, 341, 342
Emerson, Ralph Waldo, xxvi and *n*
Emotion: and social action, 52–53, 54–55
Engels, Friedrich, 244
England: consumers in, 400; taxes in U.S. and, 284
Environment: connection between religion and, 17–19, 224–25, 227; and education, 197, 200; effect of, on character, 188–89
Epiphenomenon: religious experience as, xiv, xxiv
Equality (Bellamy), 102, 105
Equality: of educational opportunity, 392
Essays in Criticism (Arnold), xxxii and *n*
Essays on Politics and Culture (Himmelfarb), xxxi*n*
Ethics: and study of social conditions, 235, 236
Europe: comparison of education in U.S. and, 393, 394
Evil: *vs.* good in existence, 31–32
Evolution: education and study of, 161–62; Macintosh on, 420–21
Ex facto jus oritur: Brandeis on, 237
Existence: encompassed by universe, 56–57; experience as proof of God's, 9–10; good *vs.* evil in, 31–32; goods in, 35; role of knowledge in shaping, 56–57. *See also* Religion; Religions
Experience: Arnold on religious, xiv–xv, xv*n*, xvii–xviii, xviii*n*, xxiv–xxv, xxvii; Bosanquet on religious, xxv and *n*; as epiphenomenon, xiv, xxvii; and formation of character, 187; imagination related to religious, 13–14; Macintosh on religious, xxv and *n*; as epiphenomenon, xiv, xxvii; and formation of character, 187; 9–10; related to belief in God, xxii–xxiii, 220, 224, 412–13, 415–17; related to religious attitude, 19–20; religion *vs.* religious, 4, 8–9, 29; religious quality of, xxiv–xxv, 4, 8–9, 10–11, 13, 23–24, 26, 426; Royce on religious, xxvii and *n*; scientific, 24; supernatural related to religious, xxviii–xxix, 3, 4–5, 27, 30, 31–32, 44–45, 53–54, 295, 428–29, 430

Faith, 56, 214, 432; allied with human values, xx–xxi, 57–58; Locke on, 15; Macintosh's view of, 418, 419; moral aspect of, 15–17, 426; as substitute for knowledge, 14–15, 28. *See also* Religion; Religions
Family: economic function of, 233
Farley, Thomas M., 356
Farmer-Labor party, 297, 298
Farmers: allotment plan for, 249–50; land value related to, 250, 255, 257, 258, 262–63,

Farmers (*continued*)
269–70; mortgage debts of, 249, 250, 255, 256–57, 269–70; need for relief of, 249–51, 257; People's Lobby on needs of, 249–51; situation of, 275, 285, 307; and taxes, 273; unions of, 250, 273

Farmers and Consumers Financing Corporation, 85

Farmers' National Educational and Cooperative Union, 273

Farmers' Union, 250

Fascism, 77–78, 93, 297, 298, 312; Niebuhr on, 401–3

Finance: Roosevelt's policy regarding, 277–78; and speculation, 254

Fletcher, Duncan Upshaw, 288

Flynn, William J., 346, 347, 362–64. *See also* Seabury investigation

Fox, Mary, 271

Frankfurter, Felix, 237

Franklin, Benjamin, 123

Freedom: educational, 206–7; minority *vs.* mass, 205–6

Freud, Sigmund, 243

"From Absolutism to Experimentalism," xii and *n*, xiii*n*, xxiii

Furriers' Union, 335

"Future of the Socialist Party, The" (Thomas), 66

Geiger, George Raymond, 299, 302

General Education Board, 117

George, Henry: moral and economic philosophy of, 61–65; social philosophy of, 299–302

George, Lloyd, 400

Glover, Katherine: interview by, 386–95

God, 423; activity allied with, 432–34, 436; Aubrey on, 435; culture and changing views of, 439–40; *a* God *vs. the*, xxi, 213–22; good related to, xxiii, 219–21, 222, 224, 225, 226; history related to belief in, 71, 216; human experience related to belief in, 220, 224, 412–13, 415–17; ideals related to, 29–30, 34–35, 36, 294–95, 430–31; love related to belief in, 220, 223; Macintosh's view of, 214, 217–18, 219, 227–28, 419; man related to, 45–46; moral ideals related to, 218–19, 227–28; as a name, xxii, 29–30, 34–35, 36, 220–21, 294, 416, 417, 431, 435, 436, 437, 439; Otto's view of, 214, 215, 224; problem of, defined, 213–14; proof of existence of, 9–10; religion related to belief in, 23, 45–46, 215–16, 228; as union of ideal and actual, xvi–xvii, 34–36, 435, 436, 437, 438, 439; value related to, 29–30, 225, 430–31; Wieman's view of, 214–15, 218–20, 221, 224–28, 412–13, 427, 430–31, 438. *See also* Religion; Religions

Goldstein, Sidney E., 271

Good: in existence, xxii, 31–32, 35; as guidance in life, 47; as ideal end, 33, 36; Macintosh on, 417–18; proponents of, 33; related to God, xxiii, 219–21, 222, 224, 225, 226; Wieman on, 412–14. *See also* Religion; Religions

Government: actions of Cuban, 310–11; and cultural values,

234; loans to farmers, 269; of New York City, 346–85; regimentation in, 88; related to economic crisis, 77, 79–80, 82, 264; responsibility of, to unemployed, 77, 254, 259–60, 262, 278, 283; policies regarding industry, 277–78. *See also* Politics; Seabury investigation
Green, William, 252
Grievance Committee: address on report of, 315–19; causes of conflict in, 330–32; and communism, 338–39, 340–42; defendants before, 320, 321, 322, 326–27, 329, 335, 336–37; and dual unionism, 335–37; hearings of, 320–21, 322, 324, 337; lists charges against Administration Group, 326–27, 328–30; members of, 320; procedure of, 321–22, 344–45; recommendations of, 342–45; on unions, 323–25, 330, 333–35. *See also* Teachers Union
Gross, Esther S., 320, 345. *See also* Grievance Committee
Growth: compared with education, 195–96, 197–98
Guterman, Norbert, 293; on Dewey's *Common Faith*, 423–25

Habit: related to formation of character, 186–87; *vs.* values in government, 234
Haeckel, Ernst Heinrich, 37
Hagan, James J., 371–72
Hanson, Florence Curtis, 124
Hardy, Ruth G., 320
Harvey, George U., 379
Hastings, John A., 365
Havana, Cuba, 311

Hendley, Charles J., 320, 345. *See also* Grievance Committee; Teachers Union
High school: progressive education and, 156–57
Himmelfarb, Gertrude, xxxi*n*
History: of American schools, 148–50, 175–78, 390–91; of changes in industry, 163–64; communism and philosophy of, 92; economics and philosophy of, 74–75; God and philosophy of, 71; Niebuhr on, 399–400, 403–5; politics and philosophy of, 71–72; related to religion, xviii–xix, xxix, xxxi, 3, 4–5, 6, 40–41, 43, 45, 48–49, 216; and social order, 205
Holmes, Oliver Wendell, 237
Hoover, Herbert C., 206–7, 277; and Citizens Conference on the Crisis in Education, 119, 120, 129; and Research Committee on Social Trends, 235
Hopkins, Harry L.: letter to, 271–72. *See also* People's Lobby; Unemployment
House Ways and Means Committee, 284
Hughes, Charles Evans: on Brandeis, 237
"Human Abode of the Religious Function, The," 294
Humanism, 224, 227, 426; secularized, 221–22, 421. *See also* Religions
Humanity, 295
Human nature: Niebuhr on, 401
Human relations: and imagination, 54, 295; related to religion, 40–58, 437
Hypostasis, 221

Ideal: God as union of actual and, xvi–xvii, 34–36, 435, 436, 437, 438, 439; in religion, 32–33, 56, 436–37

Idealism: Niebuhr on, 401, 403–4; practical, exemplified in George, 299; related to Marx and Lenin, 105; related to religion, 17; and social reconstruction, 128

Ideals: in education, 194–95, 196; related to God, xvi–xvii, xviii, 29–30, 34–35, 36, 227–28, 294–95, 430–31. *See also* Religion; Religions

Illusions: influencing social institutions, 107–8

Imagination: as creative force, 33–34; and human relations, 54, 295; lack of, in traditional education, 199; related to formation of character, 186; related to religion, 17, 29–30, 54, 431, 436, 437; related to religious experience, 13–14; related to supernatural, 47, 294–95

Income: of district leaders in New York City, 355–61; national, 252, 274, 280, 287–88; redistribution of, 64, 82–83, 256, 261, 266, 278, 282, 288; report on, 81–82, 267, 287–88. *See also* Economics; Seabury investigation

Individualism, 57; concept of rugged, 205, 207, 208, 231, 238; related to Brandeis, 238–39

Individuality, 205; according to Brameld, 244–45; related to activity programs, 172–73; related to religion, xx, 52; role in education of, 177–78, 179, 180, 183, 196, 198, 207

Indoctrination: as method in education, 178, 179, 181–82

Industry: historic changes compared in, 163–64; reform in, 296–97; Roosevelt's policy regarding, 277–78

Inflation: effect of, 265–66, 267–68; monetary, 269, 275

Ingram, Marsh, 372

Inhaltlich, 303

Initiative: in education, 196–97, 205

Inquiry: related to religion, 18–19, 22–23

Institutions: related to society, 50, 107–8

Integration: in social planning, 230–31

Intelligence: allied with emotion in social action, 52–53; allied with science, 98; related to social affairs, 51–52, 53, 54, 107–8, 109–11; and religious belief, xx, 23–25, 38–39, 40, 56–57, 432, 437, 438

Is There a God? A Conversation (Wieman, Macintosh, Otto), xxi–xxiii, xxi*n*, 213–22, 223, 417

Jeans, Sir James Hopwood, 242
Jefferson, Thomas, 162–63
Johnson, Hugh S., 280–81
Joint Committee on Unemployment, 271–72; urges unemployment relief, 253. *See also* People's Lobby
Judges: for New York City, 348–53. *See also* Courts

Kandel, I. L.: on society, 208–9

Kant, Immanuel, xxx, 9, 217
Kline, Max, 320, 345. *See also*
  Grievance Committee
Knowledge: and religion, 14–15,
  18–19, 22–23, 24–25, 28;
  role of, in shaping existence,
  56–57
Krock, Arthur, 287
Krug, Philip N., 348

Laissez faire: in economics, 206,
  297; in religion, xx, 52, 54,
  55; in social conditions, 52, 54
Land value, 277, 290; according
  to George, 301; and farmers,
  250, 255, 257, 258, 262–63,
  269–70; in New York City,
  257–58, 265; People's Lobby
  urges reforms in, 263–64; and
  taxation, 64–65; U.S. Constitution and, 266
Law: contribution of Brandeis to,
  237–39
League for Independent Political
  Action (LIPA): function of, 67;
  funds for, 307–8; political philosophy of, 67–69; stresses
  need for political action,
  69–70
League for Industrial Democracy,
  175*n*
Leboit, Joseph, 320. *See also*
  Grievance Committee
Lefèvre, Edwin, 115
Lefkowitz, Abraham, 326, 341
Legends: role of, in religions, 40
Lenin, Vladimir Ilyich, 105;
  Brameld on doctrine of,
  244–45
Lerner, Max, 237–38
Liberalism: Macintosh on
  Dewey's view of, 418–19;
  Niebuhr on, 73–74, 400–401,
  404–5; in religion, xix, 24,
  216–17, 218, 222
Liberty, 87, 88, 89–90; plea for
  Cuban, 311
Lincoln, Abraham, 162–63, 176
Linville, Henry R., 124, 326
Literature and Dogma (Arnold),
  xiv–xv, xv*n*, xvii–xviii, xviii*n*,
  xxv
Locke, John, 242; on faith, 15;
  Santayana on, 240–41
"Locke and the Frontiers of
  Common Sense" (Santayana),
  240–41
Logic, xxiv
Logical Positivism, 303
Looking Backward (Bellamy),
  102, 105–6
Loscalzo, Joseph V., 360
Love: related to belief in God,
  220, 223
Loyalty: allied with regimentation, 87

McCooey, John H., 346, 347,
  348, 349, 351, 352, 380. *See
  also* Seabury investigation
McCooey, John, Jr., 380
McCormick, James J., 357
McGoldrick, Joseph, 259; addresses bankers, 113
Machado, Gerardo, 310, 311*n*
Macintosh, Douglas Clyde, 213
  and *n*, 223; replies to Dewey
  on religion, 417–22; view of
  God of, xxi–xxii, xxi*n*, 214,
  215, 217–18, 219, 227–28
McQuade, James A.: testimony
  of, 357–60. *See also* Seabury
  investigation
Magistrates' Courts: control of
  clerks in, 373–77; investigation of, 370–77; reform of,

Magistrates' Courts (*continued*) 377. See also Seabury investigation
Mailly, Bertha H., 306
Man: place of, in Dewey's philosophy, 295; related to cosmos, 214, 217, 420–21, 435; related to God, 45–46; universe and, 37–38
Mandelbaum, Bernard, xxix*n*
Mann, Horace, 167, 390, 392
Marcus Aurelius, xxxi–xxxii
Marx, Karl, 75, 91, 298; Bellamy compared with, 103–4, 105; Brameld on, 244–45
Matrix: concept of universe as, 56, 295, 431, 438–39. See also Religion; Universe
Mechanicalism, 37
Mencken, H. L.: *vs.* Dewey on educational "frills," 141–46, 406–11
Mill, John Stuart, xxvi and *n*, xxxi and *n*, 299
Minorities: in Teachers Union, 316–19, 324–26, 327, 328, 332, 334, 336–37, 338–39. See also Grievance Committee
Misrepresentation: in Teachers Union, 316–17, 318, 327, 330. See also Grievance Committee
Mr. Justice Brandeis (Frankfurter), 237–39
"Mr. Wieman and Mr. Macintosh 'Converse' with Mr. Dewey," xxi*n*
Mitchell, Charles E., 254
Monetary reform, 296–97
Monopoly: affects economy, 63
Montague, William Pepperell, xii*n*
Morality: Arnold on, xiv–xv, xv*n*, xxv; Bible on, xxviii and *n*; compared with religion, xxvii–xxviii, 16–17, 28–29; as religious experience, xiv
Moral Man and Immoral Society (Niebuhr), 108 and *n*
Morals: as aspect of faith, xiv–xv, 15–17, 426; education for, 186–93; in religion, 5–6, 28–29, 218–19, 227–28; Santayana on, 241; and social conditions, 229
Moral values: Macintosh on, 417–18
More, Paul Elmer, xxx*n*
Morrison, Charles Clayton, 216
Mort, Paul R., 119, 129
Mort Committee, 119–20, 129
Mortgage: debts, 255, 257, 269–70, 277; debts of farmers, 249, 250, 255, 256–57, 269–70. See also Economics
Movies: influence children, 188
Mulford, Prentice [Dogberry], 176
Muller v. Oregon, 237
Murphy, Arthur H., 372–73
Mystical experience, xvi, xxx, 25–26, 27, 28, 35, 426. See also Religion; Religions
Mysticism, 25–27

Nation, 66, 305–6
National Bureau of Economic Research: on national income, 81–82, 267, 287–88
National Education Association, 167
National Grange, 250, 273. See also Farmers
National Manufacturers Association, 125
National Recovery Act: as topic in education, 160–61

National Recovery Administration (NRA), 84, 280–81, 297, 387, 388
Natural: *vs.* supernatural, 30, 37, 46–48, 294–95, 429, 434. *See also* Religion; Religions
Natural religion: concept of, 43
Natural resources: People's Lobby on, 289–90
Natural rights: George on, 301–2
Neoplatonism, 25–26
New Deal, 166, 259, 296, 297; People's Lobby on, 280–81
New Education: development in, 200; Mencken on, 408–10; subject-matter in, 199
"New England Reformers" (Emerson), xxvi and *n*
New Pedagogy. *See* New Education
New Republic, 293 and *n*
Newton, Sir Isaac, 241
New York City, 112, 121, 122, 191, 257, 265, 271; administrative functions of, 383; banks in, 114–15; bus franchises in, 365–66, 385; choosing judges in, 348–53; City Club of, 354; Civil Service Reform Association in, 356; Council in, 381, 382, 383, 384; Court of Special Sessions in, 377; departments of, 346, 361, 362, 363, 364, 365, 366, 369, 380, 381, 382, 383; incomes of district leaders in, 355–61; investigation of government of, 346–85; land values in, 257–58, 265; Municipal Civil Service Commission in, 381, 384; political party organization in, 346–54; Supreme Court in, 348, 350, 369, 377, 379; Tammany Hall in, 353, 354, 355, 362, 369, 372, 379, 382, 384, 385; zoning in, 362
New York Herald Tribune, 113
New York Times, 287, 310, 311*n*
New York World-Telegram, 364
Niebuhr, Reinhold, 71, 73–74, 110; on capitalism, 399–405; on illusions, 108 and *n*; on liberalism, 404–5
Norris, Jean H., 371
Norris-Sinclair Bill, 249

Object of devotion, 220, 221, 414–17
Object of worship, 5, 9, 28, 29, 36, 221
O'Brien, John P., 383
Olvany, George W., 362
"On the Character of Philosophic Problems" (Carnap), 303
Orthodoxy: Santayana's philosophical, 240–41, 243
Otto, Max Carl, xxi and *n*, 213; and existence of God, 214, 215, 224, 227. *See also* Religion; Religions

Paine, Thomas, 298
Parity: AAA report on, 84–85
Parker, William Stanley, 262
Patriotism: in education, 161
People's Lobby: advocates public ownership program, 285–86; advocates socialization system, 289–90; conference of, 285; on congressional duties, 287–88; lists programs for Congress, 276; on needs of farmers, 249–51; recommends land tax, 266; requests special session on debts, 269–70;

People's Lobby (*continued*)
urges appraisal of New Deal, 280–81; urges changes in taxation, 256–58, 282–84; urges land and housing reforms, 263–64; urges reduction of debts, 255; urges repeal of processing taxes, 273–74; urges revision of Revenue Act, 259, 260, 274; urges solution to banking crisis, 254–55; urges solution to depression, 261–64; urges unemployment relief, 253

People's Lobby Bulletin, 249–89

Perry, Harry C., 356

Philipson, Raphael, 320, 345. *See also* Grievance Committee

Philosophic Approach to Communism, A (Brameld), 244–45

Philosophy: according to Santayana, 240–43; American radical, 298; of Brandeis, 237, 238; and communism, 92, 244–45; of education, 194–204, 390; of George, 63–64, 299, 300–301; of history and economics, 74–75; of history and politics, 71–72; place of man in Dewey's, 295; political, of LIPA, 67–69; related to social conditions, 236

Philosophy of Henry George, The (Geiger), 299

Philosophy of John Stuart Mill, The (Cohen), xxxi*n*

Pinchot, Gifford, 286

Plato, xiii

Plenty, 81; *vs.* poverty in society, 61–62

Political economy: of George, 299–300

Politics: allied with economics, 163; and control of Magistrates' Courts, 370–77; future of technocracy in, 312; and government of New York City, 346–85; holders of power and, 76–77; influence on business of, 360–61; LIPA and, 67–70, 307; manifested in unions, 333–34; Mencken on relation of schools and, 406–7, 408; need for new interest in, 162–63; need for unity in, 74–75; Niebuhr on, 399, 400–401; parties and, 66, 79, 80, 297; and philosophy of history, 71–72; revolution in, 296, 298; and social conditions, 231, 234–35; Teachers Union and, 318–19, 338, 339

Polytheism, 294

Porter, Russell: on situation in Cuba, 310–11

Poverty, 81; *vs.* plenty, 61–62

Power: kinds of, in social affairs, 109; politics and holders of, 76–77; purchasing, 277, 280, 281

Prayer: Wieman on, 433–34

Prejudice: role of schools in eliminating, 203–4; in Teachers Union, 316–18, 322, 326. *See also* Grievance Committee

President's Research Committee on Social Trends, 133, 229, 230, 231, 235

Producers: compared with consumers, 64, 83–84, 85–86

Production, 134, 289; *vs.* consumption, 232–33; and distribution, 250, 285; farm, 287. *See also* Economics

Profit: related to unemployment, 65, 289

INDEX   459

Progress and Poverty (George), 61–62, 300
Progressive education, 151, 194; *vs.* traditional education, 153–54, 155–56, 157, 199
Progressive Group: in Teachers Union, 323, 324, 335, 337, 340, 342. *See also* Grievance Committee
Progressive integration: of Wieman, 432, 439. *See also* Religion
Propaganda: use of radio for, 309
Proposals: *vs.* assertions in philosophy of Carnap, 304
Protestantism: *vs.* Roman Catholicism in relation to God, 45–46. *See also* Religions
Psychology: effect on education of, 183; related to education, 150–51, 155, 179, 191, 409; related to religion, 3, 57; Santayana relates morals to, 241
Public Works Administration (PWA), 286

Queens County, N.Y., 346, 350–53, 360–61, 378. *See also* Seabury investigation
Quick, Herbert: on farm situation, 262–63

Radicalism: in U.S., 297, 298. *See also* Politics
Radio: used for social education, 309
Rand School of Social Science: organizations and facilities supported by, 305–6
Rank and File Group: accusations of, 325–26; compared with other groups, 340; in Teachers Union, 323, 324, 327, 328–29, 334, 335–36, 337, 341, 342. *See also* Grievance Committee; Teachers Union
Rasquin, Almon G., 348
Realism: Niebuhr on political, 404-5; religious, 422
Recent Social Trends in the United States, 229–36
Reconstruction: in education, 393–95
Reconstruction Finance Corporation (RFC), 253, 262, 286; role in helping schools, 125
Recreation: affects character, 191–92
Red-baiting: and Teachers Union, 316, 322, 326, 330, 339, 340, 341. *See also* Grievance Committee
Reform: monetary, 296–97
Regimentation: allied with loyalty, 87; economic, 89–90, 206–7; in government, 88
Relief: farmers' need for, 249–51; government role in, 254, 259–60, 268; Joint Committee on Unemployment urges, 253, 271–72; measures for, 253; under Revenue Act, 259. *See also* Economics; Unemployment
Relief Boards: composition of, 272
Religion: adaptation related to, 11–13, 14; choice related to, 6–7, 8; concept of natural, 43; defined, 4–5; Dewey's view of, xii–xiii, xxiii–xxiv; environment and, 17–19, 224–25, 227; as epiphenomenon, xiv, xxiv; function of, 44–45, 47, 48, 424, 427; Guterman on, 423–25; historic development of, xv, xviii–xix, xxix, xxxi, 3,

Religion (*continued*)
4–5, 6, 43, 45, 48–49, 216; idealism related to, 17; imagination related to, 17, 29–30, 54, 431, 436, 437; individuality related to, xx, 52; and knowledge, 14–15, 18–19, 22–23, 24–25, 28, 56–57; *laissez faire* in, xx, 52, 54, 55; liberalism in, xix, 24, 216–17, 218, 222; Macintosh on, 421–22; modes of conduct related to, 12–13; morals in, xxvii–xxviii, 5–6, 16–17, 28–29; object of devotion in, 220, 221, 414–17; Otto's views on, 214, 215; psychology related to, 3, 57; related to belief in God, 23, 45–46, 215–16, 228; relation of community to, 40–41, 42, 57–58, 431; *vs.* religious attitude, xi–xii, xiv–xv, xxvi, 12–13, 16–17, 19–20, 30–31, 56, 423–25, 429–30, 434, 436; *vs.* religious experience, 4, 29; role of rites in, 40–41, 427; Santayana on, 13; and science, xv–xvi, 3, 22–23, 27, 37, 42–43, 221, 418–20; secularism and, xviii–xix, 43, 44, 45–46, 55–56; and society, xviii–xix, 3, 6, 38–39, 40–42, 44–45, 53–56, 295, 424, 427, 428; supernatural related to, xvi–xviii, xx, xxviii–xxix, 3, 4–5, 25, 27, 30, 31–32, 44–45, 53–54, 295, 428–29, 430; truth related to, xv–xvi, 23, 27, 423; universality of, 7; Wieman on, 426–34

Religions: beliefs allied with, xv–xvi, 21–22, 23, 24–25, 38–39, 40; Christian, 22, 32, 215, 218, 219, 223, 419, 420, 421; doctrines in, 18, 23–24, 436; historic development of, xv, xviii–xix, xxix, xxxi, 3, 4–5, 6, 40–41, 43, 45, 48–49, 216; importance of scriptures to, 3; objects of worship in, 5, 28, 29, 36, 221; Otto's views on, 214, 215; role of legends in, 40; *vs.* secularism, xviii–xix, 43, 44, 45–46, 55–56; symbolism in, 28–29, 215

Religious experience: Arnold on, xiv–xv, xv*n*, xvii–xviii, xviii*n*, xxiv–xxv, xxvii; Bosanquet on, xxv and *n*; concept of, 4, 8–9, 10–11, 13, 23–24, 26, 426; as epiphenomenon, xiv, xxiv; identified with supernatural, xxviii–xxix, 3–4; imagination related to, 13–14; Macintosh on, 418; opposed to religion, 4, 8–9, 29; Royce on, xxviii and *n*

Religious function, 434

Renaissance: related to religion, xix

Rendt, David S., 346, 347, 348, 351

Republican party, 290; in New York City, 349–53, 355, 379, 382, 384

Revenue Act, 282; revision of, 259, 260, 274

Revolution: Brameld's view of, 245; as national crisis, 77; Niebuhr on, 402–3; political, 296, 298

"Revolutions in Science" (Santayana), 242–43

Rieber, Clara, 320, 321. *See also* Grievance Committee; Teachers Union
Rights: according to American Liberty League, 89
Rites: role of religious, 40–41, 427
Robert Schalkenbach Foundation, 61*n*
Rodman, Selden, 296
Roman Catholicism: *vs.* Protestantism in relation to God, 45–46
Roosevelt, Franklin D., 260, 289; administration of, 296; and banks, 254, 255; and Democratic party, 400–401; letters to, 265–66, 269–70, 273–74, 277–78; policies of, 277–79, 280, 297; related to Seabury investigation, 355, 356, 369; role of, in economic crisis, 78–79, 287, 288
Rousseau, Jean Jacques, 195
Royce, Josiah: on religious experience, xxvii and *n*
Rugged individualism: concept of, 205, 207, 208, 231, 238
Russell, Bertrand, 91

Salaries: of teachers, 116–17
Santayana, George: philosophy of, 240–43; on religion and poetry, 13
Saturday Evening Post, 115, 117
Schools: activity programs in, 179; Cuban, 311; curriculum in, 143, 145, 196–97, 388–90; economic crisis in, 112–26, 128–29, 130, 141–45, 183, 185, 386–95; effect on character of, 187, 188, 189, 192, 203–4; enrollment in, 118–19, 386–87; Mencken criticizes, 406–11; and new social order, 167–68, 192–93, 207–8; private *vs.* public, 129–30, 145; progressive, 147, 153–54, 155–56, 157, 198; related to society, 127–28, 142–44, 183–84, 185, 200–202, 203–4, 207–8; reorganization of, 183–84, 185, 192–93; role of RFC in helping, 125; taxes related to, 115–18, 121–22, 146; utopian, 136–40. *See also* Education
Schulz, George M. S., 372, 373
Schwab, Charles M.: on depression, 63
Science: allied with intelligence, 98; effect of, on economics, 97–98; effect of, on society, 96–97, 100, 101, 108–10; nature of career in, 96–97; related to religion, xv–xvi, 3, 22–23, 27, 37, 42–43, 221, 418–20; role in education of, 98–100, 195–96, 197–98; Santayana's view of, 241–43
Scriptures: importance of, xxviii–xxix, 3
Seabury, Samuel, 348, 354–55, 358, 362, 367–68, 369, 370, 380
Seabury investigation, 346, 362, 364; origin of, 354–55; purpose of, 355; recommendations of, 377, 380–85; Roosevelt and, 355, 356, 369; significance of, 377–80; some results of, 376–77
Secularism, xviii–xix, 43, 44, 45–46, 55–56. *See also* Religions

Senate Committee on Banking and Currency, 288
Shakespeare, William, 225
Shaman, 26
Share-the-Work: campaign, 307; committee, 252–53
Shelburne Essays (More), xxx*n*
Sherman Anti-Trust Law, 281
Sherwood, Russell T., 366–68. *See also* Seabury investigation
Shouse, Jouett, 89. *See also* American Liberty League
Silbermann, Jesse: testimony of, 372–73. *See also* Seabury investigation
Sisto, J. A., 366
Skepticism, xx; according to Santayana, 242, 243
Smith, J. Allan, 365
Social conditions: ethics and study of, 235, 236; *laissez faire* in, 52, 54; and morals, 229; philosophy related to, 236; politics and, 231, 234–35; topics discussed in study of, 229–30
Social Democratic party, 289
Socialism, 76–77; Niebuhr on fascism *vs.*, 402–3
Socialist party, 66–69
Social order: Bellamy on, 102–6; Brandeis on, 237; churches lag in, 46, 54–55; committees studying, 167; development of new, 297; and economics, 208, 229, 231, 232, 234–35, 312; and history, 205; Niebuhr on, 402–4; relation of education to, 131–32, 159, 167–68, 182–83, 184–85; role of teachers in, 134–35, 167, 206, 207, 208–9; schools and new, 167–68, 192–93, 207–8

Social planning: need for, 133–34, 230–32
Social Problems (George), 62–63
Social reconstruction: and schools, 127
Social relations: Brameld's view of, 244–45; supernatural and, xix, 49–50, 52, 53–55. *See also* Religion; Religions
Social struggle: Niebuhr's views on, 399–405
"Social Thought of Mr. Justice Brandeis, The" (Lerner), 237–38
Social trends: conflict in, 234–35; President's Research Committee on, 229, 230, 231, 235
Society: education related to, 127–28, 132, 133, 142–44, 151–52, 175, 180, 183–84, 185, 200–202, 203–4, 207–8; effect of child care on, 233–34; effect of communism on, 94–95; effect on character of, 191; effect of science on, 96–97, 100, 101, 108–10; emotions affecting, 52–53, 54–55; George on problems of, 65, 300–301; ideals related to, 431; institutions related to, 50; intelligence related to, 51–52, 53, 107–8, 109–11; Kandel on, 208–9; poverty *vs.* plenty in, 61–62; and public ownership program, 286; religion related to, xviii–xix, 6, 38–39, 40–42, 44–45, 53–56, 295, 424, 427, 428. *See also* Social order
Sociology: relation of, to social conditions, 229
Some Turns of Thought in Mod-

ern Philosophy (Santayana), 240–43
South Africa, 203
South African Education Conference, 194*n*
Speculation: problems caused by, 254; related to farmers, 250, 256–57; land, 265. *See also* Economics; Land value
Spinoza, Benedict, 11, 240, 241, 243
Spirit of Modern Philosophy, The (Royce), xxvii and *n*
Staley, Ellis J., 369
Status quo: education for, 181, 205, 206; organizations defending, 206; in social relations, 51
Stevenson, Robert Louis, 199
Stock Exchange, 288
Subject-matter: in New Education, 199; related to method in education, 179, 181, 182, 184–85; in traditional education, 196, 199
Success: effect on character of, 190–91; as motive for education, 177–78, 179
Supernatural: compared with natural, 30, 37, 46–48, 294–95, 429, 434; and culture, 38; as life control, 50–51; related to imagination, 47, 294–95; related to religion, xvi–xviii, xx, xxviii–xxix, 3, 4–5, 25, 27, 30, 31–32, 44–45, 53–54, 295, 428–29, 430; and social relations, 49–50, 52, 53–55
Supernaturalism, xxx, 36
Supreme Court: in New York City, 348, 350, 369, 377, 379; U.S., 238, 266, 282. *See also* Seabury investigation
Symbols: in George's concepts, 301; in religions, 28–29, 215

Talmud, xxix*n*
Tammany Hall, 353, 354, 355, 362, 369, 372, 379, 382, 384, 385. *See also* Seabury investigation
Tammany Society, 354
Tariffs: on farm products, 249, 250
Taxation: changes in, 146, 256–58, 282–83; Democratic platform on, 260; George on, 300, 301; government income and, 282–84; and land value, 64–65; and U.S. Constitution, 282. *See also* Economics
Taxes: and consumption, 259, 266, 268, 273–74, 278; in England compared with U.S., 284; and farmers, 273; People's Lobby on, 266, 273–74; redistribution of, 249, 254, 256; related to education, 115–18, 119–20, 121–22, 146, 394–95, 407–8, 410–11; waste of, in New York City, 378
Taxicabs: control of, in New York City, 366
Teachers: *vs.* Board of Education, 332; economic education of, 183, 185; Mencken on, 407–11; role in economic crisis of, 123–24; role in social order of, 134–35, 167, 206, 207, 208–9; salaries of, 116–17; training of, 164–66, 168; union organization of, 182–83, 328–29. *See also* Grievance Committee

Teachers Union: Administration Group in, 323–24, 325–26, 335, 336, 342; causes of conflict in, 330–32; communism related to, 338–42; constitution of, 341–43; criticized, 341–42; Delegate Assembly of, 315, 317, 342–43; democracy related to, 317, 318, 341, 344–45; discipline in, 343; Executive Board of, 323–24, 325, 329; functions of, 332–33, 338; Grievance Committee and, 315–19, 320–45; Joint Committee of, 320–21; minority groups in, 316–19, 324–26, 327, 328, 332, 334, 336–37, 338–39; misrepresentation in, 316–17, 318, 327, 330; need for unity in, 324, 337–38, 343–44; opposing groups in, 323, 324; and politics, 318–19, 338, 339; prejudice in, 316–18, 322, 326; Progressive Group in, 323, 324, 335, 337, 340, 342; Rank and File Group in, 323, 324, 325–26, 327, 328–29, 334, 335–36, 337, 340, 341, 342; red-baiting and, 316, 322, 326, 330, 339, 340, 341

Teagle, Walter C., 252

Technocracy, 296, 297; Bellamy related to, 105; statement on, 312

Technocrats, 62

Terror in Cuba (Révolutionnaires cubains), 310–11

Theofel, John, 346, 347, 360, 361, 378, 379; testimony of, 348–53. *See also* Seabury investigation

Third party, 297; need for, 79, 80. *See also* League for Independent Political Action

Thomas, Norman, 66–67, 69

Thoreau, Henry David, xxvi and *n*

Trade Union Unity League, 341

Tradition: in education, 175

Transcendentalism, 43

Truth: related to religion, xv–xvi, 23, 27, 423

Unemployment, 61, 64, 256, 275, 333; in April 1930, 252–53; effects of, 270, 307; government responsibility for, 77, 254, 259–60, 262, 278, 283; People's Lobby urges relief for, 253; related to profit motive, 65, 289; relief urged by Joint Committee on, 271–72

Unification: of desire and purpose, 432; Guterman on, 424–25; of ideal ends, 294

Union of Soviet Socialist Republics: communism in, 91–94

Unions, 317, 318–19; and dual unionism, 335–37; farmers', 250, 273; role of, in economic crisis, 79–80; role of, in improving education, 125–26; situation of, 333–35, 340, 341. *See also* Teachers Union

Union Teacher, 324

United States: compared with Europe by Niebuhr, 393, 394, 399–400; education in Europe and, 393, 394; radicalism in, 297, 298; socialism in, 402–3; taxes in England and, 284

United States Bureau of Internal Revenue, 267

United States Chamber of Commerce, 115, 125, 130 and *n*

United States Congress, 162, 254, 267, 275, 276; banks and, 288; and debts, 270; and farmers, 249, 250, 273; letter to, on New Deal, 280–81; People's Lobby and, 276; and taxes, 256, 266; and unemployment relief, 272

United States Constitution: history of adoption of, 161, 162; and land value, 266; and liberty, 87; related to education, 181, 206; and taxation, 282

United States Department of Agriculture: programs of, 85

United States Department of Education: proposals for, 393–94

Unity: organic, 220–21, 226, 414–17; political, 74–75; related to God, xvi–xvii, 29–30, 431, 436; in Teachers Union, 324, 337–38, 343–44

Universe: encompasses existence, 56–57; man and, 37–38; matrix concept of, 56, 295, 431, 438–39; and organic unity, 220–21, 226, 415; relation of self to, 14; as source of values, 438. *See also* Religion; Religions

University of the Air, 61*n*, 309 and *n*

Utilities: lack of public responsibility for, 286

"Utility of Religion" (Mill), xxxi and *n*

Utopia, 102; education in, 136–40

Vacuum: in education, 127–28, 199–200; in politics, 288

Value: activity and educational, 173–74; faith allied with human, 57–58; God as ideal, 29–30, 225, 430–31; Guterman on Dewey's religious, 423–25; *vs.* habit in government, 234; human, according to George, 301; land, 64–65, 250, 255, 257–58, 261–62, 263–64, 265, 266, 269–70, 277, 290, 301; in natural and supernatural relationships, xix, 47–48; spiritual, xix, xxiv–xxv, 49, 225, 232; Wieman on, 413–15, 416, 417

Value and Destiny of the Individual, The (Bosanquet), xxv and *n*

Voting: system for New York City Council, 381–82. *See also* Seabury investigation

Wagner Relief Bill, 253

Walden (Thoreau), xxvi and *n*

Walker, James J., 346, 364–70. *See also* Seabury investigation

Walker, Janet Allen, 367

Walker, W. H., 368

Washington, D.C., 124, 125, 129, 260, 285, 287, 307

Ways and Means Committee, 260

Welfare: public, 275, 286

Weston, John C., 374–75

What Is the Communist Opposition? (Wolfe), 335. *See also* Teachers Union

Whitehead, Alfred North, 420, 435, 438

Wieman, Henry Nelson, xxi and *n*, 213 and *n*, 417, 435 and *n*, 437; on devotion, 414–17, 427, 434; Dewey on, xxii–xxiii, 214–15, 218–22, 223–28, 294–95; on Dewey's *Common Faith*, 426–34,

Wieman, Henry Nelson (*contd.*) 438–40; on Dewey's view of God, 412–17; on meaning of civilization, 415, 416–17
Wilbur, Ray Lyman, 119; on crisis in education, 120. *See also* Citizens Conference on the Crisis in Education
Will: revolutionary, 424–25
Willard, Louis H., 363–64
Wilson, Dudley, 360–61
Wolfe, Bertram D., 320, 321, 335. *See also* Grievance Committee; Teachers Union

Wolfman, Joseph, 374
Women's Court, 374; graft ring in, 375–76. *See also* Seabury investigation

Youth: building character of, 186–93

Zitron, Abraham, 320. *See also* Grievance Committee; Teachers Union
Zoning: in New York City, 362
Zook, George, 387

Pagination Key to the First Edition of *A Common Faith*

The list below relates the pagination of the 1934 Yale University Press edition of *A Common Faith* to the pagination of the present edition. Before the colon appear the 1934 edition page numbers; after the colon are the pages with corresponding text from the present edition.

1:3	23:16–17	45:31	67:45
2:3–4	24:17–18	46:31–32	68:45–46
3:4–5	25:18	47:32	69:46
4:5	26:18–19	48:32–33	70:46–47
5:5–6	27:19–20	49:33–34	71:47–48
6:6	28:20	50:34	72:48
7:6–7	29:21	51:34–35	73:48–49
8:7–8	30:21–22	52:35–36	74:49–50
9:8	31:22–23	53:36	75:50
10:8–9	32:23	54:36–37	76:50–51
11:9–10	33:23–24	55:37–38	77:51
12:10	34:24	56:38	78:51–52
13:10–11	35:24–25	57:38–39	79:52–53
14:11	36:25–26	58:—	80:53
15:11–12	37:26	59:40	81:53–54
16:12–13	38:26–27	60:40–41	82:54–55
17:13	39:27–28	61:41	83:55
18:13–14	40:28	62:41–42	84:55–56
19:14–15	41:28–29	63:42–43	85:56–57
20:15	42:29	64:43	86:57
21:15–16	43:29–30	65:43–44	87:57–58
22:16	44:30–31	66:44–45	